CORRECTION SQUAD

by

SARAH STEEL

Published by **CHIMERA**
ISBN 9781780806600

Chapter One

Plumping her naked buttocks down onto her heels, the kneeling blonde inched forward until the upturned clay face in front of her rested its chin on her knees. Bending down, so that her golden mane tumbled to curtain her emerald eyes, she cupped the captive face in her hands. Already perspiring freely from her exertions, the blonde felt a trickle of sweat in her cleavage. Straining in their cups, her breasts bulged within the strict embrace of her lace brassiere.

She swore softly in her native Polish, chiding herself for not having stripped completely. She always did this better when utterly naked. Too late now, she thought. Her hands were filled with the face before her. Beads of sweat prickled her breasts but she ignored the distraction, closing her eyes into fierce slits of concentration. Splaying her fingers around the head, she worked her thumb-tips into the upturned cheeks. Pressing more firmly, the blonde addressed the eyebrows, then switched her dominant caress to the temples. Sliding her fingertips down to capture and control the chin, she bent closer - her breasts almost bursting out of their bondage - and inched her index fingers up to concentrate on the nose.

The rhythmic chatter of a helicopter broke the silence of the early autumn afternoon. That was almost the only drawback to living in a converted warehouse loft in Wapping. Too high up to be annoyed by the snarl of the traffic far below, the peace was often shattered by the assorted noises of machines transporting executives as they skimmed across the thrusting city skyscape. The helicopter peeled away over the glittering Thames, and silence filled the room. The blonde sighed, shrugging off the interruption of her concentration and returning her gaze to the passive face before her. The wet tip of her tongue peeped out between her teeth as she thumbed the face, paying careful attention to the upper lip. This was a tricky moment. Absolute concentration was essential. The lip required such a delicate touch—

'Playing with yourself again?' giggled a petite brunette who had slipped silently into the vast loft under the protective cover of the noisy helicopter and tip-toed up behind the kneeling blonde.

Startled, the blonde snatched her hand away from the face. She spat out another harsh curse in Polish.

'Touchy. I only... oh, sorry,' the brunette whispered penitently, her large brown eyes widening with remorse.

The blonde looked up, her green eyes glinting. In her open hand, she palmed the lip she had inadvertently ripped away from the face.

'Never creep up on me when I'm working. Never, ever again,' she hissed.

'Sorry.'

'Look at this. Completely ruined,' the blonde sculptress snapped, tossing aside the clay lip in disgust. Throwing a wet towel over the damaged face, she got to her feet and turned to face the brunette, her ripe bosom heaving in her anger. 'I've warned you about sneaking up on me, Beetle. Now I'm going to punish you.'

'But Krystal,' the brunette squealed, 'I was only having a bit of fun.'

'Which you will now pay for dearly. Strip and bend over. I am going to wash my hands, fetch my cane and give you four strokes.'

Beetle's brown eyes widened further and dimmed with liquid sorrow.

'At once,' came the curt command.

The younger woman obeyed the dominant blonde with alacrity, not wishing to incur extra blistering stripes across her bare bottom by provoking Krystal any further. As the blonde strode across to the bathroom, her naked buttocks rippling softly with each measured pace, the brunette pulled her blue cashmere jumper up over her breasts and head, shaking her dark curls free as she peeled it away. Nervously, she unzipped her black leather mini-skirt and wriggled out of its supple warmth. Braless, her soft breasts bobbed as she stooped to palm down her white cotton panties, bouncing as she kicked her foot free of the panties.

'As soon as you have stripped, bend over and touch your toes. I expect to find you naked and in the punishment position when I come out,' came the stern instruction from the bathroom.

Shivering slightly in her sudden nudity, Beetle poked her tongue out in defiant response, but as the handle of the bathroom door turned, she bent over instantly, squashing her breasts between her arms as they arrowed down towards her toes. The tiny toes curled up in fearful dread as Beetle heard Krystal in their bedroom opening the drawer which contained a length of bamboo. Beetle knew the cane very well: her knowledge of its whippy suppleness was painfully intimate. She shut her eyes but could still envision the twenty-seven inches of yellow bamboo. The cruel glinting wood that visited her bare buttocks with a venomous bite whenever she misbehaved - and was caught and punished by the ever vigilant Krystal. Fearful at the prospect of the stinging stripes about to scorch her bare bottom, Beetle also felt a surge of excitement moisten her prickling slit. Stretched and bending, she sensed her sticky labia part and pout as she inched her thighs a fraction apart. Her upturned cheeks tightened in a reflex as she heard the *swish, swish, thrum* of the practice strokes in the bedroom. Krystal, a perfectionist in all matters of punishment, invariably plied the wand of woe to test its degree of whippiness. *Swish, swish, thrum.* Krystal entered the studio, closing the bedroom door behind her. Soon, Beetle knew, her defenceless flesh would quiver and scald as the first of four slicing strokes swished savagely down across her buttocks. Then again, and again, and yet again. Beetle knew also that with each searing slice of hot torment came a darker delight. Each gasp of sorrow torn from her lips would be curdled by a softer note - her pleasure sobs. Beetle shuffled her feet excitedly at the thought that by the fourth crisp cut of the cane her fig would be freely weeping its sticky sweetness.

'You really can be a little pain, Beetle,' Krystal admonished, as she glanced first at the damaged clay face shrouded by the wet towel, and then at the bare bottom she was about to cane.

'I am going to punish you, my girl, and punish you quite severely. I've told you several times about creeping up on me when I'm working with my clay. You have chosen to ignore my warnings, so let this be a lesson.'

Krystal tapped the upper curve of each naked cheek smartly with the tip of the bamboo cane, emphasizing her dire words. Beetle shivered with both dread and delight at these pre-punishment preparations, thrilling to Krystal's stern authority.

'Feet together for the first two strokes. Then, and only when I say so, feet slightly apart.'

'Yes—'

'Silence! You may whimper and you may squeal but absolutely no talking while I whip your bottom. You have been very, very naughty and—'

The tense silence was broken by the shrill tone of the phone.

'Stay exactly where you are,' Krystal whispered. 'You are positioned perfectly for your punishment. I shall return.'

Placing the length of yellow bamboo on the grey carpet immediately under the bending brunette's gaze - a cruel touch, but a necessary one, Krystal mused - she strode over to the phone and picked it up.

Speaking to the caller, Krystal was cryptic and terse, giving nothing away to the naked brunette who, she knew, would be straining to catch every word. The call having ended, she saw Beetle quiver expectantly as she returned and languidly knelt to scoop up the cane. She shouldered the length of bamboo and examined the swell of the creamy buttocks beneath her stern gaze. She noted with grim satisfaction the dimple of dread in each cheek as Beetle clenched her buttocks. Krystal, still naked except for the crisp lace brassiere which held her breasts in thrall, played with her cane, crushing her breasts beneath the length of whippy wood as she rolled it firmly down their heavy flesh.

'Who was—'

'Silence!'

Beetle held her breath, her naked rump rippling imperceptibly.

Standing over the bending nude, the dominant blonde guided her cane downwards, sliding its glinting length along the cleft between the clenched cheeks. Beetle squealed, parting her buttocks to accept the wood. Krystal probed the cleft, plying the cane with consummate skill.

'Punishment postponed,' she whispered.

'P-postponed?' echoed the brunette huskily.

'That was Harrogate. We're on. Get dressed quickly. We'll catch the InterCity from Kings Cross and be there for supper.'

Night falls more suddenly when you hurtle through it at a relentless 118mph. Soon Krystal was no longer staring out at the urban sprawl but gazing into her own reflection in the black glass of the carriage window. In it, she saw also the First-Class executives peering into their lap-tops, the greenish glow of the screens turning their tired faces all the more ghostly, She switched her attention to Beetle, who guzzled cherries from a brown paper bag as she flicked through her glossie. Krystal studied her partner, younger than herself, appreciating the large brown eyes, wide mouth and her crowning glory of tumbling brunette curls. Such a beautiful head of hair - luxuriant compared to her own cropped blonde head. Those tumbling curls: so useful to clutch when taming and subduing the minx during discipline, especially a bare-bottomed spanking. Krystal's eyes devoured the swell of her partner's breasts sheathed within their tight cashmere bondage. The flesh of the bosom was warm, creamy and firm - Krystal knew them better than she did her own - and the nipples were the deepest pink, a pink that darkened to scarlet when the peaks puckered up, alert and erect, during punishment and play.

Krystal closed her eyes as she recaptured memories of her first encounter with the little brunette minx. Memories of those exciting terms at Birch Hall, their exclusive seat of education. With the initials V.W. stitched into every item of her schoolgirl uniform, it had been only a matter of days before the entire dorm had dubbed the new boarder 'Beetle'. Krystal, three years older than Beetle, had been first her dorm captain and then, later, her senior prefect. Spanking the bare-bottomed new girl had been a pleasure and Krystal had exercised her strict authority over the headstrong new girl's peach-perfect buttocks at every opportunity. Beetle had been sent to Birch Hall by her elderly parents who had despaired of ever disciplining the wilful little minx. Clear instructions to dispense chastisement as necessary had been received by the Headmistress - and so strict discipline was regularly dispensed. Krystal moistened her dry lips at the memory of those times. Since Birch Hall, Beetle and Krystal had not slept a single night apart. Beetle, an aspiring actress, had already been successful in small radio parts and had three TV ads notched up: her fourth, displaying a new French uplift bra, had been spiked in the interests of public decency, with pirated videos of the entire shoot commanding three figure sums in knowledgeable circles.

Swallowing her last cherry as she thumbed her pubis through the warm leather of her mini-skirt (a habit the brunette invariably indulged when perusing the intimate lingerie shots in glossie rag-mags) Beetle stole a cautious peep across at Krystal. Her punishment postponed, the delay had been increasing her delicious dread. Pain, Beetle reflected, was always such a pleasure from the capable hands of the strict Polish blonde. Beetle suddenly remembered her first taste of exquisite discipline back at Birch Hall. The green-eyed dorm captain had discovered Beetle eating biscuits from her tuck locker - an expressly forbidden treat - after lights out. Summoning the rest of the dorm (eight sleepy, scantily clad, girls) to witness the chastisement, Krystal had instructed Beetle to kneel on her bed: face down into her single pillow, with her knees together and her bottom raised. Biscuit crumbs still adhering to her tight vest at the swell of her bosom, Beetle had been forced to obey. Memories flooded back of her punishment in the dorm at midnight, causing Beetle to shiver - and return her firm thumb to her dampening labia. She recalled the cool touch of the dorm captain's hand dragging down her navy-blue knickers; the appreciative murmur of pleasure from the watching girls assembled in silence around her bed; the gasp of pleasure as her rounded buttocks were slowly bared; the potent threat of the punisher's palm resting lightly across her creamy cheeks as stern words were spoken; then - Beetle's throat tightened slightly at the sharp memory - the slap of the hand spanking down across her bare bottom.

Many more punishments had followed, the strict blonde graduating from plastic ruler to supple leather-soled slipper to redden the naughty young girl's cheeks. As the terms at Birch Hall passed, intense pleasure grew out of the punishments: intense pleasure for both the chastiser and the chastised. The punishments became more intimate, more private and more protracted affairs, Krystal rapidly coming to own and utterly control the younger girl's bottom.

Beetle smiled as she opened her eyes to see a station fly by in a blaze of dazzling neon: now the two women we inseparable.

The InterCity skittled across a set of points, jolting Bee out of her nipple-tightening reverie. She blinked - then blushed slightly as she met the dominant gaze of the green-eyed blonde.

'Harrogate?' Beetle inquired, surreptitiously withdrawing her busy thumbtip from her pubic mound.

'We've got a thief to catch. Private nursing home, so there's no question of calling in the police. They know who it is but can't prove it and simply can't afford any scandal.'

'Of course. Ruinous for business,' Beetle nodded.

Scandal: most of the work Krystal and her brown-eyed assistant undertook in their capacity as avenging angels was shrouded in strict secrecy. Their brief was usually to right wrongs; their instructions to avoid scandal; their purpose was invariably to punish. Beetle sank back in her seat and fleetingly thrilled to the recollection of their first assignment together - that horrible little crook, a time-share bandit. He was stinging retired couples with contracts containing more small-print clauses than the victims had remaining years in which to read them. How he had squealed under the vengeful lash of their stinging canes. Grateful relatives of the duped had paid the two girls handsomely, but punishing the crook had been reward enough. Their next assignment? Beetle closed her eyes and thought hard. There had been so many. Who had it been? Yes, of course - the Kensington society hostess they had been hired to unmask as a charity swindler. Her icy hauteur had soon melted into tears of sorrow under the heat of the fierce retribution meted out to her naked bottom. How she had writhed and squirmed beneath the lash of their leather straps.

Our purpose is punishment: the words with which Krystal always greeted new clients - and new victims. The rhythm of the train echoed the phrase, lulling Beetle into a light doze. *Punishment, punishment*, the wheels murmured. She dreamt of Krystal working the wet clay with her hands. Such capable hands, whether controlling the clay - or a whippy cane. Beetle squirmed in her sleep. When stripped naked and ordered to bend over, she would shrink slightly at the dominant touch of Krystal's firm hand on her naked shoulder. In her dream, Beetle sensed the touch of a hand on her shoulder. She squirmed and moaned softly. She felt the squeeze of the hand once more. She whimpered, shrugging off the dominant touch, fearful of the impending pain across her buttocks. Although asleep, her brain recognized the touch which signalled the cruel cut of the cane. Again, the hand at her shoulder squeezed.

'Wake up,' Krystal urged, shaking the sleepy brunette. 'We're coming into Harrogate.'

'I want her caught and punished,' the Matron repeated quietly, smoothing her nyloned thighs beneath the crisp blue of her -uniform.

'But, presumably, in a way which will avoid any scandal?' Krystal, who always conducted negotiations, countered.

'Naturally.'

They were sitting in the Matron's office in the east wing of the private nursing home, a rambling Edwardian mansion tucked away in a leafy suburb. Out in the cold November night, a chill wind whipped the wisteria. Inside the Matron's office, a gas fire hissed. Beetle studied the Matron as the negotiations progressed. She was a striking woman of forty - perhaps a couple of years more - and something of a forbidding beauty. Her pale face was free from any trace of cosmetics, and the full lips of her resolute mouth bore no lipstick's kiss. Beetle felt uneasy in her presence: the Matron was the epitome of stern authority. The note of austerity was sharpened by the seamed nylons, stiff brogues and the faint whiff of carbolic soap. Beetle sensed the Matron's eyes upon her, and quickly glanced down into the glow of the gas fire, grateful that Krystal was doing all the talking. Beetle blushed slightly and her nipples peaked firmly as she succumbed to the thought of being disciplined by Matron. After the severe spanking of her bare bottom as she lay across those nylon-seamed thighs, a dominant kiss perhaps on each scalded cheek from those soft lipstick-free lips. Beetle shuddered.

'You have suspicions, then, but no real proof?' Krystal was asking.

Matron nodded and continued with her briefing. Beetle tried to follow the discussion more closely, pushing aside her fascination with Matron's austere presence.

The facts were soon laid bare. For a not inconsiderable fee they were charged with the task of catching and then punishing a light-fingered agency nurse. Tact and discretion would be required; Krystal and Beetle proffered their guarantee immediately.

'Jolly good. When would you two girls like to begin?'

'Tonight,' Krystal replied. 'One more detail, Matron. How do you want the culprit punished?'

'*Severely*,' whispered Matron, palming her thighs with ardour. '*Most* severely.'

Directed by Matron's suspicions, Krystal studied the night duty rosta and decided to bait their trap in Orchard Wing, a suite of private rooms on the second floor of the nursing home. Orchard Wing was the responsibility of the agency nurse who was Matron's suspect.

'Be very careful,' Matron had warned them. 'Sister Oates is very clever. A slippery customer.'

'I like them slippery,' was Krystal's enigmatic reply.

By 10.45pm, the corridor lights were dimmed and the silence of the night settled over all the sleeping patients. By 11.08, Sister Oates had almost concluded the first of her rounds, checking her cosseted charges. Approaching the last room, she read from her case notes that the elderly patient within was a recent admission. Slightly confused and somewhat exhausted after a recent bout of flu, she had been admitted for rest and observation. Sister Oates opened the door and stepped softly into the darkened room. Her patient, propped up on pillows to limit congestion, was asleep. Sister Oates tiptoed over to the bedside cabinet and appraised the valuables strewn across its surface. Magpie-like, she spotted a single rope of pearls.

Under the bed, Krystal lay still and held her breath. From the moment the door had inched ajar, she had remained tense and alert. She watched the legs, sheathed in bronzed nylon, approach the bed and step towards the cabinet. She saw the white shoes inch a fraction closer and heard the dry rattle as the string of pearls was lifted up and palmed.

A softer sound told Krystal that the pearls had been pocketed. From her vantage point, she saw the shapely legs carry the culprit towards the door. Her urge to sneeze in the sudden draught from the opening door she managed to stem just as the door closed softly. *Good*, she thought. *So far, the plan is running smoothly. The bait has been taken.*

At 6.30 the following morning Krystal sprang out of her bed and set about the task of disguising herself in the domestic's uniform provided by Matron. Naked, she shivered before the full-length mirror as she stepped into her panties. The cool cotton cupped her soft buttocks deliciously. Fingering the elastic waist, she tugged the tight band that served as the gusset into her cleft, murmuring her pleasure. Next, drinking in her reflection in the mirror, she filled the deep cups of the brassiere with her heavy breasts and reached behind her back to fix the clasp. Her bosom thrilled to its bondage. The clinging white nylon uniform of a domestic fitted her as tightly as a glove. Little white ankle-socks and lace-up pumps completed her outfit. She examined herself in the mirror, tousling her cropped blonde hair and rumpling her uniform to give the appearance of a hard night's work. Shouldering a towel and grabbing a bottle of gel, she left her room and set off in the direction of the staff showers. Just like the rest of the night shift, she was looking forward to a steamy sluicing. Two nurses scampered from a shared shower, their wet nakedness pink and shining, as Krystal entered. Only Sister Oates remained, naked under her warm cascade.

Krystal stripped off her domestic's uniform and padded across the white tiles into the showers. She noticed that Sister Oates seemed to be having some difficulty with an item of jewellery around her neck. Eyes closed, her face tilted up into the hot stream of the shower, she scrabbled impatiently to open a clasp sparkling against the white nape of her neck. Feigning indifference, Krystal absorbed herself in rubbing her ripe breasts with shower gel as she luxuriated in the water - in reality never taking her eyes off the naked thief a few feet away. What a beautiful bottom the squirming nude displayed, Krystal mused as she slowly palmed her nipples into peaks of pleasure. The rounded buttocks, glistening beneath a sheen of water, were superb. A silver stream sluiced down the dimpled spine and sparkled in the dark cleft dividing the swollen cheeks. Gazing intently at the firmly fleshed rump, Krystal absently caressed and squeezed her bare bosom, supporting her breasts in cupped hands. *What a perfect peach of a bottom*, she thrilled to herself in silent rapture. What pleasure she would have when punishing it. Closing her eyes tightly to relish the thought, Krystal uncupped her breasts and dropped her hands down to spread apart her buttocks, dragging the cheeks apart until it was almost a painful sensation. Up on tip-toe, she squeezed her buttocks with her taloned fingers, offering her breasts into the stinging sluice of her shower. Seconds later, she reached out and turned the tap to cold, realizing her need to shock herself back into the matter in hand and keep her mind sharply alert. The cold water punished her nipples and Krystal gasped softly in response.

Back in her cubicle, she shivered as the towel grazed the tender erect pink buds. She dabbed at them gently, wincing slightly in her delicious torment.

'You're a new face around here, nurse,' Sister Oates called out from her shower.

'Auxiliary. Temping as a domestic. Money's good for the night shift,' Krystal grunted, pulling her towel up roughly between her parted thighs.

'Oh,' Sister Oates replied, unable to conceal a note of disdain in her voice. 'A domestic. That makes me your superior, so you'd better do as I say. Understand?'

'Yes, sister,' Krystal complied.

'Come here and dry me. Quickly, I'm in a hurry.'

Krystal assumed the mask of meekness as she obeyed. In the other's cubicle, she gathered up a warm towel and applied it to Sister Oates. As her hands weighed and then patted the splendid buttocks, Krystal perused the swollen orbs, consoling herself with the thought that shortly, before the autumn sun had streaked the grey dawn with scarlet, stern chastisement would scald their unblemished cream to a reddening shade of pain.

'I'll powder myself. You run along down to the kitchen and make sure my breakfast is prepared. I'll have something hot.'

You most certainly shall, Krystal smiled to herself as, playing the dutiful domestic, she withdrew.

'Come in, Sister Oates—'

'But I've finished my shift and my breakfast will spoil, Matron.'

'I believe,' Matron continued imperturbably, 'your duties brought you into this room a little after eleven last night?'

'Yes.' The reply was guarded, the tone defensive. Sister Oates turned in surprise as Krystal, still dressed as a domestic, stepped into the bedroom, locking the door behind her.

'An expensive item of jewellery, a single string of pearls, appears to have been mislaid. Would you be so good as to assist us in looking for it? You know what these old dears are like,' Matron shrugged resignedly, nodding to the elderly woman sleeping in the bed.

Suddenly emboldened - thinking her moment of danger had passed - Sister Oates obliged with a convincing act of searching for the mislaid pearls.

'What are you wearing around your neck, Sister?' Krystal enquired softly.

A hand flew up to the startled woman's throat.

'As a matter of fact—' She faltered - then recovered her composure - 'I have a rope of pearls. Imitation, of course.'

'What is happening?' wheezed the elderly patient from her pillows, gazing sleepily around her.

'Good morning,' beamed Matron. 'You join us at an opportune moment. Is this the person who stole your pearls?'

Oates gasped audibly.

'Yes,' croaked the feeble voice from the pillows.

'That's a lie,' hissed the accused. 'And you'll never be able to prove—'

'*That* is the person who stole a single string of pearls at ten minutes past twelve last night,' Beetle spoke now in her own voice as she briskly removed the whitened wig and sallow make-up she'd worn to age herself. Transformed from crone to nymph in seconds, she bounded out of her bed.

Panic and fear froze the face of Sister Oates into a mask of sullen hatred.

'These pearls are mine,' she asserted, a note of desperation in her shrill voice. 'This is purely a coincidence.' Her encircling accusers remained silent.

'Are you police?' Oates quavered.

'Worse than that,' Matron murmured. 'Much worse, I fear.'

'Strip,' Krystal barked.

Oates paled beneath her pretence of outrage.

'I said strip. At once. Get out of that uniform.'

'Yes,' Matron added. 'You are a disgrace to your uniform. Undress this instant, Oates.'

'B-but—'

'At once!'

Sister Oates fumbled with her belt and buttons. Slowly, resentfully, the uniform was peeled off until she stood, trembling slightly, in her brassiere, panties, nylon stockings and crisp suspender belt.

'I want you naked,' Krystal whispered in a tone of velvet menace. As she spoke

Krystal wriggled gracefully out of her domestic's uniform, then casually plucked off her own underwear, tossing her panties aside. Slowly she thumbed the pubic tuft at the base of her belly as she glared at the disgraced nurse.

'Utterly naked,' echoed Beetle, her disguise completely discarded, as she pulled the modest nightdress over her head to emerge unashamedly nude.

'I shall leave you two to your pleasantly painful duties,' Matron said softly, gazing hungrily at Oates's bare bottom as the accused woman palmed down her panties over the sheen of her nylons. 'I shall return within the hour. Will you both be breakfasting?' she asked, a carnal snarl tightening her voice as Oates removed her brassiere.

Krystal nodded. 'Big breakfasts for both of us, please. I find that dispensing punishment gives me quite an appetite.'

'P-punishment?' Oates gasped.

'Then I had better instruct the kitchens accordingly,' Matron smiled.

'Stockings.' Krystal barked.

Oates obeyed, her hands trembling as they eased the sheer nylons down her slender legs. Matron departed, locking the door behind her.

'Do you still insist the pearls are yours?' Krystal fixed her gaze on the string of pearls - the sole adornment on the naked thief.

'Yes—'

'Take it off,' challenged Beetle.

Oates made a frantic attempt to do so, her breasts bunching between her elbows as her hands worked at the clasp.

'But then you can't, can you? You see,' Beetle continued crisply, 'it has a trick catch on the lock.'

Oates dropped her hands down to cover her bosom protectively

'*Guilty*,' Krystal hissed, slowly pulling on a pair of stretchy clear plastic gloves. Splaying her fingers, she studied the effect approvingly. 'I think we've proved our case beyond reasonable doubt.'

Oates bowed her head in fearful shame, conceding her guilt completely.

'No doubt whatsoever,' Beetle replied. 'And her punishment?'

'Kneel,' Krystal commanded.

Oates made a token gesture of resistance but obeyed the curt command. Her bare bottom wobbled perceptibly as she squirmed down onto her knees, scrunching her toes into the carpet. Beetle approached the nude and bent over her, brushing her nipples against the nurse's upturned face as her nimble fingers stretched to undo the secret catch. The string of pearls slithered from the thief's neck in silence.

'Up,' Krystal commanded.

Oates rose unsteadily, vainly attempting to cover her nakedness with her trembling hands. 'Hands behind your back.'

'No, p-please—'

'Behind your back.'

Blushing deeply, Oates obeyed Krystal's firm instruction, exposing her breasts, belly and pubic thatch to the fierce gaze of her accusers. Krystal inched towards her captive. Stretching out her gloved hand, she fingered then cupped the naked left breast. Squeezing it slowly, she gazed dominantly into the frightened face.

'Before we whip you—'

'Whip me?' Oates squealed.

'Whip your naked bottom,' Krystal murmured suavely, punishing the breast within her gloved grasp. 'I will require you to write a full confession.'

'Just let me go - Please—' Oates whined.

'Silence!' Krystal captured and tormented the pink nipple between a cruel pincer of finger and thumb. The nipple thickened, then purpled with pain. Oates gasped and moaned.

'You can't do this. You've no right. The police—'

'Need not be bothered. All I want from you is a signed confession. And then your bare bottom,' Krystal whispered.

Oates whimpered.

'The pen and paper you'll require,' Krystal pointed, 'are over on that desk.'

Crushed by the stern note of authority, Oates shuffled over to the desk and sank her naked buttocks down onto the polished wooden chair.

'A full and frank confession, listing everything you have stolen from your elderly patients, both here and elsewhere. Everything, understand?'

The thief, nodding her obedience, picked up the pen. Like a naughty schoolgirl writing lines in detention before the kiss of the prefect's slipper across her bottom, she laboured over her scribbled confession. As she wrote, she peeped across at her naked accusers.

Krystal and Beetle busied themselves for the impending chastisement. Their preparations for punishment were simple: they merely had to arrange the bed to their satisfaction for the thief to receive and suffer her whipping. Two leather belts were produced, unfurled and snapped. At the harsh double crack, Oates glanced up and shivered.

Once her written confession had been completed and signed, Oates was ordered to approach the bed and to stretch out face-down into the duvet. Her pubic curls rasped softly as they brushed the gleaming satin.

'Head down, bottom up. Higher,' Krystal barked, tapping the round buttocks firmly with her straightened index finger. The nude shuddered at the touch of the plastic-sheathed fingertip as it dimpled-her upturned peach-like cheeks.

'Pillows,' Krystal nodded.

Beetle positioned two pillows between the satin duvet and the warm thighs above. Applying a gag to Oates, she smothered the rising grunts of protest and pleas for pity. The two nude punishers took up their positions - facing each other across he defenceless bare bottom that separated them.

'Excellent,' Krystal observed, dragging the tip of her supple leather belt across the crown of the vulnerable cheeks. 'To avoid scandal, Oates, copies of your signed confession will be sent to very agency—'

Oates writhed, twisting her head around. Krystal flicked the strap down across the bunched cheeks, scalding the quivering rump savagely. Oates lay still and silent, her face buried into the bed.

'At your expense, of course. You will be taken off every agency register and you will make full restitution to each of our victims. We'll see to it that you never again obtain a position of trust caring for the elderly. You will be denied,' Krystal hissed as she gathered up the length of cruel leather into her gloved hand, 'any opportunity to prey on the weak and the vulnerable. Do I make myself perfectly clear?'

Oates squirmed as she grunted her assent into the gag.

'Twenty strokes,' Krystal pronounced, relishing the sentence as she fingered the leather belt affectionately through the plastic gloves. The hide slid easily between her sheathed palms. Swallowing silently to lubricate her dry mouth, Krystal stared down at the bare buttocks she was about to blister with her belt. 'I shall administer the first eight lashes. You,' she gazed into Beetle's brown eyes, 'were superb last night. A most convincing performance. You've earned the lion's share. Give her the remaining twelve strokes, but remember Matron's instructions.'

'Severely?' the brown eyes widened.

'Severely,' Krystal echoed.

Down on the bed, the bare bottom tightened perceptibly, the cleft becoming a narrow crease between the anxious buttocks.

Crack, snap! The dark hide of the leather lashed down across the naked flesh as Krystal delivered the first of her eight searing strokes. The pliant curved domes spasmed in anguish, burning under the pink stripe of hot torment bequeathed by the bite of the belt. *Crack, swipe! Crack, lash!* Oates moaned into her tight gag, writhing as the punishment proceeded. *Crack, snap! Crack snap!* Oates bucked her hips, wriggling and twisting vainly to escape her pain.

'Hold her down!' Krystal barked.

Beetle dropped the belt she was absently rubbing against her hot slit and sprang upon the punished nude. Grappling with the hot-bottomed thief and easily mastering her, she pinned her victim to be bed then looked up with adoring eyes at Krystal.

'Got her.'

'Well done,' the dominant blonde purred approvingly, raising her strap once more.

The first eight lashes left the reddened bottom ablaze. Krystal dropped her leather belt to the carpeted floor and knelt at the bedside to examine the scalded cheeks. Oates flinched from the cool touch of the plastic gloves but Krystal gripped the firm buttocks and spread the punished flesh of the hot cheeks apart, exposing the cleft to her hovering thumbtips. The gloves cupped and ruthlessly squeezed the splayed buttocks as the thumbtips grazed the damp warmth of the shadowed cleft. Slowly, intimately, the punisher examined at close quarters the visible suffering of the punished.

Beetle picked up her belt and crushed it to her nipples as her brown eyes greedily drank in the scene on the bed. Her green-eyed blonde partner, perspiring slightly, bending down closely to inspect the hot cheeks. The shining plastic gloves, smoothing and palming the swollen mounds of ravished flesh. The penitent, stretched out face-down on her bed of pain and shame, her legs and thighs tautened in fearful expectation.

Krystal reached down and scooped up her length of leather. She doubled it up with mathematical exactitude, halving the cruel hide into a shorter strap. Slotting the belt between the striped buttocks, Krystal dragged the hide along the sensitive flesh of the exposed cleft. Oates squealed, thrusting her hips violently as she strove to rid herself of this intimate torment - her smothered protests audible despite the gag binding her mouth so severely. Removing the leather from the cleft between the bunched cheeks, Krystal buried her face down into the striped buttocks, biting softly into each mound. Nipping the creamy domes solemnly, the punisher bade the hot flesh of the punished nude *adieu*.

'Give her the remaining stripes,' Krystal said quietly, rising to her feet and moving towards the bedhead. 'Hold her by the wrists as you lash her.'

Beetle obeyed the dominant blonde's instruction, then snapped her belt harshly as she bent over the bare bottom on the bed below. *Crack! Crack!* The naked cheeks suffered the first of six double-swipes. The moans rose in plaintive response to the searing *swish, lash* of the leather. Pinning her victim's wrists together and planting her foot between her captive's shoulders, Beetle rendered Oates helplessly immobile - but superbly positioned for punishment. Beetle's slit seethed as she thrilled to her display of absolute dominance. Her brown eyes sparkled and her wet lips shone as she administered the next four savage stripes in quick succession. The leather, snapping harshly, blazed a sheen of blistering heat across the double domes of the scalded buttocks, each slice of dead hide across living flesh rocketing the squealing Oates into fresh paroxysms of torment. Eager that no centimetre of the bare bottom before her should escape the fierce kiss of her leather strap, Beetle knelt at the foot of the bed between her victim's splayed legs - forcing them apart as she inched her knees further between the trembling inner thighs. The reddened buttocks flattened slightly as Oates was forced to spread her thighs further apart - revealing to her punisher every secret detail of her body not already exposed and displayed. Crouching over the bottom, Beetle doubled up her strap and shouldered it expertly. *Crack, snap! Crack, swipe!* From her new angle of attack, Beetle scorched the inner curves of the whipped cheeks accurately, ruthlessly and unerringly. The cleft tightened to a thin flesh-crease as Oates clenched her ravaged rump, but Beetle tweaked the left buttock in a cruel pincer of finger and thumb - a silent command to the nude to spread her cheeks wide. The bottom softened and obeyed. A muffled sob escaped the gagged lips as another double dose of swiping leather visited the crimson cheeks with a vicious caress. *Snap, slash! Crack, crack!* Again, Beetle plied her supple hide across the living skin, then immediately crouched down, catlike, to crush her breasts fully into the punished buttocks. Beneath her bosom, Beetle sensed the punished nude writhe in an ecstasy of anguish.

'Keep still,' Beetle admonished, peeling her breasts away from the hot flesh - instantly pinioning the bottom beneath the splayed fingers of her controlling left hand. The whipped cheeks dimpled submissively at the dominant touch. Beetle slowly taloned her fingers and squeezed.

From her vantage point at the head of the bed, the watching blonde nodded approvingly as a sorceress might smile upon her nubile apprentice in their alchemist's lair.

'Good,' Krystal murmured. 'You must take full control during all stages of discipline. Make sure she surrenders her bottom utterly to you. Make sure that you own it completely.'

Beetle glanced up and smiled, basking in her partner's approbation. Feeling the warm drizzle of arousal seeping from her tingling labia, Beetle eased herself up a fraction before guiding her slit down against the luscious curves of the whipped bottom beneath her. Oates jerked and wriggled as Beetle's sticky lust-juice spread itself across the reddened cheeks. Squatting, Beetle ground her wet slit into the hot rump, then dragged her open wound against its firm flesh - drying her love-lips on the very cause of their wetness. Unable to see, but able to comprehend, this gesture of utter domination, Oates threshed violently as Beetle rode her supremely saddled.

'Whip her,' Krystal snapped impatiently. 'We are here for her punishment, not your pleasure.'

Chastened by the curt command, Beetle sank her bottom back on her ankles, gathered up the length of supple leather and addressed the buttocks quivering before her. Closing her eyes as she raised the belt aloft, she savoured the heady sensation of punishment and domination - relishing the helplessness of the pinioned nude; the potent weight of the strap in her hand; the imminence of another *Swish, crack* as she seared the crimson globes. Beetle felt the sweat prickle her brows, matting the dark curls at her temples. Arching back her neck, she tensed her whipping arm. The small muscles rippled in her upper arm and the length of leather shivered. For delicious seconds Beetle deliberately delayed the moment: the moment when the dark band of hide would snap down across the upturned cheeks below. Breathing slowly, she savoured the exquisite delay, licking her dry lips with the tip of her pink tongue. On her bed of sorrow, Oates jerked her hips, threatening to topple her tormentress. Beetle mastered her victim easily, clamping her thighs and knees tight against the captive torso, not so much to restrain her naked quarry but to contain the fresh trickle of warmth quick silvering from her slit. She was, for a brief but absolute moment, the embodiment of justice and punishment: a naked Nemesis.

Crack, crack! The whipping leather spoke more eloquently of punishment than any sermon ever could. A rebuke would have been wasted on Oates. These were the cruel words which she would both understand and heed. *Crack, crack!* The naked nurse moaned as her bare bottom was once more left to seethe beneath the blazing invisible flames of pain.

'Excellent,' observed Krystal, fleetingly stroking her clitoris with the tip of her plastic-sheathed thumb. 'Justice has been done.'

Beetle did not reply, but basked in her partner's approval. She gathered up the leather belt and pressed it to her mouth. In reverent silence, she kissed the hide, tasting its dark, cruel tang. Punishment, to the younger avenging angel, was a pious pleasure.

For the second time that morning, Krystal surrendered her nakedness to the stinging sluice of a hot shower. Unlike her previous visit to the showers, when she had kept an unblinking eye on Oates, Krystal indulged in the luxury of keeping her eyes closed. Behind their tightly shut lids, images of the thief persisted: Oates in the shower, her breasts bulging as she struggled with the secret clasp; Oates in the moment of accusation - her eyes widening as she sensed her impending doom; Oates, naked once more beneath Krystal's stern gaze, stretched out face-down for punishment.

Krystal opened her eyes, shuddering with delight as the shower sluiced her breasts, the cascade raking her peaked nipples. Closing her eyes, she shuddered again as she recalled the first stroke of the leather across the bare buttocks of the thief they had unmasked.

Kneeling down before Krystal, her wet bosom crushed into the blonde's shining thighs, Beetle sensed her partner's shudders and flashed her brown eyes upwards. Withdrawing slightly, she eased her breasts away from their cushion of wet flesh.

'Why have you stopped?' Krystal murmured dreamily.

'I felt you quiver. Was I too fierce?'

'It was just a memory. Come back to me. Be as fierce as you can.'

Beetle buried her face in the blonde's pubic snatch. They always celebrated a successful mission this way - naked, together, in a hot shower. As if obeying some secret rite, some ancient ritual, Krystal allowed herself to be soaped and sponged, fingered and licked, bitten and ruthlessly tongued.

'Harder,' Krystal whispered huskily.

The kneeling brunette sucked deeply at the sweet flesh and raised her face a fraction, capturing the erect clitoris between her small white teeth. Tugging gently, she teased the flesh-thorn until Krystal was arching up on tip-toe in sheer ecstasy. Sensing the blonde's urgency, Beetle buried her mouth into the pungent wetness; feeding hungrily as she would on an oozing over-ripe fig. Krystal half-screamed, the shrillness collapsing to a carnal grunt. Maddened by the sucking, the sounds of lapping down at her crotch, she thrust her hip forward and reached out both hands - clutching the mop of wet curls at her belly. With a snarl of feral pleasure, she forced the kneeling girl's face inwards.

'Tongue me.' The words were something of a pleading whimper, though Beetle recognized in them something of a stern command.

Beetle's brown eyes sparkled with lust. Gazing at the smooth white belly in adoration, she stretched out her thickening tongue and probed. This was the moment she relished. Her own slit spasmed as she gripped Krystal's soft bottom with both hands and pulled the parted thighs towards her. Kneeling in willing submission to serve and pleasure Krystal, Beetle knew that she was, however fleetingly, totally in control. The dominant blonde - now riding her face with her splayed thighs - was in fact at Beetle's mercy. It was the kneeling brunette, not the blonde who straddled her, dictating the terms. The erotic equation, the balance of sexual power, was Beetle's to resolve. And this knowledge caused Beetle to come.

Still trembling in her climax, Beetle drove her muscled tongue deeper still into Krystal. The blonde responded by gripping the wet curls tightly - and suddenly loosening her grasp to pat and stroke the head at her belly, caressing the kneeling girl as a melting warmth flooded between her thighs.

'Tongue me,' urged Krystal, the note of pleading softening her normally strict tone.

Smiling her secret smile of triumph, of control, of possession, Beetle meekly obeyed. Two-and-a-quarter minutes later, the blonde in her thrall buckled beneath an orgasm of sweet savagery. Beetle encircled the buttocks tightly as the woman both ruled and obeyed came, digging her fingers into Krystal's slippery thighs. Krystal's splayed fingers scrabbled drunkenly at the wet tiles of the cubicle, then clenched into fists of ecstasy as Beetle thumbed the cleft deep between the blonde's buttocks. A fresh climax welled up and exploded softly at the base of her firm white belly as Krystal pounded her pubis into the face of her kneeling love-slave who - for that supreme moment in measureless time - ruled her with absolute sovereignty.

Breakfast proved to be quite an unexpected banquet. With appetites sharpened by both punishment and pleasure, they set about the Yorkshire breakfast of Homeric proportions. Thick slices of Knaresborough gammon, anointed with peaches and Dijon mustard sauce, overflowed the rims of their huge breakfast-plates. The gammons left little room for the crisply fried potatoes and grilled tomatoes, asparagus spears and mushrooms seethed in white port. They left little room either for the freshly baked rolls that followed even though they were smeared with wild Wensleydale honey. Matron's specially blended Assam tea was darkly delicious and reviving. Krystal managed a second roll which she daubed with honey. She allowed an escaping golden drizzle down the length of her left thumb with her tongue-tip. Beetle, contenting herself with a pear, watched the tongue chase the sweet ooze. Flickering her green eyes above her hand, Krystal watched her younger partner peel and prepare the luscious fruit; watched as Beetle lowered her mouth slowly down upon the globe of ripe flesh; watched the lips surround, then suck before biting. By the time Beetle had dispatched the pear and patted her lips with her napkin, Krystal's thumb was glistening with the runaway ooze from her forgotten roll. Dropping the roll on her plate, the blonde bowed her head down to her thumb and licked slowly at the sticky sweetness.

'Let me,' Beetle pleaded.

Krystal rotated her wrist, her thumb now directed towards the open mouth of the eager brunette. Beetle's breasts bulged as she stretched across the table to take the honeyed thumb between her lips. The blonde shivered as she felt the muscled walls of the warm mouth tighten around the length of her straightened flesh.

'You two certainly enjoy your food,' Matron remarked archly as she entered the breakfast room. 'Any tea left in the pot?'

Slipping her thumb free, Krystal poured out a cup of tea for their host. She glimpsed Beetle, in awe of the stern beauty in starched uniform, averting her gaze from Matron and down to her plate to study the remains of her pear.

'You've been wonderful. All my problems solved,' Matron beamed over her large breakfast cup. 'And no threat of scandal. That written confession. A brilliant idea. Shan't use it, but Oates needn't know. Payment,' she continued, fishing out an envelope from her crisp uniform, 'as promised.'

Krystal nodded, pocketing the envelope unopened and the contents uncounted. The gesture, she knew, would make her partner glow with secret pride. Opening the envelope to check its contents would have been so unsophisticated. Krystal knew the depth of Beetle's adoration, and strove to keep it just so.

'I'll eventually retrieve and restore all these stolen items to their rightful owners. Some of the relatives were growing quite impatient, I must admit. Anxious about the whereabouts of their heirlooms, no doubt. Things were getting very sticky. Oates could have caused me untold damage. But with this,' Matron flourished the confession, 'her goose is cooked. I hope you roasted her well?'

'Just as the chef ordered,' Krystal purred.

Matron smiled.

'Anything else, Matron?' Krystal asked.

'No, I don't think so. Perhaps...' Matron paused, her voice dropping to an excited whisper. 'The leather belts. May I have them?'

'Souvenirs?' Krystal smiled indulgently.

'No, not exactly,' Matron replied, her tone curdling thickly.

Krystal's green eyes narrowed as she caught the darker note of desire beneath the prim vowels.

Packed and ready to depart, they waited for the taxi. It would have been a pleasantly brisk walk across the Stray - the vast park-land unique to Harrogate - to the station but the cold rain was driving hard against the windows of the nursing home.

Krystal looked up the stairs to where she knew their hostess would already be engrossed in her task for the rest of the morning. The urge to see Matron became overwhelming: Krystal succumbed.

'Just popping up to say goodbye. Stay here in case our taxi comes.'

Matron would not be in her office, Krystal knew. Turning at the top of the stairs, she headed straight for the room where Oates had been exposed as a thief - and then dealt with so mercilessly. At first, there was no response to Krystal's gentle tap at the door. Perhaps she was mistaken. *But the request for the leather belts. Surely—*

A key turned in the lock.

'Who is it?' the voice of Matron inquired.

'Me.'

The door opened a fraction.

'Our taxi's due any minute. Just a final goodbye.'

Matron smiled and, leaning towards Krystal, kissed the young blonde warmly on the mouth. Krystal peeped over matron's shoulder and caught a tantalizing glimpse of Oates. The naked thief was arranged face-down across the bed, her arms and upper thighs bound tightly together by the leather belts which had striped her buttocks earlier on. Pillows had been inserted beneath her belly, raising her reddened cheeks in passive surrender. Krystal smiled to herself. Apart from the refinement of the bondage-belts, Matron had copied their own methods exactly. Krystal frowned, puzzled by the single yellow rubber glove that lay on the carpet, tossed down next to the talcum powder, jar of cold cream and box of tissues.

'Having a little spot of revenge?'

'Yes,' Matron whispered excitedly. 'I'm spanking her. Spanking her bare bottom very, very hard.'

'The talc? And the cream?'

'I like to be thorough in the aftercare. Besides, they soften the bottom - for more.'

'And the glove?' Krystal murmured.

'So thrilling, the rubber. The firm smack of a rubber-gloved hand across a naughty bare bottom.'

'The tissues?' Krystal whispered.

'One gets so excited, spanking. I'd almost forgotten. It's a long time since I disciplined a student nurse across my knee. One gets so wet.'

They kissed goodbye, Krystal thrilling to the rasp of Matron's powerful tongue against her own. As the blonde turned to descend the stairs, her pulse hammered at her temples. Matron had discarded most of her starched uniform, remaining clad only in dark stockings, a clear plastic apron and a prim white hat. The plastic apron was clouded with the moist warmth of her arousal and the trim little hat was awry. Matron's breasts, Krystal had observed, were naked, proud and ripe. So heavy, so firm and so ripe. How deliciously they would bounce as the rubber-gloved spanking hand swept down across the suffering bottom.

The train slid out of Harrogate making less noise than the lashing rain which turned their carriage window into a silvered mirror. Denied a view of the fleeting countryside, Krystal stared into the depths of her reflected calm gaze. They were speeding back to London to their Wapping studio where there was plenty to be done: a clay face to be reconstructed; a petite brunette to be caned. Perhaps another assignment for them. They were gaining a solid reputation for the quality of their service and were highly esteemed by all who had engaged them.

Closing her eyes, Krystal pictured Oates stretched face-down across the bed, her bare buttocks obediently upturned Tightly pinioned in the leather belts of her bondage, the penitent thief would be tasting Matron's rubber-gloved fury. Krystal's wide lips broadened to a smile as she imagined the spanking hand sweeping down against the shuddering cheeks of the reddening round bottom. Later, when the sharp smacking sounds had ceased, Matron would assiduously attend to the ravaged rump, inspecting with clinical expertise the scorched buttocks before dusting them with talc. Peeling off the hot rubber glove, Matron would commence to palm and smooth the spanked bottom with her strong, cool hand. Cold cream would then be applied, worked slowly into the scalded flesh with dominantly splayed finger-tips: soothing and preparing the swollen cheeks for a fresh onslaught of the rubber-gloved spanking hand. Even now - Krystal shivered with delicious anticipation - Matron's stiff forefinger would be sliding down along the warm velvet of the cleft between the punished nurse's hot buttocks. Would the fingertip pause to rest at the tightened anal whorl? Would Matron worry the flinching sphincter in a gesture of supreme dominance? Matron, Krystal decided, would be enjoying her role as stern disciplinarian: by the time the train hurtled through Doncaster tissues would be wiping the wet warmth of arousal from the tops of Matron's dark stockings - and by the time the train reached London, the box of tissues at the foot of the bed of punishment and pain would be empty.

They split up at Kings Cross.
    'I'll take the Circle Line to Notting Hill,' Beetle said.
    She was due for an audition at Jimmy Beez's in the Portobello Road.
    'That frozen-fish ad?'
    'Swordfish,' Beetle nodded. 'But it's only a voice-over part for the tele-campaign. Samantha wants to put me through my paces.'

Cruising the plate-glass facades of Cork Street, Krystal followed the fortunes of more established sculptors by the prices their works commanded. Peter Martin, the Norwich neo-realist, was now boasting five-figure sums, she discovered.
    After a Caesar salad in Harvey Nicholls in the shrill company of TV weather-girls, she took a taxi back to the converted loft in Wapping and watched her *Wallace and Grommit* tapes.
    Beetle crept in late.
    'I'm awake,' Krystal drawled, stopping Beetle dead in her tip-toe tracks. 'Considerate of you to make no noise,' she added drily.
    The little matter of the brunette's punishment, four strokes of the cane across her bare bottom, was uppermost in the minds of each woman - though no mention of it had been made.
    'It's a bit chilly in here,' Beetle remarked, launching into diversionary tactics with an exaggerated shiver.
    'I'm sure I'll find a way of warming you up.'
    Beetle shivered again - this time at the hint of menace in Krystal's polite tone.
    'I'm sorry I'm late—'
    'You really must be cured of this habit you've acquired of creeping about,' Krystal purred. 'Remember what you made me do to my clay face?'
    Beetle hung her head, knowing that her fate was sealed. Sensing her doom she padded towards the bedroom.
    'I've switched our blanket on but the bed may still be chilly,' Krystal called out

pleasantly.

Sensing the possibility of a reprieve, Beetle turned at the door. 'I'll wriggle around a bit and warm it up for you—'

'Strip down to your panties,' Krystal interrupted suavely. 'I'll be with you in a moment. Four strokes, we agreed, did we not?'

From the safety of the bedroom, Beetle poked her tongue out over her shoulder.

'And stop pulling faces, young lady, or I'll double your punishment,' Krystal admonished, fighting to keep her smile at bay.

'Wasn't,' came the muffled, unconvincing protest through the pullover around Beetle's head.

Krystal joined the brunette in the bedroom and picked up the whippy bamboo cane.

'Bend over. Hands apart on the bed. No, leave your panties on. I will attend to them when the moment is ripe.'

With a soft whimper, Beetle obeyed, her bare breasts bulging and her dark curls tumbling as she offered her bottom up for its stripes.

'Legs together. Tuck your right foot in behind your left,' instructed the blonde, for whom the pleasures of punishment should never be rushed.

The bending brunette's bottom loomed up, stretching the sheath of cotton tightly as the cheeks burgeoned. Krystal absently traced her finger across their perfect swollen symmetry. Applying the tip of the quivering cane to the left cheek, she tapped it dominantly. Suddenly, she withdrew the cane and bent down to examine the pantied bottom more closely.

'I thought you told me your audition was for a voice-over,' she snapped, her tone waspish with jealous anger.

'It was. For frozen swordfish steaks—'

'Little liar. Your panties are on inside out and before you deny it,' Krystal's voice rose angrily, 'I saw you getting dressed this morning and they weren't then.'

Beetle remained silent, but her bottom clenched eloquently announcing her fear of the stinging wrath to come.

'Quick change under the table at Jimmy Beez's?'

'We went on,' Beetle whispered. 'To her flat. Samantha suggested it—' The words spilled out quickly now, urgent in their pleading, 'I didn't really want to but—'

'And did you get it? From Samantha?' Krystal whispered, dragging the tip of the whippy cane down the depth of the brunette's cleft.

'You mean the part for the ad?'

'What else could I possibly mean?'

Beetle swallowed silently, her mouth too dry for speech. The dominant blonde noted the brunette's taloned fingers gripping the duvet penitently.

'Keep your feet positioned exactly as they are for the first four strokes,' Krystal hissed. 'Wider apart, with your hands at your ankles for the next six—'

Beetle whimpered and started to plead as her panties were removed.

'Silence,' barked Krystal, savagely depressing the yellow cane down against the swell of the upturned cheeks.

Swish, swipe! The first slicing stroke swept down, biting into the fleshy buttocks, leaving their superb curves shivering beneath a single pink line. *Swish, swipe!* The second stroke kissed the flesh with a vicious caress, adding another blushing stripe to the deepening red of the first.

'At least *you* will be warm in bed tonight,' the jealous blonde rasped, raising her cane up above the bare bottom below.

Chapter Two

Krystal stood naked in the bathroom before the full-length mirror. With the eye of a sculptress she appraised her structure beneath the neon striplight. Her waist swept down to the roundness of her hips, conforming exactly to the prescribed proportions of neo-classical erotic perfection. Palming her buttocks, she thrust her hips forward, ruthlessly examining her slender legs. They rose up deliciously into creamy thighs meeting and merging behind the blonde snatch of her pubic nest. Above them the firm belly, and above the belly her naked breasts. They were heavily fleshed, their swollen curves thrusting in unashamed triumph. The nipples were a deep pink and semi-erect. Planting her hands palm-inwards against the clouded glass of the mirror, Krystal eased her nakedness forward, squashing her bosom into its own reflection. She moaned as her breasts bunched against the cold glass, instantly thrilling to the ache of her hard nipples peaking in protest. With a sinuous ripple of her hips, she brushed her pubis against the glass, deliberately catching her labia and spreading the lips apart. Swallowing her soft grunt of pleasure, Krystal repeated the motion, dragging her squashed breasts and belly against their mirror image - and splaying her labia even wider apart.

Remembering the strict caning she had administered to Beetle the night before, she lapsed into a reverie, gently bumping her hips and thighs into the hard glass in time with the recollection of the *swish, swipes* of her whippy bamboo across the bare-buttocked brunette. Her clitoris rose in salute to the memories, kissing the cold surface of the mirror - as did her nipples above - each time Krystal recalled another searing stroke. By the time her reverie had recaptured eight cane-cuts across the squirming brunette's bottom, Krystal's nipples were seething. Between her trembling thighs, her slit tingled and began to weep for joy. Krystal hurried the remembered strokes: closing her eyes into fierce concentration as she pounded her breasts and pubis rhythmically into the hard glass.

Suddenly, with a sobbing gasp, she arched up onto her toes. They scrabbled on the white tiles beneath as tremors of her welling ecstasy arrowed down from her belly to her thighs. At the slippery glass, her splayed fingers clawed for a hold, their pawing frantic as the naked blonde screamed softly, twice, and came. Spinning round, Krystal spread her legs wide and jammed her spasming buttocks hard against the glass, savagely forcing her cheeks apart, causing the heat of her lust to cloud the silver surface at her cleft. Grinding her rump as she orgasmed, Krystal cupped and squeezed her breasts, pleasure-punishing their moist weight with brutal tenderness.

Under the shower, she sluiced away the pungent tang of her arousal, soaping herself luxuriously between her pulsating thighs. Towelled and talcumed, she swept her fingers through her blonde crop. A faint scent of her recent excitement from her hot slit below greeted her nostrils. Orange Water. That's what she needed, she decided. An indulgent splash of her cool, fragrant Orange Water. Her fingers stretched out towards the glass shelf. Finding the solid onyx bottle, they closed around it and retrieved it to the warmth of her soft bosom. Nestling the cool onyx in her cleavage, Krystal lowered her head to unstopper it with her teeth. Pausing, she frowned. To her annoyance, the stopper was loose. Beetle, she realized angrily, had been using it again. Stealing it, despite stern warnings not behave so selfishly. Krystal dabbed absently at her nipples with the fragrance as she scrutinized her end of the shower shelf. It was as she had suspected: several items had been disturbed. Tubes of lotion had been greedily squeezed and jars of cream had been raided. Splashing a cupped handful of Orange Water against the swell of her bare bottom, then patting her glistening palm against her pubis, Krystal returned the stopper to the onyx bottle with her teeth and strode out of the bathroom, splendidly naked, intent on confronting the naughty brunette.

She found Beetle in the kitchen, dressed in an oyster silk blouse, the unbuttoned cuffs rolled up to her elbows, listening to Thin Lizzie's 'Buffalo Girl' as she poached eggs and thumbed open soft muffins for the toaster. Dancing to the hypnotic drumming and haunting bass, her bare buttocks joggled enticingly beneath the flap of the silk blouse.

Encircling her quarry with an arm, and hugging tightly, Krystal crushed Beetle's bosom within its sheath of silk. She felt the brunette easing herself away from the seething pan of poached eggs and surrendering blissfully to the embrace. Krystal pressed her bosom into the brunette, fusing herself with her captive in frank and utter intimacy before burying her face down into Beetle's neck and shoulder - snuffing deeply. Filtering out the competing aromas of freshly ground coffee and toasting muffins, her nostrils detected the tell-tale trace of stolen Orange Water.

'Toasted muffins?' the brunette asked brightly.

'I'll toast your muffins,' Krystal whispered darkly.

'No—' Beetle squealed, as the dominant blonde behind her raised the flap of her silk blouse.

'Bad girl,' Krystal murmured, squeezing the exposed left cheek fiercely, and retaining it in a merciless grip.

'Ow,' Beetle protested as she felt the fingers talon her naked buttock.

Krystal slid down to her knees, rasping her labia firmly on Beetle's bottom as she did so. Gazing directly into the brunette's buttocks, the kneeling blonde finger-traced the pink stripes bequeathed by her bamboo discipline of the previous night. Replacing the firm finger-tip with a firmer tongue Krystal licked each treacherous stripe of her cane across the creamy cheeks. Inching her face into the satin softness of the swollen globes, the strict blonde mouthed her stern warning directly into the pliant flesh. With her lips sensuously whispering the words into the brunette's swollen crowns Krystal admonished Beetle yet again - warning her not to steal from her end of the shower shelf.

Framing the soft cheek between her slender hands, and thumbing the cleft between them painfully apart, she inserted the tip of her sparkling tongue into the shadowed warmth. Krystal smiled grimly as she sensed Beetle arching up on her naked tip-toes, gasping aloud in fearful expectation. The blonde's tongue flickered: the brunette squealed.

Their entry-phone buzzed - and the muffins shot out of the toaster with a clatter - sparing Beetle further delicious torment. Krystal released her. She scampered off.

'It's Samantha,' she called from the door.

'Swordfish-steaks-Samantha?' Krystal asked from the bedroom.

'That's the one,' giggled the brunette, scampering back to rescue the poached eggs.

Krystal emerged from the bedroom wrapped in a bottle green sarong, thigh-level and cut severely at the bosom, to find Beetle and Samantha locked in urgent conspiratorial whispering. Samantha was, Krystal observed keenly, a full-breasted redhead with sky-blue eyes and a smile stretching from ear to ear. They sprang apart, Beetle murmuring something about coffee. Krystal sat down, inviting Samantha to join her at the breakfast table. The visitor tossed her head of Titian curls and called out to Beetle in the kitchen - apologizing for spilling wine on her dress at lunch the day before.

'So silly of me. Still,' Samantha babbled hurriedly, 'a quick sponge down at my flat saved the day.'

Krystal peppered her poached eggs in silence as Beetle came to stand in the doorway, her look of wounded saintliness directed at the dominant blonde. *Told you,* she seemed to be saying reproachfully, as if rebuking Krystal for the previous night's jealousy and punishment.

'Wine?' Krystal inquired, unperturbed by Beetle's martyred air. 'Beetle said it was coffee.'

'Yes, coffee—'

'No, wine—'

Beetle and Samantha squeaked in uncorroborating unison. Krystal turned her green eyes towards Beetle, gazing with cool dismissiveness at the brunette. Beetle blushed and fiddled awkwardly with the buttons at her bosom.

'I'd put on some panties if I were you,' Krystal suggested drily. 'The right way round.'

Crushed, Beetle withdrew to the bedroom.

'Do I detect toasted muffins?' Samantha asked in a bright, somewhat desperate, voice.

'Quite possibly,' Krystal smiled enigmatically. 'Coffee, Samantha?' she continued graciously. 'Or would you settle for wine?'

Breakfast completed, during which the three women had agreed that their favourite all-girl band was Kenickie, voting the wham-bam *I'm Your Car* an all-time winner, Samantha came to the purpose of her visit.

'Beetle, you've got the part. See you in the studio the day after tomorrow. OK?'

'You could have phoned,' Krystal remarked, interrupting her younger partner's squeal of delight.

'I wanted to speak to both of you,' Samantha continued, her tone becoming grave. 'I have an assignment for you.'

Her sky-blue eyes clouding as she spoke, Samantha told them how her flat-mate had recently consulted a hypnotherapist to help her to slim.

'Successfully?' asked Krystal.

'No!' Samantha shook her Titian curls violently. 'I went as well. Trying to give up smoking. It's not allowed in the studio any more. Mucks up the magnetic tape.'

Krystal nodded.

'Any good?' Beetle chipped in sympathetically.

After a slight pause, Samantha explained that both she and her flat-mate had abandoned the consultations. Both of them had been molested under hypnosis.

'We swapped notes and there's no doubt about it. All we want now is to have that

hypnotherapist—'
'Punished?' whispered Krystal.

The polished brass plate confirmed that they were at the Baker Street address Samantha had given them.

'Alex, our hankie-pankie hypnotherapist, is up on the third floor,' Krystal observed after checking the list of incumbents. 'Are you sure your panties are on inside out?'

'Mmm,' Beetle giggled. 'But I still don't see—'

'Up you go, then. I'll wait in that espresso bar opposite.'

'*What* is my problem, again?' Beetle frowned.

'Kleptomania. Stealing other people's Orange Water.'

Beetle poked out her tongue at the retreating figure of her partner before stepping inside the dull entrance to the block of 'professional' suites.

Krystal meanwhile had crossed the busy road and entered the aromatic warmth of the coffee bar - leaving the raw November afternoon to the Japanese tourists threading toward the Planetarium. She dawdled over her first coffee, then made a phone call on her mobile while waiting for her second cappuccino. Beetle joined her just as she finished spooning out the bitter-sweet froth from her second cup.

'Well?' the green eyes inquired over the rim of the glass cup.

Beetle looked flushed and tousled. 'I can't remember, really. It's all a bit weird. I had some very peculiar dreams, like you used to under gas at the dentist's. Alex said—'

'Check your panties,' the blonde said briskly.

Beetle surreptitiously obeyed. 'They seem OK.'

'On properly?'

'Of course,' the brunette shrugged. 'I'm very damp, though. You know. Down there.'

'Then we've all the proof we need. Your panties were on inside out. Remember?'

Beetle nodded, suddenly recollecting the ruse.

'Alex didn't notice,' Krystal whispered. 'After putting you under, and having a good time with you, he put them back on as he thought they should—'

'He?' Beetle interrupted. 'Alex is a she. Short for Alexis.'

'Let's go,' Krystal hissed, the pupils of her green eyes dilating a fraction. 'The riding crop' is in my bag.'

Stepping out of the lift at the third floor, Krystal followed Beetle to the dark oak door.

'She's in here.'

'Go straight in,' Krystal nodded, pausing as she entered the room to adjust the sign to 'Engaged'.

'I'm afraid I'm finished for today,' the hypnotherapist said, busying herself with some papers on her polished mahogany desktop.

'Oh, I think you'll find time to see us,' Krystal said softly.

'I'm sorry—' Alex began, her voice rising.

Ignoring the tone of protest, Krystal locked the door and walked across to the front of the desk and sat down next to Beetle.

'I really must insist—'

'There are certain matters which have come to our attention regarding your activities as a hypnotherapist.' Krystal's tone was neutral.

'Inland Revenue?' hazarded Alex, paling visibly. 'I was just about to return my self-assessment,' she lied unconvincingly.

'It is not a question of your financial probity,' Krystal continued, 'though I'm sure a visit from the tax man wouldn't go amiss. No,' her tone sharpened, 'I'm talking about gross professional misconduct. Stand up, Beetle.'

Beetle obeyed the command.

'Slip out of your things.'

'What is going on—' Alexis gasped.

'Silence!' Krystal's bark had the woman backing away towards the wall.

Having quickly unbuttoned her blouse and wriggled out of it, Beetle unzipped her tight-fitting skirt.

'I really must protest—'

'I thought I told you to remain silent,' Krystal warned the hypnotherapist, danger in her voice.

With Alexis chastened into mute anguish, Beetle continue to strip. She waggled her hips sensually as the skirt slithered down to her feet. Kicking off her shoes and stepping out of her skirt, she stood by the mahogany desk, scantily clad in a pretty bra and panties. The polished surface of the desk reflected the proud mound of her pubis - faithfully mirroring the dark wet stain at her slit.

'This is monstrous,' Alexis managed to splutter, reddening as she realized the nature of the charges levelled against her.

Krystal stretched out her hand and placed her forefinger at the base of Beetle's belly, then slid it downwards to tap the moistened panties at the pubis. Gazing at the blushing hypnotherapist, Krystal wondered fleetingly if this woman's buttocks would crimson as deeply as had her face after a taste of the crop across their nakedness.

'My colleague came to you thirty minutes ago. You squeezed her in between appointments. During the consultation,' Krystal got to her feet as she spoke and strode towards the leather couch, stroking its dimpled hide lingeringly, 'you molested her while she was under hypnosis.'

'That's a lie. An outrageous lie—'

Krystal bent down and tapped the surface of the soft leather. Raising her fingertips to her nose, she sniffed: reducing Alexis to a spellbound silence.

'Yes,' Krystal whispered, gazing over her splayed fingertip at the frightened hypnotherapist. 'There is sufficient evidence here.'

'You can't prove anything. You'll never—'

'Then, of course, there are the panties. Look at them. Now get up and examine them carefully.'

Scowling, the accused bent across the desk top, her breasts bulging against the dark mahogany as she peered at Beetle's pubic mound. Beetle remained impassive under scrutiny, shifting slightly from foot to foot, causing her buttocks to ripple within the taut sheath of her panties.

'And what do you see?' Krystal snapped.

Alexis replied sullenly that she could see nothing unusual.

'Precisely,' whispered the blonde.

Alexis frowned, uncertain and confused.

'And yet,' Krystal purred venomously, 'I personally saw to it that those panties were worn inside out for the consultation and they're now the correct way. I'm afraid you slipped up there, didn't you?'

Alexis bit her lip and swore softly.

'We are here to see that certain measures are taken to prevent you from molesting future clients!'

Turning to Beetle, Krystal asked: 'Remember Vanessa Wetherby?'

'Yes. Probably resting between parts,' Beetle nodded, casually shedding her brassiere and panties.

'I'll give her another buzz.' Krystal fished out her mobile.

Vanessa Wetherby, who graced the bar of the *Goat In Boots* on the Fulham Road when not doing occasional TV spots, answered Krystal's call.

'Beetle and I need you for that little job I mentioned earlier.'

'You absolute darlings,' boomed the reply. 'When's the interview?'

'No interview. You're uniquely qualified,' Krystal assured the former games mistress of Birch Hall who had dispensed memorable spankings. 'The job is perfect for you. Grab a cab and come at once,' Krystal instructed, giving the Baker Street address.

'She's coming?' Beetle asked.

'On her way. I spoke with her from the espresso bar while you were being fingered by Svengali here. Put her in the picture.' Krystal turned to Alexis. 'You will take her on as your highly paid assistant. Her duties will be to keep a very strict eye on you. She will attend all your future consultations.'

Alexis slumped down at her desk, her fingers whitening as they knuckled the mahogany.

'She will be reporting back regularly, but I'm sure there'll be no need for us to have to make a return visit.'

Alexis looked up, resentment glittering in her narrowed eyes.

'Spoiled your little set up here, haven't we? No, don't worry about Beetle being cold,' Krystal smiled disarmingly. 'She'll be quite busy in a few minutes. Warm work, punishment.'

Alexis flickered her eyes in fearful apprehension.

'How much do you want? I can get—'

'Get undressed,' Krystal interrupted. 'I want you naked.'

Alexis glared and began to protest.

'This instant,' snapped the blonde, angrily producing the riding crop and whipping it down across the hide of the sleek leather couch.

Alexis stumbled a few paces from her desk and slowly began to strip. For the first time, Krystal and Beetle were able to fully appreciate - while intimately perusing - the woman they were about to whip. Alexis was a strawberry blonde in her late thirties. An unarguably beautiful woman, she was approaching the very peak of her potential: grey-eyed, with a sensual pink-lipsticked mouth and a slender white neck. She reluctantly revealed her voluptuous bosom as her fingers nervously unclasped a snow-white La Perla brassiere. It was neither padded nor underwired so ripe was the bosom it embraced, the La Perla stretched and strained to tame and control the heavy breasts. The loosened bra fluttered down to encircle her red high-heels, silently joining the silk blouse which had slithered down moments before. The breasts - full, firm and proudly thrusting - rose and fell rhythmically as the semi-naked strawberry blonde grew increasingly fearful of the riding crop destined for her bare bottom.

Toying with the supple cane, Krystal's eyes devoured the ripe swell of the unadorned bosom. Dimpling the leather couch with the tip of her crop, her gaze lingered on

Alexis, on the naked breasts, on the dark nipples as they puckered up in fear. Krystal noted how the breasts bulged as Alexis struggled forward to step out of her pencil-line unzipped black skirt. Standing up straight now, naked except for her light-tan tights, the hypnotherapist tossed her head back in a gesture of futile defiance.

'Leave those on,' Krystal murmured, pointing with the tip of the riding crop at the tan tights. 'Beetle will see to them prior to your punishment.'

Beetle, who had been sitting on the desk swinging her legs, eased her soft bottom from the polished mahogany and approached the dark leather couch. With a crisp gesture, she summoned the strawberry blonde to face her. Beetle sank down to the carpet, kneeling before the trembling nude. Krystal paced around the couple, circling twice, before coming to a halt behind Alexis. She tapped the plump curves of the hypnotherapist's buttocks with her crop.

'Hands up behind your neck. Wrists together,' she instructed.

Alexis obeyed, her breasts swelling as she buried her fingers in her shining hair.

'Stay absolutely still,' Krystal warned, pressing the length of the riding crop against the swollen buttocks. 'And remain silent. She is,' Krystal continued softly, 'all yours, Beetle.'

Beetle framed the hips before her with outstretched hands. Fingering the darker waist band of the tights, she tugged gently at the glossy nylon. Slowly, intimately, she palmed the tights down, relishing the rustle of the peeled sheen across the pubic fuzz. The sudden urge to press her flattened tongue against the gusset of glossy nylon was checked by a rebuke from the ever-watchful Krystal: a stern but silent rebuke signalled by a warning tap of the crop.

The fragrance of the exposed pubis inches from her nostrils was intoxicating - but Beetle's fear of the crop was greater. Swallowing to lubricate her dry mouth, Beetle peeled the tan tights down further, fully exposing the creamy thighs as her palms inched past the knees. Soon, the svelte legs were revealed in naked splendour. Beetle drew back to examine her nude captive. Sinking her buttocks down onto her ankles, her knuckles grazed one of the abandoned red high-heels. Picking up the shoe, she raised it to her lips and licked the hide, slowly savouring its tang. Peering over the red leather, Beetle sought permission from her stern partner. Krystal wavered momentarily before nodding. Beetle clasped the shoe by the pointed toe and raised it up. Ordering Alexis to turn and present her naked bottom, she dragged the four-inch spiked heel across the swell of the buttocks before her.

'I am examining the pliancy of your bottom,' Beetle announced. 'Before I stripe your bare buttocks with the crop, I have to judge where best to plant each stroke.'

Alexis whimpered and clenched her rounded cheeks. Calling for silence in a stern tone, Beetle inserted the spiked heel into the cleft at the apex of the plump cheeks - then slowly dragged the heel down along the shadowed valley. Alexis arched on her toes and mewed pitifully.

'Now I am owning your bottom,' Beetle whispered, repeating the action with the spiked heel down along the cleft. 'Owning it utterly before I punish it.'

Alexis buckled at the knees as the spiked heel was withdrawn. 'Now it is time to tie your hands tightly and gag you,' Beetle continued, tossing the red shoe aside and rising to stand beside Alexis. Stooping briefly to gather up the glossy tights, Beetle quickly bound her captive at the wrists, leaving the hands buried in the strawberry-blonde mane. Krystal inspected the bondage and pronounced it sound. Alexis started to protest loudly, but her pink-lipsticked mouth was deftly covered and silenced with Beetle's panties: the moistened patch stretched cruelly across the imprisoned tongue within. Alexis struggled in vain, twisting and jerking violently. Krystal stilled the bound nude with a searing slice of the crop across her naked bottom.

Beetle reached out and took the crop from the dominant blonde. Releasing her hold, Krystal smiled and withdrew nodding to Beetle to commence the punishment.

'Soon,' Beetle purred, flicking the crop against the bare breasted captive, 'my crop will scorch your bottom with searing kisses. Be patient. It will not be long now. Kneel down!'

Alexis guided herself down. Pinioned against her strawberry blonde mane, her splayed fingers flexed apprehensively. Behind the tight stretch of her gag, her tongue-tip probed the moist patch.

Beetle knew that Krystal was watching every move, listening to every word. She wanted to please the stern Pole, please her and prove to her how much she had learned about the art of discipline.

'In a moment, as I promised, I will whip your bare bottom,' Beetle murmured, dropping all harshness from her voice and speaking as she would to assuage a fretful child. She was now standing directly above and in front of the kneeling nude. 'But before you are punished, you must first experience the utter helplessness inflicted on your victims.'

Krystal looked on approvingly, giving Beetle an encouraging smile.

'You must taste the shame you forced them to feast upon,' Beetle concluded, emphasising each word with a tap of the crop to the bare bosom.

Krystal signalled her eagerness to take over at this point and grasped the crop. Beetle surrendered it up to the blonde unable to mask her disappointment. She thought she had managed her victim very well. With a heavy sigh, and a resentful scowl - both of which Krystal chose to ignore - Beetle scampered across to the mahogany desk, sat down on the polished top and drew her knees up tight to her breasts.

Addressing the bound nude harshly, Krystal snarled her curt command. 'Legs apart. Wider.'

Alexis shuffled her knees obediently. Between the parted thighs, her labial lips widened in a mirthless smile. Krystal lowered the little leather loop at the crop's tip between the thighs. Flicking her wrist a fraction, she tormented the pink fleshy lips with the curl of stitched leather. Alexis moaned softly into her gag, spreading the patch of wetness even wider. At the back of her head, buried in her strawberry-blonde mane, her bound hands spasmed - fingers splayed in response to the caress of the leather below. Krystal manipulated the short crop deftly, probing and rubbing the velvety flesh with consummate skill. Soon, the hot slit had opened to receive three inches of leather-sheathed cane. Alexis writhed in her shame, anticipating her complete and absolute humiliation.

Before you suffer the stripes of your punishment, you will taste the bitter fruits of humiliation. What you have been doing is stealing. Stealing forbidden fruit. No doubt it was sweet,' Krystal murmured, dragging the curl of looped leather up against the tiny erect clitoris. 'Your greatest mistake,' Krystal hissed, 'was to steal from me.'

Beetle looked up.

'*She* is mine and *mine* alone. The other victims are numerous but anonymous. Beetle belongs to me.'

Perched on the desk top, Beetle hugged herself with delight. Krystal was claiming her for herself. Beetle thrilled to the words. Beneath her splayed bottom, the polished surface of the desk clouded with her feral heat.

'I promise you that these hands...' the crop flickered to tap each fingertip. 'And these lips...' Alexis, gagged, was forced to kiss the crop. 'Will never, ever touch forbidden fruit again.'

Intoxicated by Krystal's stern admonishment, Beetle frantically fingered her wet wound. Krystal swished the crop twice, thrumming the air with its cruel note of suffering. The sound drove Beetle's wet fingers faster and deeper into her weeping slit.

Krystal stood alongside her kneeling captive. Levelling the length of the crop below the heavy bosom, she inched the whippy wood up a fraction, toying with the bare breasts. Sensing the weight of their satin density upon the crop, Krystal gripped the cruel wood tightly. Alexis clamped her thighs together. In her strawberry-blonde mane, her bound hands jerked - the helpless fingers scrabbling in fearful dread. The leather crop caressed the swell of the breasts before shifting to hover just above the raging nipples. Krystal plied the cane adroitly to capture and control the naked bosom. She rubbed the leather sheath against the stubby peaks, teasing up the flesh-buds into points of exquisite torment. Alexis bit into the panties, her moans smothered, her grey eyes now liquid with anguish. The kneeling woman gazed up sorrowfully into Krystal's green gaze - but the dominant blonde ignored the mute pleading, continuing more firmly with the discipline and domination.

'Hypnotism,' Krystal said softly, forcing the tip of the crop under her victim's chin, 'cannot make a person go against the true nature.'

Alexis looked up tearfully.

'But it can, as you have proved, be used in a perverted way.'

Despite the crop at her chin, the strawberry blonde bowed her head penitently.

'I shall not hypnotize you. Not exactly,' Krystal purred. She flicked the crop slowly from left to right, like a metronome The grey eyes followed it obediently. *Swish, swish.* The little leather loop grazed the peaked nipples as it skimmed across her bosom. After three minutes of this mesmerizing submission to the crop, Alexis squealed and buckled, collapsing softly onto the carpet. Lurching slightly, she lay face-down, offering up her naked buttocks to the lash. Krystal stooped and traced the outline of each fleshy cheek with her quivering cane.

'She is ready for her stripes. Her bottom,' Krystal tapped the upturned rump, 'is for you, Beetle.'

She passed the crop to the petite brunette who was still perched upon the polished desk, fingering her open slit. Beetle took the crop in her wet fingers.

'Up onto the couch,' Beetle snapped. 'On your back.'

Alexis struggled across to the couch and manoeuvred herself onto her back on the dark dimpled leather.

'Legs up.'

The bound and gagged nude obeyed the curt command.

'Feet apart,' Beetle rasped, whipping the crop down across the sleek hide impatiently.

Alexis struggled to obey.

'Head between your knees. Give me more of your bottom. More.'

The strawberry blonde lay supine, her bound hands at her neck, her knees bent back towards her head.

'Punishment is the bitter-sweet delight you will now suffer for tasting forbidden fruit. Twelve strokes. On *each* cheek.'

Crack! Crack! Beetle swept the crop down against the softy bulging cheek of the right buttock, slicing it twice, swiftly and accurately. Two pink lines quickly attested to the venom of the crop across the creamy flesh. Above her blonde mane, the punished nude's feet threshed. *Crack! Crack!* Again, the leather sheathed cane sliced in against the naked buttock, the supple implement biting into the curved cheek with savage intimacy.

Beetle levelled the crop once more, holding it quivering six inches above the shining leather couch. She flicked her wrist - *crack, crack* - delivering the third double-swipe. Alexis shuddered and moaned. *Swish! swipe!* Beetle, pressing her thighs into the soft hide as she knelt at right-angles to the leather couch, swept the crop across the swell of the reddening right buttock - adding two more fierce lines of fire to the existing line of pain. *Crack! Crack!* The crop seared the helpless flesh. Gasping into her gag, Alexis started to weep gently from two places, the tears of shame trickling from her grey eyes matching the liquid evidence of involuntary arousal oozing from her hot slit. *Swish, crack!* The dozen strokes had been delivered.

'Look,' Beetle said, the leather loop pointing to the ooze at the punished nude's fig.

'Turn her over,' Krystal replied, inspecting the weeping wound.

'Up,' Beetle snapped, fingering the leather at the tip of her crop. 'Face-down and get your bottom up,' she commanded, flexing her arm as she prepared to deliver the remaining twelve prescribed strokes.

'Keep her hips up,' Krystal warned Beetle, 'or else she'll bring herself off against the hide. She's here for pain. Pain and punishment, not pleasure.'

Beetle tapped the virgin cream of the unblemished, unstriped, left cheek. Alexis eased her hips up from the surface of the leather couch.

'Get your bottom up more,' Beetle insisted, anxious not to disappoint Krystal.

The two cheeks, the one criss-crossed with pink stripes, the other a rounded hillock of satin, rose up obediently. Beetle fingered the pliant skin of the buttock she was about to whip. A double knock at the door caused her to pause.

'That'll be Vanessa,' Krystal remarked. 'Continue with the punishment.'

Swish, swipe! Swish, swipe! Beetle's naked breasts bounced she raised the crop and whipped it down, twice in quick succession. The hips of the naked woman bucked and jerked as her bare bottom seethed beneath the double lash.'

Krystal unlocked the door and greeted Vanessa Wetherby.

'Throwing a party, what?' their visitor asked, glancing across at the kneeling punisher and the writhing victim.

Swish, crack! Swish, crack! The crop spoke twice, slicing down fiercely.

'Jolly good,' Vanessa Wetherby nodded vigorously.

Swish, crack! Swish, crack! Beetle needed no encouragement.

Vanessa Wetherby was the outdoor type. Her healthy, tanned face was strongly defined. The chin was resolute. Her figure was athletic and she moved with a lissom grace. At forty-one she was still the hearty games mistress Krystal and Beetle had come to adore at boarding school. Now, as then, her thighs were powerfully developed from sprinting up and down the wing on the hockey pitch - and her hands were as strong as they had been when spanking schoolgirl bottoms in the showers.

'No slacking there,' she urged Beetle. 'I'm sure she's earned her stripes. You two avenging angels never get it wrong.'

Swish, crack! Swish, crack! Beetle's crop replied.

'Busy?' boomed Vanessa.

Krystal nodded as she embraced their friend of long standing. Vanessa knew of their exploits and warmly approved

'Exhibiting anything?'

'I might have a gallery show next month. Or in the New Year,' Krystal smiled. 'But we've been pretty busy recently.'

Swish, crack! Swish, crack! Face-down on the leather of her bed of pain and shame, Alexis suffered two more searing swipes as the crop lashed her ravaged rump.

'*You* had better give her the remaining strokes,' Krystal suggested to her former games mistress. 'That will put you firmly in control. Help you stamp your absolute authority on her. After that, keep a very strict eye on her at all times. As her assistant, you'll be present during all future consultations.'

'Capital,' Vanessa Wetherby boomed, pausing to dab her fingertip in the smear of sticky juice Beetle's slit had spilt on the polished surface of the desk top. 'You two have certainly been going it a bit this afternoon,' she laughed, drying her fingertip in her skirt. 'I'll take over,' she murmured, kneeling down alongside Beetle, her rough heather-twill skirt tickling the brunette's naked thigh. Beetle surrendered the crop and stood up, leaving the blazing bottom to its new owner.

'And what have we here?' Vanessa Wetherby whispered huskily, palming the scalded cheeks - bringing Krystal and Beetle instantly back to the changing rooms at Birch Hall when the games mistress would similarly address the bare bottom 0f a slowcoach she was about to spank. 'Have we been naughty, hmm? We are going to have to learn to behave ourselves from now on, aren't we?'

Swish, crack! Vanessa Wetherby plied the crop ruthlessly. The squeal from the whipped nude's lips only partly contained by her tight gag.

Beetle was almost clothed by the time the final stroke was administered, the sharp rasp of her zip coinciding with the searing slice of the crop.

'I'll see to her now,' Vanessa Wetherby smiled, bending down to inspect the crimson cheeks at close quarters. 'You two run along. Nothing more for you to do here. And don't forget to drop me an invitation when you have your exhibition,' she called out after Krystal.

'I won't,' Krystal smiled, closing the door behind them.

Out in the corridor, as they approached the lift, Krystal confided her delight in their choice of watchdog.

'Yes,' Beetle agreed, 'Vanessa will keep a very close eye on her. Oh, hang on a minute,' she paused. 'I've forgotten my watch.'

They returned to the door and opened it quietly. The scene inside froze them in their footsteps. Alexis was kneeling against the corner of the leather couch, her hands still bound at the wrists up behind her head. They watched spellbound as the striped buttocks spasmed and quivered as the kneeling nude dragged her pubis repeatedly up and down against the dark shining hide. Above her, clutching the tousled strawberry-blonde mane with her controlling left hand, Vanessa Wetherby towered supreme, her brogued feet planted wide apart.

'Kiss the leather, my beauty,' the dominant woman demanded.

Alexis strained to plant her dry lips against the tang of the hide.

'Now with your other lips,' whispered Vanessa Wetherby.

Alexis jerked her hips forward, planting her pubis against the leather. Her tormentress immediately tugged at her mane, keeping the kneeling nude from making contact with her leather delight.

'Yes, I know you want to come, my dear, but only if and when I say so. Understand? Now, my beauty, ride the leather one more time. If you come, over my knee you'll go for the punishment of a lifetime. Understand? That's right, ride the leather.' The taloned fingers gripped the strawberry-blonde mane tightly, driving the nude towards her climax.

'We are going to get along famously, you and I. What? You are about to come? I don't recall giving you my permission.'

Alexis collapsed onto the dark hide, her whipped bottom jerking and writhing as she orgasmed savagely.

'I'm afraid that's going to earn you a terrific spanking, my dear,' Vanessa Wetherby soothed, releasing the climaxing nude from her fierce grip. 'A terrific bare-bottomed spanking.'

The delicious threat merely fuelled the pounding hips as they ground the tormented hot slit into the dark stretch of hide.

Back in the studio loft, the night sky sparkled with the lights of sleepless London visible through the large windows. Supper had been a scratch job: grilled red mullet and a bottle of golden Chardonnay. Krystal showered first, then took her glass of wine into the bedroom. Closing her eyes, she stretched out luxuriously in their king-sized bed, conjuring up details of their trip to Baker Street. She recalled the fear-filled eyes of the hypnotherapist - and how that haunting look had deepened when proof of guilt was supplied. Krystal wriggled her toe into the colder reaches of the vast bed as she remembered the wet patch of arousal where Beetle's soft bottom had pressed its warmth into the polished mahogany. She closed her eyes tightly, her mouth now hot and dry, as she replayed the images of the stern discipline and severe chastisement meted out to Alexis. The lethal crop flickering as it seared the naked rump. Krystal counted out each stroke, rubbing her left nipple up into stiff protest with the frosted side of her wine glass.

Opening her eyes, she sipped the chilled Chardonnay. It lubricated her dry mouth, allowing her to probe its crimson secrets with her tongue-tip. Closing her eyes, she recounted the final glimpsed moments in the room up on the third floor of the Baker Street office block. Alexis, naked and punished, being propelled into orgasm by the firm hand of Vanessa Wetherby. The deliciously ironic twist did not elude Krystal: the firm hand at the blonde mane would return to fiercely spank the bottom of the disobedient therapist who had snatched her forbidden orgasm from the shining leather hide.

Draining her glass, Krystal picked a magazine at random from her bedside pile. Leafing through the illustrations often suggested ideas for her studio work. An item on large country houses caught her interest: a full-colour spread on rural retreats built by Victorian industrialists seeking instant prestige. Elaborate decorative work in vast drawing rooms yielded a riot of abstract forms: the shadows in a tiny pantry or the bars on the window of a silver-painted room provided unexpected patterns in counterpoint. Suddenly, a forlorn image in stark black and white appeared, as she turned the page. It was a photo of a small attic bedroom. Krystal focused her gaze on the door, which would have opened and closed on a room here a young maid would have lived alone, like all domestics then, in chilly isolation. Krystal's focus narrowed on the dark door-knob. The attic room would have had a small wrought-iron fireplace, but rarely would coals have been supplied for the fire. The lonely young maid, stripped of her starched white apron, black uniform and polished leather shoes, would stand at the foot of her bed every night, folding her black stockings with care. Krystal stared at the door-knob. On the other side of the closed door, a similar door-knob would beckon to the naked maid with promises of illicit pleasures each midnight - when all inhabitants of the house, except the mice, slept deeply. Rising up on her toes, the naked young woman would press her firm breasts into the cold wooden door as she eased her open wound down over the knob, dragging her splayed labia deliciously against its bulbous sphere. Slowly, groaning softly in case she woke the inquisitive parlour maid who slept next door, the young woman would lower herself fully onto the door knob, thrusting her hips forward and allowing the hard delight to enter her wetness deeply. Face pressed flat against the peeling paint of the bedroom door, the maid would shudder as her jerking hips impaled her on her forbidden pleasure, her secret knob of dark delight. Buttocks tightening, the maid would feverishly lick - then passionately kiss - the blistered paint of the quivering door as with a smothered squeal of ecstasy she came. And sometimes, Krystal intuitively suspected, the furious rattling of the door-knob would bring the wide-eyed parlour maid out from her room and into the shadows of the bleak landing. The parlour maid, who used her own bedroom door-knob in a similar fashion, would stand shivering outside the door, her hands slowly cupping and squeezing her aching breasts.

Krystal let the magazine slither to the carpet at her bedside as she lay back in the pillows and guided her fingertips down to her pulsating slit. She gently dragged her warm labia apart and dappled in the stickiness within their velvet fleshfolds. behind her closed eyelids, she pictured the naughty maid, naked and gleaming in the moonbeams, her pudendum impaled upon the door-knob. And on the landing, shivering with both understanding and excitement, the watching parlour maid, her eyes reading the meaning of the rattling, jerking knob.

What if the frenzied rattling woke the mistress? That stern-faced Daughter of the Empire, widowed by the Crimea. Investigations would be instituted and tearful confessions extracted. Would the wretched maid be spanked, bare-bottomed, across the lap of her crinolined mistress? A protracted punishment, administered on Sunday afternoon, in the gaunt library - a remote room in the east wing - so that her cries would be dismissed as the screeching of rooks in the nearby elms? Or would the strict mistress not flinch from a more public punishment? The female staff, scrubbed, shining and ready for bedtime prayers, would be summoned to the pantry before lamps were dimmed and doors firmly bolted against the night. The unhappy maid, burning in her fearful shame, would peel off her white cotton shift and then be pinned across the pine table by the capable cook and, two kitchen girls. The mistress, a lavender glove tightly sheathing the hand that grasped the bamboo cane (lovingly selected from the raspberry bushes before sunset) would approach, treading the cool flagstone floor with soft steps of menace. The cane would swish and the maid would wriggle and squeal, but the stern mistress knew her duty, and dispensed it with every evidence of mordant relish. After the caning - twelve sharp strokes across the whimpering maid's bare buttocks - the wide-eyed female staff would witness the shivering penitent as she was forced to bend and kiss the huge black Bible.

The fantasy wove itself into her dreams. Krystal sighed as she snuggled into her duvet, her right hand wedged firmly between her thighs. A muffled crash from the bathroom brought Krystal abruptly out of her reverie. *That minx has been at my perfume again*, Krystal frowned. Nothing but the onyx fragrance bottle could have made that crash in the bathroom, where Beetle was taking a shower.

Pretending to be soundly asleep when Beetle tip-toed into the bedroom, Krystal felt the younger brunette steal under the duvet and settle down to sleep. After a few silent moments, Beetle slipped her arm out and switched off the bedside light. Moonlight pierced their bedroom. Krystal smiled, remembering the maid in her moonlit attic - and the punishments meted out to her by the stern mistress. The seductive sweet scent of Orange Water stole into her consciousness. There was going to be a moonlit spanking after all, Krystal smiled as she inched down the duvet.

'Awake?' Beetle murmured.

'Mm.'

'I was thinking. We left the riding crop in Baker Street.'

'Vanessa will find a good use for it.'

'Mm.'

After a few moments of silence, Beetle rolled her nakedness to Krystal's and whispered her devotion.

'I loved it when you told Alexis that I belonged to you. That you, and you alone, owned me.'

'Did you?'

'Mm.'

'And *do* you?' _

'Of course,' Beetle squeaked.

'Then why—' Krystal pounced, swiftly pinning Beetle down to the pillows, 'do you disobey me? Why do you continue to steal my things after I warned you not to?'

'Didn't,' Beetle giggled, happy to be dominated and relishing the severity of the blonde.

'Lie still,' Krystal whispered. 'I'm going to examine you. Every naked inch of you. And if I find the merest trace, even the tiniest hint, of my Orange Water on you, I shall spank you very, very hard.'

Beetle wriggled and squealed but was easily mastered. She lay still and tense as Krystal nuzzled her neck and breasts, snuffing the smooth flesh intimately. The blonde's face swept down from the breasts to the firm belly, coming to rest a fraction of an inch from the dark pubic nest below. Slowly, tantalizingly slowly, the tongue-tip flickered out to lap at the labia.

'Beetle,' Krystal murmured, working her tongue around the tiny coils of the brunette's snatch. 'Not only can I smell my Orange Water. I can taste it.'

'Can't,' protested Beetle.

Krystal felt the buttocks tighten apprehensively as she slid her palms beneath to cup and squeeze them. Cradling the soft mounds of warmth, she held Beetle in her thrall, ending the spell with a painful squeeze. Beetle gasped.

'Out of bed this instant! Go and get my Orange Water.'

Tossing aside the duvet, and slithering out of the huge bed, Beetle scampered off into the moonlit darkness. The moonlight shadowed her rounded buttocks with its silvery glow. Seconds later, another muffled crash told Krystal that Beetle had found her perfume again.

'No, leave the light off,' she told Beetle who had bent down to switch it on. 'I know perfectly well where to find your bottom when I want it.'

'No, please don't spank me. I'm sorry,' whimpered the petite brunette. 'Don't spank me. I won't—'

'Steal from me again? Of course you won't, not after I've finished with you this time.' Krystal whispered softly. '*That*,' she continued in a tone of sweet reason, 'is the purpose of punishment. The deterrence of repeated misdemeanours.'

In the darkness, the little nude shivered anxiously.

'Come here now and get across my knee.'

Beetle submitted her upturned buttocks to the delicious threat of the hovering hand above, pressing her bosom into Krystal's firm thigh.

'Grip my ankles and keep your head down.'

Meekly, Beetle obeyed the stern blonde's command. Dreading the punishment, yet adoring the punisher, she squeezed her cheeks together tightly.

'Before I spank you, little one,' Krystal murmured, lowering her flattened palm down onto the curved cheeks of the proffered bottom, 'I have something for you.'

A shiver of expectation coursed through the naked brunette.

Quivering with both fear and delight, she dug her toes into the soft carpet. Beneath Krystal's hovering hand, the soft buttocks tightened in a protective clench.

'No. Open your cheeks,' Krystal said sternly. 'Open them wide.'

The blonde smiled in the darkness as she felt the brunette slacken and submit herself utterly, and smiled again as Beetle gasped loudly in the moonlight as her cleft was probed and the tight round cheeks forced apart. The ensuing silence was shattered by Beetle's squeal. Krystal had drizzled the ice cold Orange Water directly between the parted cheeks. Beetle moaned as Krystal's fingertip worked the ooze of perfume along the velvety ribbon of the hot cleft, worrying it deftly into the rosebud of the anal whorl. Beetle threshed in response to the stinging shock as it burned with a cold flame deep inside her innermost flesh. The dominant blonde instantly trapped the rebellious legs of the suffering brunette, pinioning them with her own powerful thigh. Beetle was trapped, rendered powerless and utterly helpless. She was at Krystal's mercy - a quality unrelated to the blonde's present preoccupation.

A further splash of Orange Water directed accurately between the wriggling cheeks rocketed Beetle into renewed spasms of exquisite torment.

'Now, my scented little jade, I think it is time I spanked your naughty little bottom.'

Smack! The first slap stilled the brunette. *Smack, smack.* The second and third stung her naked buttocks. *Smack, smack, smack.* The ensuing cracks of the firm palm across her reddening cheeks told the bare-bottomed brunette that her punishment had begun. Krystal paused, drew the naked girl across her lap and closer to her belly, and strengthened her gripping hold. *Smack, smack, smack.* The firm palm of her flattened hand swept down across the juddering crowns of the upturned cheeks, reddening her velvety flesh. *Smack, smack, smack.* The dribble of excitement from Beetle's wet slit mingled with the stinging trickle of Orange Water seeping from her yawning cleft, turning Krystal's thighs slippery and shiny. Beetle wriggled in a vain attempt to escape the blistering onslaught, but Krystal was resolute. She pinned down the squealing brunette by the nape of her neck, determined that every spank would scald the bare bottom she was chastising.

Krystal paused once more, her naked bosom rising and falling gently with the exertion of punishment, and slowly palmed the punished bottom with her hot hand. Beetle lay still, mewing softly like a kitten. Seconds later, Krystal felt the brunette's breasts peel slowly away from her supporting thighs as Beetle inched up her buttocks in mute supplication for more of the dark, delicious discipline. Krystal pretended to ignore the gesture and continued to methodically palm the ravaged rump. As Beetle jerked her hot cheeks upwards again, in a frank and unashamed request for the spanking to continue, Krystal smiled indulgently and raised her hand aloft. The Brunette wiggled her buttocks impatiently, and the blonde swept her hand down fiercely. *Smack!* Again, and again. *Smack, smack!* Beetle moaned her pleasure as the spanking hand cracked down across her hot cheeks with savage love. Then, just the darkness; the spanking had ceased. A sudden shaft of moonlight pierced the inky night - just as Krystal splashed a scandalous amount of the precious Orange Water onto the seething buttocks. Beetle screamed loudly and threshed violently but Krystal was a thoroughly competent chastiser - her grip on the brunette's neck tightened to tame and subdue the writhing nude. Beetle twisted and struggled in her sweet anguish but the blonde punisher pinned her down more forcefully. The brunette's hot bottom remained exposed and helpless beneath Krystal's stern gaze.

'More Orange Water?' came the soft whisper.

'No,' was the squealed response. 'I swear, I'll never pinch your stuff ever again.'

'Promises during punishment are so quickly made, and so quickly broken,' Krystal reflected. 'How do I know you will keep yours?'

Beetle wrenched herself free from the controlling hand which had held her pinioned across her punisher's lap and, turning to kneel down before the blonde she adored, nuzzled her face in between Krystal's parted thighs.

'I swear,' she mumbled, mouthing her obedience into the sweet tang of the splayed labia.

'Up,' Krystal whispered, suppressing her shudder of delight. 'I need to make sure that your bottom has been completely and sufficiently chastised.'

Kissing the pungent slit farewell, Beetle got to her feet.

'Turn, and give me your bottom.'

Beetle obeyed, thrusting her breasts into a shaft of silver moonlight. The pale light shadowed her deep cleavage. Her naked breasts shuddered as Beetle felt Krystal's face pressing against her spanked bottom.

'Mm. Hot,' murmured the punisher into the flesh she had just spanked. 'But just to make absolutely sure,' Krystal whispered huskily, withdrawing a little from the naked buttocks. 'Just to make absolutely sure.'

Beetle screamed, her orgasm welling, spilling and exploding as her bottom was crushed by Krystal's heavy bosom. The blonde always dominated the bottom of the brunette in this manner after a severe spanking - using her naked breasts to assess the heat of the punished buttocks. If sufficiently hot, the nipples would invariably thicken and peak.

'A perfect punishment,' Krystal purred, her breath like ripples of silk against the skin of Beetle's back. 'Perfect,' she repeated, dragging her stubby nipples against the hot curved cheeks before burying her breasts into the crimson buttocks.

Beetle buckled at the knees as she collapsed in her climax, her ragged sobs of pleasure shattering the moonlit silence.

Chapter Three

'Remember Bunny Cardew?'

'Didn't she run away to sea?' Beetle grunted, pulling up her panties.

'She is a serving Wren,' Krystal corrected, tossing aside the Polish crossword which had finally defeated her. 'She's been in touch.'

'The Royal Navy's enlisting us?' Beetle squeaked, struggling into her bra. Being heavy-breasted this operation was always a bit of a battle for the brunette.

'Well, Wren Cardew is,' Krystal conceded. 'We're going down to her base near Portsmouth after lunch. Do you think you'll be dressed by then?' Krystal inquired politely.' Or do you want me to give you a helping hand?'

Bunny Cardew met them at the station and whisked them back to her base in a dark-blue Land Rover.

'I'm in the Cygnets. We're essentially intelligence. Routine work but it's an elite squadron. Pretty illustrious outfit. Normandy beaches, Korea and then with the US Navy Seals in Viet Nam - unofficially, of course.'

'And now?' Beetle enthused.

'Now we monitor all those leaking Soviet subs up around Murmansk. Pretty dull stuff. Ever hear the call of the sea, Beetle?'

'I did a voice-over for a swordfish steaks ad last week,' the little brunette replied gravely.

'Ah, so you've become an actress,' Bunny laughed. 'More naughty than nautical, eh?'

'Beetle would rather make waves than rule them,' Krystal remarked.

Bunny Cardew nodded and grinned. 'She was a terror, I remember. Always in the soup back at Birch Hall.'

The brakes of the Land Rover squealed as it pulled up in front of a red-and-white striped barrier. Bunny snappily returned a leather-gloved salute to the sentry who waved them through. The Land Rover sped across a parade ground puddled with November rain, coming to a stop beneath three tall flagpoles.

'That one, up there on the left. The squadron's colours.'

'*Castegatur malefactor*,' Krystal read, scanning the motto on the fluttering flag.

'The wrongdoer will be punished,' Bunny Cardew translated, slamming the door and pocketing the ignition key. 'Come and meet the Cygnets.'

After a brief meeting with several members of the Mess Committee, Bunny Cardew treated her guests to an early supper. As they tucked in to the cold game pie and claret, followed by a good Stilton served with white port, she gave a detailed explanation of the problem which their visit was to address.

'So you see,' she concluded, 'the honour of the Cygnets is at stake. We simply can't have a cheat in our Squadron. Bad form and all that. But it's so very difficult for us to prove. Must be done by an outsider. That's why we've turned to you. I put your names up before the Mess Committee. Can you chaps help?'

'We'll certainly do our best, Bunny,' Krystal replied, carefully picking out more lead pellets from her cold game pie and adding them to the growing pile of shot already exhumed. 'Leave it to us. We'll play it low-key at first. Best not to arouse her suspicions. I'll sit close but not get in on the game. Try and work out her technique. If she's cheating, I'll soon know. What then?'

'Give the Mess Committee the proof they need. They'll decide,' Bunny said quietly, cutting a thin wedge of Stilton for Beetle. 'The cygnets will decide how best to deal with her.' She probed Beetle's parted lips with the sliver of pale cheese.

'*Castegatur malefactor?*' Krystal murmured.

'Precisely,' Bunny nodded, smiling suddenly as Beetle winced at the Stilton's acid bite. 'Finished? I'll take you through to the smoking lounge. The poker school should be starting up about now. I know you'll be careful, Krystal. The Mess Committee is particularly anxious to avoid a fuss. Word spreads so quickly throughout the Fleet. We'd be a laughing stock.'

Krystal and Beetle understood. They had been commissioned to defend the honour of the Cygnets, the elite Squadron of Wrens in which Bunny, their chum from boarding-school days, served. A certain Lieutenant Chandler was threatening to scupper the Squadron's reputation by cheating at poker. Swindling hundreds of pounds out of her comrades was grave enough but, Bunny had assured them, it could ruin morale and damage the vital *esprit de corps*.

Krystal signed her name in the mess book and ordered a Benedictine frappé. Taking a chair strategically near the poker school, she sat in apparent indifference to her surroundings - while discreetly observing every move and gesture of the suspected cheat.

'I'll get Beetle back to quarters,' Bunny had said casually before Krystal took up her position. 'Best if we don't appear too inquisitive. Might spook your quarry. Good hunting.' Krystal had nodded in silent response and sipped her iced liqueur.

At the green-baize table nearby, her bosom straining within her starched white skirt, Lieutenant Chandler drew slowly on a cigarette as she gazed down at her cards. Two hours later, when the crumpled notes at Chandler's elbow had grown from the thirty pounds' playing money she started with to her winnings of £186, Krystal rose and left.

Outside, the night was bitterly cold. She followed the signposts and was grateful when she reached the warmth of Bunny's quarters. It was late, so she decided to go straight to her room. She examined the key Bunny had issued to her. Number Eight. As she passed Number Seven, she heard Beetle's unmistakable giggle. No doubt they were swapping yarns about their boarding-school days, Krystal surmised: gruesome serge knickers that tickled and prickled and midnight feasts of sardines and Turkish Delight; of intenser moments, when a 'pash' was conceived and then consummated in the showers after tennis; of delicious disciplines dispensed by stern seniors across squirming schoolgirl bottoms. Bunny, Krystal recalled, had been severely caned - bare-bottomed and bent over - before the entire lower-sixth for some high jinks in the chemistry labs. 'I will not have jinks in Stinks,' the Deputy Head had accidentally punned, swishing the whippy bamboo down across Bunny's suffering cheeks for the third time, bringing a nervous giggle from the wide-eyed lower-sixth.

In between the crisp sheets, Krystal tossed and turned, tormented by the muffled laughter from the bedroom next door. With a growing jealous resentment, Krystal propped herself up on one elbow, frowning as she strained to hear. Her desire to discover what was going on in there became too great to ignore. Slipping out of bed, she stole across the room to the window, shivering in her nakedness. Inching back the curtain, she opened the window silently. The chill of the November night brought her nipples to thickening peaks of protest, puckering them in a spasm of pleasurable pain. Bunny and Beetle hadn't been secretly 'thick' back at Birch Hall, had they, she suddenly wondered. She dismissed the possibility. She knew Beetle intimately, then as now. She would have known, surely. No, she reassured herself as she shivered once more, there had been no telltale signs of dalliance in the dorm or assignations in the showers. No unexplained damp panties or abandoned brassieres. Krystal had never discovered bite marks on Beetle's naked body - other than those made by Krystal herself. Angry at her stabs of suspicion - and angrier still at the muffled giggling which fuelled them - Krystal closed her window. Then she noticed the thin shaft of yellow light lancing the darkness outside. The curtain next door, she realized, had not been drawn completely across. With the sudden fury of a jealous schoolgirl, Krystal snatched up the small looking-glass by the sink, opened her window once more and stretched out her arm into the raw night, positioning the mirror at an angle to catch a glimpse of the antics next door. She cursed softly in Polish and smothered her gasp of anguish as she was forced to press her nakedness against the cold window. The glass kissed her breasts with brutal lips, but she ignored the pain and stretched further out into the night.

Her reward was a silent film: in the small oval of glass, she caught the reflection of Beetle's mouth soundlessly laughing. The brunette was completely naked, practising to salute. As her hand rose up, her breasts rose up also, coming proudly to attention. As Beetle waggled her fingers at her temple - the bosom below wobbled in response. Bunny flitted into sight in the angled mirror, clapping her approval, her hands coming noiselessly together as the silent picture flickered in the clasp of Krystal's hand. Krystal shivered, her nipples now fiercely peaked, but held out the small mirror at arm's length with grim determination. The gap left by the incompletely drawn curtain was narrow, providing only a tantalizing glimpse of the room within. Bunny, dressed in her bra and panties, darted in and out of view, sometimes dropping out of sight as she knelt down, behind - and then in front of - the naked brunette. Krystal's knuckles whitened with cold *and* anger as she gripped the looking-glass. She watched as a pair of hands placed a peaked cap on Beetle's head, crowning her tangle of dark curls. The brunette grinned, tipping the peaked cap forward at a jaunty angle. *More naughty than nautical* - the words came back to taunt Krystal. In the glass, the blonde Pole caught the reflection of the brunette as the latter's lips parted to give another silent laugh. Krystal burned, despite the bitter cold, as she watched Bunny dress Beetle in regulation issue scanties, palming Beetle's generous breasts into a crisp cotton brassiere, then patting her bottom as the cheeks bulged within the Wren's tight panties. A white suspender belt which Bunny held against Beetle's thighs entered the framed reflection in Krystal's hand. She stared into her mirror to see Beetle gazing down, pulling the belt up to, then around, her waist and snapping it against her warm flesh. Krystal's eyes narrowed as she strove to decode the words formed by Beetle's mouth, the brunette's excitement undisguised. The suspender belt hugged the naked flesh that Krystal claimed as her own - over which she alone had sovereignty.

The hand-held mirror trembled as the watcher shivered with both fury and the biting cold. Navy-blue stockings, seamed and shining, now appeared in the frame. Krystal watched as one was draped over the brunette's shoulder, slithering down to veil the breast below. The other then was drawn slowly across Beetle's ecstatic lips - she tongued the blue sheen hungrily and snapped at it with her tiny teeth. Bunny admonished the brunette with a sharp slap across her pantied buttocks. Beetle opened her mouth to squeal, but only a silent protest at the severe spank was visible in the mirror. Krystal strained to inch the mirror further out into the November night, eager to catch more of the silent images, but the sight of Bunny bending down, then kneeling to palm the navy-blue nylon stockings up Beetle's lithe legs, was denied her. It burned brightly only in Krystal's fevered imaginings. Glimpses of their playful sport continued until Beetle had been fully dressed as a Wren. Krystal sensed her labia parting, and then felt the warm tingle of wet desire. The sight of Beetle, pert and prim in her crisp uniform, juiced the watching blonde's tormented slit. Shaken by her acute desire, Krystal withdrew her arm from the freezing night air and quietly closed the window.

Back between the sheets, her only thoughts were of Beetle: thoughts not of pleasure, but which burned for punishment. She closed her eyes and concentrated on conjuring the chest of drawers in their bedroom back in Wapping. In the drawer, still coiled up in its wrapping of tissue paper, lay a heavy leather belt. Krystal's naked body tensed as, in imagination, she opened the drawer. In the cold corners of the bed, her toes curled as the imagined drawer slid open in silent obedience. So real was the reverie, Krystal could feel the polished pine as her thigh pressed against it - she could hear the tissue paper whispering as it parted beneath her probing fingers to reveal the leather belt. Krystal could almost smell the sharp tang of the virgin leather. It was a very special belt. Hand-crafted and lovingly polished by Swedish nuns, it was at least three inches wide. Krystal had bought it purely for the pleasure of owning it, fingering it, holding it, weighing its supple potency in her trembling cupped hands. The edges were ribbed with thick stitching; waxed white cotton against the cherry red of the sleek hide. With this belt Krystal would punish Beetle. The bare-bottomed brunette would weep her penitence.

Krystal sighed as the envisioned creamy upturned cheeks burned under the cruel lash. The chastisement would be slow, searching and severe. The searing strokes would blaze across the suffering bottom again, again and yet again - and continue to do so until both ivory buttocks blushed as red as the cherry-hued leather that had set them ablaze. Comforted a little by these thoughts, and by the fingers now teasingly probing her hot slit, Krystal moaned softly and fell asleep.

In her sleep, the blonde Pole dreamed fitfully of a pert brunette covering her nakedness with the severe habit of a Swedish nun. Her nudity now clothed, the brunette asked - the words falling silently from her parted lips - for the belt. *I need you to give me the belt*, the brunette seemed to be saying. In her dreams, Krystal readily agreed.

'She is a cheat, and cheats must be punished,' Krystal said, gazing directly into Beetle's big brown eyes.

Beetle swallowed her forkful of kipper hastily and fiddled with her napkin.

'But can you prove it? We suspected it. The Mess Committee is sure that she was cheating. What a wretched business,' Bunny sighed, adding cream and a pinch of salt to her bowl of glutinous porridge. 'What next?'

'I'll play a couple of games with her in the Mess tonight,' Krystal replied, disdaining cooked breakfast in favour of an apple. 'All I have to do is catch her red-handed, and pounce!'

'*In flagrante*,' Beetle said brightly, then blushing as she was crushed by Krystal's stern gaze. Silenced, she prodded her kipper absently.

'Then we'll forget about it 'til tonight,' Bunny decided firmly. 'Come to the gym with me, you chaps. Are you game, Beetle?'

'Oh, I think you'll find Beetle game enough,' Krystal purred, placing her apple core down on her plate. 'Always willing.'

Across the breakfast table, the brunette's fingers drummed nervously on the snow-white linen cloth.

The high-ceilinged gym echoed to the squeak of pumps and the pounding of feet as a dozen trim young Wrens scampered across the polished floor. Shrill whistle blasts punctuated their exercises: one blast for press-ups; two for squat-thrusts; three for running on the spot. One piercing note forced the supple gymnasts down onto the gleaming wooden floor, where they rhythmically eased themselves up and down in a sequence of press-ups which repeatedly crushed their proud bosoms into the hard gym floor. Three sharp blasts had them up and running on the spot: dressed in sleeveless vests and severely cut shorts, the braless girls pounded their rubber pumps with vigour. Krystal's emerald eyes deepened to a shade of clouded coral as she drank in the bouncing breasts and quivering thighs. Bunny Cardew had stripped off her uniform in an adjacent cubicle, returning in tight vest and shorts to lead the Wrens through the punishing work-out.

'Come along, Beetle. Shake a leg,' she yelled.

Beetle skipped off into the changing area to emerge moments later in her bra and briefs. The Wrens greeted her with a ragged cheer. Krystal remained at the wall-bars, studying the array of beautiful young bodies being exercised so vigorously.

'Couldn't find a vest or shorts,' Beetle shrugged.

'You'll do for me,' Bunny laughed, fingering the lace trim of the cups that controlled the brunette's bulging breasts. Krystal contented herself with a reminder of the cherry-red leather belt in its nest of tissue paper back in their bedroom at Wapping. Picturing the coil of supple hide, she gripped the wall bars and smiled a secret smile.

After ten minutes, half the Wrens left the echoing gym to shower. Their shrieks and squeals under the clouds of steam, as towels were flicked and bare bottoms suffered, resounded around the gym. Bunny, Beetle and the remaining Wrens huddled together in a scrum. Krystal studied the bending gymnasts' buttocks: her eyes widening perceptibly as she gazed at Beetle's white-pantied bottom compressed tightly between the smoothly curved cheeks sheathed in navy at either side. The scrum split up, releasing Beetle who trotted over to Krystal, breathless and excited.

'Bunny says we're to make a pyramid. Watch me,' she panted.

'I am watching you,' Krystal whispered, imagining the weight of the cherry-red belt in the palm of her punishing hand. 'Every move.'

Beetle scurried back to the circle of young women who, at Bunny's command, had peeled off their vests and stepped out of their buttock-hugging shorts. Naked, they were limbering up in preparation for the pyramid.

'I'd prefer you naked, Beetle,' Bunny smiled, placing her right hand firmly on the brunette's rump and giving it a squeeze. 'You're under naval law, now. *Mine* to command.'

Beetle wriggled out of her bra, causing her bosom to bounce delightfully as her breasts were freed from the cups. Behind her, kneeling, Bunny pressed her face close to Beetle's bottom as she tugged the panties over the swell of the buttocks and slowly palmed the band of cotton down the brunette's thighs. Krystal's eyes became fierce slits of gleaming jade as they watched this act of intimacy, the kneeling Wren cheek-to-buttock with the naked brunette. Krystal's fingers curled around the imagined length of leather, assuaging the stabs of jealousy with the promise of punishment.

'First row,' Bunny rasped, rising from the wooden floor and assuming strict command. Four naked Wrens converged into a line. Breasts thrusting forward proudly, they judged the distance between their nude bodies by placing an outstretched hand on each other's left shoulder.

Bunny nodded her approval. 'Next row.'

Two Wrens bounded up and clambered up on their comrades' shoulders. Krystal fleetingly perused the widening clefts of the ascending Wrens' behinds as they climbed their wall of flesh - but her eyes flickered back to scrutinize Beetle's face, and she noted the brunette's sparkling smile.

'Steady the buffs,' Bunny shouted as the pyramid wavered and threatened to topple.

The buttocks of the supporting Wrens wobbled as they planted their feet more firmly on the polished floor.

'Up you go, Beetle. Show me what you're like on top.' Beetle obeyed, scaling her way up the naked structure. The pyramid rapidly degenerated into a shambles as the naked civilian squashed the breasts of the squealing Wrens she trod upon in her unsuccessful attempt to top the pyramid. Bunny grinned and, reaching up, cupped Beetle's buttocks in an attempt to propel her upwards. Despite this gesture of support - which drew a silent snarl from Krystal's lips - Beetle failed to make it to the top. The naked Wrens wobbled perilously. Beetle screamed, half in fear, half in delight, and the pyramid collapsed to the floor in a writhing heap of breasts, buttocks and glistening thighs.

'Never mind,' Bunny laughed. 'Into the showers.'

The gym had a forlorn feel when empty. Krystal ran her fingertip along the length of a smooth wall-bar as her mind wrestled with an annoying thought: Beetle had not brought a towel, and so Bunny would have to dry her after the hot shower.

Dinner in the Mess was a full-dress affair commemorating some minor naval skirmish in the Dutch East Indies over two hundred years ago. The Squadron's plate and silver were produced, gleaming beneath the candles punctuating the sleek stretch of starched table linen.

'We're strong on tradition,' Bunny advised her guests. 'Helps boost morale now the Cold War's melted. Former glories, and all that.'

Beetle was slightly overawed at the sight of the officer sitting opposite spreading the entrails of her pheasant onto little triangles of fried bread. Krystal, a confirmed and adventurous omnivore, had no such qualms. Bunny saw Beetle's distress and rescued her with a portion of moist breast. Krystal contented herself with a thigh, savouring the gamey tang of dark meat. Port and brandy were served, but while the brunette allowed Bunny to top up her glass, the blonde abstained - keeping her mind clear and razor-sharp for her duties at the poker table later on. The port came round from her left, and yet again Krystal passed.

In the lounge, Lieutenant Chandler was already at the green baize table, awaiting her victims. Krystal declined to join the school at first, but allowed Beetle to persuade her. Within twenty minutes, she had spotted the cheat's technique. The Lieutenant chain-smoked, frequently offering the other players at the table a cigarette.

'She's using her cigarette case to see all the cards,' Krystal whispered to Beetle. 'Get it away from her.'

Beetle suggested another round of drinks, timing her just as the crush at the bar was at its thickest.

'Steward'll come eventually,' Chandler drawled, reading her hand through a haze of cigarette smoke.

'They're busy. I'll get them,' Beetle smiled.

When Beetle returned with the tray of iced drinks, she mad a bit of a performance distributing the glasses - a ruse to distract the players as she deftly palmed the cigarette case. Twenty-seven seconds later, Chandler's eyes narrowed first in concern then in anger as she noted the loss of her silver case. Significantly, Krystal thought, the Lieutenant chose not to remark on its absence. But then, Krystal knew, a cheat wouldn't want to draw attention to her stock in trade. Chandler quickly recovered from the setback and gazed over her cards into Krystal's impassive green eyes.

'Time for a fresh pack. Cards are getting sticky.'

Krystal and the other two players merely nodded agreement. A fresh pack was brought across from the bar. Standard blue-backed service issue. The cellophane crackled as Chandler thumbed it expertly.

'I'm still banker,' the Lieutenant murmured, dealing. Krystal fingered her twenties until she exposed the pound note beneath. Chandler's eyes widened greedily. The cards dealt, bids followed. Chandler won the hand with an ace and two pairs. Krystal noted the pairs - two red eights and black tens. Krystal watched Chandler's hands beneath the glare of the bulb as they fluttered once more across the green baize. Bidding was muted, the pot amounting to a thin eleven pounds as Chandler let it go to Krystal. The next round became intense, with over sixty pounds on the table. Krystal had baited her trap. Any minute now, she knew, Chandler would pull a second stroke.

'Got you,' Krystal whispered in Polish as the cheat tabled a winning hand. Another pair of black tens. Krystal counted rapidly: two on the table; two in the pack and a ten of spades in her own hand. She stood up and tapped the green baize three times - a prearranged signal. Beetle, Bunny and members of the Mess Committee immediately flanked the startled cheat on either side.

'We are going for a little walk now, Chandler. Spot of fresh air. You will join us, won't you?'

'I don't—' the Lieutenant began.

'Be a good chap, Chandler,' Bunny hissed. 'We don't want any ugliness here.'

Chandler rose uncertainly to her feet, her face pale. 'Where are you taking me?'

'To the gym,' Bunny replied.

'Watch her closely,' Krystal warned the escort. 'She may try to throw something away.'

Lieutenant Chandler flashed Krystal a look of raw venom and inched her fingers away from the hem of her skirt.

'You have a rotten apple in your distinguished barrel,' Krystal announced to the Mess Committee.

The Committee, five senior Cygnets, sat in a row, listening to the charges brought by Bunny and her two guests against the cheat, Chandler.

'Lieutenant Chandler,' Bunny interposed, 'has been systematically cheating at poker, swindling her fellow Cygnets out of hundreds of pounds.'

'That's a lie,' the accused shouted. 'I—'

'Silence,' barked a senior Cygnet, raising a leather-gloved hand aloft. 'You will be given your chance to speak later, even if,' her tone darkened, 'it is only to plead for mercy.'

The Committee nodded, clearly prepared to entertain the notion that a plea for lenience could be allowed. The Committee motioned Krystal to continue.

'First,' Krystal explained, holding up the silver cigarette case, 'she used this. And although nobody else at the card table noted, she passed it around throughout the game.'

'Exhibit One,' Beetle pronounced, taking the silver case from Krystal and presenting it to the Committee for their scrutiny. 'It does not alter the cards in her hand,' Krystal remarked, but lets her know exactly what the other players hold. And in poker—'

The leather-gloved hand rose up once more. The Committee members were familiar with poker and understood the advantage Chandler would have gained by using her silver case. Krystal fell silent, acknowledging the Committee's wisdom.

'You're wrong,' Lieutenant Chandler scorned. 'Look at it carefully. The surface of that silver case is fully chased. It can't reflect anything. Anything at all.'

Once more, the silver case fell under the collective scrutiny of the Committee. They examined the finely chased silver surface, which seemed to support the accused's denial. The Committee looked at Krystal in concern.

'Nice try,' Krystal purred, 'but I think you'll find, if you cast your mind back, Chandler, that I said you were passing the cigarette case around. And when offering cigarettes, you do so, quite naturally, with the lid open.'

The leather-gloved hand flipped open the silver lid. The Committee gazed down into the reflective polished surface of the lid. Relieved, the members saw their collective concern gazing back.

'Bitch,' Chandler viciously hissed at Krystal. 'Purely circumstantial,' she added in a more controlled voice, addressing the Committee.

'When your cheating was detected,' Krystal resumed suavely, 'I instructed my partner here to intervene.' The blonde indicated the pert brunette to the approving smiles of the Committee.

'But we were on to you,' Bunny Cardew chipped in. 'A trap was baited and you went for it.'

'New cards. An old ploy,' Krystal explained with a shrug. The Committee looked to Krystal for further enlightenment. 'Standard naval-issue cards. All she had to do was obtain a similar pack earlier and select a few key cards for the game. She did not make the obvious mistake of using aces or court cards. She's much too subtle for that.'

Sensing her doom, the accused made a bid to escape. Bunny and Beetle grappled with her, pinioning her firmly to attention between them.

'Look for eights. Yes,' Krystal mused. 'There'll be red eights hidden on her person.'

Chandler struggled and squirmed but her efforts were futile.

'Search her,' barked a Committee member.

Beetle and Bunny examined the cuffs of the crisp white shirt. They yielded nothing. Chandler flinched as the fingers at her bosom scrabbled with the buttons. The shirt was pulled open, revealing the swell of her tightly brassiered breasts. Bunny and Beetle explored the warmth within the deep cups. Again their search proved fruitless. The Committee raised a collective eyebrow at Krystal.

'Stocking tops,' the blonde instructed, unperturbed. Chandler's sleek skirt was dragged up over her writhing thighs, exposing the sheen of her nylons and then the darker bands of the stocking-tops above. The searching hands found three playing cards wedged between the smooth stretch of nylon and the smoother skin it sheathed.

'Guilty,' barked the Committee in unison.

The accused, head bowed, slumped between her escort. Keeping a tight grip on her arms, Bunny and Beetle flanked her thigh to thigh. The most senior officer present slowly removed her leather gloves.

'Proof enough,' Krystal said, holding up the red eights for all to see.

'On this evidence, Lieutenant Chandler, we have no course but to find you guilty as charged. Before the Committee determines your punishment, it has an equally pleasant duty to discharge.'

Krystal and Beetle were invited to step forward - as the wriggling accused was dragged away to the changing rooms - and warmly thanked for their sterling services.

'There'll be a cheque and a couple of cases of decent port heading your way very soon. Wapping, isn't it?'

Krystal smiled and shook hands. Beetle stepped up to peck the stern officer on the cheek.

'You're a fine pair of chaps,' the officer said gruffly, then called out loudly for Bunny.

'M'am?' Bunny saluted as she trotted up.

'Escort your friends back to quarters, Cardew. See them across the base, then get back here for the punishment.'

'Oh, don't we get to cane her?' Beetle asked in a stage whisper.

The Committee struggled to suppress their grins.

Bunny turned and shrugged apologetically. 'Sorry to disappoint you but this is strictly a Squadron matter from now on.'

'*Castegatur malefactor?*' Krystal chipped in.

'Absolutely, old thing.'

Halfway across the windswept parade ground, Bunny paused.

'You two can find you own way now. I'd best be getting back to the gym. Sorry to cut you out of the fun, but you understand.'

'We understand,' Krystal nodded. 'See you at breakfast.'

Bunny turned into the night and hastened back to where Chandler awaited her punishment.

'I wonder what they'll do to her,' Beetle speculated.

'Something very painful,' Krystal whispered in the dark.

They walked on slowly for some thirty yards, heads bowed into the chill wind.

'Think I'll take a little exercise before I turn in,' the brunette lied transparently. 'Best to keep fit. Look at how bad I was in the gym earlier on.'

'I saw,' the blonde purred.

'Take a few turns around the parade ground,' Beetle said hastily.

'Don't go near the gym,' Krystal warned.

'Wasn't going to,' Beetle protested. Poking her tongue out at her omniscient partner, she strode off into the darkness.

Krystal watched her walk away, a shrewd smile playing on her lips. Retreating into the shadows, she stood and waited. Two minutes later, she heard Beetle scampering across the asphalt, heading back to the gym.

'Silly little minx. I've a good mind to let them catch you—'

'Please don't leave me,' Beetle whimpered.

'Are you stuck?'

'Mm.'

'Stay still,' the blonde hissed, pressing herself into Beetle's squirming rump. 'I'll try and get you free.'

Avoiding the doors, Beetle had tried to get back into the gym through a narrow window. Her wriggling legs and bottom announced that she had become stuck in the attempt.

'It's no good,' Krystal grunted. 'I'll have to push you in.'

Krystal's hands propelled the bottom up and then through the window. 'Stay where you are, I'm coming in.' She just managed to get through, joining Beetle in the darkness of the changing room.

'Thanks,' Beetle mumbled.

'They will be very, very cross if they find you. Keep quiet and move carefully.'

Ducking down to avoid detection, they crawled towards the rear entrance.

'Only wanted a quick look—'

'*And* get a quick taste of whatever Chandler's suffering. Keep down and be quiet.'

The voices coming from the gym silenced them.

'...And then check that the doors are locked and bolted,' the two trespassers heard.

Footsteps approached. The two squatted down in the shadows as a Wren strode past, locked and bolted the rear door, pocketed the key and returned to the brightly lit gym with a measured tread.

Krystal swore softly in Polish.

'We're stuck,' Beetle whimpered. 'What if we're caught?'

'Don't even think about it,' Krystal whispered. 'If they get hold of your bottom, my girl, you'll know soon enough.'

'You won't leave me?' Beetle pleaded, reaching out in the darkness to clutch Krystal's hand.

'I won't. But when we get out of this mess I'm going to see to it that you—'

The lights in the gym dimmed and expired until only two spotlights punched out a small circle of silver in the darkness below. The inquisitive couple were drawn like moths to a flame. Inching forward on their breasts and hips, they crept towards the entrance to the gym: impelled by the hope that, despite the danger they incurred, they might glimpse Chandler undergo strict military discipline. Through the gap in the door, they peered into the gym to see the uniformed Wrens standing in a circle. Sitting on the polished wooden floor, shivering in her nakedness, Chandler was slowly plaiting a twist of waxed cord. Six finished pieces of knotted rope lay in an orderly line by the side of her soft left buttock.

'An old naval tradition,' Krystal whispered, easing her body down on top of Beetle - who lay stretched face-down on a prickly mat. 'Those about to be punished had to fashion the instrument of their suffering with their own hands. Gruesome, eh?'

'Just like at Birch Hall. Remember when we'd have to go out into the kitchen garden to pick a raspberry cane for the Maths teacher to swish us with?' Beetle replied.

'Mm. Something like that.'

Beneath the weight of the warm blonde above, the brunette shivered expectantly.

'What are those little knots she's tying?'

'Trafalgar Teasers,' Krystal whispered, burying her face into Beetle's soft curls. 'They add a sting to the lash as the waxed cord swipes across the bare bottom.'

Beetle responded by waggling her buttocks excitedly against the belly and pubis of the blonde straddling her above. Krystal scissored her thighs dominantly, trapping and taming the little brunette, ensuring that the minx remained firmly in her thrall.

'Stay absolutely still and silent,' Krystal mouthed softly into the sweetly scented curls. 'They're about to begin.'

'Has Chandler not finished yet?' barked the officer in charge, pawing the polished gym floor with an impatient brogue.

'Almost, m'am,' Bunny was heard to reply.

Peeping out from their dark surrounds into the pool of light, the hidden onlookers saw their host bend down and scoop up the short strips of knotted waxed cord. Rising, Bunny offered them to the Committee for inspection.

'Jolly good,' boomed the officer, scrutinizing the whipcord intimately.

Each of the seven ropes measured twenty-one inches of potential pain. Small knots, three on each rope's tail, had been tied by Chandler's trembling fingers, ensuring that an extra sting would torment her whipped bare bottom.

'Stand up, Chandler.'

The nude stood in immediate response to the stern command. She was superbly breasted, the nipples darkly delicious against the firm creamy bosoms. Below her narrow waist, the hips were wide, and Nature had been more than bountiful with the buttocks. Chandler turned to face her punishers, swiftly presenting her ripely round bottom to the gaze of the two watchers in the dark. Beetle whimpered with delight. Her involuntary response to the beautiful bare buttocks was instantly smothered by Krystal's cupped hand. The controlling blonde felt the brunette's hot tongue pressing into her palm as, ahead of them in the gym, the heavy melon-cheeks rippled as Chandler was ordered to attention.

'At ease.'

The thighs parted, the cheeks wobbled. Beetle licked Krystal's hand feverishly, biting into the pink flesh with nipping teeth. Krystal slammed her pubis down into the rump beneath her - a dominant command for the brunette to keep still.

'Guilty as charged,' boomed the leather-gloved Wren officer. The delicious buttocks of the accused clenched in fearful expectation as the moment for the pronouncement of punishment approached.'

'Punishment number one. The Committee has determined that you write out two substantial cheques. The first to be paid to the pair who came down here to unmask you, the second to be paid to a charity of your choice. Two thousand pounds, each cheque. This will no doubt completely deprive you of any ill-gotten gains while also standing the name of the Squadron in good stead.'

'Four thousand,' Krystal whistled. 'That's a lot of lolly—'

'Sh!'

Out under the harsh spotlights, Chandler nodded, accepting her sentence meekly.

'Punishment number two: We want to see you out on the parade ground. Every morning, before lunch, for the next three months. Ten circuits, in full kit. Too many hours spent indoors have left you unfit, Chandler. Unhealthy business, sitting around playing cards.'

The Lieutenant, flinching at the irony, lowered her head in shame.

'Punishment number three.'

From their secret vantage point, Krystal and Beetle saw the naked buttocks tighten with dread as sentence was pronounced. The watching girls stiffened. This was the moment they had been impatient for - the precise details of the discipline to be dispensed. Dry-mouthed, but wet between her sticky thighs, Krystal slowly ground her pubis into Beetle, riding the swell of the brunette's bottom.

'You have jeopardized the good name of the Squadron, Chandler, and dragged the reputation of the Cygnets to the very brink of shame. Bring me the shield.'

Six willing hands promptly unhooked a large gilded shield from the breeze block wall and carried it into the silver pool of light. It was the Cygnet's coat of arms, bearing the device of two writhing mermaids in a soixante-neuf embrace. At the base of the insignia, the legend of the Squadron's motto was etched in red upon a background of unalloyed cream: *Castegatur Malefactor*.

'We are prepared to give you a chance, Chandler, to uphold the good name of the Cygnets. Bend over.'

Chandler touched her toes.

'Place the shield upon her.'

Krystal and Beetle saw Chandler's cleft widen as she bowed down to shoulder the heavy wooden shield. The poker-cheat bore it bravely, supporting its undoubted weight with her head, hands and the length of her dimpled spine. Her bending posture, the legs slightly apart, thrust her bottom up, rendering it a bigger, rounder, more vulnerable target for the impending knotted ropes.

'In a line. Six paces apart. Four strokes each. Commence.'

Seven hands tightened around the waxed cord of the seven lengths of knotted rope. The whipcords shivered in response, grazing the stockinged thighs of the seven Wrens as they formed an orderly punishment squad.

'No, don't kneel, Chandler. Get up. Feet further apart. Get that bottom up, Chandler, there's a good chap. Take your punishment like a Cygnet.'

The Committee, Bunny Cardew bringing up the rear, flexed their knotted ropes in anticipation as the bare bottom loomed up before them.

The first Wren in line stepped up smartly and planted her feet apart. Shouldering her whipcord, she snapped it down across the left buttock. *Swish, swipe!* The severe swipe left a thin vertical pink line of pain. Chandler grunted. *Swish, swipe! Swish, swipe!* Twice, in crisp succession, the knotted rope whipped down across the swell of the right buttock, bisecting the bulging cheek with exactitude. The cruel cord left a legacy of two pink stripes across the curve of creamy flesh. Chandler hissed aloud each time the waxed cord kissed her naked skin. *Swish, swipe!* The heavy wooden shield trembled as the fourth stroke - a withering slice - drew another reddening line of fire, down alongside the first.

Krystal, pressing the length of her body into Beetle's below, watched hungrily as the punisher knelt on one knee behind the striped buttocks of the punished nude. Beetle's gasp was instantly quelled by Krystal, as the knotted end of the whipcord was threaded into the cleft between the punished cheeks. Straightening abruptly, the Wren snatched at the rope, dragging it smartly up through the velvety valley of secret flesh. Chandler screamed softly as the three knots ravished the sticky warmth of her cleft. Krystal, the pulse at her throat quickening and the thorn of her clitoris now proudly erect, felt Beetle's firm buttocks jerk upwards in response to the display of delicious dominance before them in the silvery pool of light.

Swish, swipe! Swish, swipe! The second Wren had stepped up to briskly administer a couple of searing lashes, choosing to plant the length of rope horizontally across the twin crowns of the swollen cheeks. *Swish, swipe!* The third stroke licked the upper buttocks across their outer curves. Chandler moaned, parting her thighs slightly. *Swish, swipe!* The Wren swept the whipcord into the soft flesh just above the crease of the thighs. The buttocks shuddered in response - as did Beetle, grinding herself into the prickly mat beneath her as she thrilled to the whipped nude's smothered groan. Like her predecessor, the second Wren buried her length of knotted whipcord deep down between the ravished cheeks. Seconds later, she wrenched it upwards with a triumphant flourish. The heavy shield swayed perilously as Chandler writhed in an anguished ecstasy, collapsing down to crush her naked breasts into the polished wooden floor.

'Up,' hissed the third Wren, tapping the hot bottom with her knotted rope, then cracking it down savagely across the punished cheeks. The naked Lieutenant struggled up. The strokes were merciless, the suffering severe. Chandler bucked and squealed aloud as the stripes seethed her buttocks. Chandler cried out her anguish once more, her scream echoing eerily around the vast gym, as the knotted rope-tail of her third tormentress burned the darkness of her cleft.

Beetle was now threshing uncontrollably beneath her partner's straddling thighs. Krystal tamed the brunette's curls in a taloned fist, slowly forcing up the face below into her own.

'Cramp,' Beetle whispered, her voice thickened with lust.

Krystal saw through the patent lie. The brunette was coming. Fearing detection - Beetle could be very loud - the blonde forced the brunette's face down, smothering the squeals of her climax. Beetle pounded her hips into the mat as she orgasmed, her violent release fuelled by the renewed *swish, swipe, swish, swipe* as Chandler's bare-bottomed whipping continued in the gym. Under the stark glare of the two spotlights above, the reddened upturned cheeks were being searchingly lashed by the fourth Wren. *Swish, swipe!* Beetle's bottom jerked up violently in her paroxysm, her tight cheeks pounding the blonde's pubis. For a brief moment the two watchers were fused into one flesh: melded as they heard Chandler's frenzied scream when the punisher's rope swept up between her parted cheeks.

'One moment,' the senior officer barked, stepping forward to examine the striped buttocks. Lowering her leather-gloved hand, fingers slightly splayed, she carefully palmed the crimson cheeks. Chandler writhed at the touch of the supple hide against her scorched flesh. The gloved forefinger of the examining hand traced the dark shadow of the moist cleft right down to the parted labia below.

'Buck up, old chap. Another dozen and you're home and—'

The word 'dry' died on the senior officer's lips as she extracted her wet fingertip from the pouting labia.

'Punishment party,' snapped the senior officer sharply, wiping her stained fingertip across the scalded rump of the whipped nude. 'Proceed.'

Krystal snuggled down into Beetle's soft warmth beneath her. The brunette's turbulent climax had eased, and Krystal pressed her pubis firmly into the body below, her thighs wide apart, riding the taut flesh of the buttocks supporting them. Out in the pool of light, a length of waxed whipcord was being raised up once more. The sticky-wet arousal from Krystal's slit seeped through her panties and skirt onto Beetle's bottom.

Swish, swipe! Swish swipe! The knotted rope lashed down across the naked buttocks, searing them with two more lines of invisible fire.

'I want that bottom,' Krystal moaned, silently mouthing her fierce desire into the dark curls of the brunette.

'I've just had it,' the rippling buttocks pressing up into her thighs seemed to silently reply.

Krystal smiled, grinding her slit down into Beetle's bottom.

Gazing steadily out into the gym over the riot of dark curls, she relished the sight that greeted her narrowed eyes: the Wren, having whipped the bare bottom ruthlessly, was playing her knotted rope in against Chandler's heavy breasts. Krystal shivered as she saw the Trafalgar Teasers torment the peaked nipples. The nude jerked her hot bottom up in frantic response to this dark delight. Krystal started to slide into the implacable orgasm boiling up at the base of her fluttering belly. She crushed her splayed labia into Beetle's firm rump as Chandler, her punishment continuing, shivered and squealed beneath the searching rope. After the fourth swipe, the Wren knelt and plied her rope-tail between the thighs - this time inching the waxed cord up into Chandler's wet slit.

Krystal gasped as a large butterfly seemed to spread its wings wide deep down in her belly. Gripping onto Beetle's shoulders, she waited breathlessly for the waxed cord to be yanked out. It wasn't: the artful Wren drew it out very slowly, eliciting a piercing wail from the kneeling nude. Krystal started to come. Her lips twisted into a carnal snarl, she rode Beetle as she would a mustang. Beetle turned her face upwards, her eyes wide with wonder and delight. Collapsing into the sweet violence of her climax, the blonde pressed her mouth, her lips, her tongue onto those of the woman beneath her. They kissed with a silent fury.

Swish, swipe! Swish, swipe! Krystal dragged her thickened tongue across the roof of Beetle's mouth in time with the sound of the stripes being administered across the bare bottom out in the gym. Chandler was being expertly whipped by Bunny Cardew. *Swish, swipe!* Bunny seared the buttocks for the third time, judging the stroke perfectly. The knotted rope whipped down, slicing the heavy cheeks perfectly, ripping a squeal of raw anguish from Chandler's lips. Krystal drove her tongue deep down into Beetle's wet warmth. *Swish, swipe!* Chandler moaned and stumbled, her naked breasts squashed down onto the polished wooden floor beneath the weight of the Squadron's shield.

'You came,' Beetle whispered gleefully. 'You made my bottom all wet and—'

'Sh,' murmured Krystal, smiling in the darkness at the brunette's simple show of affection.

Bunny Cardew ordered the whipped Lieutenant to roll over onto her back and spread her thighs wide apart. The shield was remounted upon the gym wall then the Wrens encircled their victim once more. Krystal's eyes narrowed into fierce slits as she watched the Wrens dangle their ropes over the spreadeagled nude, some tormenting the peaked nipples, others tap-tapping against the labia between the stretched thighs.

'You're not exactly a bad chap, Chandler,' Bunny remarked, assuming command. 'Rather a good egg, I'm sure. Your punishment is concluded. No hard feelings, what? We can put this little unpleasantness behind us now.'

Bunny kicked off her shoe and positioned her nylon-stockinged left foot over the pubis of the punished nude. Treading firmly, working the darker band of nylon around her toes into the wet slit, Bunny brought the whipped Lieutenant instantly into orgasm - the curdling screech of release reverberating around the cavernous gym. Bunny bent over Chandler's breasts and trailed the rope tail of waxed cord over the nude's parted lips. Straining up, Chandler snapped at it feverishly, only to be thwarted as her dominant tormentress whisked it away.

'Show's over,' Krystal whispered, rising in the darkness and smoothing down her skirt over her thighs. 'We'll try a window in the storeroom. Quietly.'

As they crept into the shadows, they heard Chandler screech again. In the darkness, they both knew that Bunny's nylon stockinged toes would be soaking wet.

Krystal huddled against the keen onshore wind. She was cold, despite the regal breakfast of kidneys, sausage, eggs and bacon which Bunny had provided. Her green eyes scanned the greener sea. At last, she saw the launch skimming across the waves, its sleek prow nosing towards the landing stage. It slewed to a halt, bobbing gently as it rode the swell. Beetle, in her orange life-jacket, scrambled up the rope ladder, Bunny following her with the occasional prod of encouragement to the soft buttocks above.

'It was thrilling,' Beetle yipped.

'Twenty-three knots across the Sound on a choppy morning. Just giving her a taste of the navy. Can't beat it,' Bunny grinned. Krystal shivered as she recalled the three knots across the bare bottom last night in the gym. Another taste of the navy. She blinked away the thought and helped Beetle struggle out of the life-jacket. The dark-blue Land Rover pulled up.

'Thanks awfully for everything, you chaps,' Bunny said warmly. 'My driver will get you back to the station.' She unthreaded the safety harness from Beetle's slender waist, her hands lingering for a moment at the swell of the hips. She slapped Beetle's bottom tenderly.

'I'm returning her to you safe and sound,' she said, gazing directly into Krystal's green eyes. 'She's all yours.'

Bunny presented her old school chums with a souvenir of their visit to the Cygnets and then waved them off. As the Land Rover sped away, Beetle and Krystal saw the figure of Lieutenant Chandler trotting around the perimeter of the parade ground.

'Bunny couldn't tempt you then?' Krystal murmured.

Beetle blushed and squirmed.

'To join the navy,' her dominant partner added drily.

'It's a disciplined life,' the pert Wren at the wheel chipped in, laughing. 'You two chaps wouldn't know much about discipline.'

'Beetle will,' Krystal replied softly, gazing enigmatically into the troubled brown eyes of the brunette beside her.

'Stand to attention and don't lie to me. I saw you—'
'Didn't,' Beetle muttered, adding, 'Couldn't have, anyway, coz the curtains were drawn.' Beetle immediately regretted her line of defence, as it merely served to confirm her guilt.
'So, the curtains were drawn, were they? You admit to being in her room, after midnight. And you remember the curtains being drawn.'
Beetle plucked at the waistband of her panties. The scolding was making her a little damp at the crotch. Her thumb tip rubbed at her slit absently as she looked over her shoulder, with a defiant toss of her curls, to sullenly accuse Krystal of being mean and spying.
'About face! And put both hands where I can see them,' the blonde commanded.
The brunette reluctantly obeyed, straining to interpret the sounds as Krystal opened the third drawer in the chest and rustled the tissue paper.
'You were fantastic, catching Chandler out like that. I was so proud of you,' Beetle enthused.
Fingering the coiled leather belt farewell for now, Krystal closed the drawer, sliding it home softly with her thigh. She'd decided not to discipline her little brunette's bottom with the belt now. How could she? Beetle was so loving and, in her own haphazard way, so loyal. And yet the minx had been very, very naughty. She most certainly would be taught a lesson. A little navy discipline, perhaps.
'And all the Cygnets thought you were gorgeous. I heard them in the showers—'
'Be quiet,' Krystal whispered, managing to sound stern. 'I was going to whip your bottom—'
'No, please—'
'But I've got something different planned for you now.'
Beetle whimpered. Krystal saw the pantied buttocks tighten.
'A partnership is very similar to being in the ranks. It demands exclusive devotion to duty. I know you try to be loyal and...' her voice became a thrilling whisper '...sometimes almost succeed. So, this will be for all those little failures. Bend over.'
The brunette's buttocks rose up as her head of dark curls descended to the duvet.
'Hands on the bed.'
'But I didn't—'
'Legs apart. Wider,' Krystal continued imperturbably, fingering the white cotton panties stretched across the burgeoning bottom. 'These are not yours, surely?' The question was crisp, the tone waspish. Krystal dragged the panties down.
'B-Bunny gave them to me. Something to remember the Wrens—'
'And Bunny gave this to me. Head down.'
Krystal reached across the duvet and picked up Bunny's parting gift. It was a Bosun's Rod, twenty inches of the smoothest polished ivory. After sweeping the length of Beetle's spine with the blunt knout, Krystal brought it to rest pressed into the cheek of the left buttock. Beetle shivered at the touch.
'Exclusive devotion to duty often means denying oneself. When one serves, one obeys. One struggles to stay above temptation; to be rigorously loyal. I spoke just then of self-denial. An admirable quality. It is so important.' Krystal, propelled the bending

nude further down across the duvet.

Beetle started to protest but the duvet smothered her pleading.

'Something here for you, Beetle. From Bunny. A taste of the navy. A taste of naval discipline - perhaps not as sweet as you imagined it to be. Open your legs wider,' she hissed, kneeling down before the bending nude's buttocks.

Beetle's labia peeped out shyly as she obeyed the blonde's curt command. Krystal inched the blunt knout of the boson's rod towards the wet, pink, fleshy lips. As the tip of the shaft kissed the weeping slit, the bending nude gasped, then moaned.

'A present from Bunny,' Krystal whispered savagely, rotating the ivory phallus five times before thrusting it in two inches. Beetle gasped aloud and clenched her buttocks. A shiver rippling down the silken inner thighs betrayed the brunette's pleasure as the blonde's guiding hand controlled the probing shaft.

'Please,' begged Beetle. 'Harder, faster. Please.'

Beetle dug her fingers into the duvet as her slit accepted the rod. Down on the carpet, her toes scrabbled frantically. The delicious discipline was dispensed slowly, a measured half inch at a time. Beetle squirmed as the shaft entered her wet warmth. Krystal deliberately paused: her happy victim shuddered and mewed pitifully for more. But Krystal was teaching her little partner a strict lesson. She was in supreme control and Beetle, naked and bending, utterly in her stern thrall.

'Please,' Beetle begged, her bare bottom rippling with spasms of frustration. 'Please.'

'The Persian poets wrote at length of one pleasure greater than a pleasure consumed: it is the haunting delight of a pleasure denied—'

'Oh, please,' the brunette moaned, thrusting back her hips and buttocks in an attempt to cheat Krystal's controlling hand. Krystal smiled knowingly and deftly retracted the length of white ivory a fraction, denying Beetle her desire.

'A pleasure denied,' the blonde whispered. 'I want you to reflect upon the wisdom of the Persian poets. Consider the paradox of how much better it is, how much sweeter, to suffer a pleasure denied. Think carefully,' Krystal mouthed her words slowly into the soft creamy flesh of the left buttock, 'should you ever again be tempted into any engaging little encounters.' The blonde finished her words of warning by licking, then nipping and biting the heavy cheek of the bare buttock.

Offering up her bottom submissively to Krystal's cruel mouth, Beetle hung her head in penitent shame. Shuddering in her torment, she muttered a full contrition. Krystal withdrew the rod slowly, sighing contentedly as Beetle whispered her confession and sobbed her atonement. The dominant blonde wiped the glistening rod on the duvet and tapped it against Beetle's bare bottom. All that remained to be determined, she mused contentedly, was a penance.

'Up onto the bed. No, kneeling. Face-down. Legs wide apart.'

Beetle scrambled happily onto their bed, dimpling the mattress with her elbows, knees and toes. Krystal stroked the velvety labia with the tip of the Bosun's Rod, cunningly managing to drag its polished smoothness against Beetle's tiny pink clitoris. The duvet drowned the shrillness of the brunette's squeal of joy. Guiding the first three inches of the shaft between the sticky fleshfolds, Krystal probed the kneeling nude until six, seven and then a full nine inches of firm delight had disappeared. Catching the stem of the shaft between both palms, she rubbed slowly, rotating it clockwise, then anti-clockwise. Beetle's bottom bounced, jerking rhythmically as she harmonized her body with the length of ivory inside her - the pillow enveloping her face muffling her purrs of pleasure. Krystal gradually increased the speed of rotation until her palms flew together in a blur. Beetle squealed, pounding the duvet with clenched fists.

'Harder, faster, please,' she screamed, panting as she implored to be impaled. 'Please, oh please—'

'Pleasure denied,' the dominant blonde murmured, withdrawing the glistening shaft in one swift snatch, 'is a much better motto for you than *Castegatur Malefactor*, isn't it, my sweet?'

Beetle groaned as she clamped her thighs tightly together.

'Isn't it? Or would you prefer—' Krystal drew the tip of the ivory rod, as she would a cane, across Beetle's bare bottom.

'Yes,' Beetle sobbed, choking on her welling climax.

'Then we will say no more about your episode with Bunny Cardew,' Krystal whispered, urging the tip of the cool ivory shaft down between the brunette's buttocks. 'We will consider the matter closed.' The Bosun's Rod paused to worry the sticky anal whorl. Beetle moaned. 'I forgive you. Sleep now, my little minx. No, keep your fingers up on the pillow where I can see them. There will be no release from your sweet agonies tonight. Suffer, my little one,' Krystal whispered huskily, tucking Beetle in under the duvet. 'I will place our little souvenir here, between your thighs. Do not attempt to pleasure yourself with it. Remember the Persian poets. No cheating, Beetle. For you, it must be a pleasure denied.'

Beetle grunted her reluctant obedience.

'And don't forget, if you try anything in the darkness, I will know. I will hear you, sense you, smell you. As they say in the navy. I will be on watch.'

Chapter Four

Trevor MacDonald beamed at them from the television set and invited them to join him after the break.

'What time are you on?'

'Twenty-two sixteen: fifteen is the network slot,' Beetle said solemnly, trying to sound very cool and professional.

'You mean just after quarter past ten,' Krystal sighed. 'And now you'll get talc everywhere.'

Beetle, naked and briskly towelled after her shower, was sprinkling talc over her shoulder. 'I'm trying to powder my bottom,' she pouted. 'Keep it nice and soft for you.'

'Give it to me.'

Krystal palmed the bare buttocks slowly, spreading the sheen of talc across the silky mounds of warm flesh.

'Mmm,' Beetle purred. Suddenly, she jumped up and down, her breasts bouncing freely. 'Look, I'm on,' she squealed.

'Quiet,' Krystal insisted, gently spanking the joggling bottom to calm the brunette down.

The ad for swordfish steaks flashed before their eyes as they stood facing the TV holding hands.

'You were marvellous,' Krystal enthused, kissing Beetle and squeezing her left breast affectionately. Trevor MacDonald, back with the news, looked mildly surprised as Krystal lowered her lips and sucked hard on the proffered nipple.

'To your success.'

They sipped from their celebratory glasses of champagne.

'Didn't last long,' Beetle remarked, dabbing at her pubis with a corner of the towel. 'It took ages to do in the studio.'

Krystal scooped up the remote and aimed right between Trevor MacDonald's eyes. He shrivelled to a dot. 'Let's go out for a slap-up supper.'

'Sure? You've been busy all day at your clay.'

'Already booked. It's a new place near Farringdon. Fish restaurant. They do swordfish.'

Beetle grinned as she struggled into her skin-tight spangled dress.

Beetle ordered swordfish and a green salad.

'The carp - how is it cooked?' Krystal inquired.

'They do him in sherry. Very nice,' their pretty little Portuguese waitress said, frowning with concentration. 'Very succulent. My name is Pastora,' she tapped the badge on her bosom.

'And a bottle of Dom Perignon—'

'Ooh,' Beetle squealed.

Their waitress, petite and perfectly formed, beamed at Beetle. The brunette gazed back, drinking in the honey-coloured skin, the dark eyes, the ripe bosom and the shapely waist. Krystal noted how, as she bent across the table to rearrange the silverware for their fish course, Pastora's fingers fleetingly brushed against Beetle's forearm. Beetle's eyes widened a fraction at the touch. The little waitress, her breasts heaving within the restraining crisp white apron, pressed against Beetle as she placed rolls and butter on the table.

'How you like the swordfish?' she asked, standing close to Beetle's chair, her thigh grazing Beetle's elbow.

'What do you recommend?' Beetle flirted.

'You like him poached or you like him grilled?'

'Grilled,' Krystal answered. 'My partner does not approve of poaching, or being poached.'

Beetle blushed and lowered her eyes. Pastora wrinkled her brow, giggled and departed, her plump bottom swaying temptingly beneath the tight sheath of her black velvet uniform.

Their meal was served promptly, Beetle receiving extra attention with the pepper mill. Krystal eyed the entwined fingers of the four hands around the thick shaft as she watched over the rim of her champagne glass.

Seconds later the pert waitress returned to their table. 'Salad?'

'For me, Pastora,' Beetle said, looking up eagerly.

'You like me to toss it for you?'

Krystal forked her carp-in-sherry-sauce in silence as Beetle and the pretty waitress playfully oiled and salted the green salad. Beetle licked at the virgin oil glistening on her fingertips. Pastora took the brunette's hand and wiped the fingers gently with a napkin.

'Sticky fingers, no? Always sticky fingers after tossing.'

Beetle giggled.

'Let me do it,' she pleaded.

Pastora surrendered the large wooden spoon, the pen dropping from her bosom as she bent down. Retrieving it, Beetle grazed her knuckles up the tanned leg as far as the thigh of the velvet mini-skirted waitress.

'Put him back, no?' Pastora purred, offering her bosom to the brunette.

Krystal's teeth closed over her carp in silent anger as Beetle slid the silver pen down between the perfect breasts and clipped the top onto the crisp apron.

The pen arrowed directly down into the shadowed cleavage, separating the swollen breasts. Beetle's thumbtip dimpled the satin swell of the left breast during the delicate manoeuvre.

'He is a naughty pen, no? Thank you.' The voice was warm and intimate.

Beetle hastened to placate Krystal. 'How's your carp? It looks—'

'Hi, you two! What are you doing?'

It was Mandy Winwood, their poetess friend. Krystal detected a strong whiff of brandy as Mandy seated herself a little unsteadily at their table.

'Celebrating Beetle's ad on the TV tonight,' Krystal replied.

'Great.' Mandy hiccupped.

'The ad was for swordfish,' Beetle explained. 'That's what I'm having for supper.'

'What's that?' Mandy asked, peering dubiously at Krystal's plate.

'Sherried carp.'

'I adore cerry-sharp.'

Krystal's suspicions were confirmed. The poetess was tipsy, and when Mandy Winwood was tipsy, Mandy Winwood was sad.

'What's the matter?'

Krystal listened attentively as Mandy unburdened her sorrows. Her portfolio of poems - erotic Sapphic verse - had been submitted for the Cup of Lesbos prize.

'My editrix claims she mislaid them but in fact pinched the best bits and passed them on to her partner. And who won the prize?'

Krystal nodded. 'Copyright?'

'I was foolish. Working to deadline, I trusted her with my only copy. But I can remember them,' she added quickly. 'I can remember every word.'

Nearby diners turned in amazement as Mandy loudly recited no less than twenty-six lines from *Forbidden Fruits*, a torrid depiction of lustful longings fulfilled.

'Yes, yes,' Krystal soothed, stemming the flood of references to split figs, oozing plums and firm, succulent melons. At the next table, a dark-haired woman was fingering herself as her scampi congealed, neglected, on her plate.

'Have some coffee with me and we'll sort it all out tomorrow.' Krystal ordered two coffees, and asked for the sweet trolley Beetle.

'Such treats,' Beetle squealed, clapping her hands in delight. She stood up to peruse the tempting confections on display, pressing her body closely against Pastora's as they stood thigh to thigh at the trolley.

'Tell me more,' Krystal invited, now that the coffee had sobered the poetess up a little. 'I think I might be able to help. I do so hate injustice. I burn to right a wrong.'

Their heads almost touched over the table cloth as Mandy repeated her woes. At the sweet trolley, Beetle and the waitress giggled as they chivvied a coy profiterole onto a plate, their hands together on the silver slice.

Supper completed, the three friends prepared to depart. At the next table, the dark-haired diner, now recovered, ordered crepes suzettes. Pastora was gamely preparing the delicacies, but at the crucial moment her lighter failed to ignite. Beetle came to her rescue, slipping her a book of matches. Krystal signed their bill and shepherded Mandy out to a taxi. Returning, the blonde retrieved the matches while Beetle was busy securing another taxi. Flicking the cover open, Krystal's green eyes narrowed as she read Beetle's mobile phone number scribbled inside.

They walked past the British Museum towards the offices where Mandy's dishonest editrix waited expectantly.

'Just a profile with pix,' Krystal had suggested over the phone.

'Which magazines?' came the reply, already hooked.

'Syndicated. Very big circulation. Might mean a TV interview tie-in. We'll include the prize-winner too.'

'Ah, Prudence. Yes, she's scooped the Cup of Lesbos.'

'Noon, tomorrow?' Krystal chose that time as it meant the other offices would be empty, the occupants busy Christmas shopping or securing prawn and avocado rolls.

'Noon it is.' The barely concealed excitement of the voice had made Krystal smile.

'Here we are. Camera ready?'

Beetle tapped her leather case.

'Follow me.'

They were glad to be out of the raw December wind. The aroma of fresh coffee led them to the door. It was opened by a tall brunette with stunning legs and a wide smile. The office, Krystal noted, was typical of the 'small press' poetry publishers. Vanity and chaos held equal sway. A black porcelain frog with agate eyes squatted on the fax machine. Withered asters in a vase drooped over the filing cabinet.

'And this is—'

'Prudence?' Krystal anticipated her, determined to keep the upper hand. 'The Cup of Lesbos prize-winner.'

The heavily-breasted redhead nodded but preserved an aloof silence.

'We'll do the pix straight away,' Krystal continued suavely, as coolly professional as if she interviewed twice a day, every day.

Beetle was convincing, adjusting the lighting and encouraging her two subjects to sit closely together, embracing as they pored over a smudged typescript.

'Known each other long?' Krystal began her questioning, clicking on a small tape recorder. 'Helps me when I do the write-up,' she explained.

After six minutes, Krystal turned to the redhead, who had maintained a cold silence throughout.

'Could we have a few lines?'

'That might not be possible, my dear,' the editrix interposed, fussing protectively over Prudence. 'Copyright, and all that.'

'Ah, yes, copyright,' Krystal murmured. 'I just thought a snatch from one of the prizewinning poems.'

Vanity won through, and the redhead capitulated.

'Is this altogether wise, Prudence?' the editrix bleated.

'Be quiet. You fuss too much. I shall,' Prudence condescended, turning to Krystal, 'recite.'

'From *Forbidden Fruits*, perhaps?' Krystal ventured.

'How on earth did you know that?' Prudence gasped, flattered and confused.

The editrix broke in anxiously. 'Perhaps we had better not—'

'Research,' Krystal replied, ignoring the interjection. 'You'd be surprised how important it is to get all the facts absolutely right.'

'Very thorough of you,' the editrix conceded. 'I am always thorough. Prudence?'

The poetess coughed gently and, rifling through some sheets of paper, extracted one from which she started to declaim:

'Down from ripe melons to plum sticky sweet,
Now split wide open its juices to weep—'

'—There with my tongue tip I linger then dip
And at thy hot nectar wantonly sip'

Krystal concluded the stanza with the lines she had been taught by Mandy.

The paper in the hand of the redhead rustled nervously. For the very first time, Prudence stared directly into Krystal's green eyes. Standing by the desk, her hand at her pale face, the editrix blinked, her wide eyes startled by Beetle's sudden flashbulb. Recovering her composure, she asked in a strained voice how Krystal could possibly have known the lines.

'Research. I told you I was thorough. More, please, Prudence.'

In something of a daze, the redhead glanced down at her sheet of typed verse and, in a mechanical tone, read:

'Soon demon sharp darts of urgent desire
Our naked limbs blaze with passionate fire—'

'My finger so firm glides deeply within
Between your smooth peach cheeks softer than sin'

Once more Krystal concluded the verse to the astonishment of Prudence.

'Impossible,' rasped Prudence, rising up from the desk.

'Got the pix, Beetle?' Krystal asked, ignoring the poetess.

'I think we've got more than enough,' Beetle nodded.

'I just don't understand...' the editrix faltered.

'I think you do. Those lines were not penned by Prudence. They were entrusted to you by Mandy Winwood. She submitted them to you, her editrix, and in doing so,' Krystal's voice dropped half an octave, 'lost what was rightfully hers to win - the Cup of Lesbos.'

'No, that's—' Prudence hissed.

'Beyond dispute. We are here to see justice done.' Prudence turned on the editrix, abusing her savagely.

'Be quiet,' Krystal rasped. 'You will both listen to what I tell you and you will obey me. Understand? We have got enough on you to ruin you both. Do I make myself plain?'

'Fool,' the redhead snapped at the editrix. 'I told you it was dangerous, stealing her poems.'

'Don't blame me, you vain little beast. If your talents were as big as your ego—'

Krystal smiled as she sauntered across to the blinds and closed them. 'Lock the door, Beetle.'

Their recriminations spluttering into silence, the editrix and the redhead addressed Krystal.

'You'll never prove—'

'I'll deny—'

'You will disclaim the prize and see to it that the Cup of Lesbos is restored to the rightful winner,' Krystal said, silencing their protests. She unbuckled and removed the leather belt from her svelte waist. 'But first, you must be punished, Prudence, take this,' she passed the leather belt across the desk, 'and give the editrix six strokes.'

Prudence gasped, her trembling hand barely able to grasp the length of supple leather.

'Get across the desk,' Krystal ordered the editrix. 'Skirt up, panties down. Beetle, put her in position to receive her stripes.'

The editrix shrieked in outrage but Krystal merely held up the tape recorder. 'We have it all here. You have no option but to take your punishment.'

Quelled into sullen silence, the tall brunette stumbled towards the desk.

'Bend over,' Beetle commanded.

The editrix obeyed, easing herself across the desk top submissively. Beetle's fingertips swept up the lissom calves, pausing for a moment at the hem of the skirt. Seconds later, she had thumbed the skirt up over the hips and peeled the pale-pink panties down, leaving them in a restricting stretch just above the knees.

Krystal walked around the desk and examined the bare bottom. Turning, she picked up the black porcelain frog from its perch on the fax machine and placed it at the edge of the desk.

'Take your hands away from your bottom. Place them on top of the desk. No, further. Grasp the frog and hold it down while you are being whipped.'

Her face pressed down onto the desk top, the editrix groped blindly in front of her, her fingers seeking for and grasping the frog.

'It's all her fault, you know,' Krystal murmured to Prudence. 'She's got you into this mess. No prize for you, and a severe punishment for her to come. I trust you'll stripe her hard.'

A soft snarl was the only reply Prudence could make as, raising the leather aloft, she planted her feet apart. Fuelled by a sudden fury, she lashed the bare buttocks before her. *Swish, swipe! Swish, swipe!* The belt whipped down, scalding the naked cheeks. *Swish, swipe! Swish, swipe!* Two more searing slices of the hide across living flesh. Across the desk top, the editrix squealed and begged to be spared the remaining strokes.

'Shut up,' muttered Prudence angrily. 'I told you it was a stupid idea, stealing her lines.'

Beetle's flashbulb exploded as she photographed the punishment in progress.

Crack, snap! Crack, snap! The leather whipped down twice more, rocketing the bare-bottomed editrix into renewed paroxysms of anguish. She squealed loudly as the belt barked across her reddened cheeks.

'You've ruined everything,' Prudence hissed.

Krystal stepped forward and relieved the redhead of the leather belt. 'Now you,' she ordered. 'Skirt up and across the desk for your six strokes.'

'No,' Prudence exclaimed, backing away. 'It was all her idea to steal the poems. It was all her fault—'

'Across the desk, bare-bottomed, at once,' repeated Krystal imperturbably.

The redhead made a futile bid to escape but Beetle grappled her from behind and mastered her easily.

'Before you are whipped, Prudence, I must thank you,' Krystal continued.

'Thank me?' the redhead echoed, confused.

'Mmm. We hadn't much on either of you by way of proof. We bluffed our way in and hoped for the best. You have been most obliging. A full admission, as good as a confession, all here on my tape. It was a case of Mandy's word against yours, but now,' Krystal switched off the cassette and pocketed it, 'we've got it all.'

'Moron—'

'Idiot—'

The editrix and the redhead exchanged their venomous recriminations for a full half minute before Krystal interposed, cracking the leather across the desk top.

'Take the belt and stripe her well,' she instructed the editrix as, crushed and defeated, Prudence inched up her skirt and lowered her tights to her thighs. Beetle arranged the redhead across the desk, then dragged the dark tights down to the knees of the prostrate poetess. Prudence, too, was given the black porcelain frog to hold during her punishment. She gripped onto it tightly, clenching her buttocks as she surrendered the round cheeks to the impending lash.

Scalded by her own stripes, and by the redhead's open treachery, the editrix was eager to use the belt. *Swish, crack!* 'If you were a better poet—' *Swish, crack!* 'I wouldn't have had to do it.' *Swish, crack!* 'You are nothing but a second-rate scribbler.' *Swish, crack! Swish, crack!* 'You will never, ever win—' *swish, crack!* 'a prize.'

Panting from her exertions, the editrix stumbled forward, steadying herself by taloning the hot rump with her splayed fingers. Prudence squealed as her ravished buttocks suffered this fresh torment and, in a reflex of agony, she let the porcelain frog slip to the floor and shatter.

'My frog, my beautiful frog!' In a frenzy of rage, the editrix raised the belt and lashed it down three times more. Prudence jerked her buttocks, writhing under the vicious onslaught.

'Stop,' thundered Krystal. 'There is more punishment to come, but only when I deem it. Give me the belt and get across that desk.'

Surrendering the leather, the editrix joined the redhead, and Beetle stepped forward to bare her bottom once more.

'I think it is time for a little poetic justice,' Krystal mused, fingering the warmth of the supple belt. Gazing down at the two whipped bottoms, she noted with satisfaction the red lines that had developed across the ivory-cream of the suffering cheeks. 'I propose to see just how good you are as poets. I will give you the opening line of a couplet. You will each have a chance to complete it, observing the strict rules of both rhyme and rhythm. Understand?'

The bared buttocks joggled as the cheats nodded in unison. Krystal handed the belt to Beetle. 'Be ready to stripe them on my command. You may,' she addressed the pair across the desk, 'hold hands during this punishment. There is no use in your falling out. You are equally at fault in this sorry matter and will suffer equal torments.'

The two bottoms inched closer together as Prudence and her editrix nestled into each other.

'Beetle, prepare yourself.'

Shouldering the belt, the brunette positioned herself behind the upturned cheeks.

'Complete this couplet, Prudence: "Cruel supple length of cool whippy cane..."' A pause followed. Krystal tapped the desk top. 'I'm waiting,' she whispered.

'"Lash me slowly, again and again",' Prudence said huskily.

'Not very good, I'm afraid. Too much reliance upon repetition and padding. A marked lack of alliteration. Altogether, a weak line. Four strokes, Beetle.'

Whipping the length of the hide smartly down, Beetle delivered the four prescribed strokes with a staccato *crack, crack, crack, crack!* Prudence moaned, grinding her exposed pubis into the desk as the searing strokes licked into her defenceless flesh in rapid succession. The fourth slicing stripe elicited a shrill squeal from the redhead's parted lips.

'Try again,' Krystal invited. 'Give me another, more lyrical, line. Let's see if you can come up with a prize-winner, mm?'

Prudence pressed her face against the desk top, her bare cheeks tightly clenched beneath the hovering leather.

'"Cruel supple length of cool whippy cane..."' Krystal prompted.

'"Pour down thy sorrow of bamboo rain",' Prudence whispered softly, her breath clouding the polished desk top.

'Much better, though owing much to the Imagists, I suspect. Mallarme would be flattered. Still,' Krystal continued suavely, 'plundering others' work is well within your scope, isn't it, Prudence? Worthy, I'm sure, of a small prize. Four more strokes, Beetle.'

The brunette raised the belt: the bare bottom shivered. *Snap, crack! Snap, crack!* Prudence groaned, her hips jerking rebelliously at each slicing stroke. *Snap, crack! Snap, crack!* The thin leather added more reddening lines to the scalded cheeks, blazing them with a fiery pain.

'And now you,' Krystal addressed the editrix. 'Your turn to complete my little work in progress.' She repeated the couplet's opening line.

'"Bite-stripe my cheeks, bestowing sweet pain",' the editrix blurted, the words tumbling out disjointedly.

'A reasonable grasp of the principles of rhyme,' Krystal commended, 'but sadly amiss in matters of metre and rhythm. Give her four.'

'No, please, no—'

'Silence,' the dominant blonde rasped, quelling the protest. 'You must learn, and learn well, that as the late Dr Johnson observed, good poets borrow but only great poets steal. You are neither great nor good. Beetle.'

Swish, snap! Swish, snap! The superb legs threshed in their bondage of tight panties as the leather lashed the buttocks above. *Swish, snap! Swish, snap!* The bare cheeks seethed and the hot bottom bucked and bounced as the editrix squealed her torment.

'And again. I want a better line.'

The editrix remained sullenly silent.

'"Cruel supple length of cool whippy cane..."' Krystal murmured, reaching across to take the scalded flesh of the left buttock between a firm pincer of finger and thumb.

The editrix screamed softly and hastily rattled out the words to complete the couplet.
'"Across my buttocks bare rule sovereign".'

Krystal relinquished her grip on the soft cheek. 'Very, very derivative. An echo of the minor Victorian voices. Nothing to trouble Tennyson. Six strokes, please Beetle. I like to see effort rewarded.'

The editrix wriggled and squirmed under the *crack, crack, crack!* of the whistling leather belt as it bit mercilessly into her buttocks. Beetle dispensed the stinging six with vigour, relishing the subtle change from crimson to scarlet as the naked bottom burned.

'Stay exactly where you are, both of you,' Krystal commanded. 'Beetle, type out this letter for me.'

As the blonde dictated - and the brunette typed - a letter refusing the Cup of Lesbos and returning the prize, explaining that there had been an oversight resulting in the prize going to the wrong recipient and not to Mandy Winwood, its rightful winner, the pair across the desk top comforted each other, their mutual vehemence melting under the fierce heat of their shared suffering.

'Prudence, sign this and then fax it.'

The redhead pulled up her dark tights and smoothed down her skirt. Having signed the letter, she faxed it off.

'When the Cup of Lesbos is with its rightful owner,' Krystal concluded, tapping her tape cassette, 'you will receive this and the film from Beetle's camera.'

The week before Christmas was hectic, and Beetle was not having much luck with her mobile.

'Who was it?' she cried, scampering into the room in response to its shrill command.

'Couldn't get to it in time,' Krystal lied, holding out a pair of hands she'd just deliberately smeared with wet clay. 'Sorry,' she shrugged.

That evening, the mobile trilled again. Beetle retreated into the bedroom with it, only to re-emerge seconds later complaining that the battery seemed to be dud. Krystal, feigning sympathy, suppressed her smile as she shoved the battery she had earlier switched for the almost spent one deeper down the side of the sofa.

The following afternoon, Beetle was browsing in Bond Street. Her mobile rang and the sultry voice of Pastora from the restaurant several nights ago huskily suggested coffee, giving an address just behind the Barbican. The taxi that whisked her across London became snarled up in the inevitable rush-hour jam along London Wall. Beetle skipped out and skittled along the wide pavement, her excitement mounting, her hot slit tingling, as she approached the flat. The entry phone buzzed her in. Breathless after her two-hundred-yard dash, Beetle blinked in the December tea-time darkness of the unlit flat. A sultry voice instructed her to go straight along to the bedroom and undress. Surprised but happy to obey, Beetle went into the darkened room and unzipped with trembling fingers. A voice from just beyond the doorway whispered silkily, expressing great pleasure at Beetle's arrival.

'Are you naked, yet?'

'Mmm,' Beetle giggled.

'And your bottom, she is bare?'

Beetle confirmed that she was utterly nude.

'Your bottom. How you like her done?'

'Done?' Beetle repeated uncertainly.

'I cook her for you. Really well done, or scorched?'

'Pastora?' Beetle's voice faltered. 'Is that you? You sound just like—'

'Krystal?' Krystal purred in her own natural voice.

Beetle squeaked, surprise and alarm sharpening her tones.

Krystal stepped into the bedroom and snapped on the light. Beetle automatically shielded her bottom with cupped hands.

'I'm so very pleased to find you naked, for naked is exactly how I require you for your punishment.'

'I don't understand,' Beetle blurted. 'You're not supposed—'

'To be here? And why shouldn't I visit Mandy? Hmm?'

'Mandy? You mean—'

'This is Mandy's flat. Why, Beetle, whose did you think it was? Pastora's, maybe?'

'Yes, no, I don't—'

'Kneel,' Krystal snarled softly. 'Hands on your head. No, look at me.'

Beetle gazed up sorrowfully at the blonde she knew was about to punish her bare bottom severely.

'Mandy has been invaluable to me. Making those phone calls, just to whet your appetite. Then providing me with her flat. A little honey trap, and you, my little fly, have flown right into it.'

'So Pastora—'

'Didn't even get time to memorize your phone number.'

Beetle blushed, muttering something about offering to help the little Portuguese waitress improve her English.

'Pastora can make herself perfectly understood. Your presence here is proof enough of that. Across the bed.'

'No, please. It's nearly Christmas—'

'Your bottom will still be very sore on Boxing Day. Across the bed at once.'

Beetle obeyed, offering her bare buttocks to the fury to come.

'Mandy,' Krystal called out.

The high-heeled footsteps echoed as they approached the bedroom.

'Hi, you two. Having fun?'

'Fond of salads?' Krystal asked innocently.

'Love 'em.'

'Then you'll have oil, vinegar, pepper and a large wooden spoon.'

'Yep, sure have. Need 'em now?'

Krystal nodded. The naked buttocks across the bed tightened.

Mandy returned, bearing the wooden spoon and condiments. 'I was just looking at my prize, Beetle. The Cup of Lesbos. Thanks for all your help.'

Beetle grunted into the duvet, poetry being the last thing on her mind.

'May I stay and watch?' Mandy asked. 'I adore discipline and you are a bit of an expert, Krystal.'

'Be my guest,' the blonde Pole bowed, acknowledging the tribute. 'Beetle has been very, very naughty. She knows she deserves to suffer. Don't you, my sweet?'

Beetle grunted softly again.

'We didn't hear you properly. *Again*, please,' Krystal instructed, padding across to the bed, wooden spoon in hand.

'Yes,' whispered Beetle hoarsely. 'I have been bad and deserve to be punished.'

'And how shall you be punished, Beetle?' Krystal demanded.

'On the bottom. On the bare bottom. Severely.'

'I'm going to use this wooden spoon for your chastisement,' Krystal said, sitting down on the bed and depressing the swollen crowns of the naked cheeks firmly with the spoon. 'A fitting punishment, don't you think? I seem to recall you having lots of fun with Pastora, tossing the salad.'

Under the pressure of the spoon, the soft buttocks trembled.

'We'll dress the salad first, before using the spoon. Over my knee.'

On the bed, Krystal arranged the naked brunette across her lap.

'Bottom up, please. No, you know how I want it. Bigger and rounder.'

Beetle offered up her buttocks as bidden.

'A little olive oil. Not virgin, I'm afraid, but it will serve.'

Beetle mewed as the golden droplets splashed down into her cleft. Krystal stemmed the trickle, dabbling down between the creamy cheeks with her fingertips, and spread the oil over her buttocks. The smoothing palm ensured that every inch of the warm, satin pillows of flesh glistened beneath the sheen. Mandy, her back to the door, sank slowly down to her knees, her bottom squatting on her heels, as she gazed spellbound.

With stern authority and consummate skill, Krystal thoroughly oiled the naked rump. *Crack, spank!* Plying the wooden spoon down across the gleaming cheeks, Krystal elicited several squeals from the punished brunette. *Crack, spank!* Again, and then again, the wooden spoon spoke. Beetle writhed under the searching swipes of hard pear-wood across soft flesh.

'A little vinegar,' Krystal, cool and dominant, murmured.

Beetle squeezed her reddening cheeks as the droplets of dark brown liquid scalded the sensitive ribbon of flesh deep within her cleft. 'No!' she protested, jerking her hips.

'Silence,' came the stern command.

Mandy, her skirt riding above her thighs, stroked her hot slit, pausing to tease up her clitoris. Her eyes were clouded with lust and she shuddered each time Beetle moaned.

Crack! Crack! Crack! Pinning the brunette down, the blonde whipped the spoon harshly across the naked buttocks, lecturing Beetle sternly on fidelity, obedience and loyalty. The words stung the little brunette as severely as did the spoon. Tears of contrition were soon being shed, soaking Krystal's thigh.

'Salt and pepper,' the blonde mused, thumbing the hot cheeks wide apart.

Beetle squealed, dreading the searing torment promised by condiments sprinkled into her cleft.

'No,' Krystal soothed. 'You have been punished enough.' Ordering the brunette to remain face-down across the duvet, Krystal took the glistening spoon and, crossing the bedroom, knelt down before Mandy.

Mandy looked up, parted her thighs wide and stretched her arms up against the door behind her. Krystal lowered the spoon down between the parted thighs until it touched the smiling, welcoming labia. Mandy grunted softly, stiffening slightly as the spoon caressed her pubis, slowly at first and then with ruthless accuracy. Arching up, Mandy signalled her approaching climax.

Peeping from the bed, Beetle hammered the duvet with fists of jealous fury. 'No,' she shouted hotly. 'Me, not her! Me!'

Krystal smiled at the anguish in the brunette's voice. Pumping the spoon savagely, twisting it a little so that its curved edge ravaged the clitoris, she brought Mandy to a loud orgasm. Pounding her buttocks against the door behind her, Mandy shrieked as she came, drowning the sorrow-sobs of misery from the red-bottomed brunette abandoned across the bed.

CHAPTER FIVE

'Panties off'?'

'Keep them on. When my editor commissioned a centrespread, that's not what she had in mind.'

Beetle giggled, squirming her nylon-sheathed legs as she compressed her thighs into the zebra hide. Brazilia, Lady 'Nuts' Collingham's youngest, concentrated on adjusting the zoom between a delicately prinked finger-and-thumb pincer until the swelling curves of Beetle's pantied bottom sharpened into focus.

'Legs straight,' Brazilia commanded. 'No. Turn your left foot in a little. I want those seams perfectly aligned.'

Beetle obliged, but the impatient sigh escaping from Brazilia's aristo-decadent red lips signalled that the result was still far from satisfactory. Approaching the sofa across which Beetle was arranged to display the lingerie collection to full effect, Brazilia knelt and swept her fingertips up over the nyloned curves of the inner leg. Beetle gasped aloud, clenching her thighs together.

'Open up,' came the stern instruction. 'And don't tighten your cheeks,' the strict voice continued. 'I want smooth buttocks in every shot,' Brazilia warned, admonishing the left cheek with a slap.

Beetle mewed a token protest and snuggled once more into the warmth of the animal skin. The striped fur tickled her pubic plum as it probed the stretch of her black silk panties.

'Stop wriggling.'

'It's the zebra. It itches.'

'You can give yourself a good scratch later, my girl. Just be patient. I must get these shots. I'm way behind my deadline—'

'Beetle,' Krystal's voice interrupted in tones of velvety menace, 'if I have to come over there to give Brazilia a hand, I promise you it will be a very firm one.'

'Sorry,' came the whimpered reply.

Krystal sipped her coffee and gazed meditatively at Beetle's writhing buttocks over the brim of her big red mug. Sensing the eyes of her partner fixed upon her upturned cheeks, Beetle hastily arranged herself exactly as the photographer wanted her, assuming the required pose.

'Why all the rush?' Krystal asked, putting her mug down firmly onto a coaster bearing David Mellor's face. 'I thought the shoot was completed before Christmas.'

'It was,' Brazilia grunted, bending down over her SLR. 'Hold it.' The automatic motor whirred and the zoom lens devoured the beautiful bottom and lithe legs poised before it. 'Perfect.'

'Can I get up for a moment?' Beetle whined, 'I think I've swallowed a zebra hair.'

Without waiting for permission, she skipped across the room to where Krystal sat curled up on her sofa. Reaching down, Beetle picked up the big red mug and gulped down two mouthfuls of coffee. From the ring-stained coaster, the face of David Mellor grinned inanely up at the bulging, bouncing breasts above. Beetle obliterated the face with the mug and returned to the zebra skin, absently scratching her pubic snatch before resuming the required pose.

'Take a longer break, Beetle,' Brazilia said. 'Then change into the next outfit. The scarlet one, but just panties, suspender and stockings. No shoes this time. I'll take you up on tip-toe.'

Krystal finished the coffee, nursing the warm mug against her heavy bosom. Three feet away, Beetle peeled off her black satin ensemble and wriggled coquettishly into the scarlet silks.

'So?' Krystal pressed, nodding to the SLR on its tripod. 'Is this backup stuff?'

'No,' Brazilia sighed, shrugging. 'Some of my best prints were pinched.'

'Pinched?'

'Up at Linton Hall. I went home for the customary yuletide jollies. Mama had quite a houseful, but made the mistake of dishing out an invite to Penny Cakebread.'

'Heard of her. Sharp customer.'

'One of the sharpest, and not above stealing other people's ideas. Or their maids.'

'Go on,' Krystal murmured, absently covering up David Mellor's face with the empty coffee mug.

'We had foxes at the kitchen dustbins on Boxing Day. Woke the whole household by setting off the infra-red alarms. We all trooped down thinking it was the fire bell.'

'Sounds exciting.'

'Total shambles. Then Cambridge, the butler, gravely announced that the party assembled to shiver in the Orangery was incomplete. Estrelle Colette—'

'The French actress?'

'Yes. Both she and her maid were missing. I went upstairs with him and Penny Cakebread skulked behind. We found Estrelle whipping her maid—'

'Under the mistletoe?' giggled Beetle.

'*With* the mistletoe,' Brazilia replied drily. 'Cambridge was, as ever, impeccable. Advised us that he had taken the precaution of summoning the brigade but that the likelihood of a conflagration was minimal - all this as he was untying the naked maid from the four-poster. Penny Cakebread's eyes were as big as saucers.'

'What fun you have in the Shires,' Krystal murmured. 'Beetle,' her voice now sharp, 'stop playing with those suspenders or I'll dress you myself. And you wouldn't want that, or would you?'

Beetle, who had been tapping her labia with the stretchy scarlet silk, instantly snapped the waspie around her slender waist. Bending to adjust it, she risked poking a tongue at her stern partner.

'And so Penny Cakebread pinched the maid.'

'Decamped the following day when we were all out at a point-to-point.'

'Taking some of your best prints, too?' Krystal added lightly.

'Mm,' Brazilia nodded, absorbed in the foil-wrapping of a fresh film cartridge. 'Came to see me on Christmas Eve. Tried to rope me into some dodgy promotional work. Wouldn't touch it, of course, but once in my room she spotted the lingerie shoot. Took quite a fancy to three of my best shots.'

'Can she put them to any use?'

'Yes. Her PR agency is always busy. They'll be in syndication by the spring. Copyright's so difficult with pix. I wouldn't have a leg to stand on in court.'

'One pair of stockinged legs is very much like another,' Krystal countered carefully.

'Not exactly,' Brazilia replied, reloading the SLR with the cartridge. 'Not when they're shot with this for background,' she continued, striding over to the sofa and holding the zebra hide aloft. 'My trademark.'

'One zebra's very much like another,' Krystal almost whispered.

Two of Brazilia's fingers poked through the striped hide.

'Uncle William bagged this beauty in '53 out in Nyassaland, before it became Malawi. Look.' The fingers waggled like a can-can dancer's provocative legs. 'Came back from the club one night to find it paddling in the swimming pool. Had one too many Sundowners and was sozzled - Uncle William, not the zebra. Bang! Bang! That's how I got my exotic prop.'

Krystal nodded. 'Penny Cakebread should be taught the difference between "yours" and "mine". And taught pretty severely.'

Beetle, smoothing the scarlet stocking on her left leg between flattened palms, looked up quickly. Krystal winked, drawing a warning finger up to her lips for silence. Beetle nodded.

'Can't make any fuss,' Brazilia shrugged. 'She's quite a big spider in the London PR web. Ditch my chances if I shouted "foul".'

'Perhaps you're right. How did our little French flagellant take the loss of her maid?'

'She wept. They were very close. Altogether, it was a pretty sticky Christmas up at Linton Hall. But it's great of you both to let me do these shots. Anything ready for your exhibition next week? Thanks for the invite, by the way.'

'Just one new piece you haven't seen yet. I'll show you.'

Krystal rose and went across to her studio.

'Beetle,' Brazilia commanded, her slender hands smoothing the zebra skin across the back of the sofa. 'Over you go, my girl, and spread 'em. No, not like that. Stay still while I arrange you for the shot.'

Beetle held her breath and crushed her braless bosom into the zebra skin as she felt Brazilia's slender fingertips skimming up along the glistening sheen of her stockinged inner thighs to fleetingly caress the swell of the buttocks above - alighting where the scarlet silk of the taut panties had disappeared into the shadow of the deep cleft. Exhaling slowly as she relished the intimate attentions of the aristocratic photographer, Beetle smothered her soft moan as Brazilia's deft index finger probed between the joggling cheeks and hooked out the band of silk that bit so fiercely into her flesh. Decorously arranging the panties so that both the anal rosebud and the fig-like labia lower down were screened from the searching lens of the SLR, Brazilia stood back, inspecting her handiwork. Beetle shivered deliciously under the intense scrutiny - and at the cool kiss of silk at her secret, most sensitive, flesh.

'Two holes in the zebra, maybe,' the cool aristocratic drawl chuckled, 'but we can't have any other holes in this shot.'

Beetle squirmed as her pertly upthrust bottom received a sharp spank of encouragement.

'Give her a couple more, just for good measure,' Krystal urged, returning from her studio.

Spank! Spank! Spank! Brazilia obliged. Beetle squealed, digging her stockinged toes into the carpet.

'Like it?' Krystal enquired, holding up her latest creation.

Turning, her left palm resting dominantly across Beetle's spanked bottom, Brazilia squinted at the clay object.

'It's been catalogued as "Accusing Finger" but I'm not sure whether to display it this way.' Krystal held the study of a rigid index finger spearing up out of a clenched fist horizontally. 'Or this way.' She turned it, palming the perspex base so that the finger jabbed at the ceiling above.

'Pointing up,' Brazilia said firmly, slapping Beetle's left cheek decisively. 'Makes it more meaningful. Sort of existential.'

Krystal considered this, nodded her agreement and turned back towards her studio door. She paused. 'Beetle?'

'Mmm?' came the response from lips pressed into animal hide.

'I don't want you going anywhere near my pieces. Understand? Keep out of the studio and touch nothing.'

'I won't,' Beetle murmured obediently. 'Promise.'

With the tremulous sweep of Brazilia's fingertips at her inner thighs and, more deliciously, tracing the swell of her tightly pantied cheeks still prickling her memory, Beetle towelled herself down and bounded out of the shower for the bedroom. Krystal and Brazilia had gone out to rent a film - *Nil By Mouth* - which had been shot on the Hackney estate Brazilia and her titled chums had once squatted in, until complaints from the binmen about all the empty Krug bottles had brought about their eviction.

Beetle lay on her bed, face upwards, squirming her naked buttocks into the sensual warmth of the silk duvet. Remembering the svelte touch of those dominant fingertips at her stockinged legs and then the adjustment of the tight silk at her hot cleft, Beetle cupped and squeezed her heavy, stiff-nippled breasts, slowly and punishingly. Legs splayed wide apart, she felt the wet bubble burgeoning at her pouting lips below. Minutes later, after inching her fingertips down to her pubic fringe - to rub and pluck at her heated pussy - a snarl of frustration broke through her teeth.

The images fuelling her excited pussy-play swam tantalizingly in and out of focus, eluding her spinning brain just as her orgasm eluded her frantic fingertips. Then she remembered the 'Accusing Finger'. The hard contours burned brightly behind her eyes: seven inches of cruel clay. So smoothly executed. So firm. The image of Krystal's masterpiece of Neo-Realism burned brighter - as brightly as would be the burning stripes bequeathed by Krystal's punishing bamboo in the morning if Beetle's disobedience was discovered.

'Won't touch it. Just look,' Beetle lied to herself as she scampered naked from the bedroom into the forbidden studio. A glimpse of the phallic splendour would be sufficient, she felt, to rocket her into the orgasm she desired.

It was there, on the perspex plinth. Larger than life, it winked temptingly in the gloom. Beetle approached, her heart hammering, her dry lips parted expectantly. The rigid erection of clay was thicker than she had supposed. *Finger.* Her eyes closed as she remembered once more Brazilia's fingers at her defenceless legs, thighs and upturned buttocks. *Finger.* She saw Krystal's raised finger wagging at her sternly during the admonishment not to enter the studio. Her hot slit juiced as she shivered between the opposing forces of dread and desire. *Finger*. Scooping up the exhibition piece, Beetle cradled its hard length to her bare bosom, crushing the cold clay shaft against her protesting nipples.

Back in the intimacy of the bedroom, she examined her prize minutely, then sprawled back on her bed. Pressing the tip with savage tenderness into her nakedness, she drew the hard clay finger down in a diagonal sweep across her belly, paused at her hip then angled it down to nudge the wet labia which greeted it with a warm, widening smile. Lightning bolts of delight flickered down her body, raking her pulsing flesh with shivers of anticipation and burning delight. Heated thoughts and images blazed across her inner eye: Brazilia, the cool aristocrat, dominantly fingering her; Krystal's own hands working the wet clay - hands which spanked and caned so ruthlessly, working their wicked magic across cheeks soon to be set on fire. Beetle started to come. Eager to relish the clay erection, she probed herself brutally, tenderly, but it proved impossible to guide it into her aching warmth. The perspex plinth was too difficult to manipulate at arm's length. Beetle cried out in a frenzy of frustration, accidentally grazing her stiff little clitoris with the fingertip. She screamed softly as she collapsed into a renewed climax - a fierce convulsion which squeezed her mercilessly within its velvet fist. Wet with sweat, Beetle blinked and sat up and sighed.

Impaling herself upon the finger became an erotic obsession. Blind to reason and caution, she knelt up on the bed, positioning the perspex plinth between her thighs. Eyes tightly shut, she squatted down, lowering her parted thighs onto the erect spear of baked clay. Riding the shaft, she squealed and came twice in savage succession. Gripping the impromptu dildo with her tightened, spasming muscles, she shrieked long and loud as she came yet again, the ferocity of this climax toppling her and spilling her face-down into the cool pillows. Writhing, she ground her seething breasts into the silk duvet, rasping her nipples into the deliciously cool fabric. Gasping, she jerked her hips and clenched her buttocks as her tiny fists pounded the bed - a pummelled surrender to the next climax welling up and threatening to... snap! Beetle froze. Her eyes opened, already fearful and disbelieving. The finger had cracked and sheared off the plinth. Clutching her hair, then her breasts, in despair, she turned her head and stared in horror as, with a soft plop, the wet finger dropped out of her and onto the silk duvet. *Accusing Finger*. Her throat tightened. *Accusing Finger*. It pointed at her, unswervingly and directly at her bottom. The bottom which would now be whipped for her flagrant disobedience.

Beetle shuddered and moaned. Already she could hear the dry rattle of the bamboo cane as Krystal took it out of the drawer. Already she could feel the flesh of her bottom tighten as, ordered to bend over, the cheeks were offered up, perfectly poised for punishment.

'Hell,' she muttered. Gathering up the broken digit, she dried it on her thigh and scrabbled about at her bedside table. Her panicking fingers found a tube of eyelash fixative. Krystal would never know. It was the work of seven agonizing minutes to squeeze enough of the sticky glue onto the base of the perspex, set the broken finger back in position, test it gingerly, and then return it to the dark studio.

'But Brazilia said not to—'

'I know. And we won't. Not exactly,' Krystal smiled.

They were lunching at the Oxo Tower. Down below, the broad Thames looked tired and sluggish in the grey January

half-light. Further downstream, they could just make out the neon lights of the National Theatre dancing on the silver water.

'So?' Beetle pressed. 'We've got a bogus appointment to see Penny Cakebread at two—'

'And one to see Estrelle Colette any moment now.'

'And you haven't brought a whip or cane or anything—'

'Ah,' Krystal broke in imperturbably. 'She's come.'

They turned to watch as the French actress - currently linked in the lifestyle columns to a minor royal from the House of Bohemia - elegantly glided her way through the tables towards their own. Chic in Chanel, she strode confidently, holding her head high like the thoroughbred she was.

'No names,' Krystal smiled. 'It is a strictly confidential matter, Mademoiselle.'

On the YSL masque of the French actress, a perfectly applied eyebrow arched inquiringly.

'Merely a matter of restitution,' Krystal soothed. 'And, of course, the pleasure of retribution.'

The perfectly lipsticked mouth succumbed to a pout of anticipation. 'Retribution?' the Gallic accent purred deliciously.

'Your maid—' Krystal began.

'*Ma petite Solange qui j'adore,*' Estrelle confessed in a sudden spate of torment.

'She is to be returned to you,' Krystal assuaged. 'As I said. This is a matter of repossession.'

'And? You spoke of retribution,' purred the actress, her mouth lubricating with the anticipation of punishment.

'No doubt you will deal with la petite Solange as you see fit, Mademoiselle. I was referring to the punishment of the stealer, not what may or may not await that which was stolen from you.'

'When I get her back, I propose to have—'

'Chablis, Mademoiselle?' Krystal interposed suavely. 'I've ordered sole Veronique.'

Penny Cakebread received them, as arranged, in her private office.

'Well?' she rasped, flashing them a glance of doubt as Krystal and Beetle, tricked out as simpering Sloanes, fizzed girlishly and giggled.

Krystal did the talking. Jangling her chunkiest gold bracelets and pitching her spiel quickly, she baited the trap. 'So you see,' she concluded, 'we've simply oodles of capital but no experience and we have to be so very careful with Daddy being tipped for the Cabinet.'

'But everyone is getting into lingerie,' Penny Cakebread countered. 'Market research shows that it's easier to buy a bra than a book. What have you come up with that's so special?'

Krystal produced several samples of the Portuguese lace items, stressing their low unit cost and high mark-up price. Penny Cakebread, despite her initial scepticism, began to thaw. After four more minutes of Krystal's carefully prepared pitch, the PR supremo grew positively warm.

'And you say these figures have been audited?'

Krystal nodded, letting it be known that her Daddy knew a nice little chap in a merchant bank.

'I see.'

She's hooked, Krystal thought. She's just working out how much it's worth to her.

'But why should I represent you in this venture?'

'We need the best. We've seen your work in—' Krystal larded her words with the names of magazines her research had unearthed.

Penny Cakebread, susceptible to professional vanity, nodded and smiled.

'And they all talk about you in Daphne's,' Krystal lied. Aware of the South Kensington watering hole where reputations were made - and shattered - over plates of inkfish risotto, Penny seated herself behind her large desk.

Gotcha, you bitch, Krystal thought.

'But you young things don't have a clue how expensive it is to launch. Overheads are enormous.' She bowed her face over a calculator. A red-nailed finger jabbed greedily at the buttons. She glanced up. 'The photo-shoot alone, if you want top-notch glamour girls—'

'Top notch, natch,' Krystal nodded vigorously.

This was Beetle's cue. Up to now, she had merely grinned. 'That's why we want you,' she burbled.

'I think I may be able to manage your promotional launch—'

'No, you,' Beetle insisted shyly. 'We want you to model for the photo-shoot.'

'Me?' the PR shark snorted, for the first time stumbling slightly along the yellow-brick road she had been treading so carefully. 'Me? Model?'

'Absolutely,' Krystal chimed in. 'You see, our exotic line is aimed for the early-thirty-somethings. About your age.'

Penny Cakebread, a superb specimen at forty-three, flushed becomingly. Krystal could see vanity wrestling briefly with shrewd business acumen. No contest. Vanity won.

'Oh please,' Beetle wheedled, 'say you'll handle all our promotional stuff and be our model. Why not try these samples on. We know you'll look great.'

Penny Cakebread, a glamour model twenty years ago (dubbed the girl who put the rump into crumpet) flushed delightedly, and succumbed. Accepting the sheer Portuguese silk stockings from Beetle, she weighed their airy nothingness across an open palm.

'Self-support,' Krystal murmured, 'so no suspenders. And as it will be leg shots, don't bother with a blouse or panties.'

'Mmm,' gushed Beetle. 'Let's see your lovely legs.'

Penny Cakebread slowly unbuttoned the sleeves, then the bodice, of her starched white blouse. It flapped open, revealing the ripe swell of her bosom uplifted by white cups of crisp cotton. The blouse slithered to her feet. The grey pencil-line skirt, unzipped and palmed down over rounded thighs, joined it.

'This is your work?' Krystal asked, picking up a green leather-bound portfolio. 'I'll just flick through it,' she continued, not waiting for an answer.

Soft rustlings teased their imagination from the corner of the luxuriously appointed office, as Penny changed into the sample lingerie. Krystal and Beetle, heads together, glanced at the stills as Krystal flicked through the album. They scanned the most recent entries. Christmas, and Brazilia's loss, had been only a week or so ago.

Just as Penny sauntered back across the carpeted floor to the large desk, sleek and lithe in the freshly donned stockings, they spotted the stolen stills. A pair of shapely legs, as supple as they were slender, rose up from the spiked stiletto shoes: the model wore nothing other than a pair of sheer bronze tights. Her cheeks bulged temptingly within the sheen of the 15 denier nylon. Her thighs pressed into a zebra skin.

Beetle stood up and distracted the PR guru, gently fingering the darker band of Penny's self-support stockings and making appreciative noises, leaving Krystal to pore over the stills. Reaching into her clutch bag, Krystal surreptitiously withdrew a small magnifying glass. Through this opaque third eye, she scrutinized the hide - and found the two bullet holes made by Uncle William's gun. Pocketing the glass, she snapped shut the green leather-bound portfolio. Nodding to Beetle, she stood and walked across to the edge of the desk.

'That's marvellous,' she enthused. 'Just turn around once more. No, face the desk. That's great.'

Penny became putty in their manipulative hands.

'Now that's perfect, isn't it?'

'Mmm,' Beetle agreed. 'Exactly what we want.'

'Bend over. A little more. Try to get right across the desk.'

Penny obeyed. Krystal saw the white cups of the swollen brassiere kiss and then crush against the polished surface of the executive desk. As Penny bent down, her bottom bulged, the luscious flesh stretching the panties that firmly controlled the cheeks within its taut bondage.

'Excellent,' cried Krystal, clapping her hands in an explosion of loud delight.

The office door opened softly and closed even more quietly. Estrelle Colette trod the deep-pile carpet in her silent lizard-skin shoes.

'Are you absolutely sure?' thrilled the bending semi-nude, waggling her hips and wiggling her superbly ripe rump (a woman still capable of putting the rump into crumpet) invitingly. 'I'm sure I don't deserve—'

'But you do,' snarled Estrelle, brushing the two girls aside as she pounced. 'You deserve everything I'm going to give you.'

Binding and gagging her victim was but a moment's work for the accomplished disciplinarian, who took advantage of both the element of complete surprise and Penny's obliging posture. Beetle and Krystal stared in amazement at the display of brutal efficiency as the startled mouth bit into the fierce gag; as the panties were whipped down and tossed aside; as restraints were applied to the wrists of the outstretched arms and smartly clicked into place.

'Legs apart,' Estrelle ordered crisply. 'Wider.'

The thighs parted a timorous three inches. Estrelle grasped the hair of the bowed head in her taloned hand. Her fingers tightened. 'Wider, bitch.'

Krystal and Beetle watched in awed silence. Obedient to the stern command, the cheeks joggled as Penny Cakebread's legs splayed wide apart. They exchanged appreciative glances as two more restraints snapped into place, binding each ankle to the opposing legs of the desk.

Still struggling - a frenzied writhing of resentful rebellion - Penny's bosom slammed down on the desk top. Through the white cup at her bulging left breast, a thickened nipple punched the calculator's buttons until the green digital display passed through 14 million and became an 'E' for error. Tightly gagged, the bending, bound woman could only grunt her muffled fury. Estrelle dragged her thumbnail up between the parted cheeks. Penny's thighs stiffened and froze. Estrelle repeated the dominant gesture, subduing her near-naked victim completely.

'Don't go,' Estrelle said, 'whoever you are.' She winked at her accomplices. 'Stay and watch how business can be transacted unofficially. Sometimes it pays to bypass timely and expensive litigation. Settlements can be achieved as I propose to demonstrate. This bitch,' Estrelle continued in a cool voice, thinks nothing of breaking the law of copyright on intellectual property. That is how she crawled up from the back-street studio to this penthouse suite. But she made the mistake of stealing something very precious from me. The goods in question—'

The goods. Krystal and Beetle immediately imagined the pert little maid, demurely naked, bound to the four-poster, her naked bottom criss-crossed with the mistletoe's loving kiss-lashes.

'—I now consider lost. I will not accept them back. But I demand and will achieve complete and utter satisfaction this afternoon. You, bitch,' she whispered vehemently into Penny's ear, 'will be whipped twice. Once for the theft and then again for my loss. You can keep Solange but I think you'll find the price painfully high.'

'Whipped?' Beetle squeaked, keeping up her pretence of surprise.

'Gosh,' Krystal supplied supportively. 'They'll never believe us at Daphne's.'

Across the desk, Penny groaned through her gag at the impending loss of her reputation.

'And we can't do business with a thief,' Krystal gasped in well-faked horror. 'Not with Daddy so close to a Cabinet seat.'

Penny groaned again, this time at the loss of such easy money.

'A whipping,' Beetle purred excitedly.

'Not a whipping, dear girl. Not a whipping, exactly. I prefer to punish with this.' Estrelle flourished a short, broad, wooden paddle. The handle was tightly bound with shining red leather, and the blade was rectangular, about a foot in length, fashioned from smoothly polished pear-wood. Estrelle thrust the paddle blade in front of Penny's face. Glimpsing the instrument of her torment, the large eyes blinked then filled with sorrow.

'Lick it, bitch. I want you to taste the wood.'

A brief struggle ensued but the agile Frenchwoman easily tamed and controlled her victim, taloning the tumbling hair in a fierce grip, holding the captive face-down and forcing the lips to kiss - and the tongue to taste - the paddle.

'Kiss it again.'

In the loud silence of the room, the three onlookers witnessed the subjugated near-nude press her trembling lips against the polished pear-wood blade.

'Remember this during your punishment,' Estrelle whispered softly, dragging the blade slowly down Penny's spine until it rested upon the swell of her upturned cheeks. 'I seek nothing in compensation for my painful loss. Nothing more than your tears of contrition.'

Krystal and Beetle knew they were in the presence of a supreme dominatrix. Sitting close to one another, hand in hand, thighs pressed tightly together, they drank in every gesture, every nuance of the superb display of domination and humiliation, certain that an even more thrilling demonstration of discipline was to follow.

Estrelle paced herself. All her movements were exquisitely slow. Unbuttoning the sleeve-cuffs of her crisp blouse, she rolled them up to the elbows. Then she kicked off her shoes, using her toes to tidy them away under the desk. Next, she unzipped the citrus-lemon chic Chanel skirt that hugged her buttocks and thighs. It fell to her feet with no more than a whisper of sound. Stepping out of the skirt, Estrelle displayed her lithe graceful legs, tightly sheathed in dark-navy tights. Beneath the blue sheen of the tights, under the darker band that bit into her waist, a wisp of white silk graced her pubic mound. Slowly, maddeningly slowly, her red fingernails dabbled at the twelve pearl buttons running from her arched throat to the base of her belly. The blouse flapped open, allowing her satin-smooth breasts to spill out; braless, in loose and lovely freedom. The dark nipples were already aggressively peaked in anticipation of the pleasure of bestowing pain.

Estrelle stood, legs slightly parted, close to her victim. Inching forward, the shiny material of her dark-blue tights grazed Penny's ripe thigh. Bending over suddenly to check the bondage at the left ankle, Estrelle crushed her breasts into the helpless buttocks beneath them. Penny squealed and bucked, writhing at the dominant touch of flesh upon flesh, of breasts upon buttocks. The punisher quelled the rebellion with an imperious fingertip with which she dimpled the softness of the right cheek. Krystal and Beetle gasped as they saw Penny freeze into quivering submission, a surrender as abject as it was absolute.

Taking a step back from the bare bottom, the Frenchwoman paused to inspect it intimately. Gripping the handle of her paddle in her right hand, she lowered it, firmly depressing the swollen crowns of the upturned cheeks. A spasm of fear thrilled down Penny's taut legs, shivering the captive flesh from thigh to bound ankle as the pear-wood kissed the satin skin of the rump above. Estrelle seemed dissatisfied, and placed the paddle on the desk top. Stooping, and causing her spilling breasts to bulge, she fished up her pert Chanel skirt. She folded the soft material in half, then quartered it. Using it as a pillow, she positioned it level with hips and belly as they pressed onto the desk below, taking care that the pubis snuggled firmly into its welcoming softness. This had the desired effect of thrusting the bare bottom upwards a perceptible amount, making the naked cheeks rounder, firmer and more inviting.

Picking up the paddle and palming it reflectively, Estrelle inched closer to her quarry. Guiding the tip of the flattened blade between the Chanel skirt and the pubis above, she positioned it and took her hand away, leaving the labia pressed devotedly into its polished wooden surface. Swiftly mounting the desk - and the shivering woman across it - Estrelle presented her buttocks to Krystal and Beetle as she straddled then squatted down upon Penny. The bulge of the blue-nylon-sheathed buttocks squashed down onto the creamy naked bottom beneath them. Bending forward, Estrelle's fingers sought and found Penny's brassiere clasp. Penny screamed softly as the brassiere was brutally dragged away, snapping loudly into the wooden desk top to leave the quivering bosom crushed painfully against the unyielding hardness. Beetle cupped her own breasts and squeezed as she watched Estrelle hold the white brassiere up in triumph before pressing it to her mouth, cramming her face into the empty warmth of the left cup. Beetle could see that the Frenchwoman's eyes were now tightly closed. Suddenly, they opened wide, then narrowed fiercely.

Tossing the brassiere aside, she dismounted from her perch of subjugated flesh to address the bare bottom once again. Kneeling down before it, she noticed as if for the first time the stockings Penny had put on to model. Bringing her palms together around the thigh, she gently eased down the left stocking, leaving it furled just above the shackled ankle. Estrelle brought a gentle severity of touch to the other leg, silkily fingering the stocking down with hands that would soon deliver savage punishment.

For Krystal and Beetle, it was bewitching to behold. The tender cruelty and the stern intimacy of the punisher kneeling before the bared bottom and making the last-minute preparations. Their eyes followed every sweeping gesture, missing nothing of the delicacy soon to become discipline so dire.

Rising, Estrelle plucked the paddle from where it was wedged between the skirt and the pubis of the penitent nude. After examining it closely, she bit into the pear-wood at a spot where the labia had wept. Removing the polished blade, she pressed her lips against Penny's wet deposit, then licked every inch of her instrument of punishment.

'I see you are wet already, bitch. You have grown sticky with impatience for your pain. Be warned,' she snarled softly, 'if you stain or spoil this expensive Chanel skirt, I will double your chastisement.'

At this deliciously terse threat, Beetle gasped - but was instantly silenced by Krystal. Estrelle turned briefly and bowed, mockingly accepting Beetle's unarticulated admiration. Returning to the bare bottom, she tucked the folded skirt tightly under the splayed thighs, pubis and lower belly and wedged the blade of the paddle once more beneath the warm weight of the bending nude. Positioning her hands down over the buttocks, she gripped and squeezed the helpless flesh-cheeks, scrunching their satin softness then spreading them savagely apart. Satisfied with the suffering she had inflicted, she forced her thumb tips down into the heat of the yawning cleft. Penny Cakebread bucked and writhed as the red nails raked the sensitive ribbon of velvety flesh in unison but was competently quelled into whimpering quiescence by stern commands for silence.

Removing the paddle and grasping its red leather handle tightly, the dominatrix probed between the heavy cheeks, nuzzling an angled corner of the blade against the rosebud sphincter. Despite the bondage at each ankle, Penny rose up on tip-toe in response to this intimate outrage. Easing the polished pear-wood away, Estrelle replaced it with a straightened index finger - this time probing deeply the tightly muscled warmth beyond the anal whorl. Beetle mewed softly like a kitten: her palms now pressed together and forced down between her thighs. She came, soaking her panties and filling the office with the feral tang of her arousal.

Maintaining her posture of supreme dominance, Estrelle lithely mounted the desk, and her victim, once more, pinioning the buttocks she was about to set ablaze between her scissored thighs. Penny grunted thickly as the probing finger entered more deeply during the manoeuvre. Facing her spellbound audience now, the dominatrix squeezed her knees: the dark-blue tights bunched the bare cheeks between them in a painful pincer, forcing the cleft to become a severe crease. Estrelle withdrew her finger slowly and took several agonizing minutes to examine the spreading wet stain on the blade of the paddle. Bucking and twisting, Penny tried to topple her tormentress. *Crack.* The pear-wood spoke - a harsh, cruel note. The nude's futile effort had earned her a searing stroke of the polished blade across her exposed cheeks, the scalding slice an instant reward for her last-ditch rebellion.

Krystal felt her sticky labia pout within her soaking panties. She pressed herself closer to Beetle. They sat in absolute silence, tense and expectant for the flurry of punishing strokes to commence. Never before had they witnessed such strict preparations before the administration of discipline.

The tantalizing suspense was sustained. Estrelle was a consummate dominatrix. Savouring each pre-punishment moment, she refused to force the tempo, her every action deliberate and meticulously performed. Returning the paddle to the desk, she slid it beneath Penny's heavy breasts, rasping the pain-peaked nipples with the blade. The nude screamed softly as the wood which had just scalded her buttocks now tormented her bosom. Addressing the bared bottom again, Estrelle spread the swollen cheeks painfully apart. Lowering her face, she tongued the shadowed flesh between the taloned globes.

Beetle squirmed on her chair as she glimpsed the thick muscle of the Frenchwoman's tongue wetly gouging the cleft. She tightened her grip on Krystal's hand and squeezed, finding the accepting palm wet with the sweat of voyeuristic arousal.

Substituting the thin edge of the paddle in place of her tongue, Estrelle rasped the pear-wood blade between the tightened cheeks as if it were a saw. The bound nude whimpered through her gag, her body now loosening into the slack of surrender and total submission. Twisting at the hips, Estrelle turned, reached out and swiftly undid the gag.

'Do it. Do anything. Do what you want with me,' Penny moaned softly in lust-thickened tones, the heat from her parted lips clouding the polished surface of the desk.

The Frenchwoman reapplied the gag, her face a mask of stern triumph. 'I intend to, bitch. It is not your permission I seek. Only your suffering.'

This time, Krystal orgasmed, openly knuckling her pubis as the hot wet release scalded her clamped thighs.

Crack! Crack! The double blow of the paddle split the silence as a vicious swipe scorched each peach-soft cheek in rapid succession. The ivory spheres burned with vivid blotches where the wood had kissed them so passionately. *Crack! Crack!* Again a double-dose of the searing paddle swept down to turn the pink flesh an angrier crimson.

Beetle sat on the very edge of her chair, thrilling to the unfolding drama of domination and discipline. Delayed by the exquisitely controlled preparations, the punishment being administered was delicious to behold.

Crack! Crack! Smacking down into each suffering cheek, the paddle was plied with a fluency and easy grace that belied the severity of each scalding stroke. *Crack! Crack!* the swiping wooden blade sought out and mercilessly ravished every inch of the naked buttocks.

Beetle's fingers flew up to her mouth, dragging down her lower lip. Krystal's eyes narrowed, drinking in every detail. Estrelle, they realized, was an accomplished chastiser and skilled disciplinarian. They knew that Penny was suffering as she lay bound over her altar of agony, attended to by this high-priestess of pain.

Swiftly kneeling up, Estrelle thrust the paddle between Penny's thighs and squeezed them together. Trembling, her quivering flesh seemed to draw the very heat out of the captive wooden blade. Bending forward, the dominatrix dabbled her red-nailed fingertips down between the reddened cheeks into the pronounced labia beneath. Withdrawing her fingers, she stretched her hands out, palms down, as if watching her vermilion nail-varnish dry. The fingertips waggled, their wetness sparkling.

'You were warned, bitch. If you have stained my expensive Chanel skirt with your liquid sorrow, even with the merest drop of your contrite weeping, your misery will be limitless.'

Penny squealed, threshing in renewed anguish.

'Examine the skirt,' Estrelle instructed Beetle. 'Let us see if the bitch has dared to disobey.' Squatting down heavily, the Frenchwoman's nylon-sheathed buttocks pinned the nude firmly to the desk.

Beetle got up as if in a dream and approached. Dry-mouthed and with a rapid pulse plucking at her throat, she insinuated the splayed fingers of her right hand between the hot flesh and the desk, shuddering as her knuckles grazed the moist labia of the punished nude. Scrunching her fingers tight, she slowly dragged the skirt out. Penny grunted as the soft serge rasped her clitoris, and clenched her buttocks together. Unable to resist the overwhelming temptation, Beetle fleetingly caressed each red sphere of seething satin.

'Show me the skirt,' Estrelle hissed impatiently, pressing the broad blade of the paddle against the buttocks to contain and control them totally.

With trembling fingers, Beetle opened up the folds of warm cloth. A dark stain was revealed. Estrelle snatched it up and, twisting round from the hips, thrust the wet stain on the skirt into the face of the victim she straddled.

'Double punishment, bitch. You were warned.'

They heard Penny Cakebread's squeal despite the tight gag.

Springing down from her mount and off the desk, Estrelle knelt down facing the reddened buttocks. Weighing the paddle ominously in her right hand, she steadied her left hand - palm inwards - against the swell of the left cheek.

'She's going to beat each buttock separately,' Krystal whispered softly. 'That is how the ancient Chinese advocated the punishment of females. One buttock at a time, with the punisher always in close contact with the other cheek. It is such an intimate method. By holding the left cheek while chastising the right, the punisher is fused with the punished.'

Beetle wanted to reply, but her tongue was too swollen and her mouth too dry. The simple words she wished to speak remained unsaid. She nodded, her dark hair flouncing.

Crack! Crack! Gripping one buttock fiercely, Estrelle ravished the other with her wooden paddle.

'She can sense every twitch, every spasm of response. She can almost feel Penny's pain,' Krystal's voice curdled. 'It is truly the perfect way to punish. I must remember the next time you are across my knee, bare-bottomed.'

Beetle gulped.

Estrelle was now licking and softly biting the crimson buttock she had just paddled. Burying her face deeply into the hot flesh, her moans mingled with Penny's softer cries of carnality.

At first, the Frenchwoman did not hear Krystal speak.

'We'd better be getting along,' she repeated. 'We've got to find ourselves another PR agent,' Krystal said loudly, assuming the guise of a squeakily excited Sloane. 'They'll never believe this at Daphne's.'

The man from the *Guardian* nibbled the ear-loop of his horn-rims pensively. The bloke from the *Sun* nibbled the end of his cheese straw hungrily. Krystal gave the former her manifesto on neo-realism and the latter a bottle of the reasonable rouge ordinaire the gallery had provided.

Peter Martin, aglow with excitement at his former pupil's exhibition, had come down from Norwich. Vanessa Wetherby had descended from Fulham, and a taxi had delivered Mandy Winwood together with a group of Krystal's loyal friends and admirers.

The evening was going well. The young woman from 'Kaleidoscope' (who had hoped to cover the Flemish mime troupe in Camden Lock) remained aloofly indifferent until Beetle started to fiddle with the small microphone pinned to the Radio 4 bosom.

Everybody confessed to 'liking' Krystal's pieces even if they failed to fully 'understand' them. Buyers swelled the throng. Red dots began to appear on the tide cards.

By nine minutes past seven, six of the clay exhibits had been sold. Then Vanessa Wetherby spotted the 'Kaleidoscope' scout - mistaking her for one whose bottom she thought she had become acquainted with back at Birch Hall. Krystal panicked, then relaxed. At least, she thought, tonight's radio review would be stimulating.

The gallery, tucked behind the Mile End tube station, was small but the ambience was terrific. Each of Krystal's exhibits was individually mounted and competently spot-lit.

Peter Martin oiled the wheels of the press. 'I like the neurotic sensibility frozen in form,' he supplied helpfully.

The *Guardian* scribbled busily.

'Saw those Three Graces once,' the *Sun* drooled. 'Now that's what I call Art. Tasty Tottie Trio,' he pronounced in tabloid-speak.

Then disaster! With a loud snap, the 'Accusing Finger' cracked and collapsed. The cosmetic glue Beetle had used was unable to resist the heat of the spotlight above. A general buzz of dismay filled the air. The *Guardian* clicked his pen officiously and started to review his review. The 'Kaleidoscope' girl, thrilling to Vanessa's firm hand at her bottom, craned for a closer look. Krystal stood transfixed, the Polish curse frozen on her lips. A tear welled up in her eye.

'Ah, kinetic art. How avant garde,' Peter Martin burbled gallantly. 'Such an original concept, procuring movement out of stasis.'

The *Guardian*, relieved, beamed. Nodding vigorously, he took notes.

'Two pieces in one,' purred Mandy Winwood, joining them. 'Duality in singularity,' she continued gamely. 'The "Accusing Finger" becomes the "Broken Promise" and we, the audience, are all guilty.'

The 'Kaleidoscope' scout, not wishing to be upstaged by the press, took up the theme. The evening developed into a riot of intellectuality celebrating Krystal's Neo-Realism. Even the *Sun* took pix.

Later, in a quiet corner, Krystal quizzed Beetle. 'Eye-lash fixative?' she echoed angrily. 'Why?'

'The finger sort of broke,' the minx mumbled. 'I didn't know it wouldn't stick.'

Further inquiries proved impossible as the departures were underway. But Krystal was furious. She beckoned to Vanessa Wetherby.

'Jolly good show, what?' boomed their ex-games mistress.

Brazilia bounced over. 'You'll never guess,' she squealed. 'Penny Cakebread's going to the States. Says London's too hot for her. Wonder what she means?'

'I wonder,' Krystal murmured.

'And she's gone right off anything French. Just seems to haunt Daphne's every day, eavesdropping on all the tables. Gone quite paranoid. Still, I'm glad she's out of the picture.'

Brazilia bounded off to console Peter Martin, whose BBC2 feature 'Taking It In From The Rear' - an innocent photographic survey of tradesmen's' entrances to houses of historic importance - had been hounded off the airwaves by a posse of tory MPs, the Bishop of Frinton and a motion of censure tabled by the Women's Institute.

'Poor Peter,' they all chorused.

Krystal, the chastened Beetle and Vanessa were left by themselves.

'Good show, Peter and Mandy chipping in like that. Saved the day.'

'But not *your* bacon, my girl,' Krystal whispered, restraining Beetle who was sidling off on tip-toe. 'Vanessa, I want you to take Beetle over to that private office. Get the truth out of her.'

'The truth?'

'The truth about "Accusing Finger" and how it came to be glued—'

'Oh, have no fear,' Vanessa boomed, collaring the minx. 'I'll get to the bottom of it.'

'I'm sure you'll do that in any case,' Krystal smiled.

'Just like old times, what?'

Beetle squealed as she felt her silver mini being yanked up over her bottom and Vanessa's strong fingers plucking at, then easing down, her tights.

'Up.'

Beetle dipped her tummy and raised her buttocks obediently. Vanessa thumbed down the panties, dragging them to a restricting band at Beetle's trapped knees.

Spank! The hand gripping Beetle's neck tightened around the nape as its partner swept down across the exposed buttocks. *Spank!* Beetle wriggled as her bottom blazed.

'Stay still while I smack your bottom, you naughty, naughty girl.'

The last four words of the admonishment were loudly punctuated by four sharp spanks as, in blistering alternation, the naked upturned buttocks suffered the cruel caress of the firm palm. Beetle wriggled and squirmed in a renewed effort to escape the severe chastisement, but Vanessa - just as she had been back at Birch Hall - was in total control of the bare bottom before her.

There was a brief pause. Beetle started to confess, taking care to omit the more intimate details of her unhappy escapade. Vanessa, a shrewd old bird, resolutely spanked the truth out of the squirming minx. Another pause followed, during which Vanessa's spanking hand savoured the satin texture of the firmly fleshed cheeks with a slow circular motion.

'How exactly did you use it as a dildo?'

Beetle's cheeks blazed hotly - two with shame and two with pain.

'Or did you squat down on it? Hmm?' Vanessa pressed.

Taking Beetle's silence as an admission, the ex-games mistress laughed mirthlessly. 'This is only a taste of what Krystal's going to give you, young lady.'

A triple staccato broke the sullen silence as the spanking hand cracked down, flattening the swell of the soft peaches and reddening them deeply.

'We have a close bond, you and I,' Vanessa murmured, taking a pincer of the spanked left buttock between her forefinger and thumb.

Beetle squealed as the pincer tugged at her soft flesh. 'We share the same initials. V.W.'

'What?' Beetle muttered, her lips pressed into the warmth of her stern punisher's thigh. 'Oh, yes. I'd never thought of that,' she sighed, forgetting for a moment the delicious threat of the hovering hand above her bare buttocks.

Two severe spanks reminded her.

'Has she confessed?' Mandy Winwood grinned, entering the room. 'Krystal's furious. I wouldn't like to be in your shoes later on, young lady. At least I *think* I wouldn't,' she added ambiguously, remembering a brief encounter with the Polish sculptress the previous summer.

'Beetle has been very sensible,' Vanessa conceded in a matronly tone. 'We've had a little chat.' She spanked the cheeks sharply.

'And they say the art of conversation's dead,' Peter Martin countered, joining them. 'Private party, is it?'

Beetle squirmed, hating yet curiously enjoying the experience of being bare-bottomed - and spanked - so publicly.

'The thing is,' Mandy said, 'my taxi is coming and I'm taking three back with me. Can you put Peter up for the night?'

'Delighted to,' Vanessa boomed expansively.

Peter awoke from the reverie of studying Beetle's hot bottom. Are you bringing Beetle back home too?' he asked hopefully.

'She's got a very important date to keep with Krystal and a whippy bamboo cane, I believe,' Vanessa replied, absently rubbing the cheeks she had just punished. 'But I'm in possession of some curious prints I'd like your professional opinion on, old chap.'

Mandy knelt and stroked Beetle's face tenderly as the conversation turned to seventeenth-century Italian erotica. Peter seemed quite knowledgeable on the subject.

'Bye bye, Beetle,' Mandy laughed, tilting the spanked girl's face up and kissing her lightly on the tip of the nose. 'Sorry your brush with modern art has been so painful.' She left, Peter following to see her off.

Spank! Spank! Spank! Lubricated by the brief discussion of erotica, the wheels of Vanessa's mind turned quickly back to Beetle's upturned buttocks.

Beetle squeezed her hot cheeks and buried her face in her punisher's warm-nyloned thigh.

'They've nearly all gone,' Krystal sighed as she came into the room, closing the door behind her. 'What has she to say for herself?'

Chuckling fruitily, Vanessa repeated Beetle's confession.

'Wait there, ' Krystal snapped angrily. 'Hold her down.'

Krystal vanished, returning seconds later with the erect finger - minus its perspex base. 'Hold her down tightly,' she commanded, kneeling down alongside Vanessa's knees. 'I'm sorry I underestimated you, Beetle. I didn't know you had such an appetite for the arts.'

Beetle froze, sensing the tip of the hard clay finger as it teasingly worried her sticky labia.

'You must have all the art you can manage,' Krystal purred.

The tip of the finger probed, and then the entire length slid in with ease. Vanessa grunted. Krystal sighed. Beetle gasped and moaned.

'Continue with her punishment,' Krystal rasped.

Pinning Beetle down, Vanessa ravished the bare buttocks across her lap as Krystal plied the thick shaft ruthlessly and with increasing vigour.

Chapter Six

Beetle scampered around the breakfast bar, her surreptitious glances at the clock betraying impatience. Plates were whisked away and crumbs wiped before Krystal had swallowed the last morsel of croissant.

'What's the hurry?' she drawled. 'Anxious to see me gone?'

Beetle blushed furiously. 'Of course not. Just don't want you to be late. Big day.'

Pulling on her gloves - and delaying her departure by slowly flexing her leather-sheathed fingers - Krystal wondered aloud whether she had time for another mug of coffee. Beetle's response was to dance frantically and point to the clock.

'The foundry in Bow has been in business since 1601. I'm sure they'll still be there at 9.30.'

Pouring the contents of the coffee pot down the sink, Beetle poked her tongue out in silent reply. Seeing Krystal at the door, she rushed across to her.

'See you later. Good luck at the foundry,' she gushed, opening the door and almost propelling Krystal out. A look of relief spread itself across her beautifully made-up face as the door closed.

Turning away from the hastily closed door, Krystal frowned. Beetle was a lazy little monkey. Indeed, she frequently had to spank the minx for 'slutting' (as such indolence was termed back in their Birch Hall days). And *she* never had her face on before noon. Shrugging off her suspicions, the sculptress merged from the greystone block in which they lived, tucking her blonde head down to brave the late January wind. Outside the converted warehouse, she turned left. She'd grab a cab at the top of the street. Then straight to Bow.

She was excited. For years she had hoped to cast a bronze. Peter Martin had always said she would be at her most creative when working the dull metal. Now, after the success of her exhibition, a sponsor had come forward. Krystal had all her ideas in her notebook - her notebook? Damn! With Beetle virtually chasing her out this morning, she had left it in her studio.

Impatiently retracing her steps, Krystal re-entered the warm interior of the warehouse. The lift took ages to respond. At last it hissed to a gentle stop and the doors slid silently apart. A very pretty young Postgirl stepped out. Krystal noticed that the second and third buttons of the uniform shirt were undone at the voluptuous bosom. Krystal noted the girl's deep-carmine lips. Turning to watch the retreating figure, her eyes followed the slender hips, the swelling curves at the hips and pert buttocks swaying almost insolently as the tiny black pumps nimbly took her out of the building.

Up in their penthouse loft, Beetle looked flustered. She was pink and doing her 'busy' routine - picking up cushions, punching them and throwing them down haphazardly. Krystal read the signs. Going into her studio for the notebook, Krystal spotted on the breakfast bar a glass that had evidently, and recently, contained milk - something which neither woman drank on its own. It was smudged with carmine-red lipstick.

Emerging, notebook in hand, she saw that the glass had gone.

'Any post?' she asked nonchalantly.

A crash from the kitchen sink where Beetle was continuing to be busy, told Krystal all she needed to know.

'I'll take the service stairs this morning,' Krystal murmured, stepping down from the weighing scales. Naked, her soft buttocks joggled as she trod the carpet. 'I could do with the exercise.'

Beetle, distracted by the clock, voiced her agreement.

'So you think I've put weight on, do you?' Krystal challenged. 'Prefer a trimmer bottom, I suppose?' she added, thinking of the pert little Postie with the unbuttoned blouse.

Beetle shook her head. Running across the room to the nude blonde, she knelt down and buried her face in the heavy bottom. Kissing and then licking each swollen cheek lovingly, she mumbled into the soft pillows of warm flesh. 'You're perfect just the way you are. But—'

'But?'

'You could use the stairs. Just for the healthy exercise.'

And avoid meeting little Miss Postbag. Krystal concealed her smile as she strode into the bedroom. She would, she decided, dress very slowly this morning - extending Beetle's agony.

'Do you like this bra?' Krystal asked, emerging several minutes later, still nude except for the black La Perla cupping her ripe breasts.

'Great,' Beetle replied, slapping her thighs impatiently.

'Or what about this?' Krystal said, emerging once again, naked except for the white Wonderbra that gave her bosom such a deliciously bulging uplift.

'Fantastic,' Beetle cried, her troubled eyes on the clock.

Krystal weighed both brassieres in her hands back in the bedroom, then decided on an ivory basque. The distinct possibility of discipline was in the air. She always felt better suited to dispensing discipline when tightly sheathed in the intimate feminine bondage of a basque.

Shouting out her goodbye she left, closing the door loudly behind her. Skittling down the wrought-iron stairwell, her echoing steps rang out like a chattering Ouzi machine-gun fired in short bursts. Enough to convince Beetle who would be listening behind the door. Reaching the third level, Krystal paused, turned and, slipping off her shoes, quietly tip-toed back up to the top floor.

Through a crack in the swing doors she watched and waited. The lift rumbled in the depths of the building, then began its ascent with a whispered whine. It came to rest. The doors opened and Krystal saw the pretty young Postie skip out. Before she had taken her finger off the bell, Beetle opened the door with a welcoming smile. Krystal's eyes narrowed jealously as she watched the trim uniformed hips and bottom disappear and the door close firmly behind her.

Four minutes became eight, and still the pert Postie failed to emerge. Krystal's bosom grew heavy, the weight of her warm breasts filling the basque that cupped and squeezed them. She was glad she had chosen the basque. Its firm embrace controlled and disciplined her soft curves just as she would later be controlling and disciplining Beetle's silkily contoured bottom. Eight minutes became twelve. Sighing resignedly,

Krystal descended the iron stairs slowly, as if weighed down by a duty to the discipline she would have to dispense upon her return that evening.

'No, stay where you are, Beetle. Supper will have to wait. This is a matter, I'm afraid, which cannot.'

Beetle froze on the sofa, her white teeth biting into her lower lip.

'You're getting a lot of post recently,' Krystal continued. Her tone was pleasant, almost casual.

Beetle blushed, but sought sanctuary in silence. 'Did you by any chance receive post this morning?'

'No.'

'Beetle—'

'Yes,' the minx changed her plea. 'But it was only junk mail.'

'Show me, please.'

'Junked it.'

'Then bring me the bin-bag.'

'Threw it away,' Beetle countered - the relief in her tone all too transparent.

'I thought you might, so I took the trouble of retrieving it,' Krystal whispered, holding up the black plastic bundle. 'Now, I wonder what we're going to find in here.'

Beetle's letter was on the top. It was a recorded delivery, like the others buried halfway down among the teabags and fruit peelings. All were unopened; when opened, all of them were empty.

'Addressed in your own handwriting, too. So what have we got if we put all this together, hmm?'

Beetle squirmed.

'It can only mean that you are deliberately sending empty recorded deliveries to yourself so that you can—' Krystal paused, tantalizingly allowing the minx a loophole.

Beetle went for it. 'I'm doing a bit of hush-hush consumer research for—'

'Pretty little thing, the Postie, isn't she? Bright red lips and an unbuttoned uniform. What did she get besides milk, Beetle?'

'Nothing,' Beetle - beaten but blustering valiantly - retorted.

'I think we need to discuss this matter in depth. In the bedroom.'

'There's nothing to discuss—'

'In you go, my girl. Strip, then stand by the bed. I will join you in a few minutes when I have finished my wine.'

'No, please. I'm sorry—'

'And be so good as to get a cane out of the drawer,' Krystal added suavely. 'I'll use the clouded silver Indonesian bamboo, I think. So satisfyingly swishy and supple.'

'Oh, please—' Beetle whimpered.

'Bare-bottomed and bending,' Krystal rasped, the note of finality in her severe tone crushing all further delay.

Krystal sipped her chilled Soave and, unbuttoning her right cuff, rolled up the silk sleeve of her blouse in preparation for the impending punishment of Beetle's bare bottom. Her throat tightened at the thought of the whippy Indonesian cane striping and slicing the upturned cheeks of the shivering minx. Another sip from the frosted glass eased her pleasurable discomfort - but did nothing to assuage the tightness around her peaked nipples which had thickened in a salute to the promise of pain.

The politely old-fashioned knocking brought her to the door. A well-preserved silver-haired gentleman, not unlike a rural dean, presented and introduced himself.

'Cambridge?' Krystal responded warmly. 'Come right in.'

Declining the chilled Soave, he succumbed to an amontillado sherry.

'Lady Brazilia informed me of a generous service you performed on her behalf,' he began.

It took several minutes for the dignified family retainer to achieve the purpose of his visit. He was still hedging cautiously when Beetle, naked and carrying the cane, emerged from the bedroom.

'Shall I withdraw?' Cambridge suggested.

Beetle scampered back into the bedroom with a shrill squeal.

Krystal saw the butler's eyes widen appreciatively as they followed the retreating buttocks.

'Just a little domestic difficulty. It can wait.'

'Then I will explain my position,' he continued, polishing off the glass of sherry.

Beetle, more or less dressed, joined them moments later.

'Lady Brazilia had an unswerving habit of coming to me after her evening bath when she was in some trouble, some difficulty. I would wrap her in a towel and sit her on my lap and she would confide in me.'

Krystal nodded understandingly. How kind this loyal servant must have been to the children growing up in that huge rambling pile, Linton Hall.

'Last week, after her bath, she came to me. Sat on my lap and told me how you had avenged—'

Krystal gulped her Soave. Lady Brazilia must be a bit of a lapful now!

'The Lady Pistachio, her elder sister, has never been as trusting,' Cambridge observed. 'Which may explain her present difficulties.'

Cambridge, with Lady 'Nuts' Collingham's blessing, had come to Krystal and Beetle for assistance.

'Pistachio is stage-struck. That, for her mother Lady Collingham, is bad enough. What is worse, however, she has become entangled with a vile specimen. They tour together in a minor rep company and are in fact currently in Salisbury with *Hamlet*, Lady Pistachio playing the part of Queen Gertrude and her beau taking the role of Hamlet.'

Topping up his tipple, Krystal encouraged him to continue. 'An unfortunate alliance?'

'Extremely so,' he nodded gravely. 'The bounder, passing himself off, since his last prison sentence for fraud and deception, as Larry Lollard—'

'Heard of him,' Beetle squeaked. 'He stinks.'

'Beetle has an Equity card,' Krystal explained. 'She gets all the gossip.'

'Lady Collingham is convinced that he is using his unofficial connection with the family purely for his own advancement and—'

'Milking the family funds?' Krystal hazarded.

Cambridge eyed her over the rim of his sherry glass and nodded. 'Precisely so, my dear. Nine thousand, to date.'

'It'll be sticky going if they're actually engaged.'

'A munificent arrangement on his part. He deceives her regularly in every town they visit.'

'If Krystal and I tailed him,' Beetle volunteered, 'we could get enough on him to—'

'Lady Collingham has already engaged the services of a private investigation agency. Regrettably, as she feared, their reports were wholly conclusive,' Cambridge replied. 'What we have now is an unpleasant situation which needs—'

'Correcting,' Krystal whispered.

'A little more of the duck, my dear?'

Beetle grinned. 'Is there any more of that lovely cherry sauce?'

'Cambridge?' Lady Collingham queried.

The butler appeared at Beetle's elbow, supplying the minx with a silver sauce-boat.

'So very good of you to put us up,' Krystal said, raising her glass of Hock to her hostess.

'Salisbury being only an hour from Linton Hall, it seemed appropriate,' boomed the aristocratic voice from the other end of the long, candlelit table. 'You must return next month for the rough shoot I'm putting on.'

Silently attentive, Cambridge filled Krystal's glass.

'And what did you make of the performance tonight?'

Krystal and Beetle had attended a performance of *Hamlet* in Salisbury earlier. 'Patchy,' Krystal replied with candour. 'Ophelia was under-rehearsed, and the lead was weak. Lady Pistachio, as Gertrude, showed some promise, but—'

'Do not apologise for my daughter's shortcomings, my dear. If by some miracle you manage to sever her relationship with that swine, I will see to it that she attends drama school and pursues her acting career with a more reputable company. Have you given the matter any further consideration? Was your visit to the Assembly Rooms profitable this evening?'

'Well, we are at least familiar with the layout, now. Tomorrow night is their final performance in Salisbury. And rest assured, Lady Collingham, it will most certainly be his final bow.'

'He has deceived my daughter,' their hostess fumed, beckoning for the cheeseboard.

'Beetle got the stage door gossip,' Krystal continued. 'He is sleeping with the stand-in for Ophelia right under Pistachio's nose.'

'How very Shakespearean,' Lady Collingham snorted, chivvying the Stilton. 'I'd like to cut off his couplets.'

'He put powdered glass in the real Ophelia's face cream,' Beetle supplied in a rush. 'She scratched her face and had to withdraw. It's an old backstage trick. Larry Lollard got his own girl in, a lap-dancer from a Soho clip-joint. They're at it like rabbits all the time.'

Lady Collingham blinked uncomprehendingly.

'He nobbled the overnight declaration and slipped in a ringer,' Krystal translated, waxing horsey. 'They go the pace in the gallops,' she added.

Born in a saddle, Lady Collingham grasped Krystal's meaning.

'We must save Pistachio from any further humiliation and pain,' she grunted, tackling the Stilton with renewed vigour.

After lunch in a pub in the busy market square the next day, Krystal made some calls on her mobile.

The *Guardian* replied wanly but declined the journey down to Salisbury, citing a severe head cold which, he felt, a hackneyed 'Hamlet' would do little to alleviate. The *Sun*, however, was at a loose end.

'Any nookie?'

Krystal explained that the play positively dripped sexual passions, adding, 'I promise you a front-page scoop.'

In the 'Kaleidoscope' office, the Radio 4 girl initially demurred. Krystal promised an evening of ground-breaking experimental theatre. 'And Vanessa Wetherby will be sharing your box.'

'Kaleidoscope' promised to be there.

The Assembly Rooms in Salisbury were a splendid example of eighteenth-century Italianate exuberance. Housing a full-size apron stage, with proscenium arch and orchestra pit, they boasted a warren of changing rooms backstage.

Being Thursday, market day, the seats were full by 7.15. The plush crimson curtain rippled and the houselights dimmed. Culture had come to Salisbury and the populace had turned out *en masse* to be enlightened.

Up in the circle, the *Sun* noisily guzzled his Mars Bar, much to the annoyance of a powdered dowager and her retired colonel escort. Secluded in their box, Vanessa and the 'Kaleidoscope' scout bitched about the dress-sense of Channel 5 presenters.

Deliberately deepened cleavages and Beetle's Equity card got the avenging angels past the stage door. Backstage, they bided their time in the shadows. Larry Lollard's dressing room was easy to find. It was the biggest. They heard the dull thudding of the drum roll. The curtain would be parting and the bleak opening battlement scene underway. Planned down to the split-second, their own little drama now began to unfold.

Act I came and went, drawing only polite applause, a response which had become more enthusiastic by the time Larry Lollard, sleek in his black doublet and hose, brought the crimson curtains together, at the end of Act II scene ii, with a rather histrionic 'Wherein I'll catch the conscience of the King'.

That was their cue. They slipped into the star's dressing room, awaiting his arrival for the eight-minute break in strategic darkness: a darkness the continuation of which Beetle assured by covering the light switch with elastoplast.

Poring over the text, and then a reading script, the two avengers had worked out that Hamlet would be off-stage (sipping chilled Guinness according to backstage gossip), leaving almost the entire cast of King, Queen, Polonius, Ophelia, Rosen-what-ever-his-name-was and the other one, Guildenstern, on stage.

'And the Attendant Lords,' Beetle reminded Krystal, 'so we won't be disturbed.'

'And Hamlet goes back on stage—'

'For his big "To-be-or-not-to-be" number, with only Ophelia in the footlights.'

'Perfect.'

They jumped him in the dark, covering and smothering his gagged face in a huge damask cushion-cover, borrowed for the purpose from a wing-chair in the billiard room at Linton Hall. Pulling down his hose, Beetle - her right hand fastidiously. sheathed in a plastic surgical glove - fished out his flaccid length and started to pump vigorously. Krystal peeled off her polo-neck and slacks, revealing an inky black Lycra catsuit. A ginger 'Harpo' wig and Donald Duck mask later, and she was ready or her entrance as Hamlet - the alienated experimental version.

'Wottcha think?' she hissed, displaying her incongruous costume.

'You'll knock 'em cold,' Beetle grinned, bringing her struggling but subdued captive to his first spurting climax. Beetle deftly aimed the stream of silver upwards, so that it splattered down over his doublet.

'Pity about the breasts,' the minx murmured, tilting her head sideways as she considered Krystal's unDanish bosom bulging within its sheath of gripping Lycra.

'You didn't complain in the bath this morning,' Krystal replied, remembering Beetle's lips at her nipples in the warmth of the early-morning foaming tub.

'Two minutes,' Beetle warned, pausing in her vigorous pumping to check her watch. 'Got the—'

'Yep,' Krystal asserted, tightening the leather harness at her waist. The thongs across her haunches bit into the swollen cheeks as she screwed the yellow banana dildo into its socket. 'I'm off.'

'Break a leg,' Beetle grunted.

Larry Lollard squirted another stream of hot release as Krystal closed the door.

It is a time-honoured tradition in the playing of the role that Hamlet, entering stage right, in Act III scene I, should find the audience - from Stockholm to Seoul - silently moving its collective mouth as if declaiming the opening line 'To be or not to be...'

And the good and the great gathered in the Assembly Rooms of Salisbury that Thursday (market day - spent mostly in the pubs) did not fail to keep up the tradition. At least they all opened wide for 'To be...' - and kept them agape in horror and dismay at the spectacle unfolding before their eyes.

Fluffing up her 'Harpo' wig and fingering her banana dildo as it nodded ponderously between her thighs, Krystal peered out from behind her lurid Donald Duck mask and, with a few seconds left before the great soliloquy scene, decided to dispense with the attack on Shakespeare's finest and to go instead for the girl.

In her recent days as a lap-dancer in Compton Street 'Ophelia' had become skilled at repelling the excited advances of peers, public schoolboys and piss-heads. But nothing Compton Street had taught her had prepared her for tonight.

Ripping away her maidenly cotton shift, Krystal grabbed the banana. Borrowing, but adapting heavily, from Macbeth she roared: 'Is this an erection I see before me?' and, spinning the dumbstruck erstwhile-stripper around and down onto her knees, promptly proceeded to perpetrate an unnatural act. The banana, being well-oiled, slid easily between the cheeks of the writhing girl.

Salisbury's Assembly Rooms held its breath for an instant but already mutterings began to break the pause. Sitting in frozen outrage next to the *Sun*, the dowager bayed for the management. Beside her, the retired colonel, more at home at Ascot, raked the stage with his opera glasses. His commentary was ripe and vivid.

On stage, Krystal grappled with the now-naked Ophelia, turning her onto her back and pinning her down. Ophelia screamed twice: once at the sight of the Donald Duck mask bearing down on her, and again as the probing fruit thrust up inside her. With the distinctly unShakespearian scream of 'Fyffes!' she fainted dead away. Krystal rose, spotted an unguarded exit, and scuttled off the stage, just as the curtain fell heavily down and the audience sprang to its feet.

'Prince Porks Suicidal Nun,' was the *Sun's* first scribbled impression, instantly changed to a snappier headline for Friday's edition: 'DIRTY DANE'S BANANA

BONK'. Minutes later, despite the dowager's elbow in his ribs as she struggled for the exit, he was in touch with the night editor via his crackling mobile.

The more agile citizens of Salisbury had already stormed the stage and were now flooding the warren of corridors behind. Krystal was only a couple minutes ahead of them. Beetle meanwhile was bringing the official Hamlet to a fifth groaning climax - his doublet and hose now sticky with spattered semen as the bogus one returned. Whipping off her wig, mask and dildo, Krystal pulled on her jumper and slacks as Beetle released Larry Lollard. The bemused and shagged-out actor flinched slightly as Krystal showered him with a hip-flaskful of fine old reserve cognac from Cambridge's pantry.

The two women decamped, mixing with the surging lynch mob and being carried towards the exit just as the sirens of the police cars could be heard over the hubbub of the rioting crowd. They could hear the splintering of wood as the star's dressing-room door was smashed down.

Radio 4 listeners did not get the advertised feature on Jeremy Irons that night. A very confusing account of an extraordinary *Hamlet* was given over a live link from Salisbury. Listeners throughout the land heard the approaching sirens - an ambulance for the hysterical Ophelia and a police van for Hamlet - synchronized into one deadening blare.

Taking with them a distressed and mystified Pistachio, still dressed as the Queen of Denmark, Krystal and Beetle taxied back to Linton Hall.

'Cambridge followed it all on "Kaleidoscope", such a loyal lap,' Lady Collingham beamed, 'and I gather there were confused reports of town-centre disturbances coming in on The News At Ten. Cook never misses her date with Mr McDonald.' She was presiding over a scratch supper of savouries on toast, claret and strong black coffee. 'I am indebted to you both. Simply indebted. My cousin is on the Bench of course and so it will all be going to Crown Court.'

'On what charges?' Beetle asked, sipping her claret.

'I can think of a half-dozen that'll earn him a three stretch at least,' Lady Collingham surprised them with her jailbird jargon.

'And Pistachio?' Krystal murmured solicitously.

'Gone right off the whole idea of acting,' the relieved mother sighed. 'Damn girl wants to be a nun. And now, I'm for my bed. Cambridge will see you to your bedrooms.'

'Will you take a turn in the herb garden?' the butler purred into Krystal's ear. 'The thyme and the rosemary particularly are not to be missed on such a frosty night as this. I will see to madame,' he continued suavely, capturing Beetle by the elbow, 'and come for you in about ten minutes.'

Cambridge was quite right. The crisp night air was suffused with the penetrating aroma of sage, basil, oregano and mint. Krystal closed her eyes, listening to an owl hooting somewhere over the stable roof. The mint evoked memories. *Mint*. It haunted her memory deliciously...

She was bathed in sunshine. It was a glorious summer day sometime in their final year back at Birch Hall. Up on the Big Field, backing onto the coppiced beechwood through which a path trailed to the nearby village of Steeple Parva, all the Upper School were out for the last hockey match of the season. Coltish girls - lithe and lissom - were charging up and down the shaven sward, pleated skirts flipped up across their rounded buttocks. Navy knickers against the soft cream of thighs. Squeals of excitement splitting the air and beads of perspiration trickling down between warmly bunched bosoms.

A shrill whistle freezes the entire field. A foul. Two willowy girls bend, perspiring brows almost touching, hockey sticks locked like the antlers of rutting stags. A second shrill whistle blast unfreezes the players on the field. A fierce tussle and more gleeful shrieks. A collision of soft bodies - bosom to bosom, thigh to thigh. One blonde-maned beauty tumbles, rolling in the grass, her thigh and left buttock grazed green. She rises, plucking at the snagged navy serge at the cleft between her soft cheeks...

Krystal opened her eyes, sniffing the strong tang of mint once more then closing her eyes and remembering. Remembering slipping her hand into Beetle's and running up towards the edge of the coppiced beechwood. There, in the long grass, with the shouts of distant hockey players mixing with the cries of skylark up above, Krystal and Beetle crushing their bosoms down into the sweet sedge, bruising the pennyroyal beneath their bodies so that the warm air became perfumed with mint. Dazzled by the sun blazing above them, they had stripped slowly, offering their pubescent nakedness to the balmy summer zephyr - and then to one another. Krystal remembered the softness of the Beetle's breast and the firmness of her nipples. She remembered the smoothness of the buttocks beneath her sweeping palm, and the slight rasp of the dark pubic fuzz against her questing knuckles. She remembered the sweetness of Beetle's wet mouth - and the heady pungency of pennyroyal n the warm air.

Grinning suddenly, Krystal wondered at the tabloids' headlines tomorrow. 'Bard'stard Banned From Boards', perhaps? No. She'd leave it to the experts.

Cambridge loomed out of the darkness. 'Shall we go up?' he invited.

Krystal shivered, glad to regain the warmth inside. She followed him up the sweeping staircase, turning left at the top.

'Not that way,' he cautioned, politely motioning Krystal away from the corridor leading to the room she had shared with Beetle the previous night. 'I thought perhaps...' he murmured, opening a large oak door.

Through the door, Krystal caught a glimpse of Beetle's naked back. The brunette was standing facing the bed, her arms and legs tethered, spreadeagled, between the two posts at the base of the four-poster bed.

'Krystal,' Beetle whimpered softly, her face twisting round to look over her shoulder.

'I believe that when we first met, a couple of days ago, I interrupted a little domestic difficulty which you were about to resolve,' Cambridge said deferentially to Krystal. 'I thought perhaps that you might wish to resume—'

Krystal smiled and kissed him on the cheek.

'Krystal!' Beetle bleated, clenching her buttocks and squirming between the dark wooden posts.

'Gag, madame?'

'Thank you, Cambridge,' Krystal nodded.

The butler obliged adding, as he condemned Beetle to enforced silence with a tight wedge of cotton, 'I'm afraid I cannot supply you with any mistletoe, as the season is over. However, I took the liberty of cutting a hazel switch from our own copse down by Home Farm.'

'How kind,' Krystal replied, accepting the thin rod and slicing the air with it. It thrummed with a whispered note of menace. 'Thank you, Cambridge.'

'No,' he bowed gallantly, 'thank *you*, madame. The Lady Pistachio's future, thanks to your good offices, is now quite secure. Goodnight, madame.'

'Goodnight, Cambridge.'

The massive door closed behind the butler. Beetle struggled in her bondage but the ropes were tightly knotted at her wrists and ankles. Twisting and jerking her head, a cascade of Beetle's dark hair came down to curtain her eyes. Krystal delicately parted the fringe, then stepped back to peruse the naked peach-like cheeks waiting to be whipped. She tapped the left buttock sternly with the tip of her whippy hazel rod, causing it to tighten in a spasm of fearful response.

'Interfering with the Royal Mail is a very serious offence,' she began, emphasizing her words with an admonishing tap of the switch against the curved cheeks. The hazel rod rested across the twin spheres of warm satin. 'The post must not be touched.'

Swish! The punisher took a silent step back and with a supple flick of the wrist, brought the wand of woe slicing across the helpless buttocks. Beetle writhed in her bondage, tossing back her head in anguish.

'Interfering with the Postie carries an even harsher penalty,' Krystal murmured, dropping her voice down an octave.

Swish! The second cutting slice bequeathed another thin red line across the quivering cheeks. Beetle squealed into the tight gag. At the bedposts, her bound wrists writhed in futile desperation.

'Postie must not be tampered with.'

Krystal proposed to administer seven strokes across the bare bottom of the naughty minx. Seven, to commence with. She always avoided dispensing the obvious stinging six, preferring an odd number. Part of Beetle's torment, she knew, would be trying to guess if the fifth - or the ninth - would bring the suffering to an end.

Swish! Swish! Flicking the hazel switch expertly, Krystal delivered the third and fourth slicing strokes in succession. This time, the squeal of response was audible despite the binding gag. Four red lines burned angrily across the swell of the creamy rump, each betraying the fierce Judas kiss of the slicing rod.

Krystal paused and, stepping back, stretched out her arm. Levelling the tip of the cruel switch against the bare bottom she slowly traced each weal from left to right across the punished cheeks. Beetle arched up on tip-toe in response to the nuzzling cane-tip as it fingered the flesh it had just lashed. Demonstrating her absolute dominion over the buttocks before her, Krystal proceeded to trace where she proposed to place the ensuing stripes. Slowly, deliberately, the hazel rod score soft indentations across the unblemished flesh. Krystal knew that each delicate sweep of the wood across the fearful flesh would burn brightly in Beetle's anxious imagination. Krystal was right: Beetle's toes turned white as she trod the carpet in an ecstasy of torment.

Swish! Cutting through the air, the rod sang an evil note of pain before biting into the poised buttocks. Krystal paused once more, intent on pacing the punishment. Holding up the rod, she inspected it intimately before dragging it slowly through a pincered finger and thumb, thrilling to its supple potency and pliant menace. Flexing the switch once more, she raised it up for the sixth time.

Swish, slice! Swish, slice! The concluding stripes were planted down across the upper curves and then - with a deft flick of her wrist - up into their lower swell. Beetle gasped and clenched tight her whipped cheeks, forcing her cleft into a barely visible flesh-crease.

An equally stinging short sermon followed. Dragging the tip of the cruel switch down Beetle's spine - from the nape of her arched neck to the dimple at her cleft between the striped cheeks below - the blonde warned the bound brunette on the foolishness of infidelity, the dangers of disloyalty and the inevitability of punishment and pain.

Placing the length of smooth hazel down on the carpet at the side of the four-poster bed, Krystal stood directly behind Beetle. Fully clothed against her naked, bound victim, she felt her hot slit pulse as the thrill of dominance, the raw frisson of erotic power, flickered down from her tightening belly to her wetness below. She drank in the intoxicating feeling of being in absolute control of the bare-bottomed girl, bound and writhing only an inch from her bosom. Tipsy with the heady draught, Krystal exhaled, causing her peaked nipples to push out the cashmere jumper and prink the naked flesh of Beetle's soft back between the straining shoulders.

Grunting softly, the dominant blonde thrust her hips forwards, crushing her pubis into the hot bottom with an almost contemptuous display of arrogance. Seconds later, to control her flinching victim, Krystal reached out to cup, then squeeze, Beetle's bare bosom. She relished the warm weight as it filled her gripping fingers and juiced her panties as she felt the erect nipples piercing her palms. Burying her face into Beetle's musk-scented hair, she swallowed to lubricate her parched throat before whispering her final words of dire admonishment.

Beetle writhed in an attempt to escape this intimate attention, her bottom shuddering and flinching away from the rasp of Krystal's skirt. Krystal smiled, drawing the naked minx back into her own warmth with a tweak at the nipples. Squeaking, the nude responded, thrusting back her hot bottom into Krystal's thighs.

'I own you completely,' the blonde snarled softly. 'And I am not willing to share. Understand?'

Beetle slumped, surrendering completely.

'Understand?' whispered the wet lips at her ear. Signalling her penitence and contrition, she hammered her whipped cheeks into Krystal's pubis as far as her restricting bondage would allow.

Relishing the homage, Krystal allowed herself to come.

Gripping her partner's captive breasts with fierce lust, she ground her pantie-sheathed clitoris into the punished bottom, raking it across the velvety flesh-mounds.

Moments later, still welded into the nakedness of her bound victim, Krystal reached out and untied the ropes at each outstretched wrist. Beetle's arms relaxed and she rubbed the chafed flesh gratefully. With an imperious forward thrust of her hips, Krystal propelled Beetle face-down along the bed. The whipped nude was still tied at each ankle, causing her buttocks to rise up from the satin duvet. Sprawled helplessly, thighs splayed and rounded cheeks offered up submissively, Beetle moaned into the cool silk.

'Arms out. No, completely straight. Touch the pillow with your fingertips,' Krystal commanded, stooping to pick up the hazel switch. 'Palms down flat,' she added, her orders delivered in the sternest of tones. Dimpling the bed of pain with one knee as she addressed the striped bottom, she noted with satisfaction that the buttocks, in this new position, were fuller and rounder. Upthrust and vulnerable, each cheek presented itself as a ripe, lusciously fleshed, temptation for the lash.

Crack! Sweeping down, the hazel wand made a sharper note than before when it swished in against the buttocks. *Crack! Crack!* Beetle's fingers taloned the duvet and dragged the heavy silk down to smother her squeals. *Crack!* Threshing in response to the searing stroke, Beetle shuddered and dipped her tummy, causing her whipped buttocks to arch up superbly, exactly as Krystal, the consummate disciplinarian, had calculated. *Crack!* The severity of the fifth cutting slice set the crimson buttocks ablaze, the flames of pain licking at the swollen curves.

Krystal depressed the quivering hazel switch down across the bare bottom, and, stretching out, loosened the tight gag at Beetle's mouth. Wriggling and squirming, the naked brunette turned her face sullenly away.

'Look at me.'

Fearing the threat of instant pain, the dark hair flounced and her pale tear-stained face turned to gaze up sorrowfully at her chastiser.

Bending down, Krystal kissed the pouting lips softly, slowly and sweetly. The sullen lips beneath Krystal's responded. Tongue tips quivered, parried and touched. Angling the hazel rod up above the buttocks with her left hand, Krystal caressed Beetle's face with her right. Planting a deep kiss in the hungry lips, she cracked the switch down, searing the soft silk of the curved cheeks with the unexpected stroke. Beetle squealed and drove her tongue deep into her punisher's mouth. *Swish!* Another slice lashed the scalded buttocks. Burying herself face-down into the duvet, the nude punched the soft silk with fists of resentful fury. Wriggling, she struggled to escape, forgetting in her anguish the shackles at each ankle.

'Be still, little one, and submit. You must accept and embrace our punishment,' Krystal purred, recapturing the tear-stained face and kiss-licking the salt pearls away. Beetle's whimpering melted into a kittenish mewing as she strove to snuggle up against her strict tormentress. The blonde kissed each tear-jewelled eye, and kissed the buttocks once more with a final stroke of the whippy wood.

Tossing the switch aside, Krystal straddled her partner and, easing her heavy buttocks and scissoring thighs up, slowly began to strip. Shorn of her jumper, blouse and brassiere, Krystal squatted, plumping her bottom directly down on the striped cheeks below. Gently rocking back and forth, she rode the brunette lightly, delighting in the rhythmic bobbing of her ripe breasts. Clamping together her stockinged thighs, she squeezed the trapped peaches fiercely. Beetle moaned her sweet agony into the silk at her lips. Krystal wriggled out of her skirt and, snapping her suspenders, peeled off her stockings. Only the white cotton panties - biting into the hot cleft between her cheeks - remained. Pinning Beetle down firmly at each shoulder, she lowered her belly onto the swell of the whipped buttocks and dragged herself upwards, peeling her panties down against the hot cheeks. Beetle submitted completely to the sweeping of the hips and pubis along the line of her cleft. Slowly, the panties were peeled away, drawing a thin spindle of liquid desire from Krystal's wet labia. The thread of her sparkling arousal broke, splashing down onto the warm flesh below. Beetle cried out, a loud shout of carnal celebration. Collapsing down onto her victim, Krystal's sticky flesh-lips kissing the bottom, she rolled from hip to hip, smearing her juices triumphantly.

'Forgive me,' Beetle moaned - her first words of contrition since being whipped.

'I have forgiven you,' Krystal whispered. 'And now that I have punished you, it is time that I pleasured you.'

'P-pleasure?' Beetle stammered.

'Wait. You'll see.'

Scrambling off the bed, Krystal bent over and kissed each striped buttock, pausing to lick the reddened flesh with her strong wet tongue, then succumbing to sucking deeply and softly biting the firmly fleshed peaches. She sensed Beetle coming to orgasm - the stiffened belly and the taut thighs - so withdrew her face and arrowed a straightened index finger down into the yawning cleft.

'Open wider,' she urged in a voice from which all the earlier stern iciness had melted.

The spasming cheeks, signalling the imminent climax, obeyed. Krystal fingered the cleft firmly, with slow, deliberate strokes. Just as the orgasm erupted, she probed the anal whorl burying her stiff finger in Beetle's muscled warmth. Fuelled by the kiss of the whippy rod across her cheeks and then the dominantly tender finger inside her, Beetle climaxed long and loud.

Abandoning her partner to the shuddering paroxysms of her ecstasy, Krystal skipped across to where she had thrown down her bag. From it, she fished out a supple leather harness and a yellow banana dildo.

Hearing the slight jingle of the harness as it was threaded around the thighs and across the buttocks, then snapped into place, Beetle dragged herself up onto one elbow and stared over her shoulder through bleary eyes.

'What—' she began.

'It was a spare. Just in case. Didn't need it, though. So I thought I'd save it for a special occasion—' Krystal left the sentence unfinished as she approached the bottom of the bed.

Beetle inched her buttocks upwards invitingly.

'No,' Krystal murmured, fingering the yellow shaft that thrust out proudly from her pubis. 'I won't have you in bondage. I want you in my arms.'

The blunt tip of the banana raked Beetle's thigh and inner leg as Krystal knelt down to untie each ankle. Slithering from the bed, Beetle sprang into Krystal's arms. Lips to lips, nipples to nipples, they delighted in their reunion.

'Up,' commanded Krystal, cupping Beetle's hot cheeks.

The minx wrapped her arms around the blonde's neck and clamped her legs amorously around the hips below. Locking her heels, she dug them into the swell of Krystal's firm buttocks.

'Closer,' whispered Krystal.

Beetle obeyed, impaling herself on the blonde - and onto the thrusting dildo.

Cradling and rocking the minx tenderly, Krystal worked the thick banana dildo up into Beetle's welcoming slit a hip-jerk at a time. Beetle spilled her warm breath into Krystal's neck, and her warmer juices onto the taut belly at her thighs.

'Can you hear bells? I can,' Beetle murmured dreamily.

'I should hope so,' Krystal gasped, giving her all.

They did not hear the polite tap-tap at their door, nor did they notice Cambridge, moments later, standing in the doorway.

'Ahem!'

The banana slipped out, wedging itself between Beetle's splayed cheeks. She writhed, struggling to reinsert it.

Trained to disregard whatever he may discover in the course of his duties, the English butler wears the mask of discretion. Cambridge butled at his best, batting his eyelid only twice as Beetle's sticky fingers guided the banana back up inside her. Grabbing Krystal's ears, she squealed and pleaded to be pumped. Krystal pumped.

'Forgive me madame but I came to inform you that there is no cause for any alarm. The bells now ringing...'

Krystal gasped, mid-thrust, and staggered slightly under Beetle's weight. Beetle was insatiable, and continued to ride both the blonde and the banana ruthlessly.

'...may be disregarded,' Cambridge managed to continue in a slightly strangled voice. 'They merely indicate the presence of foxes at the dustbins. The little fellows...' he struggled bravely as, spurred on by Beetle's drumming heels at her buttocks, Krystal humped frenziedly, '...have a weakness for cook's leftovers. Especially the *boeuf á la Melvyn Bragg.*'

'Thank you, Cambridge,' Krystal grunted.

'No, thank *you*, madame.'

CHAPTER SEVEN

'No croissants?'

'Nope.'

'Or muffins?'

'Or muffins,' Beetle said sweetly.

'What, then?' Krystal demanded, waving a buttered knife.

'Crisp bread. I'll do you a grilled grapefruit if you like,' the minx added helpfully.

'I'm starving,' Krystal muttered, mourning the loss of the crisply fried bacon, scrambled eggs and buttery toast the bleak February morning demanded. 'How long is this latest health kick going on for?' Krystal queried, already tiring of her partner's latest enthusiasm.

'You should follow my example,' Beetle replied piously.

'Thinking of dragging me down to your gym?'

'No—' Beetle said quickly, a little too quickly. She blushed.

Krystal's eyes narrowed as she crunched into her wafer-thin crisp-bread smeared with blackcurrant preserve. She noted the pink cheeks on Beetle's face but chose not to pursue the matter directly.

Minutes later, as Krystal was rummaging for a custard cream in the kitchen, Beetle emerged from the bedroom, sporting a figure-hugging leotard. The stretched Lycra managed to reveal more than it concealed of her exquisite curves. Cut thigh-high, it left her rounded buttocks almost bare. Cut low at the cleavage, it left most of her bosom bulgingly exposed.

'Like it?' The minx twirled.

'Come here,' Krystal murmured, abandoning her futile search for carbohydrates. 'Let me have a closer look.'

'Wait,' Beetle squeaked. 'Sticky fingers.'

Grasping Krystal's wrists, she guided each hand in turn up to her mouth, sucking away any traces of the blackcurrant preserve.

Withdrawing her glistening fingers, Krystal knelt, turning the minx around and steadying her plump cheeks between the frame of her firmly upturned palms. Fingering the taut lycra she tried to stretch it across the swell of the cheeks. Beetle jiggled impatiently, so that the leotard shrivelled into a thin band at her cleft. Krystal knuckled the left cheek tenderly.

'You really ought to wear a size bigger, Beetle,' she observed, appraising the bare buttocks intimately.

'Don't I look good in it?' the brunette pouted.

'Too good,' purred the blonde. 'Turn around.'

Beetle presented her pubis to Krystal's steady gaze. Her eyes flickered up, meeting the bulging breasts. Through the stretchy ice-blue lycra, the damson-dark nipples thickened and peaked as Krystal's fingertips traced the outline of Beetle's smooth thighs.

'Isn't it punishing, this daily workout at your gym?'

'Not a gym,' Beetle said emphatically. 'The "Fit As A Fiddle" is a body enhancement studio,' she pronounced, quoting from the brochure which had persuaded her to join. 'And you get a personal fitness trainer.'

'Qualified?' Krystal asked absently, as if already bored with the subject.

'Svetlana is terrific,' Beetle gushed unguardedly.

Flickering her eyes up across the swell of the lycra-bound bosom, Krystal caught the sparkle in the little minx's eyes.

'Svetlana,' Krystal echoed softly.

'Oooh, she's a big, tough, Russian battle-axe. Quite frightful, but she takes a very scientific approach to balancing optimum body mass with ergo dynamic calorific...' Beetle burbled, citing the brochure's blurb. She was speaking a shade too rapidly for someone with nothing whatever to hide.

'You'd better get your coat, then,' Krystal said, rising. She gave the retreating bottom a playfully sharp spank. 'Mustn't be late for the battle-axe.'

Beetle lay on the leather couch, fingering the lycra at her labia. Snuggling her soft buttocks into the warm hide, she savoured the luxury of her private cubicle in Fit As A Fiddle. Basking in the gentle heat from the solar panels above, she inhaled the aromatic air suffused with exotic oils and squirmed with pleasure as her near-naked buttocks kissed the polished surface beneath their warm weight.

Svetlana, her twenty-six-year-old blonde pony-tailed personal fitness trainer approached, her white pumps squeaking on the pristine tiles. The tall Russian beauty wore a cropped white vest that squeezed her prominent bosom voluptuously, tiny white shorts that hugged her hips and bottom and white cotton ankle-socks. The virginal innocence of a gymnastic goddess from the Upper Sixth was betrayed by the insolent sway of the tightly sheathed breasts and buttocks, the carnal glint in the grey eyes and the knowing smile spread as thickly as the crimson lipstick across the wide and pouting lips.

Beetle gazed up into the steel-grey eyes and shivered expectantly.

'Up,' Svetlana snapped. 'Onto the scales.'

Beetle, thrilling to the stern command, obeyed instantly. On the scales, her toes trod the soft rubber as she squeezed her buttocks tightly.

Spank! The Russian's palm swept down across the near-naked right cheek. It reddened and wobbled in response. 'You have gained twenty-six grammes,' she barked. 'You have not obeyed my strict instructions to eat sparingly, have you?'

Beetle bowed her head in shame, hating the shimmering red figures of the digital display at her scrunched toes.

Spank! The reddened cheek blushed crimson. 'Have you?' Svetlana insisted.

'I ate doughnuts,' Beetle confessed.

'How many?'

'Three.'

Spank! Spank! Spank! The stinging palm delivered one searing spank for each forbidden doughnut.

'I must do something about the extra weight. Then,' the Russian continued, taloning and squeezing the spanked buttock dominantly, 'it will be, I think, treatment Number Four.'

Beetle shivered, the frisson of delicious dread fingering the soft flesh of her inner thighs.

'On the couch,' came the crisp command. 'Face-down,' the fitness trainer instructed, tapping the leather impatiently.

Beetle's bosom squashed down into the couch as she stretched out, crushing her nipples into its supple warmth.

'It has been scientifically proven,' Svetlana continued, thumbing the buttock she had crimsoned, 'that the most efficient way to burn off calorific excess is corporal punishment, sharp discipline. Findings from the Research Institute at Minsk confirm this. Our glorious swimmers, athletes and ballerinas submit to discipline to keep their buttocks slim. In their thirst for gold medals, they are prepared to suffer to stay trim. I will deal with your bottom in a moment,' she murmured, her finger hooking out the leotard buried deep down in Beetle's cleft, 'and when we have burned off those wicked calories, we can progress with treatment Number Four.'

To Beetle's dismay, the deliciously strict Russian left the cubicle. Beetle wriggled across the expanse of polished leather, thrilling to the sensation of her proud nipples rasping against the hide. To Beetle's delight, stern Svetlana returned, weighing a table-tennis bat in her left hand as she stroked the dimpled rubber surface with her right thumb.

'Table tennis is an excellent sport for developing the suppleness of the wrist,' she declared. 'And it is the favourite method in Minsk for abolishing those calories.'

Beetle felt the tingling touch of tiny spiders scuttling down her spine. She raised her hips up from the leather, peeling her moist pussy away from the smooth hide as she offered her bottom up to the bat.

'Stretch out completely. Arms out. Grip the leather,' Svetlana ordered, levelling the bat across the bunched cheeks then firmly depressing their ripe swell.

Forced back down into the couch, Beetle felt her sticky labia kiss the sleek surface.

'Remind me. How many grammes have you gained?'

Beetle's parted lips tasted the feral tang of the hide as she whispered her response: 'Twenty-six.'

Svetlana did some abstruse calculations, using the Minsk formula, aloud in her native Russian tongue. 'According to the experts who pride themselves on this punishment regime, eleven strokes should prove satisfactory,' she concluded, slipping back into her heavily accented English.

Crack! Crack! Crack! Whipping the bat down in a searing staccato, Svetlana set the bunched cheeks ablaze. At each swiping stroke of dimpled rubber across quivering flesh, the bat flattened the curved cusp of each punished cheek.

Crack! Crack! Crack! Again, the cruel bat viciously caressed Beetle's proffered buttocks.

'You will learn to obey me absolutely. Your diet is calculated in strict accordance to Minsk. As is your discipline. I do not want to see any further body-mass gain. Understood?' She brought the bat down twice more, leaving the wobbling cheeks a deepening pink blotched with a reddening sheen.

'Yes,' whispered Beetle, grinding her pussy furtively into the leather.

Crack! Crack! Crack! The concluding three strokes were delivered with ruthless accuracy. Beetle suppressed her squeal as she hammered her nipples and weeping labia into the dark hide.

'And now,' Svetlana hissed, lowering the bat down to tame and control the writhing buttocks, 'treatment Number Four.'

'It's only pasta and a salad. I could do you scampi,' Krystal called out from the kitchen. 'I've just come back from Bow. It's so hot in the foundry, I could drink gallons.'

'Not hungry,' Beetle lied, enviously glimpsing Krystal's tempting lunch, especially the salad, glistening under the drizzle of extra virgin oil. 'OK at Bow?'

'Yep. They've agreed to do my Girl On A Horse.'

'Good job that Korean bank paid up before they wobbled,' Beetle said sympathetically, deftly pinching a forkful of pasta while Krystal raided the fridge for Chablis.

'They don't even want it now. Or their money back.'

'Great, you can flog it,' Beetle smiled, unzipping her kitbag and tossing her skimpy leotard into the laundry basket. 'I'll go and shower.'

'Fitness routine on schedule? Did you feel the burn?'

Hiding her blushes, Beetle scampered for the shower.

Silently putting down her forkful of pasta on her plate, Krystal tip-toed across to the laundry basket, thumbed out the ice-blue leotard - still warm from Beetle's body - and palmed it open for inspection. Spotting the dark stain where the stretchy fabric hugged at Beetle's pubic mound, she fingered it slowly sensing the wetness. Lowering her face down into the Lycra, she closed her eyes and sniffed deeply. Raising her head up, like a tiger that has feasted on its prey, her eyes opened: into fierce slits of anger.

'That was Vanessa. Seems she's got a little job for us.'

'Great,' Beetle grinned, greedily swallowing the last of her bap filled with a fried egg and two sausages. 'What? Where?'

'Very delicate stuff, and a bit complicated. Remember she put up Peter overnight in Fulham after the exhibition?'

Beetle, remembering the spanking across Vanessa's knee, nodded pinkly, and bent her face down to lick ketchup from her thumb.

'They saw off a bottle or two between them, and Peter opened up to her.'

'Peter and Vanessa?' Beetle squeaked, her ketchuped thumb forgotten for the moment.

'His heart. Spilled out his worries. Got a problem. Blackmail. Former lover is keeping letters of a highly intimate nature. Highly personal, not to say embarrassing.'

'Peter's?' Beetle squeaked again. To her knowledge, the Norwich man led a singularly saintly existence devoted to the arts.

'No his sister Chloe's. Told you it was complicated.'

'Isn't she an MP?'

'Almost. Jumped on the New Labour bandwagon and is up for selection in the Midlands. Split up with Max a year ago last Christmas. Max took it badly. Turned sour. Now her ex wants several thousand or the selection committee will get some pretty fruity bedtime reading—'

'And Chloe won't be gracing the green leather of the back benches with her bum.'

'Matthew Parris couldn't have put it better. We've agreed - Peter, Chloe and Vanessa - to buy 'em back. I hate blackmail.'

'Don't we get to—'

'Chloe just wants the letters back.'

'So Max goes unpunished,' Beetle sighed.

'I didn't say that.'

'Today, I shall administer treatment Number Seven. Minsk recommends it strongly for keeping the bustline trim. It is especially recommended for those blessed with bountiful breasts,' Svetlana purred (in exquisite English that would have brought a tear of joy to her language tutor's eye) cupping and savagely squeezing Beetle's lycra-bound bosom.

'Treatment Number Seven?' Beetle gasped, her tongue thickening in her dry mouth.

'Up on the couch,' Svetlana snarled softly. 'On your back.'

Beetle's buttocks bunched as she backed into the hard leather. Steadying herself with outstretched hands down on the polished hide, she pressed her knees together and swung her feet up.

'Legs apart,' the Russian ordered, dominantly fingering Beetle's inner thigh half-an-inch below the pubic mound.

Beetle's arousal bubbled into the lycra holding her labia as she promptly obeyed.

'Stirrups,' the fitness trainer explained, pulling down the two jangling adjustable chains from the ceiling. At the end of each chain, black leather and steel stirrups twisted slowly in suspension about Beetle's naked feet.

'Up,' Svetlana ordered.

Beetle obliged. With each foot firmly secured, the beautiful Russian, breasts bouncing within her tight vest, yanked down the counterweight. Her blonde pony-tail swished from side to side as she hauled, raising up Beetle's arrowing legs, toes pointing directly at the ceiling. So severe was this bondage, most of Beetle's rounded buttocks were exposed below.

'Take these. One in each hand,' the stern voice instructed.

Beetle, elbows flexed and opened palms upturned, accepted the dumb-bells uncertainly.

'Push them up until your arm is straight.'

Beetle pushed up with both arms, raising them to their painful limit. She gasped aloud as her breasts tightened, her bosom bunching between her upper arms.

'One by one. One at a time. How do you say?' Svetlana searched her word-memory bank. 'Alternatively, yes?'

Beetle found this easier, though the handheld weights were growing heavier and more irksome.

'Minsk recommends sixty push-ups and so sixty you shall do. As and when you slack,' Svetlana murmured, 'I will be here, to encourage you, so.'

As she hissed her final word, she sliced a short cane in across the surface of the leather couch, so swiftly it made no shadow, whipping the bamboo into the tightly rounded cheeks of Beetle's exposed bottom.

Beetle squealed.

The cane swished in again, leaving a thin red weal across the perfectly poised cheeks.

'Silence. You must not disturb the other clients.'

Beetle whimpered softly, dreading the moment when her heavy arms - already burning - swayed and buckled under the dumb-bells. Imagining the moment, and the bite of the bamboo that would follow instantly, Beetle groaned.

Swish, slice! The supple cane skimmed across the polished ride, scalding the proffered cheeks with a third cruel stripe of crimson pain.

'Minsk warns that many of those undergoing treatment Number Seven achieve orgasm within nine minutes. Let us see if we can better that record, eh?'

The cane swished again, and Beetle screamed softly.

'Silence, I said. You must not disturb the next cubicle.'

Next door, basking in her solar rays, Krystal's eyes narrowed behind her glinting Raybans.

The late February sun hung on the horizon, low and heavy like an orange. Despite the warming late pub lunch of rabbit pie, chips and Medoc, Beetle shivered as she trudged behind Krystal. They followed the snaking white wooden rail that separated them from the racetrack.

'She said the fourteenth fence. This it?'

Beetle, hands deep in her pockets, chin buried in her roll neck, looked up guiltily. 'I forgot to count.'

Krystal sighed, turned and nodded slightly as she counted the dark birch fences punctuating the green shaven sward stretching back to the starting post of Worcester Race Course.

'Fourteen,' she confirmed. 'We'll wait.'

'Funny place to meet,' Beetle murmured, shivering.

A dank mist was rolling up the course from the river that flanked it down in the meadows.

Krystal shrugged. 'Her choice.'

Beetle reached over the white rail and palmed the supple birch twigs compacted to form the hurdle. She squealed, snatching back her hand.

'Birch,' Krystal remarked. 'The flagellant's favourite. Just imagine a bundle of those beauties whipping down across your bare bottom.'

Beetle did and shivered, though not this time from the cold.

The quartz light-beams of a Range Rover raked the sky as the sturdy four-wheeled drive crested the low hill and caught Beetle and Krystal in their glare, dissipating the gathering gloom. To the west, the sun was sinking into the purple smudge of the now indistinct hills. Before them, the Range Rover bucked doggedly on the wet turf. At last it slewed to a halt, engine idling, fifteen yards from them. Ducking under the white rail, Krystal and Beetle shielded their eyes against the powerful headlights and approached slowly. As they neared, the engine died and the lights dipped.

'Hi, I'm Max. We talked on the phone yesterday.' The ash-blonde smiled, getting out and slamming the door. 'So sorry to drag you here but I've been with the vet since cock crow and I've got a meeting with some owners in the Steward's Office in an hour.'

Krystal scanned the honest face. Max was indeed a beautiful woman. Just as she had been surprised to hear the soft warm voice on the telephone yesterday when arranging the meeting, she was again surprised to find no trace of greed, malice or spite - features associated with blackmailers - in the clear blue eyes, chill-blushed cheeks or shy smile of welcome.

'You owners love all this cloak-and-dagger stuff, don't you?' Max teased. 'So, what is it to be. Dam or sire?'

Krystal blinked. She liked to be in control. So far, she was adrift. 'Dam or sire?'

'To bring to stud. Or would you,' Max continued, 'prefer to draw from the frozen sperm bank?'

Krystal shook her head, and turned to silence Beetle who had giggled. Instantly taking in the mud-spattered Range Rover, the taut cream jodhpurs and black leather riding boots of its driver, she realized the source of the misunderstanding.

'No, we're not here for stud services, Max. The business matter I mentioned concerns Chloe.'

'Chloe?' Max gasped, genuinely delighted. Krystal saw the blue eyes widen as fond memories flooded back. 'Chloe asked you to come and see me? Why? Where is she? How is she?'

Krystal wondered if this was all an elaborate pretence. Uncertainly, she simply repeated that Chloe had sent them.

'But who are you?' Max gushed. 'I can't remember meeting—'

'Friends—'

'What is she up to these days?' Max interrupted, clearly excited.

'She sent us to collect her letters, Max.'

Max looked back blankly. 'Letters? I don't understand.'

'Her letters to you.' Before Krystal could mention the matter of payment, Max laughed.

'Oh, yes,' she managed, still chuckling warmly. 'If Chloe wants them back she can have them. Hot stuff,' Max grinned. 'I'll dig them out and post them—'

'We've come to collect them,' Krystal gently insisted, sensing the moment of truth approaching. She'll name her price any minute now, Krystal thought, feeling the weight of the banknotes in her pocket.

'Chloe can have them, but I'll have to speak with her first, you understand. Don't be offended,' Max added hastily, 'but I have to make sure.'

Krystal nodded.

'I'll give her a ring,' she said emphatically. 'Hop in. I've time to get you back to the stables before my meeting.'

The interior of the Range Rover was comfortable and warm. Max did not talk, electing to drown the silence with Vivaldi.

Beetle whistled appreciatively as they cornered a paddock and pulled up in front of a pink-stone cottage. A row of stables stood to the left, all the doors swung shut for the night.

'We only rent it,' Max said apologetically as they climbed out onto loose gravel. 'We hope to buy - when Henrietta stops chucking all our money at the bookies,' she muttered.

Krystal noted the remark and filed it away under M for motive in her memory bank.

Downstairs, over generous gin-and-gingers, Krystal and Beetle conversed softly.

'Not at all what I thought,' Beetle whispered. 'So open and frank. And no mention of money. She hasn't asked for any.'

'I don't believe she ever did,' Krystal murmured.

Upstairs, drawers and cupboard doors were being frantically opened and closed as the hunt for the love letters got underway.

They looked at the red, white and grey chalk etchings on the far wall. From the Euston Road school of the late 1930s they were a series of Lesbos and her handmaidens. The themes of domination, discipline and desire were executed in boldly sensual curves. The sinuous curl of a leather whip in one scene ensnared the plump buttocks it had just lashed. Next to it, parted lips yearned for the swollen breast - with vermilion nipple peaked - which was withheld only an inch above. In the third, slender hands cupped and parted creamy buttocks, holding the whipped cheeks in their thrall. Beetle stood up and tip-toed across, peering up at the lubricious prints.

Footsteps thumping hurriedly down the stairs sent the minx scuttling back to her gin-and-ginger.

'Can't seem to find them anywhere. Tell you what - Krystal?'

Krystal nodded.

'I'll give Chloe a ring and explain. They'll turn up. Have you got her number?'

'Haven't you?' Beetle challenged.

'It was with the letters,' Max shrugged.

'I can give you her brother's,' Krystal suggested.

'Darling Peter,' she squeaked, delighted. 'Would you?'

'What about your meeting,' Krystal reminded her.

'Oh, hell, yes. Look, I'll get Henrietta to run you back into Worcester for your train. Leave the number with her and,' she lowered her voice a fraction, 'you won't, please, say anything about her heavy betting, will you?'

She went out in a rush. They heard the Range Rover spit gravel and roar off.

Moments later, a tall, closely cropped redhead, ten years older than Max's twenty-seven, entered the cottage through the kitchen. She was smoking a thin cheroot. A curl of smoke closed her left eye. 'Max asked me to give you two a lift to the nation,' she said with scant charm. 'Ready?'

'Just finishing my gin,' Krystal replied, her eyes narrowing a fraction.

'Friends of Max?' Henrietta, her athletic body hidden in frayed denims and a waxed Barbour, inquired casually as she pretended to tidy up back numbers of *Horse And Hound* and *The Field*.

'Friends of an old friend,' Krystal countered, briefly signalling to Beetle for silence. 'Just a little business matter to settle. A small transaction.'

'We could use some cash just now,' Henrietta grunted. 'How much?'

'I believe you know how much,' Krystal said softly. 'Four thousand was the price agreed with Chloe, wasn't it?'

Henrietta dropped the magazine she was holding, and left it on the floor at her feet.

'Max knows nothing of this. I have the letters,' the redhead explained. 'She doesn't even know I found them. Wait here.'

Returning from the kitchen with a shortbread tin in her hand, Henrietta prised open the lid.

'Here they are. Got the money?'

'Bookies getting impatient?' Beetle chipped in, earning a scowl from Krystal.

Henrietta's eyes narrowed dangerously. 'What has that prattling bitch told you?' she snarled.

Beetle's eyes were drawn to the prints on the wall. There, she saw Max's doom etched out in red, grey and white: the depiction of dominance and discipline as the lash ensnared her whipped buttocks of the naked woman prostrating herself at the feet of her punisher. Following Beetle's gaze across to the triptych of Lesbos and her love slaves, the redhead laughed softly.

'Let me see a few of the letters,' Krystal said.

'Have you got the money? All of it?'

'The letters,' Krystal demanded.

She took several sheets of pale-blue paper from Henrietta's outstretched hand. Scanning the first two, she read the indiscretions, the promises and the carnal longings of a turbulent mind. On the third, she saw the coils of pubic fuzz sellotaped next to Chloe's exuberant signature.

In silence, the rest of the letters were exchanged for the bundle of banknotes.

'We'll make our own way back to the station,' Krystal said curtly.

'Why are we waiting here?' Beetle whispered, shivering in the darkness of the tackle room. The air was heavy with the raw tang of oiled leather.

'Unfinished business,' Krystal replied. 'She'll be in here soon to hang up the bridles. Keep quiet.'

As Krystal had predicted, Henrietta backed into the tack room, staggering under the weight of martingales and harnesses. Using an angled elbow, Krystal snapped on the light.

The assortment of leather dropped to the flagstone floor as she stepped back, startled.

'I think you forgot to give me something,' Krystal said.

Henrietta's eyebrows framed the unspoken question.

'Copies,' Krystal explained.

She caught the brief frown on Henrietta's face then watched the mask of pretended puzzlement attempt to conceal the deception.

'Copies?' she blustered, almost convincingly.

'Four thousand for the originals was such easy money. You are bound to come back for more.'

'There are no copies,' Henrietta snapped.

'Blackmail is such a potentially lucrative business,' Krystal observed suavely, 'and with your debts, no doubt you hoped to milk it.' Krystal jerked her head to Beetle. 'Now,' she hissed.

It was the agreed signal for Beetle to scoop up one corner of the rope net - used for bales of straw around the stables - and for Krystal to snatch up the other. Henrietta shrieked and clawed, but they easily overpowered her and bound her in the web of hemp.

'Hands!' Krystal ordered.

Bending over their quarry, Beetle tied a short leather thong around Henrietta's wrists. 'Get the net off and strip her naked.'

Beetle struggled valiantly but the task proved too difficult for her unaided. Krystal, having gagged the cursing mouth, helped the minx. Soon, they had Henrietta utterly naked, bound at the wrists.

'Back into the net,' Krystal murmured.

They wrapped the wriggling nude tightly with the knotted ropes. The heavy breasts bulged in their bondage and the bare buttocks, burgeoning through the diamonds of biting mesh, ripened roundly in their savage bondage.

'Position her for punishment,' Krystal ordered succinctly, sauntering over to select a riding crop from a hook on the wooden wall. 'Get her across that bale.'

Beetle simply tugged at the net, causing the writhing nude to topple and sprawl, breasts down, over the broad bale.

Krystal swished the crop down. Its slicing thrum sounded eerily menacing above the gagged groans. Krystal tapped the swell of the proffered buttocks. 'Pin her firmly.'

Beetle pounced, rendering the blackmailer completely helpless by straddling and squatting on her.

'I am going to whip you,' Krystal announced sternly, worrying the naked cheeks with the little loop of leather curling from the tip of the crop. 'The first dozen or so you have already earned. Those strokes must and will be administered. Understand?'

Henrietta redoubled her struggles to escape. A swift, cruel slice with the crop stilled her. She cursed through her gag.

'I will give you a chance to speak, eventually. If and when you decide to reveal the whereabouts of the copies you have made, then and only then will your suffering...' the crop swished '...cease.'

Bucking and writhing as her bare bottom crimsoned, Henrietta snarled through her gag.

Crack! Crack! The whippy crop spoke twice, the harsh strokes lashing down in quick succession, slicing across the bunched cheeks below. Henrietta's squeal was silenced by the gag. She wriggled and writhed, but Beetle's pinioning thighs held firm. Jerking her wide hips in response to the cutting lash, Henrietta's splayed labia crushed into the bale, forcing the flesh-lips into its teasing prickle. *Crack! Crack! Crack!* The whipped blackmailer grunted into her tight gag. At her back, her fingers spasmed above the leather-bound wrists, signalling her anguish. Again, the jerking hips forced the unprotected pussy into the golden stubble, raking the wet flesh with tongues of flame. *Crack! Crack! Crack!* Krystal whipped the crop down, savagely reddening the swollen cheeks with weals of crimson.

Beneath the unyielding weight of Beetle's dominating buttocks, the netted nude crushed her breasts in to the stubble - ravishing her nipples ruthlessly. *Crack! Crack! Crack!* The triple echo of the withering crop snapping down across the proffered bottom sang out harshly, to be instantly drowned by the groans of suffering from the sensual mouth behind the gag. Rasping her nipples into the sharp straw, the wretched blackmailer squirmed and jerked as her buttocks danced under the whip again, hammering her pubis into the stubble and subjecting her sensitive wet flesh to exquisite torments. *Crack! Crack!* The hungry crop bit into the netted globes, the leather-sheathed cane bequeathing two more angry red lines across the swollen curves of the meshed cheeks.

Powerful headlights fingered the darkness outside, blinding for a split-second the tackle room window with their sudden dazzle. Crop poised to slice down again, Krystal registered the sounds of the Range Rover lurching to a stop, a door being slammed in temper, feet crunching gravel as they hurried towards the tackle room.

The door burst open. 'Henrietta, you bitch—'

Crack! Max froze wide-eyed in the doorway as she saw the crop swish down to slice the jerking buttocks. *Crack!* Another swiftly followed, licking the scorched cheeks with a tongue of fire.

'What the hell—' Max gasped.

'I'm afraid I've got some distressing news for you,' Krystal broke in, shouldering her crop and treading her foot dominantly onto the buttocks she had just blistered. In a calm voice, she described Henrietta's blackmailing intentions. Max sat pale-faced on the cold flagstone floor.

'This is both her punishment *and* a persuader.'

'Persuader?' Max echoed bleakly.

'She's kept copies. She'd planned to twist the screw a little tighter next month. Then again, and again. I want those copies.'

'And you shall have them,' Max murmured decisively.

'What brought you back?' Beetle asked, puzzled at the sudden return.

Max remained silent for a few moments. 'I may as well tell you,' she shrugged. 'I had to leave, I was so embarrassed. Two trainers said they'd paid her, in cash, last month—' Max pointed angrily at the striped buttocks bending across the bale '—and a feed merchant said he hadn't received the money I'd given her to pay him. I've been cleaned out.' She broke down, sobbing. 'Every last penny.'

'She demanded four thousand for Chloe's letters. The cash is probably in the shortbread tin in the kitchen. I'm so sorry, Max.'

Max stood up, peeling off her jacket and rolling up the sleeves of her lemon jumper. 'Give me that,' she whispered, holding her hand out for the crop.

'Don't get involved,' Krystal suggested. 'I'll deal with her. All I want are the copies for Chloe.'

'I'll get them for you,' Max promised, snatching the crop and grasping it tightly.

Waving Beetle and Krystal away, Max straddled the redhead, riding the whipped buttocks with her tight jodhpurs. Stretching down, she loosened the gag. A torrent of vile abuse poured from Henrietta's distorted lips.

Swish! The crop lashed the bare bottom, eliciting a shrill scream from the whipped nude.

'Silence, you bitch,' Max almost whispered. 'You poisoned Chloe's mind against me, didn't you? I see it all now. Then you sucked me in, but only for my money. Well, that's all gone and, when I've finished with you here tonight, I'm going too. Where are the copies?'

Henrietta, cursing, denied the existence of any copies. Max stood up.

'Help me with her,' she commanded, taking total control. 'I want her out of the net and up on that hook,' she said, pointing up with the tip of the quivering crop to a hook protruding from a thick rafter.

The rough mesh of knotted ropes rasped the punished buttocks as three pairs of hands unwound the net from the bound nude, Beetle knelt down and, pressing her face into the nude's belly, encircled her arms around the whipped cheeks. Hugging the captive fiercely, she awaited the command to lift.

'Wait,' Max ordered, standing directly behind Henrietta. 'I must make her tell us where the copies are.'

Beetle glanced up at the bare bosom. At each nipple a cruel pincer of Max's finger and thumb tweaked and tugged at the punished flesh.

'Where are they?' Max demanded.

Beetle felt the spasms of response rippling against her face as she hugged the squealing blackmailer.

'Well?' thundered Max, ravishing the nipples ruthlessly.

Beetle gasped as Henrietta's hips jerked, forcing her wet slit into Beetle's face.

'Stop—' the redhead screeched, quivering in torment. Sullenly, she blurted out her hiding place.

'Replace the gag and hang her from that hook,' Max instructed, before dashing out into the darkness.

When she returned, bearing bundles of banknotes and paper, Henrietta was suspended from the rafters, her naked body twisting slowly.

'Give these to Chloe,' Max panted, breathless from running. She handed the bundles to Krystal.

'What will you do?' Krystal asked, clearly concerned.

'I'll use this,' Max replied, misunderstanding the question. She took down a driving whip from the wall, snapping it harshly against the flagstone floor. The *hiss-crack* of the whipcord caused the suspended buttocks to clench.

'I mean after you have punished her?'

Max stood next to the nude, her face an inch from the bare bottom. At the height of Max's knees, Henrietta's pink heels wriggled as her feet trod the empty air. Carefully, methodically, with the driving whip clamped between her thighs, Max bound the heels together with a length of twine. 'Will you two wait for me in the Range Rover? I'm leaving tonight. As soon as I've finished here.'

Krystal and Beetle departed in silence. Sitting in the warmth of the Range Rover, Krystal in front, Beetle on the back seat, they heard the first whiplash crack-snapping in the tackle room.

'Seven-thirty,' Beetle whispered thickly, rubbing her cheek where Henrietta's sticky slit had kissed it.

From the tackle room came the sound of a second stroke being administered. The silence in the Range Rover grew loud. Closing her eyes tightly as she wriggled down her slacks and panties, Beetle conjured up the images etched in red, grey and white on the living-room wall: Lesbos and her love slaves. The snarl of the whip broke the silence of the night for a third time, and Beetle shuddered as her thumb tip found her clitoris. In her mind's eye, the rounded buttocks in the prints were replaced by the image of Henrietta's bare cheeks. *Crack!* The oiled whipcord lashed out once more. Beetle's thumb worked down between her hot parted thighs. She saw, in delicious motion, Max's bosom heaving as the whip hand was raised. The flicker of the lash jagging out to kiss and stripe the naked cheeks, the suspended nude twisting and writhing as her body jerked in torment. The heavy cheeks, each buttock crimsoned, bore a fresh strip of scarlet.

Orgasming frenziedly, Beetle ground her soft buttocks into the supple leather seat. Arching back her head, eyes shut and lips parted wide, she rode the soft hide as paroxysms convulsed her body with renewed fury. Her climax spilled into a second and then a third orgasm, each implosion fuelled by yet another searing slice of the whip.

'Eight-fifteen,' Max grunted, slamming the door.

Beetle, who had been dozing, sat up and furtively pulled up her panties, relishing the crisp cotton at her hot stickiness.

'I'll get you two to the station for nine.'

They sped through the country lanes in a silence broken only by the distinctive hum of the powerful engine. As they approached the orange sodium lights of Worcester, Krystal unpocketed the love letters and banknotes, placing the bundles down between the front seats.

'Where will you go?' she asked softly.

Max shrugged, blinking tears from her eyes.

Krystal placed her hand gently on the hand gripping the steering wheel. 'Why not take the letters back to Chloe yourself?'

'Stay in the bedroom until I say you can come out.'

Beetle's muffled voice protested that she would be late for her workout.

'And keep your eyes closed,' Krystal warned, ignoring the minx's impatience.

'It isn't my birthday,' came the speculative voice.

'Not exactly,' Krystal grunted, struggling with plastic wrapping. 'Get undressed,' she ordered. 'I need you naked.'

Beetle squeaked with delight as she struggled with her tracksuit.

Winning her battle with the plastic wrapping, Krystal stood back and perused the gleaming exercise bike.

'Eyes closed?'

'Yes,' Beetle giggled.

'I'm ready for you now.'

'Coming,' thrilled the minx.

'You will be,' Krystal whispered, palming the leather saddle. 'You will be.'

Beetle made a meal of entering the room, eyes closed. She managed to bump into two chairs and the sofa before her firm thighs brushed against the cold steel frame of the bike. 'Ooh,' she cried. 'For me?'

'For you,' Krystal nodded. 'Now you won't have to go to Fit As A Fiddle. I'll keep you in shape in future. Up.'

Beetle, naked, straddled the bike, snuggling her buttocks around the soft saddle. Tentatively stretching her pointed toes down for the rubber pedals, she gripped the handle bars. As she slowly pedalled, her bosom rose and fell rhythmically.

'This,' Krystal explained, tapping the digital display, 'tells you both your speed and the distance travelled.'

'Thank you,' the minx gushed. 'It's beautiful.'

'Try for five kilometres at twenty-five kph.' Krystal invited.

'Gotcha,' Beetle nodded, biting her lower lip in exaggerated effort before powering her sleek thighs. The green digits danced as she pedalled, clocking up the kilometres.

'Faster,' Krystal purred, skimming her fingertips down over the curve of the dimpled spine, then splaying her fingers out to caress and squeeze the bulging buttocks below. 'Show me exactly what you can get up to in the name of exercise.'

'Up to?' the guilty voice of the minx echoed nervously.

'Thirty? Or just what is your limit, I wonder?'

'Ah,' Beetle gasped, relieved. Shrugging off the fleeting threat as her own guilty anxiety, she concentrated on the figures in the digital display. 'Look,' she squealed, 'I'm doing thirty-two kph. I bet I get up to more than you supposed.'

Krystal eyed the rippling buttocks hungrily but made no comment. 'Just keep pedalling.'

She withdrew, emerging from her studio with an armful of extras. 'No,' she warned, 'don't turn round.'

Beetle whimpered impatiently. 'I want to see.'

'You will, soon enough. Just a few little improvements I'd like to try out.'

'Finished,' the minx gasped, steadying the pedals with whitened toes and easing herself back on the saddle. Between her loose breasts perspiration glistened.

'Bottom up, please,' Krystal ordered, tapping the bulging cheeks imperiously.

Thrilling to the dominant touch, Beetle eased her buttocks up.

'I've a saddle here I think might improve your performance.'

Inching up her globes of creamy flesh, Beetle stood on her pedals. Krystal twisted the saddle sharply and removed it, fingering the sticky warmth where Beetle's slit had kissed the leather so passionately.

'You take such an interest in me,' Beetle sighed. 'I'm so lucky.'

Krystal bent and picked up the replacement - a thin racing model. She slotted and screwed the saddle into the frame securely, tightening it with a tiny silver spanner. 'Wait,' she whispered, as the hovering buttocks dipped. She anointed the devilishly moulded four-inch anal plug rising up out of the narrow strip of leather with clear lubricant jelly.

'Can I sit now?' Beetle moaned plaintively, her rigid arms quivering under the strain of supporting her weight.

'One moment, please. I want this exactly right,' Krystal murmured, bending down once more to scoop up the riding crop she'd taken from Max's tackle room as a souvenir. 'Exactly right.'

Beetle waggled her rump and squealed impatiently.

'Down,' came the crisp command. Standing directly behind Beetle, her nipples just grazing the bare back in front of her Krystal tapped the bottom with the crop.

Beetle tensed, thighs rippling with a frisson of fear, at both the stern note of authority and the touch of the crop on her cheeks. Hearing the strict edge to the blonde's voice, she clenched her buttocks and lowered them slowly. As the tip of the anal plug nuzzled her sphincter, she wriggled and squealed.

Pacing around so that she could worry Beetle's nipples with the cruel crop, Krystal crushed the leather-sheathed cane against the bosom's heavy swell.

'I said, down,' she snarled, her grip on the leather tightening as the trapped breasts bulged.

Spreading her cheeks painfully to cover - and enclose - the rubber plug, Beetle gasped aloud as she straddled the saddle, and gasped again as the lubricated shaft entered her anal whorl.

Crack! The crop whipped across the bunched cheeks. Beetle screamed softly.

'Ride,' Krystal thundered, tracing the smooth flesh of Beetle's thigh with the loop of leather at the tip of the crop. *Crack!* A second thin line of crimson fire scored the creamy buttocks. 'I think you will find that I can provide all the exercise that's good for you.'

Beetle pedalled sullenly, pushing up the stuttering speedo.

'Faster,' ordered the blonde. Breasts bouncing, the naked brunette obeyed. 'I want you up at thirty, minimum.'

Beetle groaned.

Swish, crack! The crop kissed the bare bottom savagely.

'Ride.

'Krystal—' Beetle wailed.

Swish, crack! Again, the unerring stroke crimsoned the defenceless cheeks with a fourth weal.

Tearfully, Beetle bowed down into her task, pedalling furiously as her whitened knuckles gripped the handle bars.

'I have it on excellent authority that this treatment will keep you in trim,' Krystal whispered silkily. 'It comes highly recommended, from Minsk.'

'Krystal, I'm so sorry, so very—'

'Ride,' urged the blonde, raising the crop once more over the bulging buttocks. 'Ride.'

Chapter Eight

The March sunshine had London bustling before lunchtime. On the broad, brown Thames, gulls mobbed the tourists cruising up to Tower Bridge. On the busy roads, taxi drivers risked pastel sports shirts.

Beetle, frolicking as she haphazardly spring-cleaned, danced naked to the Rolling Stones. Bending to polish the TV screen, she saw the window cleaners' cradle rise up and come to rest outside their living-room window. 'Brown Sugar' belted out, with Jagger at his most priapic. Glimpsing the expressions of the two window cleaners change from surprise to a wide-eyed appreciation of her bare bottom, she waggled it at them and launched into a raunchy dance. Sliding her palms from her throat to her breasts, she cupped and tenderly squeezed their warm weight, spinning round briefly to offer them to the window. Twisting round again, she splayed her quivering legs wide until her buckling knees brought her dark snatch down against the TV screen. Grinding her buttocks rhythmically, she arched her head back, cascading her hair down her back, and pantomimed an orgasm. Clutching her hair in assumed ecstasy, she jerked her bottom out, spasming her cheeks as she feigned a climax.

Out on the dangerously swaying cradle, with pumping hands fisting their erections, the two guys roared their approval, the foaming squeegees abandoned in their buckets.

Beetle suppressed her grin. She had them hooked, and was now about to exploit them fully - as a cat will torment its captive mouse. Rolling the can of polish across her breasts, crushing her nipples brutally, she dragged the cylinder down over her belly and clamped it between her thighs. Turning full-frontal to the watching faces, Beetle kept up the pretence of ignoring their presence. Fingering the can, she twisted it, rotating its hard length between her wet labia. The guys fisted themselves furiously, their faces screwed up in exquisite agony. Throwing aside the can, Beetle suddenly knelt, then rolled head-over-heels towards the window, snatching at an abandoned black stocking en route. Coming to rest on her back, her long legs raised and splayed, she offered her bare bottom to the watchers' wide-eyed adoration. Biting into one end of the sinuous black stocking, she stretched its shining length between her breasts and down to her wet slit. Grasping it and guiding it against her pink clitoris, she jerked her head back, dragging the stocking against her flesh.

She closed her eyes, ignoring the dull thud of fists at the window. With a clenched hand behind her hot buttocks gripping one end of the stocking, her teeth clamped around the toe-end of its sleek stretch, she succumbed to a real orgasm. Relishing her sense of power over the appreciative onlookers, she squirmed and wriggled in a frenzied climax. Fuelled by the illicit thrill of exhibitionism, her paroxysms were powerful: pounding the carpet with her free hand and her clenched buttocks, Beetle came furiously. A second climax followed almost immediately. The carpet under Beetle's wet slit sparkled with her juices. She clamped her thighs together hugging the delight of teasing and taunting the helpless faces at the window. Wallowing in her orgasm, she luxuriated in the forbidden delights of erotic dominion. Through slyly parted eyes, she saw the first window cleaner shudder at the thighs, his clenched fist a blur as it skimmed his throbbing shaft. Then he went rigid as, eyes squeezed shut, he pumped a thin stream of silver into the window. Beetle giggled deliciously and ravished herself once more, this time collapsing in a writhing frenzy, her shrieks of carnal delight torn from snarling lips. Panting, she rolled over, crushing her painfully peaked nipples into the carpet. In the reflection of the TV screen, she saw the mouth of the second window cleaner open wide to groan silently as he spurted his hot sticky chorus of approval.

Beetle rose, smoothly palmed her breasts and belly before dabbling her fingertips in her glistening pubic nest. Treading the carpet with measured steps, she became skittish once more and danced. The Stones were still rocking, the throbbing bass became the pulse at her throat. Avoiding eye contact with her passionate admirers beyond the glass, she bowed. Grinning, they broke into rapturous silent applause, their clapping hands coming together soundlessly high up in the sky above Wapping. Like a diva, coolly indifferent to her devotees, Beetle stepped up to the window and pressed her nipples into the cold glass the outside of which bore the tell-tale smears of liquid applause.

Her breasts and stomach pressed against the cold glass, naked to their searching gaze, Beetle once more felt the forbidden thrill of her intoxicating triumph. She dragged her sticky labia against the glass as though against their upturned faces - almost rocketing herself into another climax. Through the half-inch thickness of icy glass, an intimate distance fixed between the watchers and the watched, she saw the lust for her nakedness burning in their hot eyes. Exultant, she drew her hands together above her head, entwining her slender fingers deliciously. Turning slowly, tantalizingly, she waggled her bottom at them with pert insolence, simultaneously inviting and dismissing their adoration, and walked back into the centre of the room. Ignoring their pummelled request for her to return - for an orgasmic encore - she stooped, offering her wet plum and bulging buttocks to their feasting eyes. She picked up the remote control, aimed it casually over her naked shoulder, and pressed the yellow button. Silently, the pink curtains swished together, bringing her scandalous exhibitionism to an abrupt end.

'Window cleaners come?' asked Krystal.

Beetle snorted into her mug of lemon tea. Wiping her wet chin and mouth with the back of her hand, she struggled to nod soberly. 'Yep.'

'Not very thorough, were they?' Krystal frowned, approaching the expanse of glass and stooping to peer at the smears of semen. 'See?'

'Pigeons?' Beetle suggested brightly, despite the hammering of her heart in case her shrewd partner should start digging too deeply into her earlier escapade.

'Some little bird caused it,' Krystal replied softly, tracing the outline of each stain with a stern gesture. Her narrowing eyes turned their suspicious gaze from the glass to Beetle's pious face.

The minx flushed as she polished ever more industriously at a bookcase.

The traffic crossing Battersea Bridge had slowed to a sluggish trickle. Sitting behind the wheel of her gleaming new Freelander, Krystal sighed impatiently.

'You know I need the boot space now that I'm branching out into bronze. It's no joke getting onto a bus with a sixty-pound cast under your arm.'

Beetle, more vain than practical, had wanted something sporty. Something like the red MG two-seater Krystal had instantly vetoed. Gazing at the Volvo in front, she sulked in silence.

They crawled over Battersea Bridge and turned towards Pimlico. Beetle, fickle as the April sunshine, melted out of her sulk. 'Can't I have a go?'

'Perhaps,' Krystal murmured. 'Depends on your behaviour. You've been very naughty recently, I can't think why we get our windows cleaned three times a week. Can you?'

Beetle became suddenly engrossed in her role of dutiful navigator. 'Left and then left again,' she announced, burying her nose in the A-Z.

The back streets of Pimlico became narrower. Cats sat on battered Cortinas and children whizzed up and down on mountain bikes. They were friendly streets. They turned into the terrace of red-bricked houses.

'Number eighty-four,' Beetle counted. 'And there's a space.'

Peggy Lamb, Vanessa Wetherby's daily help, received them with cups of strong brown tea and a plate of assorted cakes.

'My niece is a good girl,' the elderly woman said firmly, dispelling any doubt on the matter.

Krystal saw the pink blotches of discomfort on Peggy's cheeks, and responded soothingly. 'Vanessa assured us of that. But there has been a little difficulty?'

'She's a music student. Plays the cello.' She showed them a photo of a thin blonde wrapping her thighs around the upright instrument. 'But the fees are so expensive.'

'She works part-time?' Krystal suggested.

Peggy nodded.

'Very sensible. As a nanny, I believe?'

'Yes,' the aunt smiled proudly. 'Her agency finds her occasional evening and week-end hours.'

'Is that how she met Billy Box?'

'The agency sent her. She said it was a bit peculiar, what with him in London all week rehearsing for that TV show of his, "On The Box", and his family down in Buckinghamshire all the time. They have a farm—'

'What happened?' Krystal pressed, stemming the garrulous flow.

Peggy offered the plate of small cakes. Krystal declined politely. Beetle wolfed two.

'My niece *is* a good girl,' Peggy pronounced again, causing Beetle to giggle into her cake.

Krystal maintained a patient silence.

'They were alone in his big mansion. He made suggestions. Advances. You know,' Peggy dropped her voice to a whisper. 'She wouldn't have any of it, got up to leave. But he stopped her at the door, accusing her of stealing something. A gold cigarette lighter. Said he'd get the police. She was frightened, what with him being famous and everything.'

'And?'

'My niece *is* a good girl,' Peggy said, a tear winking in her left eye. 'But you see, my dear, she was frightened...'

'And the name of the agency?' Krystal murmured, anxious to avoid causing the sweet old lady any further distress.

'Why can't I drive?' Beetle, pert in her pink-and-white nanny's uniform, protested. 'You said—'

'I know what I said,' Krystal retorted, turning off the Old Brompton Road. 'When you can explain to me the sudden popularity of our windows, then I'll let you drive.'

Beetle squirmed her bottom in the soft leather seat. 'Remember the drill?'

'Yep. One freelance nanny, from the Safe Pair Of Hands agency.'

Krystal guided the Freelander under the cherry-blossom trees lining the exclusive South Kensington cul-de-sac. 'In you go.'

Billy Box looked surprised - then delighted - to discover the candy-pink-striped minx on his doorstep.

'Must be my mistake,' Beetle apologized, three minutes later. 'I'm sure the girl at the Safe Pair Of Hands agency gave me this address.'

Running his hand through his flowing golden mane, Billy Box opened the door wider, his tone enthusiastic. Inviting Beetle in, he assured her that there could very well be a position for her.

Inside the grand drawing room - tastelessly but expensively upholstered in black mohair and gold - Beetle was given a huge brandy alexandrine. No mention of duties required, references sought or rates of pay were made. Tossing his luxuriant mane, Billy Box boasted of his phenomenal success. Soon, the brash TV celebrity was, as Peggy had warned, making suggestions. In lurid detail, he sketched out some positions he hoped Beetle might assume.

Putting-down her untouched drink, Beetle shook her head firmly and rose to go.

'Pity,' he shrugged, flashing the insincere smile adored by millions.

Beetle raised an eyebrow, sensing that something in the remark and the tone in which it was said made it more than a hackneyed compliment.

He caught her expression. 'Pity about you being a little thief.'

She froze.

'I'll have to call the police, I suppose. I saw you take it,' he said distinctly, holding up a gold watch.

Beetle protested hotly.

'Shut up, silly bitch. I know and you know you didn't. But who do you think the police will believe. Pity,' he said softly, 'you wouldn't let me get you into a good position.'

Beetle slumped back down onto the squashy leather sofa. 'That's better, petal. Just you finish your nice drink and then show Billy Box what you've got hidden under that nice nanny's uniform.'

Beetle gulped down the brandy alexandrine.

'Up you get, petal. Strip. Slowly,' he commanded, checking Beetle's trembling fingers at her cuffs, 'we've got lots of time. No, turn around. Full-frontal.'

Beetle slowly unbuttoned each starched white cuff, tossing them down. Billy Box scooped them up, undid his ornate dressing gown and threaded them onto his exposed erection. Fingering the inverted watch at her left breast, Beetle plucked it off, then slid her hand inside the pink striped nanny's uniform to palm and squeeze her bosom.

'That's it, petal. Get hot.'

Planting her stockinged legs wide apart, Beetle undid each tiny button, from the broad belt at her waist up to her throat, then wriggled down the tight bodice of the uniform dress over her shoulders, revealing her bosom. She jiggled vigorously, causing her breasts to wobble as they bulged in their brassiered bondage.

'Yes,' Billy Box snarled thickly, the white cuffs dancing on his throbbing shaft. 'Yes.'

The door-bell rang imperiously.

'Shit!' Jabbing a quivering forefinger at Beetle's swelling breasts, he ordered her to freeze. 'Back in a minute,' he grunted.

He returned, silent and sombre, with Krystal.

'Know your way around a studio floor, don't you, Billy?'

Krystal asked politely.

He scowled.

'Floor manager for a spell, weren't you?'

He trousered his hands beneath the dressing gown sullenly.

'Then this,' Krystal continued, easing the nanny's uniform down to Beetle's belly-button and cupping the Wonderbra gently, 'should come as no surprise.'

Krystal unclasped the white bra that hugged and bunched the ripe breasts within. Billy Box's eyes stared wildly as Beetle's breasts were bared.

'Underwired,' Krystal whispered, fingering the warm cups, 'for sound.' Offering him a glimpse of the empty brassiere cup, she pointed to the tiny silver transmitter.

'A body mike. You bitches—'

'Silence!' Krystal commanded. Fishing out a mini-receiver, she held it up and softly pressed the playback.

Billy Box's voice filled the room, damning him with every taped utterance. He sat down, golden mane in his hands, as his words came back to haunt him. Beetle filled the empty cups of her bra with her warm breasts, snapping the straps across her shoulders. Seconds later, she had buttoned the crisp uniform up to her throat.

'Kneel,' Krystal thundered.

He looked up, startled, then laughed contemptuously.

'I'm afraid I'll have to get the police,' Krystal continued. 'Think of the scandal, the publicity. Box Productions would start to slip in the ratings even before the court case—'

He knelt.

'Got a bit of a thing about nanny's, haven't you, Billy? Time you were taught a lesson. Tonight, I will be your governess. A very strict governess. Nanny here will assist. Strip.'

He fumbled reluctantly at his dressing-gown cord. Krystal strode across to the telephone. Turning her back to him, she picked up the receiver and dialled, calling out the number of Box Productions as her finger tapped each button.

'Don't,' he begged, his hands scrabbling and pulling off his clothes.

'That's better,' Krystal purred, her back still turned. 'Obey your governess and your nanny, and you won't suffer.' She paused. 'No more than you deserve to, anyway.'

His muffled whimper of alarm was drowned by the gold velour sweatshirt smothering his face.

'You will address me as Miss and nanny as Nanny while we deal with you,' Krystal instructed, every inch the stern governess. *Deal with me?* Billy voiced the unspoken question with widening eyes.

'Teach you to respect Nanny from henceforth, and punish you for the disrespect you have shown. I have been in touch with the agency,' she continued suavely, 'and find that there are at least seven instances of gross misconduct on your part.'

Naked and kneeling, he submitted in silence to having his hands bound tightly above his buttocks. He struggled slightly, eyes bulging, as they gagged him with one of Krystal's bronze nylon stockings.

'Word is that Billy Box has a bit of a thing about nannies,' Beetle remarked, kicking off her shoes and inserting the toes of one black-stockinged foot beneath his balls.

He clamped his thighs together, trapping her foot.

'How dare you?' Krystal thundered. 'How dare you oppose Nanny? Open your legs at once.'

Wide-eyed with surprise and fear, the kneeling man obeyed. Krystal immediately strode behind him, placed her foot on his neck and forced the helpless TV star face-down into his black and gold carpet.

'Nanny is very cross with you. She is going to be very strict with you. Very strict indeed. You have been naughty and so you must - and will - be punished.'

'Up,' Beetle ordered.

He remained kneeling, averting his face from the minx's dominant gaze.

Beetle joined Krystal behind him. *Spank! Spank! Spank!* Bending, Beetle delivered three severe swipes, her firm palm scalding his defenceless cheeks. He grunted softly, his buttocks reddening from the smarting punishment.

'Nanny told you to get up,' Krystal remarked. 'Up,' she snapped. 'And obey Nanny instantly. Understand?'

He nodded, avoiding her searching gaze. Staggering to his feet, he allowed himself to be frogmarched between Krystal and Beetle up the stairs and into the ornate bathroom.

'Nanny, I think little Billy needs a nice cooling shower. He got a little overexcited earlier on,' Krystal remarked, twisting the cold tap on full.

Beetle grinned. Taking a bound arm each, they propelled him into the freezing sluice. He gasped, his anguish audible despite the stocking gagging his mouth.

Threshing like a penned bull, Billy Box tried to shoulder his escape from the icy fingers raking his vulnerable flesh. They pinned him to the peacock-blue tiles - Beetle pressing a toilet brush into his balls, Krystal opting for a slightly more decorous loofah pinned at his chest.

'Four minutes,' Krystal said. 'Nanny wants you to stay there for four minutes until you have cooled down a bit.'

Beetle, primly consulting the inverted watch at her breast pocket, counted out each half-minute in plummy, nannying tones as their victim writhed.

'Four minutes,' Beetle confirmed, slowly twisting the cruel bristles at his balls.

'And nanny will have no hesitation in putting you straight back under the nasty shower if you are a naughty boy again,' Krystal whispered, unwinding the soaking stocking from his lips. 'Understand?'

'Yes, Miss,' he whimpered, his wet mane curtaining his eyes in a yellow slick. Rising to his feet, he slipped, slumped down and groaned.

'Now, I think, a proper wash before Nanny spanks you and gives you your supper. What do you think, Nanny?'

'An excellent idea,' Beetle enthused. 'Up,' she instructed, tousling his dripping mane. 'And I think we'll have a hair cut. Nanny likes her little man to be neat and tidy.'

He staggered to his feet. 'You wouldn't bloody dare—' he blustered angrily, forgetting his fear in a sudden rush of vanity.

Krystal quickly applied a block of soap to his mouth, forcing it between his teeth. Gagged, he spluttered helplessly.

'How dare you speak to Nanny like that. My goodness, little man, how your poor bottom is going to suffer.'

They pushed him across to the hand basin.

'A washed bottom before punishment,' Beetle said brightly, generously soaping a nail-brush until the fierce little bristles foamed. 'Bend over legs apart.'

Choking on the gag of soap, he remained stubborn, defying her instruction.

'I'll hold him,' Krystal intervened. Reaching down, her firm hand clasped his flaccid penis and pulled him to the sink.

Deftly palming a face-flannel, she wrapped it around the drooping shaft and eased it over the rim of the cold porcelain basin. He rose up on his toes in response. Krystal squeezed the flannel. Billy Box's legs parted and he bent, offering up his buttocks.

'That's a sensible little chap,' Beetle said approvingly, rasping the soaped nail-brush between his cheeks and raking the exposed cleft ruthlessly.

'Give Nanny your bottom,' Krystal instructed, squeezing the thickening flesh.

He bent lower, spreading his feet wide apart, surrendering his sensitive flesh to the skimming nail-brush.

'Nanny insists on having a freshly scrubbed bottom to spank,' Beetle hissed, savaging the cleft mercilessly.

He screamed softly through the gag, and, lurching forwards, pressed his face into the mirror above the sink.

Krystal gripped the flannel tightly, squeezing the erection within it, and pumped slowly, deliberately. Suddenly, he staggered and slumped. Krystal grabbed and steadied him, taloning his wet golden hair. Forcing his perspiring face back against the cold glass above the sink, she noticed the thick veins at his pulsing temples. She pumped fiercely as Beetle rasped the cleft between his splayed buttocks with the nail-brush. Stiffening, his tense body suddenly buckled, his whitened toes grinding into the cork mat. He groaned. Rolling his forehead into the mirror, he shuddered and ejaculated into the flannel.

'Kneel,' Krystal thundered.

Exhausted, he slumped down on his knees.

Fingering the flannel disdainfully, Krystal opened it up across her upturned palm. She levelled it before his eyes. 'Just look at what you've done, you naughty little boy. Nasty, sticky mess. I'm afraid Nanny is going to have to be very firm with you.'

Pinning him belly-down across the toilet seat, she offered his bare buttocks to Beetle, who spanked him long and hard. Renewing his violent struggles, he almost escaped her sweeping palm.

'Mount him,' Krystal advised tersely. 'He must be made to learn that Nanny is the boss.'

Beetle hitched her uniform skirt up to her thighs and plumped her soft buttocks - and moist pubis - down onto his back. His writhing fingers scrabbled at her cotton sheathed labia. She prised them away firmly. 'Naughty,' she whispered sternly. 'Mustn't touch Nanny there.'

The rain of pain commenced. Straddling and riding him, she punished his bottom severely. *Spank! Spank! Spank!* From her new position of supreme dominance, she reddened every inch of his clenched buttocks.

'Supper time,' Krystal remarked, helping Beetle to dismount. 'Up.'

He rose drunkenly.

'On all fours.'

He obeyed, shivering with fear at the sight of the hairbrush in Beetle's hand.

Crack! Crack! Crack! The hairbrush spoke harshly, echoing loudly in the tiled bathroom.

'Downstairs to the kitchen on your hands and knees, you wicked little boy,' Beetle instructed, directing him with the bristle side of the brush against his scalded cheeks.

Krystal stayed his progress, jabbing her foot down onto the nape of his neck. 'Wait.'

His knees shuffled to a clumsy halt. At his hot bottom, the fingers of his bound hands flexed anxiously. Krystal removed the gag.

Under the fierce glare of the neon light in the hi-tech kitchen, Beetle emptied two cartons of yoghurt into a cereal bowl and picked up a teaspoon.

'Nanny is going to feed you,' Krystal announced, guiding his reddened buttocks down onto the seat of a hard wooden chair.

'Mmmm, nice yoghurt,' Beetle purred, sitting down on the table in front of him, her skirt riding high up her thighs. 'No looking up nanny's skirt, mind,' she warned archly as she parted her knees wide.

He closed his eyes, opened them in confusion then hastily averted his gaze.

'Look at me when I'm talking to you,' Beetle said crisply. He returned her gaze.

'How dare you peep up Nanny's skirt. I'm going to have to cane your bare bottom after supper, do you hear?'

He twisted his face away in alarm. Krystal caught him by the ear, dragging his head around to face the table and the thighs splayed wide upon it. 'And then I'm going to cane your bare bottom for being so rude. Rude little boy. Look at Miss when she's speaking to you.'

He writhed, helpless between their pitiless domination.

'Every naughty little boy wants to peek at Nanny's pussy,' Beetle whispered, fingering her labia through the cotton panties. 'But those who do - and are caught, like you - have to be especially punished.'

Slipping off the table, casually brushing his erection with her thigh, she sauntered across to the cupboard. Returning, she opened the Worcester sauce and the mustard she had secured, adding them to the pineapple yoghurt. Back up on the table, directly in front of her captive, she stirred the vile mixture with the feeding spoon.

'Special punishment,' she whispered. 'Open wide.'

Krystal nodded her approval. Dropping down on one knee beside his chair, she slipped her hand, palm upturned, between the seat of the chair and his soft, exposed flesh. Cupping his balls, she squeezed.

'Open wide for Nanny,' she insisted.

'That's better,' Beetle announced, spooning the dreadful mixture into his mouth. 'Swallow it all down. We don't want you playing your hamster tricks and spitting it out later, do we?'

Krystal squeezed hard. Billy Box swallowed harder.

Every time his lips met the spoon in a tight line of resistance, Krystal punished his balls. Soon, he had been forced to take every disgusting spoonful. Beetle wiped his lower lip with the spoon - a devilish touch of nanny-supremacy.

'Still hungry? Does my little chap want some more? I think he does. You are a growing boy, aren't you,' Nanny mocked, tapping the tip of his quivering erection.

Behind the wooden struts of his chair, his bound wrists writhed, the fingers twisted in frustrated rage. Krystal noted the temper tantrum and sank her fingers into his golden mane. Controlling him utterly, she dragged his head back, presenting his upturned face to Beetle.

The minx had slipped her uniform dress down over her right shoulder. Unburdening her bosom from its deep cup, she palmed one breast, gently weighing its soft warmth. Guiding her nipple down to his mouth she traced his lips using the stiffened pink peak as a lipstick.

'Suck,' she barked. 'Suck Nanny.'

Sucking tentatively at first, soon his eyes were bulging as he took the nipple - and most of the swollen breast - into his mouth.

'Harder,' Beetle hissed. 'Nanny is going to feed you.'

Between his thighs, his throbbing erection twitched.

'Harder,' Beetle commanded, burying her bosom into his face.

Dominated by her soft warmth, he drowned slowly, groaning as he spurted his hot liquid release onto the front of her uniform.

They had no cane, so they used a wooden spoon across his bottom, giving him the punishment they had promised - plus an extra sharp dozen for spoiling Beetle's prettily pink striped dress.

Back on the lurid carpet of woven black and gold, he lay curled up asleep, still bound and gagged. An hour passed, during which they drank Krug and cut off all of his hair. He awoke to the buzz of his own electric razor rendering him completely bald.

'No tears. Be a big brave boy for Nanny,' Beetle warned, grasping his ears as Krystal plied the skimming blades.

Sobbing with shock and rage, the golden boy of prime-time sludge buried his face in the carpet.

Crack! Crack! The leather belt bit into his proffered cheeks, his fingers splayed in a paroxysm of pain. Spinning over onto his back he glared up at them, mouthing obscenities through his gag.

'Perfect,' Krystal whispered, drawing the buzzing razor down to his pubic curls. 'Try explaining this to Mrs Box.'

He froze, impotent and helpless, as she shaved him intimately. The nuzzling shaver excited and terrified him. Before she had removed the last wisp of blonde pubic fuzz, his organ was thick and rampant.

'Look, Nanny, our little man is excited again,' Krystal murmured, switching off the razor, and gently teasing it down the muscled shaft. 'I wonder why? Is he dreaming of Nanny, hmm? Naughty thoughts of Nanny's nice starched uniform?'

His erection quivered under her fingertips.

'Of Nanny, in her private room, getting undressed. Is he troubled by naughty dreams of Nanny, nearly naked, pulling down her stockings? Peeling down her panties? Hmm? I wouldn't be at all surprised,' Krystal said almost conversationally to Beetle - utterly ignoring the nude man in her thrall, 'if this naughty little fellow didn't peep through cracks in doors.'

'Do you like to peep at Nanny? Catch her breasts in the looking glass as she bends to powder her bottom after a bath?'

Pulsing painfully, the erection nodded his guilt.

'I think we had better take steps, painful steps, to cure our little chap of this little peccadillo once and for all.'

Wrapping the leather belt around her fingers three times, she stood up, dangling the limp lash, deliberately allowing the leather to tease the knout of his shaft. He writhed.

'So naughty, peeping at Nanny,' Krystal purred, pushing a footstool against his thighs and then treading him down over it. Belly-down across the red velvet, his buttocks rose up to kiss the dangling hide. Stooping, Krystal removed the gag.

'Do you peep at Nanny?' she inquired, fingering the leather.

He remained stubbornly silent.

'Answer the question,' Krystal urged, trailing the belt against his buttocks.

'Yes, Miss.'

'You may now apologise to Nanny.'

'Sorry, Nanny.'

'And to make sure it never happens again,' Krystal continued, treading him down firmly and pinning him across the red velvet, 'repeat after me.'

Beetle stood five feet away, unbuttoning her uniform.

'Nanny's uniform,' Krystal barked.

As Beetle loosened the last button and wriggled out of the striped pink-and-white dress, she heard his hoarse voice echo Krystal's words. *Crack!* The belt snapped witheringly across his bottom.

'Nanny's brassiere,' Krystal said crisply.

'Nanny's brassiere,' his dry lips croaked.

Crack! Beetle peeled off her white bra just as the leather spoke once more, its supple tongue harsh against the suffering cheeks.

'Nanny's panties.'

'Nanny's panties.'

Crack!

The painful catechism - and prompt responses - continued, punctuated only by soft rustlings from the near-naked Beetle and the fierce swipes of the cruel belt.

Nanny was now nude, except for one black stocking. Seamed and shining, it hugged the curves of her lithe leg, the darker band of the self-support biting into her creamy thigh.

'Nanny's stocking,' Krystal thundered.

'Nanny's stocking,' the whipped man echoed.

Crack! Yet another searing stroke added its mark across the crimson cheeks. Krystal lowered her arm, letting the limp leather dangle at her thigh.

'Kiss Nanny's stocking,' she instructed.

Beetle arched her stockinged foot, positioning the prinked, black nyloned toes at his lips on the red velvet stool.

'Kiss,' Krystal commanded, whipping the leather belt down viciously.

The stroke across his buttocks jerked him over the red velvet, driving his shaft into its softness. He screamed softly and pressed his lips submissively into the stocking's sheen.

'Lick,' Krystal insisted, swishing the leather down once more.

He obeyed, his tongue thick and sticky.

'Again,' came the command.

Beetle turned, dropped down onto all fours, and guided her rump into his face. He flinched, but Krystal's foot at the nape of his neck and the leather in her hand lashing down on his buttocks urged him on. Grunting thickly, he buried his face into the parted buttocks.

'Lick, little man,' Krystal hissed. 'Lick Nanny until the leather is silent.'

Crack! Crack! Crack! The first three strokes of the snapping leather belt - the first three of the severely administered extra dozen - were applied mercilessly. As the last slice exploded across his blazing cheeks, Billy Box groaned and rolled from the foot stool onto the floor. Krystal gazed down at the sticky patch of darkening wetness staining the red velvet - where her victim had, hips pumping and whipped cheeks clenched, just come explosively.

'Poor sore bottom,' she whispered. 'Nanny will make it better.'

Broken and spent, he merely groaned incoherently.

'Nanny will have to see to that immediately, won't she?'

'Ice cubes?' Beetle suggested.

'What a thoroughly sensible idea, Nanny,' Krystal smiled.

An hour later up in the master bedroom, a triumph of rococo vanity, he knelt bound and blindfolded before his full-length mirror.

'I'm sorry,' he whimpered. 'Very sorry—'

'We hear your apology but you see, little man,' Krystal interrupted, bending to tap his bottom with her slipper, 'I'm rather afraid it isn't good enough.'

'Please, Miss,' he whined. 'I want to—'

'In a moment, Nanny is going to take your blindfold off. Then, as you gaze into your own repentance, your bottom is going to be soundly slippered. If you come, splashing your naughty stickies onto the mirror, the consequences will be dreadful to contemplate. Too dreadful.'

Her stern words had the desired effect: his shaft quickened and rose. Sensing his own response, the bound victim quivered with apprehension.

'Too dreadful,' Krystal whispered, trapping his erection against his hard belly with the soft sole of the slipper. He groaned as she rubbed and rolled the imprisoned spear of flesh.

'To come when being punished by Nanny is forbidden. Nanny knows you want to go across her warm stockinged thighs and soak her nylons with your sticky wickedness as she spanks you. But it is forbidden.'

He buckled and shivered, grinding his belly - and his erection - into the slipper's rubbery torment. Digging his toes into the carpet, he seemed to be bracing himself for orgasm.

'Silly boy,' Krystal purred, unwinding the blindfold. 'For a brief moment you have regained your sovereignty over your bottom. It is purely your decision. Ejaculate, and you will suffer.'

His protests were drowned as Krystal applied the blindfold as a gag. Beetle's black stocking silenced his carnal groans. Signalling to Beetle, dressed once more in her pink striped uniform, she handed her the second slipper. The two accomplices knelt, squashing his bound nakedness between their breasts and thighs. His erection flickered in a throbbing salute to their intimate proximity.

'Bend,' Krystal murmured.

He obeyed, bringing his eyes down against the mirror to meet those staring back hollowly from the glass.

The two kneeling chastisers pressed their slippers against his buttocks, each dominating a cheek with the controlling kiss of cold leather.

Swish, swipe! Swish, swipe! The supple soles grew warm as his cheeks blazed fiercely. Harmonizing the discipline, they synchronized the searing strokes so that every five seconds, both buttocks burned beneath the double blows. In the mirror, they saw his eyes screw up and the sweat glistening on his freshly shaven head. Angrily erect, his shaft throbbed, his climax imminent.

Swish, swipe! Swish, swipe! Beetle paused, applying the warm sole of her slipper beneath his balls. She teased them with short dominant taps. Lurching, he slumped against the glass, pumping a silvery squirt up into its own reflection.

'Bad boy,' Beetle murmured, loosening the gag.

'Sorry, Nanny.'

She massaged his balls with her upturned slipper. 'Nanny warned you about nasty stickies, didn't she?'

He bowed his head.

'Didn't she?' Krystal demanded.

'Yes, Miss,' he mumbled contritely.

Picking up the black nylon stocking where Beetle had let it flutter to the carpet, Krystal pushed it loosely between his teeth. Using her slipper, she pressed his face into the mirror. 'Wipe it clean. Nanny will inspect it presently. If the mirror is not spotless, you will be whipped.'

Shivering, he crushed his face into the glass, dragging his gag across the dripping semen.

Krystal froze, her slipper falling to the floor. Her eyes narrowed. Suddenly, she understood the peculiar business of the window cleaners. Looking sharply across the room at Beetle, she saw the minx, head bowed, unconcernedly plucking at the cotton gusset of her panties clinging to her wet slit.

'Did he sign it?'

'Yep. And the cheque. I didn't know the fees at music college were so much.'

'Excellent,' Krystal nodded. She had typed out a brief note, addressed to Peggy, which started with the words 'Your niece is a good girl.' Apologizing profusely for any distress he had caused, Billy Box - under the shadow of the strap - had signed the letter and the substantial cheque which was enclosed.

Krystal licked the envelope. 'Dress him in your uniform. I have a phone call to make, then we're all going for a little ride.'

It took longer than expected to track down the *Sun* to a pub in Hammersmith. It was a punk revival night. Communication was difficult.

'Billy Box? I've been waiting to scoop that poop for ages. When and where?' the *Sun* replied.

Krystal considered. 'How long would it take you to get to the V&A?'

The *Sun* said that he'd never heard of the pub.

Krystal explained. 'Ten minutes?'

'Traffic's light on the Cromwell Road. Ten minutes it is.'

'He'll be tied to the front doors.'

'Good.'

'In a pink nanny's uniform.'

'Better.'

'And he's bald,' Krystal concluded.

'Great,' the *Sun* approved. 'Make a fantastic spread.'

Beetle dithered between the gold lame track suit and the sweat shirt with matching shorts.

'Is he dressed?' Krystal demanded.

Beetle nodded, jerking her thumb over her shoulder. Krystal looked, quickly suppressing a broad grin. The bald TV star, gagged and blindfolded, his hands bound, stood confused in the pink striped uniform and slightly wrinkled black stockings. The bodice was unbuttoned down to his navel. The bra looked ridiculous.

'Quickly. We've got to get him to the V&A.'

Beetle gazed at the fashion icon. 'Bit postmodern, don't you think? Are you sure they'll have him?' She giggled. 'Did you raise the *Sun?*'

'He'll be there.'

'Not much of a story, really,' Beetle murmured. 'Should see the way they party at the Mansion House. I've seen MPs—'

'This,' Krystal flourished the cucumber snatched from the salad box at the bottom of the fridge, 'should make things interesting.'

'What's so special about that?' Beetle frowned.

'It's where they'll find it that counts.'

He made page 314 of Teletext before midnight. The flickering blue script spelled out his disgrace, guising it with the gloss of a suspected breakdown. 'Billy Box has been working very hard recently,' the spokesman from Box Productions was quoted. 'Time for an enforced rest.'

Beetle squinted at the screen.

'You should wear your glasses more. I've warned you.'

'I can see,' Beetle protested, poking out her tongue.

'You won't need them for the pix in tomorrow's *Sun*,' Krystal observed.

'Can't wait for the morning,' Beetle laughed.

'Neither can I,' the blonde replied, pacing slowly across to the window. Fingering the curtain apart, she gazed out into the neon speckled night. 'Neither can I.'

The curtains remained drawn despite the late morning sun. Beetle, bare-bottomed and bending across the sofa, struggled vainly. Krystal had made sure that the red silk ribbon binding her ankles together had been tightly tied.

The whine of the electric motor protesting at the strain announced the arrival of the window cleaners' cradle. Soft fists thumped at the glass, demanding another erotic display.

A black leather glove picked up the remote control. A black-leathered finger jabbed the yellow button. The curtains shivered and opened, revealing the cradle and two eager-faced 'We Take Panes' cleaners at the glass. They had returned for more.

Their mouths fell open in silent wonder as, through the window, they saw Beetle bound and naked, offering up the rounded cheeks of her bunched buttocks to their unswerving gaze. Beside the bare-bottomed minx, Krystal stood flexing a cane. Ignoring the men cheering and waving at the window, she turned smartly to address the soft cheeks across the sofa, depressing their ripe swell with the whippy bamboo.

In her taut black-leather basque, deeply cleavaged and cut high at the hip and buttock, elbow-length gloves and black fishnets, her feet arched in shining black stiletto shoes, she brought prominent bulges to the trousers of the white-overalled cleaners.

Levelling her sparkling cane against the proffered cheeks, she raised it, allowing it to hover. The bare bottom below quivered with delicious dread. Krystal kept the cane aloft for an agonizing thirty seconds before whipping it down. Kneeling instantly, she traced the crimsoning line bequeathed by the cane, dragging her leather-sheathed index finger slowly across the punished cheeks.

Beetle's hips jerked and her tethered ankles squirmed in their red-ribboned bondage as the second stroke sliced down across her bottom. Raising the cane up to her lips, Krystal flickered out her pink wet tongue, lovingly licking the cruel wood. Down on one knee, she moved her face close to the heat of the whipped cheeks, this time to lick the searing scarlet weal.

At the window, the cradle swayed dangerously as the onlookers celebrated with fistfuls of stiff flesh.

After the third stroke, Krystal crushed the cane to the proud swell of her bosom. Down at the striped cheeks, she crushed her bosom into their proud swell. Rising gracefully to administer the fourth, she whipped the bamboo down then thrust it between her clamped thighs. The cradle rocked violently outside, lurching drunkenly to the left. Krystal knelt, caressing the hot bottom with her leather-sheathed pudendum.

Eight strokes later - each celebrated by the whipper with a dominating flourish over the striped bottom of the whipped - Krystal turned towards the window, and bowed.

Both men had ejaculated. Spent, and staggering slightly, they gripped the guard rail, steadying themselves against the dangerous tilt of the cradle. On the window, two splashes of warm appreciation dribbled slowly downwards. Scooping up the remote control, Krystal paced slowly towards the glass, her black stiletto shoes treading the carpet with measured menace. She sauntered up to the window. Tapping her cane tip against the glass, she mimed the silent reproach 'you've missed a bit' - then turned her leather-bound buttocks to their fevered gaze and paced back into the room to tower over the hot bottom across the sofa. Then she knelt. Fashioning her index finger up into a cruel curve, she aimed directly at Beetle's shining slit. Inch by inch, the black-leathered finger approached the wet pink lips. Just as it nuzzled the splayed labia, Krystal pointed the remote over her shoulder and pressed. The curtains drew silently together.

Almost immediately there was a shout, then cries of alarm from outside. Another yell of raw fear brought Krystal to the curtains. She dragged one open by hand. The cradle had slipped its right cable, and was dangling dangerously at an acute angle. Both men clung on for their lives as the smoking cradle's engine shrieked impotently.

Nine yellow-clad firemen later - not to mention the Simon Snorkel platform like a prehistoric monster at the window - the drama was over. The crowds dispersed from surrounding streets and the faces from the high-rise windows all around their block.

For Beetle, a more intimate drama was about to unfold.

'Come out here at once,' Krystal yelled, banging her fist on the bathroom door.

'Shan't. You'll only cane me,' Beetle retorted.

Krystal, still smouldering after the ribald comments of the crew of Wapping's Green Watch, was intent on dealing with Beetle. Severely.

'Just come out here. We'll discuss it,' she lied.

'No. Wasn't my fault they insisted on cutting my red ribber with special equipment.'

Green Watch had arrived so quickly, they discovered Beetle still bound at the ankles. It had taken four men five minutes to cut the bondage - in reality, a two-second one-handed job.

'I'm sorry they caught you on video in your basque,' the small voice behind the door said.

Krystal fisted the door angrily. 'Come out here.'

'Not till you've calmed down,' Beetle giggled.

'I am calm,' Krystal shouted.

'At least you had a basque on. All I had was a red bottom. They took ages taking video footage for their training film, didn't they?'

Krystal, reminded of the indignity, pummelled the obstinate wood with renewed fury.

'Promise you won't cane me?' the minx murmured.

'Promise,' Krystal sighed. 'I caned you to teach you a lesson, though you never seem to learn.'

'Bully.'

'You were caught red-handed and so I gave you a red bottom.'

'No cane?' Beetle pressed.

'No cane.'

'Promise?'

'Promise.'

The door clicked. Beetle emerged.

'But I am going to spank you severely,' Krystal declared, grappling the minx by the nape of the neck. Having dragged her squealing prey across to the sofa, she dragged her across her knees.

'Not fair,' Beetle whispered into the black sheen of the fishnets as she snuggled deliciously into the warm thighs of her cruel chastiser.

Chapter Nine

'Lean forward. More. Let your breasts tumble freely. No, a bit more. Spill them.'

Beetle obeyed the stern blonde's strict instructions.

'Now squeeze your thigh into the sofa. Tighter. And the knee. Foot up another four inches.'

The knee flexed, the naked foot rose, toes pointing directly down.

'Good. I like that. Keep it exactly like that,' Krystal enthused. 'Head back.'

'Like it is when I come?' Beetle whispered.

'Like it is when you come.'

Closing her eyes, Beetle raided her very short-term memory for a recent bout of ecstasy. Finding one almost immediately, her face flickered with recaptured delights.

Naked astride the sofa, Beetle was sitting for Krystal who was busily sketching her Girl On A Horse for the first of hers the foundry at Bow had promised to cast. Riding the soft sofa, Beetle squeezed her thighs, simulating the action mastering the beast between them.

'Sit still.'

The minx considered risking a covertly poked tongue, but decided against it. Her bunched buttocks, poised pertly on the sofa, already made too tempting a target for Krystal's firm hand.

The blonde hummed a half-forgotten tune from her Polish childhood, totally absorbed in the challenge of capturing Beetle's generous curves and supple limbs on paper with her pencil.

The winking lights of the approaching helicopter caught Beetle's eye before the drowning chatter of its engine disturbed her ears. She twisted, dimpling her buttocks, to watch. 'Don't move. It's only the police,' Krystal warned, engrossed in capturing the ripe round bottom.

The helicopter clattered across the night sky of the city, skimming the thrusting tower blocks. Like a gnat above a pool of snapping pike, it was powerless to prevent the dodgy deals going down in the depths below.

Following the little red tail-light, Beetle leaned back. As the police spy-in-the-sky disappeared, eclipsed by the NatWest tower, she overbalanced and toppled down from her perch, her naked legs sprawled inelegantly in the air.

'Beetle.'

'Sorry,' the minx mumbled, urgently scrambling up to remount the sofa before Krystal decided to lend a very firm hand.

'Just sit still.'

'Yes, Krystal.'

The minutes passed, the silence broken only by the scratching of the blonde's busy pencil.

Beetle eased her labia up, peeling them away from the tickling prickle of the sofa. It was no good. The prickle intensified, fuelled in part by Beetle's mind wandering back to the delicious spanking she had happily suffered across Krystal's lap after breakfast. A warm stickiness oozed and her labia spread, making her perch an almost unbearable mount to ride.

She squirmed, grinding her soft cheeks down into the sofa.

'Beetle.'

'It tickles,' the minx pouted. 'It's tickling my bottom.'

'I'll tickle your bottom for you if you don't stay quiet,' Krystal warned. 'And don't think I won't find the cane. I know you've hidden it - and I know perfectly well where.'

Beetle squealed. 'No, please. Look, I'm sitting very still now,' she gasped, wriggling as her clitoris grazed the fabric. 'Ooooh.' Her thigh quivered as her leg straightened, arrowing down the side of the sofa and breaking out of the required pose.

'That's it,' the blonde snapped in exasperation, tossing her sketchpad aside and bounding across the room before the naked minx could escape.

Breasts bouncing as she struggled, Beetle begged for her bare bottom to be spared. 'Please don't spank me, please don't spank me, please don't—'

Spank! Silencing the minx with the first, Krystal quelled her wriggling victim with the second sharp smack. Crisply administered, the third and fourth stilled each squirming cheek. *Spank! Spank!* Inching her pink bottom up submissively as she hugged her punisher's thighs, Beetle thrilled to the delicious discipline.

Krystal paused, after the ninth spank had flattened wobbling globes, to inspect the crimson cheeks. Beetle squealed pleasurably as the punishing palm revisited her hot bottom, this time to sweep in smooth circles across its ravished flesh. Krystal palmed the buttocks firmly, dominantly, smiling affectionately at her now-snuggling captive.

The smell of Beetle's freshly washed hair filled her senses with the remembered smell of the new-mown meadows frolicked in when they first encountered one another back at Birch Hall. The sweet scent of soap - and of freshly showered girl - brought her straight back to those forbidden shared showers after punishing cross-country runs on crisp autumnal mornings.

Drowning in her happy memories, Krystal absently thumbed Beetle's warm cleft, parting the firm buttocks gently and probing the anal whorl with her thumb tip. Then, moments later, with her tongue tip.

Beetle mewed like a kitten at its cream. Wriggling, she turned, offering her mouth, breasts and dark pubic nest up in utter surrender to Krystal's eyes, mouth and hands.

Krystal feasted, slowly and steadily, like an epicurean at a banquet. From the sweetness of the lips to the salt beads of perspiration spangling the breasts below, her hungry mouth sampled the delights of female nakedness. From the pale firm flesh of the shoulder and the bosom to the darker succulence between the thighs, her tongue and mouth rejoiced as they appeased their raging appetite.

Gathering Beetle by the wrists and pinning the minx to the carpet, she raked the helpless nude with a fierce tongue. Grinding her bottom with delight into the carpet, Beetle suddenly broke free from the dominant blonde and turned over, crushing her breasts and pubis beneath her own weight. Krystal mounted the proffered rump immediately, pinioning Beetle completely between her straddled scissoring thighs. The minx thrust her buttocks upwards, crushing their sensual swell up into the blonde pubic snatch and rubbing the wet labia with her soft cheeks.

'Ride me,' she whispered hoarsely into the carpet. 'Ride me.'

Easing herself a fraction up from the bare bottom, Krystal dragged her splayed labia across its rounded warmth. Again, and again and then again, she swept her hips sinuously down as she crushed her wetness into the willing buttocks. Cunningly managing to graze her clitoris on each descent down the supple flesh cushions, Krystal guided her sweet little thorn firmly across the swell of Beetle's left cheek. Sensing its presence, the minx wriggled to ensure maximum pleasure.

Krystal rose up on her hands, steadying herself clear of the bare bottom in an erotic press-up. Beetle stretched out luxuriously beneath, certain in her knowledge that soon the warm weight above would crush down onto her nakedness and explode in orgasm over her bunched buttocks.

'Use me,' she urged thickly. 'Use me,' confiding her dark desire to the carpet. Waggling her bottom she seduced the wet labia into a slow descent of her cresting buttocks.

Melting out of her frozen press-up, Krystal closed her eyes and rasped her pubic snatch against the bare bottom. The smell of Beetle's hair and body - a sweetness tinged with the feral tang of arousal - maddened her. She opened her eyes. The tumble of Beetle's dark hair, submissively spread over the carpet, inflamed her. The pulse at her tight throat quickened as her eyes took in the pale shoulders, the dimpled spine, the narrow waist. Her hungry gaze came to rest on the swollen peaches of Beetle's spanked-pink buttocks; and Krystal devoured them with ravenous eyes.

The heat at her slit intensified, the burning softness within now a lava flow of her molten juices. Astride the soft buttocks, she clamped her legs and thighs tightly together. Squashing her pubis into the rounded cheeks, she rocked from side to side, sliding her wetness into the imprisoned bottom. Beetle responded, rolling from hip to hip.

Fused, flesh to flesh, they quickened the tempo of their mutual pleasuring. Three minutes later, Krystal rose up on her elbows, splayed her thighs wide and recommenced the downward sweeping of her hips and belly across Beetle's bottom. Once more, her stiff clitoris traced the firm contour of the left cheek. Slowly at first - until the rasp of her flesh caused her throat and bosom to tighten - then more rapidly, she powered her hips towards her climax.

An invisible hand squeezed at the base of her belly. The spasm forked down like lightning, burning her with its soft pain. Krystal came once.

'Witch,' she yelled, spanking Beetle's bottom savagely as she shuddered.

She came again.

'Bitch,' she cried softly, burying her face into the bare shoulders to lick, suck and bite.

The third orgasm erupted deep within her muscled warmth. The seething wetness at her slit surged. Krystal hammered it violently into the submissive buttocks.

Groaning a precious endearment, she writhed frenziedly across the bare cheeks in slippery ecstasy.

They lay in blissful silence together, each listening to the other's rhythmical breathing. Krystal thought she could heat her own heartbeat. She sighed - it was only her hot blood singing in her ears.

'You haven't come like that since Christmas Eve,' Beetle gurgled happily, remembering the struggle that she, as Santa, in a scarlet bustier and silk panties, had put up filling the blonde's stocking.

'You are supposed to put the present in the stocking on the end of the bed,' Krystal grinned, reading Beetle's mind. 'Not in the stocking still on the leg.'

Laughing, they rolled into each other, soft bosoms colliding, and kissed deeply and slowly. Tongue tips vied for supremacy. Krystal's thicker muscle easily conquered Beetle's pink wet stretch of velvet. Mouths peeling apart, they separated at a mutually understood signal. With the effortless grace of a cat, Krystal mounted Beetle, squashing her buttocks into the minx's breasts. The blonde shuddered, murmuring her delight in her native Polish tongue, as she sensed the brunette's peaked nipples dimpling her splayed cheeks.

'Open,' Krystal purred, sliding her finger down over Beetle's pubis.

The minx squealed expectantly and parted her thighs, admitting Krystal's bending face into her wet warmth. The blonde's tongue lapped, then probed. Beetle clenched her buttocks, her taloned fingers clawing the carpet at her hips. The blonde's lips sucked fiercely. Beetle clutched at the carpet, frantically rolling her head from side to side. Then her teeth found the erect clitoris, and nipped tenderly. Beetle buckled under the exquisite torment, jerking in her paroxysms as she approached climax.

Grinding her hot bottom firmly into the minx, Krystal ravished the sweet flesh between the parted thighs with her whole mouth, eating ferociously as a lioness would at her kill. Beetle's buttocks pounded the carpet as she started to come. Sensing the orgasm, Krystal withdrew her mouth and applied her thumbtip to the clitoris, worrying the tiny pink thorn ruthlessly, prolonging and extending the ecstasy as one climax collapsed into the upsurge of the next.

Panting and glistening beneath a fine sheen of sweat, Beetle lay gazing up in adoration at the bottom pressing down upon her bosom. She tensed as Krystal bent down towards her parted thighs - her tension increasing to a rigid thrill as two firm fingers, then a third, probed her deeply. Beetle clamped her thighs together to hug and capture her delight, but Krystal's hand was as strong as her wrist was supple. The probing quickened as it deepened. Within minutes, the brunette was pounding the carpet once more as her swelling climax surged - spilling over into the sweet hot spasms of another orgasm.

'How do they do it?' Beetle asked, perched once again on the sofa in the Girl-On-A-Horse pose.

Through the chicken sandwich at her mouth, Krystal muttered a few technical details, half-heartedly answering the distracting question. Her pencil was capturing every detail of her model - still perspiring from several orgasms - recording the triumph in the thrusting breasts; the smile of supreme satisfaction on the curved lips; the sparkle of ecstasy in the exultant eyes.

She finished one sandwich and bit hungrily into another.

'They work from this sketch, that's why it's so important,' she explained, gesturing with the sandwich. 'Their computer scans it, coughs up a virtual model. From that, they make a bronze cast. Then,' the sentence was punctuated by another deep bite into the delicious chicken salad on rye, 'the finished statue is developed from that, allowing for adjustments. Dimensions.'

'And how do they—'

'Be still. I've nearly finished. Look,' Krystal conceded. 'I'll put the TV on. No sound though, I must concentrate.' Licking the mayo from her thumbtip, she picked up her pencil and shaded the inner slopes of Beetle's cleavage.

'OK.' Beetle nodded happily, wrinkling her nose at the screen.

When Krystal looked up once again - to capture the perfection of the taut nipples - she saw Beetle squinting.

'I've done your face. You can put your glasses on.'

'Can't find them,' Beetle lied.

'Vain little beast,' Krystal chuckled. 'But you really should wear them,' she added seriously, a note of protective concern in her voice.

'Don't need them,' Beetle countered, screwing her eyes up.

Krystal shook her head and returned to her sketch, concentrating hard on capturing every nuance and evidence of the minx's state of naked ecstasy.

'Newsnight' filled the screen. Beetle squealed, pointing at the fleeting images excitedly.

'That's Max.'

'Quick. Turn up the sound,' Krystal shouted.

Beetle scrambled from the sofa, stumbled, and scuttled across to the remote on top of the set. Jeremy Paxman's eyebrows shot up as she approached the screen, bare bosoms bouncing. Reaching up, she pawed for the remote, crushing her breasts into Jeremy's speechless mouth.

Almost too late, the sound boomed out along with another flash of Max among a rosetted throng outside a bleak hall. She was holding up Chloe Martin's arm in victory.

'New Labour got in,' Krystal remarked. 'With the mid-term blues, they were lucky,' she added shrewdly.

'They're back together,' Beetle burbled romantically.

'Puffins,' Beetle squealed delightedly.

The Freelander scrunched to a halt, ten yards from the edge of the steep Welsh cliff.

'Won't be a minute,' the minx gasped excitedly, scrambling down and racing towards the wind-whipped heights.

In the warmth of the four wheeled drive, Krystal turned to their old school chum 'Tiger' Cubb. 'When did you start up Ysdrgg?'

'Four years ago. Started small, just Petra and myself, kept it that way. Emphasis on quality, not size. We service pretty big clients now.'

Krystal listened as 'Tiger' Cubb outlined the development of Ysdrgg, the exclusive Management and Assessment Centre she had formed after leaving the Army with the rank of Major.

'Put all my money into it and it paid off,' Tiger concluded.

'When did you first start to suspect Petra?'

'Picked up a few whispers on the network,' the former Major sighed. 'No proof, but several clients were unhappy with the high grades some of their female trainees were awarded.'

'Petra's trainees?'

Tiger nodded.

'Money?' Krystal asked.

'Probably not. More like special favours. If I don't nip it in the bud my name will be mud. Need the proof.'

'With Beetle as bait, we'll catch her. What then?'

'I'll deal with her my way,' Tiger muttered darkly. Suddenly, twisting her face at the window, she cried out in alarm.

'Beetle,' Krystal shouted, staring in horror at the empty cliff top.

They charged across the turf and knelt down into the wind. Below them, two hundred feet down, the sea boiled.

Thousands of puffins filled the air, breasting the updraught on tiny black wings. Thousands more huddled at the face of the steep cliff. The noise was deafening.

'Can you—'

'No,' Krystal gulped. 'No sign of her.'

'She's slipped. She might be clinging to a ledge further down.'

'We need a rope.'

The comical little birds gazed up inquiringly at the two frantic pale faces peering down over the cliff top. Krystal cupped her hands to her lips. Blinded by the tears in her eyes, she yelled out Beetle's name. Only the screams of wheeling guillemots replied. Choking back a sob, she cried out again.

'Yes?' the minx asked brightly, standing behind them.

Tiger almost tumbled over the edge in surprise.

'Where the hell?' Krystal thundered. 'We thought—'

'Had to pee,' Beetle shrugged. 'Aren't the puffins sweet?'

'Get back inside,' Krystal commanded, pointing angrily at the vehicle.

'Want to see the puffins,' Beetle pouted.

'Inside.'

They drove. Ten minutes later, Tiger put her hand on Beetle's shoulder.

'This will do,' she observed, scanning the terrain.

It was a bleak hillside, but down in the valley dense pines offered good cover. In the silence after the engine had died, they heard the mournful cry of a curlew competing with the wind.

'Ysdrgg is only two miles over the next hill,' Tiger pointed. 'We'll get out here.'

Krystal helped Tiger with the tent, sleeping bags and rations.

'We'll walk from here. Get down in those woods then establish a command post up above Ysdrgg.'

Krystal shouldered the pack.

'Sure you're OK.?' Tiger asked.

'Yep.' Beetle gripped the steering wheel.

'Remember. Don't flirt, or do anything to encourage her,' Krystal warned.

'Shan't,' the minx promised.

'You're just another management trainee from KBZ Petro-chemicals. I've done all the paperwork,' Tiger continued. 'Petra won't suspect a thing. And we'll be watching all the time. Remember the signal?'

Beetle nodded.

Krystal held up her powerful field glasses and waggled them. 'I'll be watching very carefully,' she murmured. 'So be careful. No mistakes. Ysdrgg is very important to Tiger. If Petra is trading assessments for favours, we need to catch her at it.'

Beetle's eyes widened. She giggled.

'Beetle.' Krystal's tone was stern.

'I'll be good,' the minx squeaked, starting the engine.

They watched the Freelander bounce along the track. 'I wonder if Petra will succumb?' Tiger muttered.

'If Beetle doesn't tempt her, nobody will,' Krystal replied.

Ysdrgg was a collection of white-washed stone cottages and outhouses clinging onto a steep Welsh hillside. Beetle nosed the car gingerly down the dirt track and drew up alongside a long-abandoned sheep pen.

A tall young woman strode purposefully out to meet the minx. Glancing down at her clipboard, she confirmed Beetle's name and the firm sponsoring her on the course.

Beetle smiled. 'Am I late?'

The hazel eyes flickered up from the clipboard and gazed steadily at Beetle's smile.

'Better come inside and meet the others. Just in time tea,' Petra said at length, her sensual thick lips moving slowly.

Beetle climbed out, her tightly denimed buttocks bulging invitingly. Petra licked her lips, pressing her clipboard tightly to her bosom. As she ran her fingers through her chestnut curls, the hazel eyes devoured Beetle's soft curves.

'Got a pet name?'

'Beetle.'

'Beetle it is, then. Best to be informal. We've got a couple of punishing days ahead.'

It was growing dark. The Welsh hills rose up out of the gathering mist to merge indistinctly with the low thick clouds. Inside Ysdrgg, oil-lamps were produced, their yellow light bathing the spartan whitewashed walls with a warm glow. The other five female candidates sat in silence completing multiple-choice personality assessments.

Beetle chewed her pencil and frowned, her mind full of puffins.

'Time's up, everybody,' Petra announced. 'Better get to bed early. Busy schedule tomorrow.'

The Armani-suited career girls handed in their test papers smugly. Beetle's was unfinished. Glancing at it, Petra smiled.

'Do you usually wear glasses?' she speculated, shaking her head at all the blank spaces on the answer sheet.

Beetle nodded. 'Forgot them.'

'Never mind. We'll see how you shape up on the physical side.'

In the converted cow byre, Beetle rolled over in her squeaking iron-framed bed. Despite the extra blanket Petra had given her, she was cold. The other five course members were soon fast asleep, their laptops and chic attire neatly arranged on chairs. Beetle's jumper, brassiere and jeans lay crumpled on the floor.

Beetle lay in the stillness, still preoccupied with thoughts of puffins. Looking around her, she tried to picture the building fifty years ago, when girls from the Land Army would have tended the dairy herd.

Snuggling her head down into her single pillow, Beetle closed her eyes and palmed her nipples slowly, gently crushing her firm breasts as she conjured up a hot summer night all those years ago.

Up in the violet light of dusk, a lark would be pouring out its sweet cascade of liquid song. A thousand feet above, three Hurricanes hummed deeply as they winged out on coastal patrol, the pilots keeping their eyes peeled as they gained height over the Western Approaches.

A hot summer night. The cattle would be moving softly in their straw. Outside, silent as they drank their beer, sat two Land Army girls, Betty from Reading and Flora from Swiss Cottage. Betty, the bubbling shop girl, with peroxide blonde hair and knowing eyes, and Flora, the assistant librarian, shy and inexperienced. Like thousands of other girls from offices, shops and factories, these two had left their towns and cities to lend a hand on the land, sacrificing their summer to help bring the harvest in.

Betty and Flora. Beetle's fingers pinched and pleasured her nipples into fierce peaks of pain. Betty, complaining of the sticky heat, peeling off her fatigues. Now she stood in the dusk, clad only in a white cotton brassiere and regulation issue knickers. Flora, gazing shyly, still dressed as correctly as the neatly dust-jacketed books in her Swiss Cottage library.

Beetle's fingertips spidered down to caress her tummy, drumming on its taut skin, then further down to dabble at her pubic nest. Wriggling her bottom firmly into the bed, she parted her thighs a fraction then a little more. Stroking and rubbing at her silky, warm labia, she willed Flora to unbutton.

Betty approaches, shadowless in the dark. Their thighs brushed. Flora avoiding Betty's knowing eyes. Betty's fingers at the stubborn buttons. Betty's fingers sliding down Flora's milky skin, inching down from the shoulders to the warm spine. Flora's eyes wide with wonder as Betty unclasps her brassiere. (Beetle squeezed her thighs together, trapping her wet fingers.) Flora surrendering her brassiere - the cups peeling away to expose the full breasts just as the huge moon comes out to shadow their deep cleavage. Betty, the naughty shop girl, her hand firmly cupping the left breast. Cupping and squeezing. From Flora's parted lips, the low moan of delicious awakening. Treading out of their knickers, both are naked now. Holding hands, they seek the secrecy of the haystack.

(Beetle's fingertips teased her clitoris, tugging and tweaking it up into a tight little throbbing thorn of flesh. She rolled over in her bed, trapping her hand at her slit.)

The naked land girls scramble up the ladder. (Beetle grunted into her pillow as she pictured Betty's wide cheeks opening to reveal the dark, delicious cleft.) In the hay, bosom to bosom, they kiss. Pinning Flora into the prickling straw, Betty's lips stray from the eyes to the lips below. A token wriggle of resistance from the Swiss Cottage girl. Betty, firm now, uses her tongue. Flora's timorous thighs tremble and part. Shyly at first, then wider. Wider than they have ever been before. Betty's fingers - the red nail-varnish chipped - clutch and squeeze Flora's helpless buttocks. A low moan. The cattle answer from the byre. The land girls embrace. Their slits juice up and kiss.

Suddenly, above them, the roar of three Merlin engines as the Hurricanes chase a night-time bomber - a Dornier Do in their gun sights as it banked to swoop down on a Liverpool-bound convoy. The sound of machine-guns firing. Now the Hun is losing height, black smoke pluming from its starboard engine. A harsh staccato. Red, silver and gold tracers streak across the night sky. The Dornier Do disintegrates in a fireball. The sky is full of flame and fury. Then silence.

Cowering in their haystack, Betty shields Flora. The naked librarian clings to the shop girl, burying her face into the soft ripe bosom. Silence settles on the Welsh farm as the Hurricanes circle for the last time, straighten their flight path and beat it lack to base. In the haystack, Betty's wet tongue laps at Flora's belly, then traces a glistening line down to the parted labia.

Beetle's fingers scrabbled frantically as she fuelled her imminent orgasm. In her fevered imaginings, Betty's head was buried between the screaming librarian's clamped thighs, licking, lapping, sucking and softly biting the sweet pink flesh. Thrusting her buttocks up, Beetle started to come...

A brilliant light pierced the darkness, catching Beetle like a rabbit in a quartz beam.

'Better get some sleep,' Petra's voice whispered, the tone curdling as the torch raked the jerking buttocks on the bed below. 'You'll need all your energy for tomorrow,' she added.

Grunting in her climax, Beetle gazed up drunkenly with lust-bleary eyes. The torch clicked. In the darkness, a firm hand sapped Beetle's quivering bottom.

Breakfast was bland but substantial. With top-notch blue-chip companies sponsoring the candidates, Beetle thought, Ysdrgg could at least run to decent coffee. She sipped the supermarket blend without enjoyment.

Clothed in the white vests, tight shorts and pumps provided by Petra - who was herself warmly swathed in a quilted Barbour over her track suit - the six candidates were invited out for a physical appraisal.

'Stamina is what we look for,' Petra concluded her brief introduction. 'We'll start with a dozen press-ups.'

Clicking her pen, she scribbled on her clip board.

'Commence.'

The six young women, suddenly becoming competitive, dropped down to the lush grass and began. The shapely blonde from Nomura International reached the halfway stage first, but the trim-buttocked brunette from Glaxo passed her on the ninth. Bottoms taut, bosoms thrusting, they battled their way towards the required number of repetitions. Five white-vested girls rolled over, groaning as if they had just been ravished. Beetle, struggling on her tenth, lagged lamentably behind. Petra approached. Straddling Beetle, she raised her foot and guided it down onto the minx's plump rump.

'Eleven,' she counted, pressing down, then easing up as Beetle's buttocks rose.

'Twelve,' she concluded, treading the soft flesh firmly.

Beetle elbowed herself up, pushing her buttocks against the dominant foot at their curved swell.

'Excellent,' Petra nodded, ticking the sixth box on her char. 'Running on the spot. Commence.'

The six girls scrambled up and, elbows pumping and rounded bosoms bouncing, trod the turf rhythmically.

Petra stood behind Beetle, tapping her bottom with the clip board.

'Knees higher. Higher,' she urged.

Three hundred yards away, Krystal gazed steadily through powerful field glasses. Their magnification was so great, she could see where the tight shorts bit deeply into Beetle's cleft.

'Our fish is rising,' she observed, crouching behind the yellow blaze of a flowering gorse.

'You picked the perfect bait,' Tiger replied, her knuckles whitening around her binoculars.

'Team-building produces mere passengers. What I am looking for today is leadership,' Petra announced, escorting the group across the field to an eight-foot brick wall. At its base lay telephone poles, ropes, pulleys and netting. 'During this exercise, the object of which is to get Beetle up and over this wall, I will be assessing each of you for the following qualities: forward planning; communicating ideas effectively; the ability to command; and evidence of an analytical approach to problem solving. Go.'

The five candidates filled the Welsh hillside with their opinions, suggestions and conflicting ideas. Petra stood to one side, her arm casually around Beetle's waist. At length, the Nomura International blonde picked up the net and ordered the trim-buttocked brunette from Glaxo to assist. Approaching Beetle, they netted her and hauled her to the wall. The morning dragged. Five times a complicated erection of poles, ropes and pulleys rose up against the brick obstacle. Five times Beetle's squirming buttocks bulged through the netting as she was hoisted aloft - almost, but never quite, clearing the wall.

Petra gave a shrill blast on her whistle and walked over to where Beetle dangled. 'I've seen enough to allow me to assess your dynamic leadership skills,' she announced. 'Go in for a quick lunch, and then rest.'

They turned, Glaxo deliberately tripping the Nomura blonde. Instant conflict was avoided by a screaming blast from the whistle at Petra's sensual full lips.

'What about me?' Beetle squealed, her bottom bouncing against the bricks.

'I'll see to you,' Petra purred, lowering the net until Beetle nestled against her bosom. 'I'll see to you.'

'She's swallowing the bait,' Krystal remarked, watching every intimate detail through her powerful field glasses. 'Hook, line and sinker.'

Tiger looked up from the scratch lunch she was preparing. 'I'll sink her,' she muttered, peeling the red wax rind from an Edam cheese. Palming the curl of crimson skin, she clenched her fist angrily. 'And give her plenty of lines. Red ones, across her bottom.'

Petra sent the pack off on an exhausting cross-country orienteering run in the afternoon. Beetle did not set off with them.

'Go and have a shower after this morning's exercise,' Petra suggested silkily.

Watching the retreating figures of the other five girls slithering down a muddy slope, Beetle needed no second invitation.

Under the delicious sluice of warm water in one of the converted outhouses, Beetle relished her shower. Soaping her breasts vigorously, she offered them up to the drumming droplets, thrilling as her nipples thickened and shuddering with delight as the soapy curds caressed her thighs.

'Just been looking at your overall assessment,' Petra announced, pulling back the plastic curtain. Her eyes widened at the sight of Beetle's shining bare bottom.

Beetle squeaked with surprise and dropped the soap. Bending to retrieve it, the cleft between her cheeks deepened. The pulse at Petra's tight throat quickened.

'Not good,' she murmured. 'Just how important to you is the prospect of promotion?'

'Very,' Beetle replied, soaping her left cheek.

'Very?'

Beetle nodded and rasped the creamy soap against her fuzz.

Petra stroked her fingertip down between Beetle's shoulder blades. 'I could massage the results if the promotion means so much to you.' Her fingers were now at Beetle's bottom. 'Massage them,' Petra whispered, palming the left cheek firmly. 'If I asked you to come and see me tonight, after lights out, what would you say?'

'What time?' Beetle replied huskily, inching up on her toes in response to the firm finger probing her clenched cheeks.

'Make it ten thirty.'

'She's swallowed the bait,' Tiger said, letting her binoculars rest against the swell of her chest. 'Look.'

Krystal raised her field glasses. 'Where?'

'Third building from the left. The shower block. She's made her move. Beetle's given the signal.'

Krystal adjusted the focus. The small red towel draped the window ledge - their agreed signal - told the watching eyes what they needed to know.

'She'll wait 'til dark, if I know Petra.'

'We'll move in at eleven,' Krystal nodded.

The returning pack, tired and mud-spattered, were suppered, showered and quickly asleep after the rigours of their orienteering exercise. At ten-twenty-five, Beetle eased herself up on one elbow. The iron bed frame creaked. Slipping out gingerly, the minx tip-toed through the row of beds. It was just like being back at Birch Hall: where the penalty for being out of bed after lights out was a severe spanking over the knee of the divine dorm senior - and the penalty for succeeding in getting clear away from the midnight dorm was an even more delicious punishment at the hands and mouth of the waiting Krystal. Beetle grinned, remembering the many occasions when she had indeed been caught - and the even more numerous occasions when she had made it to Krystal's bed.

Gently closing the door behind her, she instantly regretted her bare feet as she skipped across the damp grass. Shivering, with only her panties for protection, she tapped gently on Petra's cottage door.

Inside, a log fire blazed, perfuming the air with the sweet scent of last autumn's apple-tree logs. Beetle saw the leaping flames reflected in two large wine-filled glasses.

Petra, curled up naked on a soft rug before the fire, motioned the minx to join her.

'I kept my promise,' the nude on the rug whispered. She dangled the assessment sheets between a teasing finger and thumb. 'Going to keep yours?'

Beetle was bending, about to kneel.

'Stay there,' Petra murmured softly. 'Face the fire. I want to warm you up.'

As Beetle stood obediently in front of the orange flames, Petra knelt behind her. Beetle felt nipples sweep against the backs of her thighs. Seconds later, firm fingers were peeling down her panties.

'So soft,' Petra murmured, licking the curved cheeks she had just bared. 'So soft.' Grunting, Petra buried her face deeply into the proffered buttocks.

The door opened, the cold draught causing the orange flames from the apple logs to leap.

'Caught her,' Krystal announced.

'Bitch,' Tiger whispered.

Petra gasped at the sound of Tiger's voice. Beetle felt the warm breath fan her buttocks.

'Up, this instant.'

Petra scrambled up to stand on trembling legs. Beetle scampered across to Krystal.

'I didn't do anything. Only what you said.'

'I believe you,' the blonde Pole murmured, hugging the shivering minx closely and kissing her soft dark hair. 'We came just in time. Go and get dressed.'

Tiger had snatched up Beetle's assessment sheet and was scrutinizing it carefully. She held it out for Krystal's inspection.

'It's exactly as I suspected. All the grades revised upwards. I can't believe she'd betray me like this.'

'You're wrong,' Petra shouted hotly. 'I didn't—'

'Silence, I'll deal with you presently. Where do you think you are going?' she snapped.

Petra replied sullenly that she was going to get dressed.

'Don't bother. Just stay exactly where you are. I want you naked for the rest of the night.'

Petra, shielding her pubic nest protectively, whimpered.

'To punish, not to pleasure,' Tiger growled.

Petra's hands cupped her buttocks, a futile gesture against the impending pain.

Beetle returned clothed. 'What now?'

'I've been meaning to evaluate the stamina-testing routine,' Tiger mused. 'This seems as good an opportunity as any. Outside,' she ordered Petra.

'But I'll freeze,' the nude wailed.

'I'll keep you warm, have no fear.'

'Haven't used this since I was a Major,' Tiger confessed, lovingly fingering the length of her leather-sheathed crop. Capturing its tip in her left hand, she flexed it. Satisfied with its whippy action, she nodded, then sliced the empty air with it, smiling in response to the cruel note singing out in the crisp night air.

Despite the gag they had just fastened around her lips, they heard the nude moan.

'We'll try the zig-zag first,' the former Major decided, driving Petra across the grass towards the assessment course with sharp strokes to the bare bottom.

Beetle and Krystal followed, cuddling each other for warmth. They came to a halt at the start of the zig-zag course: ten rubber tyres, half-buried in the ground, planted in an erratic line at ten-yard intervals. The rubber above ground had been whitewashed. They looked like ancient burial stones in the thin moonlight.

'Thirty seconds is about par for this course,' Tiger announced, consulting the stop watch in her gloved hand.

'Kneel.'

Petra, gagged and naked, obeyed.

'Go.'

Petra sprang - urged on by the swish-slice of the crop across her rising rump - and sped towards the first rubber tyre. As she dropped down to crawl through it, the crop kissed her bunched cheeks with another cruel swipe.

Swish, crack! In the darkness, Beetle and Krystal did not have to strain to see the naked Petra's progress. Each time the nude bent to negotiate a tyre, Tiger's crop sliced down fiercely, burning its encouragement into the helpless bare buttocks.

Swish, crack! Swish, crack! Trotting behind her victim, Tiger monitored the whipped nude's time with a stop watch - never missing an opportunity to crack the crop down.

'She's certainly putting her through the hoops,' Krystal murmured.

Beetle, snuggling into the blonde, smothered a giggle.

The ex-Major escorted the stumbling nude back to the start-line. 'Twenty-seven seconds. Best time yet. Mind you, I gave the bitch every encouragement.'

They walked across the field in the moonlight, Petra shivering despite her hot stripes, to what 'Tiger' referred to as 'The Net'.

It was five feet wide, and stretched for fifteen yards across the grass. Made of knotted hemp, it was part of an old drift net that they had salvaged from the beach and pegged out for candidates to crawl through.

'Eighty seconds is the record for this. Let's see what she can do tonight,' the stern voice barked, as the tip of the quivering crop flipped up the edge of the net.

Petra, cradling her bosom, hesitated.

Swish, crack!

Petra scrambled down to, and then under, the net, wriggling frantically as she struggled under the taut ropes. Kneeling, Tiger shadowed the progress of the squirming nude. As the bare bottom rose, undulating the knotted hemp, the crop lashed the smooth cheeks. The soft bottom dimpled beneath the biting net as Petra stalled. Two fierce slices spurred her on.

Nine times the crop spoke, cracking down with its tongue of fire to lick the bunched cheeks, setting them ablaze.

Krystal and Beetle joined Petra's tormentress as the punished nude scrambled up from the far end of the net.

'Seventy-two seconds,' the ex-Major remarked, enclosing her stop watch in her gloved hand.

Beside her, head bowed, Petra snivelled. Tiger levelled the crop at her betrayer's nipples. Rubbing the leather-sheathed cane harshly against the stiffened peaks, she launched into an angry denunciation of Petra's crimes.

The fierce reprimand ceased. 'No tears,' she snapped, controlling the bare bosom with her whippy crop. 'You must have known how damaging your selfishness could be for our operation at Ysdrgg. Now you must pay the price in full. Move.'

Swish, crack! Petra almost stumbled as the crop sliced down across her buttocks.

Swish, crack! 'We'll see how you cope with The Wall.'

The dawn broke, reddening the eastern sky with streaks of scarlet almost as deep as the blaze of pain on Petra's soundly whipped buttocks.

'The crew will be up in an hour. Just gives me time for an important bit of intelligence gathering,' the ex-Major grunted, positioning Petra over an oil drum, the crop depressed at the nape of the nude's neck.

'Intelligence?' Beetle echoed, gazing at the striped cheeks.

'Damage limitation. Need to know exactly how many favours she's enjoyed by abusing her position as assessor. I need names, dates,' Tiger grunted, stooping to bind her victim's wrists together, then kneeling to weld the ankles with a length of cord.

'An hour? That gives you plenty of time. And, speaking of time, we'd better be going,' Krystal observed. 'Got to beat rush-hour traffic.'

'Here?' Tiger replied, amazed.

'In London. This evening,' Krystal laughed.

'Ah,' Tiger nodded. 'No traffic hereabouts. Nothing to beat but bare bottoms.'

'Aren't you going to take her gag oft?' Beetle asked.

'No, not yet. No need to rush. This,' the punisher remarked, flexing her crop, 'will do all the talking to begin with.'

Bound and helpless at her back, Petra's hands twitched, fingers spasming in a starfish of fear.

Beetle played with her little soft toy puffin - a surprise present from Tiger to go with the substantial cheque - as Krystal talked on the phone.

'I have to go out,' Krystal announced, putting the phone down. 'If the foundry rings with any queries, just check my note pad. All the details are there.'

Bouncing the puffin along the edge of the sofa, Beetle turned its brightly coloured beak towards Krystal and ventriloquised her reply.

Krystal sighed. 'It's important. The foreman has had to go up to Norfolk to see about a cracked bell and today's the day they're going to do Girl On A Horse.'

'A cracked bell?' the puffin queried.

'Seems all this Lottery money is kitting out the kingdom with bells for the Millennium. If his assistant asks any questions, just refer to these.' She tapped the note pad by the phone.

'OK,' the puffin replied.

'Beetle.'

The minx stuffed the puffin down the side of the sofa and jumped up. 'Relax. I'll handle it.'

They kissed, and Krystal went. Beetle returned to the sofa and turned on the TV. A short item on the recently completed Greenwich Dome failed to hold her attention - Beetle was bored. After all, she could see the real thing from her window. She turned the TV off, just as the Esso tiger sprang across the wide screen.

Tiger. Beetle suddenly remembered a snatch of poetry from her Birch Hall days. How did it go? Yes. She'd got it. '...Burning bright, in the darkness of the night...' Striped. Just like Petra's bottom after the crop, bared and poised over the oil drum under the threat of more punishment. Burning bright. How Petra's buttocks had burned under Tiger's stripes.

Easing her skirt up, she fingered her pussy through her tights. Two sleepy and lazy to remove them, she plucked at her pubic nest through the warm bronze sheen of nylon. The tickling torment juiced her labia. They peeled apart, welcoming her finger with a broad smile. Locating her clitoris, she trapped its sweet thorn beneath the tight stretch and teased it with a slowly rotating fingertip. Firmly, tenderly. Soon she felt the inner surge of a warm ooze.

The images of Petra's punishment rekindled in her mind. The bending cheeks, offered up to the crop, being whipped as the nude struggled through the rubber tyres. The wriggling bottom, caught in the knotted rope web, jerking as the crop lashed down across the upturned cheeks. The finger at her wet tights worked harder. Squeezing her thighs together, Beetle rolled onto her back and surrendered to a protracted orgasm - then promptly fell asleep.

The ringing of the phone broke into• her contented nap. Leaping up, she took a step - and fell, forgetting that she had pulled her tights down to her knees just before she'd climaxed.

The phone rang on. Hobbled by her tights, Beetle hopped across the carpet kangaroo style. It was the foundry wanting to double-check the dimensions of Girl On A Horse.

'Nine long by twenty high,' Beetle squinted, stubbornly refusing to obey Krystal's instructions to wear glasses.

'Nine what?' the voice asked.

Beetle was stumped.

'What does it say? After the numbers?' the voice from Bow insisted.

Beetle squinted. The 'ins' for inches blurred into the 'm' for metres. She took a deep breath and a deeper risk.

'M,' she said, yanking her tights up over her bottom.

'OK. Metres it is.'

'I don't believe it,' Krystal whispered, her face pale and eyes heavy with sorrow. 'Were you wearing your glasses?'

'No. Yes. I forget—'

'Twenty metres. That's over sixty feet of Girl On A Horse. Over sixty feet. Didn't you even think? Who is going to want a sixty foot statue of you, starkers, on a horse?'

Beetle shrugged, taking refuge in silence.

'I need a long, stiff drink. You'd better go to bed.'

'But it's only just gone seven,' Beetle squeaked.

'I'm too tired to cane you now, Beetle. But if you stay I might just find the energy to teach you the difference between inches and metres.'

Knowing it would be a painful lesson, Beetle went into their bedroom.

As Krystal uncorked a full-bodied Medoc, Beetle held her mobile close to her face and whispered as softly as she could. Jumping at the sound of the Medoc's cork in the next room, she scribbled down the number the operator gave. She dialled again. At last, the answer-phone at the other end kicked in.

'Millennium Office? I want to leave a message.'

Chapter Ten

Beetle was ostentatiously wearing her glasses. She wore them everywhere - even in the shower. Twice, Krystal had had to rescue her slippery nakedness as she wandered around the studio, colliding into everything. Perched on the tip of her nose, the glasses gave Beetle an expression of quizzical insouciance that was proving increasingly maddening for Krystal.

'I've mastered a new game. I'll teach you, if you like,' Beetle declared.

'Mmm?' the blonde murmured, poring over another unfathomable Polish crossword.

'Fanorona,' Beetle continued, memorizing the text on the side of the large box she had just read. 'A game once played by Madagascan royalty, derived in part from Alquerque, that noble game from ancient Egypt.'

'Oh, you mean draughts.'

The minx poked her tongue out from behind the safety of the large box.

'I'll spank you.'

Beetle squealed and jumped up from the sofa, scattering the pieces all over the carpet. Krystal rose solemnly and approached. Treading on a sharp piece of the strewn Fanorona, she yelped.

'Come back here and pick these up,' the blonde thundered, jabbing her finger down at the carpet.

Beetle, down on all fours, obeyed.

Spank. The hovering palm could not resist the temptation of the upturned cheeks. It succumbed. *Spank.* It succumbed again.

'Not fair,' Beetle pouted, wriggling her rump as she stretched deep under the sofa.

'Don't forget,' Krystal said sternly, 'there is still a punishment outstanding.'

Beetle had not forgotten. Punishment pending. The phrase haunted her, juicing her slit and filling her imagination with delicious dread.

'A small matter of a sixty-foot bronze,' Krystal concluded.

Beetle deployed a diversionary tactic. 'Try to keep the evening of the ninth free,' she said innocently.

'The ninth? Why?' Krystal grunted, struggling to lift the sofa to free Beetle's trapped arm.

'You'll see.'

Vengeance and punishment brought them to the opulence of the West End. Beetle and Krystal entered the exclusive antique shop and closed the door on the bustle of Bond Street. Under the cold eye of a smooth young man seated at a gilded Italianate desk, they browsed at the display of small silver items.

Emerging from behind a green curtain, an assistant struggled into a coat. Saying goodnight to the man at the desk, she departed.

A spoon from the court of James II detained Krystal. Bending, she studied the rat-tail design, using the glass front of the cabinet to monitor the dapper young man at his desk.

The other two customers, whispering excitedly in Spanish, lingered for a few moments at a polished pear-wood table that was probably beyond their means, and then departed. Beetle and Krystal were alone with their unsuspecting quarry.

'I'm closing shortly,' the bored voice from the desk drawled, sensing no sale in his final customers.

Krystal's acute ears caught the lazy vowels that only good claret and inbred arrogance can produce.

'Looking for some French silverware. Seventeenth century. Possibly Nantes,' Krystal said.

The smooth young man flickered his eyes from Beetle's charms to Krystal. 'Nantes,' he murmured, pursing his lips.

'Seventeenth century,' Krystal replied.

'Tricky,' he countered, slowly building up to a sale, exploiting the psychology of disappointment and doubt. 'Tricky.' His eyes priced Krystal's Gucci shoes and smart Milan leather jacket.

'Candlesticks,' Krystal suggested. 'How much would they be?'

'A pair, if perfectly matched,' he said suavely in a voice of the expert he pretended to be, 'would be quite a catch.'

He was speaking Mayfair. Krystal decoded the price.

'Why Nantes?' he asked, guardedly.

She had a prepared answer. 'I saw some charming pieces at Lady "Nuts" Collingham's,' Krystal murmured, fingering the breasts of a marble nymph.

'Linton Hall?' he nodded, failing to disguise his grudging interest in the potential buyer.

'Candlesticks,' Krystal decided firmly. 'How much did you say?'

He hadn't said, not directly. He spread his hands expansively. Beetle, who had been appraising some indifferent majolica, returned to the door, clicked the lock and drew down the blind.

'How much did you say?' Krystal repeated.

'What do you think you are doing?' he demanded angrily.

'We do not wish to be disturbed,' Krystal purred, 'while negotiating the price.' She commandeered a ted velvet-cushioned chair and sat down.

Relieved that no robbery was threatened, he discharged his momentary frisson of fear in waspish anger. 'The price is not negotiable.'

'So you do have a pair?'

His knuckles whitened as he pressed his fists down on the gilded desk, hating to be bettered so easily. The advantage, he conceded, was now with her. 'I dare say I might.'

'I dare say you do.'

'Four thousand,' he snapped, gathering up some paperwork and tidying it fussily. Relenting slightly, in case the sale went awry, his tone softened back to the urbane drawl. 'That is, to be sure, if you find them agreeable.'

'That's quite a steep mark-up. You gave three hundred only for them.'

She could have sworn he buckled slightly at the knees. Recovering himself, he shot a swift glance at her. She met it with a cold gaze.

'How—'

'Three hundred. My friend noticed their loss when visiting her aunt. The aunt, who is, as I am sure you are fully aware, one pearl short of a necklace, had lost her cheque book and so was temporarily unable to purchase cat food for several strays she has acquired in her basement area.'

'Business is business. It's perfectly legal. I made an offer, she—'

'Is vulnerable. Sharp practice is sharp practice. It's perfectly immoral.'

'I must ask you both to leave,' he insisted, rising to his feet behind the desk in an effort to assume control.

'Not *without* the candlesticks, and not until,' Krystal paused, lingering on the words, 'the penalties have been paid.'

'Penalties?'

'Penalties.'

He sat down behind the desk. 'I have my finger on an alarm button. Leave immediately or I will press it.'

'Beetle?'

The minx, who had been fingering the pubic mound of the same marble nymph whose bosom had detained Krystal, turned. 'Now?'

Krystal nodded.

Beetle unbuttoned her raincoat. Peeling it off, and stepping out of her shoes, she stood in naked splendour on an Afghan rug.

'Beetle is now being recorded on both of your video cameras. Press that button, and you will certainly have some explaining to do to the police.'

Beetle, kneeling - her heels supporting her heavy buttocks - began to finger and pinch her nipples.

'Get her out of here,' the man hissed.

'Who are you afraid of? The police? Or the owner?'

Stripped of any pretence of being no more than an assistant working late night Bond Street hours, he paled.

'Can she return the money?' he said slowly.

'Cats have healthy appetites. The candlesticks, please, at once.'

He bit his lower lip. Krystal knew why. The pieces of exquisite Nantes silverware would have already been listed on records. No doubt the owner would miss them immediately.

'I'm waiting,' Krystal whispered.

Beetle grunted as she punished her swollen breasts within hands that cupped and squeezed.

'I'll get them,' he snarled. Disappearing behind the curtain, he returned almost at once, billowing the curtain as he clutched the candlesticks. 'Here. Take them. Take them and go.'

'Not until you have paid the penalties.'

'P-penalties?' he stuttered, staring in horror as Beetle press the bristles of an Edwardian silver-backed hairbrush between her thighs.

'There will be no repayment.'

'But I'll have to juggle the books.'

Not for the first time, Krystal supposed.

'I will have to bear a big loss. Pay the penalty, as you put it.'

'Penalties. You not only cheated my friend's aunt, you humiliated her. Exploiting her infirmity and weakness in our book is humiliation. Now you too must taste humiliation. Take off your clothes.'

He protested angrily, although his eyes never for one moment left the pale bristles raking Beetle's labia.

'I thought I told you to strip,' Krystal said calmly, remaining poised on her velvet-cushioned chair. Her coolly collected *mien* rendered her all the more intimidating, all the more dominant.

His erection was already quite proud, despite his fear and shame, when he emerged naked from behind his desk.

'Down,' Krystal pointed to the brightly coloured rug. 'On your back.'

Reluctantly, he obeyed.

'Beetle is going to sit on your face and ride you until you ejaculate. Technically,' Krystal continued in a prim tone as if discussing a piece of Dresden china, 'this is known as "queening". A most fitting humiliation, I think, for you. To be utterly dominated and used by a woman. Have you ever been queened? I think not. What is your name?'

He remained silent, watching the minx as she fingered herself furiously.

'Mr Scott-Bannerman, I asked you for your name.'

'William,' he replied, failing to mask his resentment at Krystal's knowledge of his surname.

'William. Willy,' Krystal chuckled. 'Well, Willy, down on the Afghan with you.'

'Please—' he protested, still kneeling.

'Down,' Krystal thundered.

Horror mingled with enchantment in his eyes as he stretched out on the soft rug. Beetle was on him like a cat on a kipper, her bottom burying his face.

'Commence,' Krystal said, clapping her hands twice. Beetle's toes strained into the Afghan as she rocked on her haunches, sweeping her cleft and sticky slit across his face. His shaft stiffened and throbbed.

'No tongues, Willy. Put it away this instant. Beetle is here to punish, not pleasure you.'

He came, forty seconds later, his hot spurts spattering Beetle's left shoulder - and the delicately acid-etched lalique vase four feet behind her. Grunting, he struggled to withdraw his sweating face from beneath Beetle's buttocks.

She clamped her thighs, trapping him. Helpless, he surrendered to the heat of her flesh.

'Again,' Krystal barked, clapping her hands like a Chinese mogul summoning a naked concubine to his sheets of silk.

Beetle bounced enthusiastically, riding him pitilessly. He came - groaning a note of rising protest - once more. His hot spurts left Beetle's breasts glistening. Droplets of semen slid slowly down from her nipples onto his belly. Sensing them, he writhed.

'Stay perfectly still, Willy, during your humiliation, or your bare bottom will surely suffer - more than I intended it to.'

Trapped beneath the feral heat of the cleft smothering his face, he tensed. They saw his fists claw frantically at the exotic rug. Exchanging glances, they smiled. Krystal nodded.

The minx worked adroitly with her wet slit, dragging it dominantly over the imprisoned face beneath.

'Not coming, Willy?' Krystal taunted.

Moments later, the shaft thickened and rose. At last, his body surrendered to a shuddering orgasm - the climax wrenching a wail from his lips. As his hips jerked and pumped, Beetle's soft buttocks drowned his shriek of anguish.

'Ten strokes,' Krystal instructed.

Beetle dismounted and rolled him over onto his front. Utterly spent, he offered no resistance. She palmed the silver-backed hair brush, then applied its polished surface across buttocks. They reddened quickly under the savage onslaught. He grunted his suffering into the rich Afghan. *Crack! Crack!* The sweeping hair brush blistered his buttocks - Beetle pinned him down firmly at the neck as he writhed to escape. *Crack! Crack!* After the tenth stinging swipe, she devilishly applied the pale bristles, dragging them cruelly across the scarlet cheeks.

Tossing the hair brush aside, Beetle rose to accept a tissue from Krystal's outstretched hand. Bending, she dried between her thighs and stuffed the wet tissue into his mouth. Krystal nodded her approval and supplied the minx with another. She rolled her victim onto his back once more and, gathering up his flaccid penis between the silver blades of exquisite Hanoverian sugar tongs, held it up to be dried with the tissue.

Krystal wrapped the candlesticks separately and placed them in her bag.

'Ready?' she asked Beetle.

The minx, back in her raincoat and shoes, nodded.

'We are going now. But your problems are not quite over yet, Willy.'

Rising up on one elbow, he shook his head slowly as if dazed. 'Not over?' he managed to gasp.

Krystal pointed to the pair of security cameras angling down from the ceiling. 'That system is tamper-proof. The feed goes directly to a control centre. They view every inch of the tape twice a week. I know, Willy, because I took the trouble to check. Next viewing is tomorrow afternoon. And you have every reason to fear the wrath of your employer, haven't you, Willy? Lady Creighton-Stern comes from an illustrious line of flagellants. At least we've given her a couple of pointers as to how best to punish you. Cheerio.'

Beetle whispered urgently into the phone. 'She's in the shower. Be quick.'

'She's not in the shower now,' Krystal whispered from the doorway, her naked body sparkling with diamond droplets.

The minx squeaked and slammed down the phone.

'Who were you speaking to?' Krystal demanded.

'Nobody. Wrong number.' Beetle evaded capture and bounded over the sofa.

'You're up to your naughty little monkey tricks again, I can tell. Come here.'

'No, it isn't like that. I'm—'

'Yes?'

Beetle was determined to keep her secret, so she surrendered to the blonde's lap and submitted her bared bottom to a sound spanking. Krystal's breasts joggled and bounced as her palm swept down repeatedly in a stinging staccato across the upturned buttocks.

'Take that as a warning against doing anything you shouldn't or as a punishment for already having done it.'

Beetle's brain struggled with both the logic and the tortured syntax of Krystal's words.

'Understand?' the blonde rasped.

'Understood,' the hot-bottomed brunette whispered.

'Sure?'

'Yes, Krystal,' Beetle murmured, squirming.

'You've been far too busy on that telephone recently. Busy and furtive. Don't know what you're up to, but when I do—'

Spank! Spank! Spank!

The firm hand spelt out the dire warning across the crimson cheeks.

When Krystal had returned to the bathroom to dry herself with a warm towel, Beetle - rubbing her buttocks ruefully - risked a quick phone call.

'Vanessa? Have you told Peter? I'll let Mandy know. Krystal? No. She doesn't suspect a thing.'

The vast Belgravia flat seemed small and cramped in darkness. A sodium streetlight gave the room they crouched in an air of unreality. In the weird light, Krystal appeared to Beetle like something from a Lou Reed album sleeve.

'What are you eating now?' the blonde whispered fiercely.

'Ice cream,' the minx replied softly. 'Found a tub of chocolate chip in the fridge. Want a lick?'

'We came here to work, not for a picnic, piglet. What have you scoffed?'

'Ginger bread, some Brie and a peach.'

'But you had a huge plateful of bubble and squeak—'

They froze and crouched lower down behind the large armchairs in the darkened room. In the surroundings, Beetle's hand brushed against a slender statue of a cat. The cold touch at her flesh alarmed her. She smothered a squeal.

'Be quiet. It's them. They're at the door,' Krystal warned.

Straining their eyes in the darkness, they heard the key scratching in the lock. Soft rustlings followed. Moments later, a slender silhouette passed across between them and the sodium streetlight outside the large bay window.

'Now,' Krystal hissed.

Rising silently to maximize the element of surprise, Beetle and Krystal simultaneously switched on powerful torches, directing the beams at the source of the faint sounds. Two beautiful airline stewardesses, pert in their trim uniforms, shrieked as they blinked into the yellow glare.

'Stand absolutely still,' Krystal commanded. 'Beetle. The door.'

The minx scampered into the hallway, locked the door and returned to find the room bathed in a sparkling blaze from an overhead candelabra. In the strong light, the stewardesses shivered.

'Sit, and start explaining,' Krystal ordered, pointing her extinguished torch at a leather Chesterfield.

One of their captives, a sharp-eyed blonde, attempted to bluster. 'We have a perfect right—'

'Breaking and entering. Burglary,' Krystal added, nodding at the silver cigarette case the svelte blonde had attempted to pocket. 'We have been waiting for you. We know all about you and have done for some time. It was just a matter of getting the proof - the proof needed before punishment can be dispensed.'

The sharp-eyed blonde, astounded, sat back in the leather Chesterfield. Beside her, a sullen, firm-breasted brunette scowled in silence.

'Catching you was easier than we expected, because you grew too greedy.'

'How did you know we would—' the sharp-eyed blonde began.

'You were expected,' the voice of a man entering the front door interrupted. The accent was heavy. Greek.

All four faces turned to see the tall bronzed man stride into the room. His steel-grey eyes were narrowed in anger.

'Mr Demosthenes,' the stewardesses gasped.

'Have you all the proof you need? Are you completely sure?' he asked Krystal, ignoring his employees.

Krystal nodded. 'As I predicted, they let themselves in. We surprised them as they were picking up the best items.'

'I will give you one chance to explain your coming here tonight,' the Greek demanded. 'Speak.'

The sharp eyes blinked. 'Two passengers—' she faltered, then took a deep breath as her brain whirred. 'They became friendly on the flight. They gave us the keys to this flat. Told us to make ourselves at home,' she added defiantly.

'Lies,' Mr Demosthenes thundered. 'You have done this before.'

'They target passengers on the flight out. Give them plenty to drink, then become playful, taking them back to their cabin deck or the toilet to pleasure them.'

'Then, when the passengers are asleep, these two take wax impressions of their house keys. *You* have easy access,' he grimaced, turning to address the stewardesses, 'to the computer for passengers' address and return flight date. Burglary by design.'

'The passengers wake up in Bonn or Davros, by which time you've returned to London on the next fight, with days, even weeks to take your pick,' Krystal concluded.

'No, you've no proof. No proof at all,' the sullen brunette snarled, speaking for the first time.

'Silence,' Mr Demosthenes roared. 'Though you may make as much noise as you like when being punished.'

The two uniformed girls huddled closely, united in their fear.

'A pattern emerged,' Krystal shrugged, modestly accepting the Greek's renewed thanks. 'All the clients who fly on your executive jets are wealthy. Wealthy people are creatures of habit.'

He nodded.

'Once they have flown with your exclusive airline, they do so again and again. Several were burgled while abroad. And the only link was the staffing detail your computer printed out. These two were on every flight on which there was a subsequently burgled passenger - *and* were back in London to do it.'

'Is that why you phoned last week? To have their bags secretly searched?' he asked.

'I had to be sure of their methods. Tablets of soft wax were found in the make-up compacts.'

The brunette burst into tears.

Mr Demosthenes opened a fumed oak cabinet and poured himself a drink. Tossing back his head, he drained the glass in a single swallow. Turning angrily, he ignored the sharp eyes widening with surprise at the ease with which the Greek made himself at home in this flat.

Jabbing a finger at his employees, he shouted at them furiously. 'Whores. You target your man. Ply him with drink and then pleasure him. When he sleeps, you pounce.' He threw his empty glass into the fireplace. It shattered in four hundred pieces.

Pale and shivering, the two culprits curled up in fear, their pertly uniformed bottoms squirming on the dull leather Chesterfield. Neither dared to speak - whether to deny or plead for mercy.

Krystal closed her eyes, imagining their crime. She pictured the Lear jet, in the pale blue and gold livery of Demosthenes, streaking high above the Alps. The pretty stewardesses, polite, attentive, responding to every whim of the tycoons in their care. The champagne. The crush of a breast or the caress of a thigh as more champagne is served, the shapely girls deliberately rubbing their uniformed softness up against the rich men strapped into their seats. Targets, to be teased and tamed - then inflamed. Krystal ran her tongue over her dry lower lip. She briefly imagined the sulky-mouthed brunette. She saw the heavy-breasted girl kneeling, blouse open and red lips parted, as a lust-engorged tycoon spears his shaft up between her swollen bosoms, his stiff excitement trapped by the tight band of silk between the bulging cups of her brassiere. Shuddering, he empties himself into the smooth warm pillows of flesh. Her red lips widen approvingly. His carnal scream of delight drowned by the roar of the jet engines as the Lear streaks towards Bonn. Later, her slender hand insinuates itself into the inside pocket. An expensive leather pouch yields up a key. The key yields up its pattern to a soft wax tablet concealed in her palm.

'Supposition and circumstance,' the sharp-eyed blonde on the Chesterfield snapped. 'You cannot prove—'

'I can prove everything,' Demosthenes growled.

'And what are you doing here, in—'

'My flat?' he chuckled, enjoying the game.

The blonde slumped back, confused and frightened.

'Come on up,' the Greek barked into his mobile, which he had unobtrusively produced and dialled.

'Yes, boss,' came the smart response, barely audible above the brunette's sobbing.

'Get the door,' he asked Beetle.

Beetle ushered in two handsome men. They grinned sheepishly at the girls on the Chesterfield.

'Nice ride,' one of them winked at the brunette.

'Silence,' Demonsthenes barked.

The underlings stood stiffly to attention.

'Not, as you were led to suppose, two fat pigeons for your pot, but two of my security team.' The Greek spread his huge hands wide apart. 'How can I thank you two?' he beamed at Beetle and Krystal. 'A most ingenious plan. You spun the web. These two little fleas jumped straight into it.'

'Sticky ending,' Krystal murmured. 'Are you going to prosecute?'

'And become a laughing stock? Robbed, on my own planes, by these two bitches? Ruin the name of Demosthenes. No.' His voice dropped to an eerie whisper. 'I will not hand them over to the authorities. I will see to it that they are punished properly.'

He dismissed the two men with the words, 'Bonuses for you two next month.' Beetle saw them to the door, and then locked it behind them. Returning, she saw Demosthenes pick up a cushion, plump it up, and sit down comfortably.

'Would you draw the curtains for me and fix me an iced rye?' he asked Beetle. Settled comfortably, he sipped his drink after toasting Krystal and Beetle. He looked at the miscreants. 'My home,' he said softly, waving his glass in a broad sweep. 'You chose the wrong target my dears. Those who cross Demosthenes always suffer.'

'Do you want them whipped?' Beetle asked brightly, topping up his glass with rye.

On the Chesterfield, the sharp eyes widened in horror.

'You two,' the Greek grinned at the avenging angels, served me very well. I will see to it that you are handsomely rewarded. But as for the punishment of these two - I reserve for myself. Strip them and tie them up. Then you may go.'

Beetle took the sharp-eyed blonde, Krystal the shivering brunette. They struggled, but were easily overcome. Beetle unzipped the tight pencil-line skirt and relished the moment when it slithered down over the bronze nyloned thighs to reveal suspenders and snow-white pantied buttocks.

'Naked?' she murmured to the Greek.

'Naked.'

Binding the captives at their wrists and ankles, using bronze nylon stockings peeled from trembling legs, and Beetle arranged them, belly down, buttock by buttock, across the leather Chesterfield.

'Excellent. You have placed them together, side by side,' Demosthenes grunted. 'They stole together, hand in glove as the saying goes. Now they must suffer together.'

Taking a last look at the bunched cheeks poised for impending pain, Krystal and Beetle departed.

'Damn. I forgot to return his key,' Beetle sighed, pocketing the key Demosthenes had given them to effect the surveillance and spring the trap.

'Don't bother him now. We can post it. I expect he's got his hands full.'

The Freelander went around Sloane Square for the fourth time, drawing glances from the policewoman in the doorway of Peter Jones.

'What's wrong?' Beetle asked.

'Did you see his belt?' Krystal murmured.

'Studded with diamonds. Bit OTT don't you think?' Beetle grinned.

'Imagine what that would do to a bare bottom.'

Beetle's grin faded. She fell silent. Krystal nosed the Freelander round Sloane Square for the fifth time. The policewoman grew interested. Muttering into the radio at her collar, she gave the vehicle licence number to her control.

'Krystal,' Beetle whispered. 'That belt.' She shuddered.

'I know.'

As the Freelander sped back towards Belgravia, Beetle spoke only once. 'They only ripped off super-rich playboys, after all.'

The shrill scream - instantly followed by sobs - stopped them in their tracks at the door. Using the stake-out key, they entered softly.

They saw Demosthenes, his silk shirt open to his navel, swaggering above the naked bottoms. The veins at his neck bulged, giving him the likeness of a bull in a rage. From his clenched right fist, the diamond-studded black leather belt dangled, dragging its tip across the cheeks it had just lashed. Across the swollen creamy hillocks of their bare bottoms, a single searing weal blazed. The hide of the Chesterfield was wet where the punished nudes had crushed their sobbing faces into its dull sheen.

'Put that down,' Krystal whispered softly from the doorway.

Six eyes flashed up to greet her: four tear-stained, two glinting with a dark lust.

'Get out,' Demosthenes roared. 'You'll get your money.' He swallowed deeply from the bottle clasped in his left hand. 'These are my employees. I, Demosthenes, own them, body and soul. They dared to steal from my clients. I can do what I like with them.'

As if to prove his point, he snapped the leather down, licking both bottoms with a single stroke. Squealing in anguish, the nudes jerked their scalded buttocks, allowing both Beetle and Krystal a glimpse of the second red weal. Bound and helpless, the naked stewardesses writhed as their punished cheeks seethed.

'You are wrong,' Krystal said firmly. 'They may deserve to be whipped, but with a crop or cane. Not that,' she hissed, pointing at the obscenely decorated leather belt.

'Stripe their bottoms by all means. That is justice. But what you are doing is—'

'Go. Now. Or I swear I will give you a taste of this,' he roared, bloated with raging lust.

'Not without these two—'

Krystal was prevented from completing her threat by a voice from the door behind her. 'Is that your Freelander parked outside, miss?'

'Yes, it is mine,' Krystal replied, surprised by the intrusion.

'You were observed—' the voice broke off. Stepping forward, the policeman whistled softly as his gaze took in the whipped nudes on the leather Chesterfield. 'What's all this, then?'

His question was met by silence.

'Come on, what's going on?' his colleague demanded, eyes riveted to the two scarlet stripes across the proffered buttocks.

'Private party,' Beetle blurted out in her best Bermondsey. 'We just like giving this gennelman a bit of a good time, don't we, dearies, eh?'

The policemen exchanged knowing glances.

'No 'arm in it—' Beetle's voice whined, trailing off into silence under Krystal's astounded stare.

'Oscar-four,' the policeman called in. 'Send round a trolley to - what number Belgravia Square would this be, sir?'

The Greek was already on his mobile to his solicitor.

The 'sweet trolley', Met police shorthand for the white windowless Sherpas that cruise Mayfair for tarts, arrived. Belgravia twitched its lace as the four girls and the Greek were bundled aboard.

Money talks. For Demosthenes, it purred softly in the tones of a mohair-suited solicitor. The Greek tycoon was out of his cell - no charges pressed - within the hour.

'It's us poor workin' girls wot gets the blame,' Beetle shouted out, warming to her part. A stern policewoman loomed in the cell door. Beetle shut up and sat down.

Beetle, Krystal and the two chastened stewardesses chatted amicably into the night as their plastic cups of undrinkable coffee grew stone-cold. In the morning, agreeing to a shared story, all four pleaded guilty to being common prostitutes at Knightsbridge magistrates.

The *Sun*, sliding onto the well-worn press bench on the chance of a juicy Society snippet, choked on his chocolate bar as Beetle and Krystal were put up before the Bench. He choked again - the frowning Clerk first offering him water and then threatening to have him removed - at the sound of Beetle's Bermondsey vowels.

'What's the story?' he sniggered, catching up with them in Hans Crescent.

'Glorious morning,' Krystal replied a little stiffly.

Beetle giggled.

'In,' the blonde commanded, yanking open a taxi commandeered to take them to their marooned Freelander in Belgravia.

Beetle paused, snatched a whispered exchange with the *Sun*, and got in.

'Thinking of handing in my belt and hanging up my crop,' Krystal remarked as they drove east along the Embankment.

'And closing down the Correction Squad?'

'Yes. Though I'll always keep a couple of spare canes handy,' the blonde said, giving Beetle a meaningful look.

'I'm sorry. It's all I could think of. Those poor girls and that dreadful Greek. I was frightened—'

Krystal could no longer hide her smile. She drew the Freelander over to the curb.

'And now we won't even get paid and we'll be broke—'

'Don't worry,' the blonde murmured. 'Look what sharp eyes slipped me in the cell last night.' Krystal produced the silver cigarette case. 'Sort of thank you.'

'It's beautiful. All sparkly,' Beetle gasped.

'Good job that Greek has the habit of studding everything with diamonds.'

Beetle whistled.

It was the evening of the ninth. Beetle had been skittish with mounting excitement all afternoon. Unfortunately for her, Krystal mistook the signs. Unable to keep a secret, the minx was bursting to share the information burning in her brain. To the blonde, this behaviour merely signalled the edginess brought on by guilt.

As Beetle had scampered around, humming, Krystal had grown increasingly grave. By teatime - walnut cake and Gunpowder tea for Krystal, a vodka and cola for the nervous minx - the blonde had become quiet and remote. By the time the lemon sun spread itself across the dancing Thames, a distinct frost chilled the air between them.

'I want you to explain something to me,' Krystal called out from the bedroom. 'Come in here.'

Beetle skipped across to the bedroom door. She saw the blonde, head bowed, sitting on their bed.

'I've been examining our phone bill. You seem to have been making an extraordinary number of calls.'

Beetle managed to conceal her triumph and simply grinned. Krystal, she realized, had not discovered her secret.

'Would you like to tell me what's going on?'

'Nothing,' the minx replied, blushing as she lied.

'I'm afraid I know you only too well,' Krystal reeled off a stream of Beetle's 'little lapses' which had punctuated their years together.

'That's not fair,' Beetle cried, stung by the catalogue of sins. 'I thought you had forgiven me—'

'But not forgotten. Not entirely,' the blonde murmured. 'Are you going to tell me whose number this is? Or this? Or this?'

Beetle shook her head.

'Can't? Or won't?'

Beetle squirmed.

'Panties down,' Krystal said suavely, getting up to collect the bamboo cane.

'No—'

'This instant. You were given a chance to explain. I want you bare-bottomed across the bed, Beetle.'

As the minx struggled to remove her panties, Krystal flexed, then swished, the whippy wood. Her buttocks bared as instructed, Beetle bent over the bed. The blonde swished the cane down once more, slicing it into the duvet. Beetle's knuckles gripped the soft silk in fearful response.

'I will commence with at least six,' Krystal purred, tapping the bunched cheeks dominantly. They clenched at the kiss of the thin cane against their softness.

'Six?' Beetle protested.

'Six names from your most recent examples of infidelity.'

Thinking the threat of the strokes had passed, Beetle relaxed slightly. Her soft buttocks joggled.

Swish, swipe! Krystal called out Pastora's name - the Portuguese waitress who had caught Beetle's eye. *Swish, swipe!* The cane cut across the cheeks, leaving a second thin stripe. The second stroke was delivered along with the name Bunny, the flirtatious wren; the third was accompanied by the mention of Beetle's adventures during the making of the swordfish ad. Each stroke was administered with a name from Beetle's register of misdemeanours.

After the stinging sixth stroke, Krystal levelled the cane against the swell of the striped bottom.

'As you see, I have every reason to doubt you. Now, what have you to say for yourself? About all these mysterious phone calls?'

'Trust me, Krystal. Please,' the minx implored, swivelling round and burying her face in the blonde's pubis.

Tossing the cane down on their bed, Krystal clutched a cruel handful of the penitent's dark hair. Gently, she eased the minx away. Beetle stared up, her eyes bright and shining.

'Trust me,' she whispered.

The taloned fingers relaxed their dominant grip.

'Have you forgotten? It's the ninth,' the minx said.

'And?'

'You promised to let me take you out tonight. We agreed. The ninth—' Beetle's voice rose in panic.

'Where to?' the blonde relented.

'Surprise,' the brunette grinned.

They took a cab. Krystal agreed, reluctantly, to be blindfolded so that Beetle's surprise would be complete.

The minx had difficulties with the cabby.

'The Millennium Dome,' she mimed, anxious that Krystal would not hear her destination.

'Huh?'

Beetle sketched the outline of the Dome with her hands. 'St. Paul's?' he hazarded.

Beetle shook her head impatiently. Then, jerking up her jumper, she finger-traced the outline of her left breast.

'Mount Mandelson,' the cabby mimed, grinning broadly. Laughing, he turned the cab towards Greenwich.

Krystal felt the heat of the television lights. Guided by Beetle, she walked obediently along a soft stretch of carpet. A shrill fanfare made her flinch. *What sort of do*, she wondered, *would both minor Royalty and Beetle attend?* She felt herself being steadied and stilled in the centre of an excited, hushed circle of onlookers. Then the blindfold was removed. Krystal stared. Blinking her eyes, she stood transfixed.

At the heart of the Dome, the sixty-foot bronze statue was causing a sensation. Krystal's eyes were sparkling with tears as she hugged the minx.

Up on a plinth, the image of Beetle, naked astride the horse, dwarfed all those below.

'The spirit of young Britannia urging on her hopes and desires for the next century, forward into the future...' the *Guardian* scribbled. 'Conceived in bronze, this Icenic beauty straddles the centuries—'

'Great tits,' the *Sun* murmured appreciatively. He nudged the *Guardian* suggestively with his elbow. 'Look at that expression on her face.'

Beetle rejoined Vanessa, Peter and Mandy, who were toasting Krystal's success for the fifth time. Flashbulbs and champagne corks filled the air.

Gazing up at Beetle's ecstasy frozen in bronze, the *Guardian* agreed. 'A remarkable face, one that is, perhaps, the embodiment of youth and beauty. It has, dare one say, almost spiritual qualities.'

If they had a ladder - which they didn't - and the nerve to climb it, the gentlemen from the press would have been able to see that between the thighs of the bronze girl the labia gently peeled apart.

The *Guardian* was reminded of something existential: 'She has the look of one heroically facing things to come.'

The *Sun* was closer to the truth: 'More like the face of one who's come already.'

Thanks for reading!

Did you enjoy **Correction Squad**? We hope you did (needless to say), and if you did you can also order Sarah Steel's **The Collector** as a paperback from **Amazon**.

'Not too fast. Punishment must not be rushed. Pace her pain so that both her body and mind can savour it slowly,' Dr Stikannos whispered. The wheelchair rattled as he inched his metal mask towards her whipped cheeks. 'Four more,' he pronounced. 'But slowly, my dear. The pleasure of pain is a feast. But it is a banquet,' he added darkly, 'that must be taken leisurely, by both the punisher and the punished.'

Lured into the lair of the cruel connoisseur Dr Stikannos to catalogue his priceless collection, Emily becomes subject to his perverse whims. Her submission ignites the jealous fury of his very personal assistant - and Emily's naked flesh suffers fresh stripes from Ursula's vengeful crop and cane.

A sale is arranged: Emily the star attraction - and the prospective bidders are invited to inspect and intimately examine the 'slave' each desire to possess. Forced to taste the bittersweet torments of domination and discipline, Emily struggles to escape the dark delights and exquisite agonies of her servitude.

www.ingramcontent.com/pod-product-compliance
Lightning Source LLC
Chambersburg PA
CBHW051456050726
47593CB00005B/2095